"Why are you here?" Sabine asked.

"I don't suppose you'll accept saving you from an intruder as an answer," Doug replied.

"Not likely, since I had it handled." Sort of.

As nice as it would be to believe that, he couldn't have known she'd needed saving at that very moment. She had to stay upright. If not, Doug would probably throw her over his shoulder and take her to whoever he reported to for that questioning he'd threatened her with.

Was he friend or foe? He acted as if he cared. But then at times he was like a runaway train. Nothing would stop him from getting what he wanted.

He broke into her thoughts. "Thinking about running again?"

"I was—" Her voice gave out. Sabine touched her throat. It was tender from the intruder's grip. She sucked in a deep breath. It was all she could do.

"Sabine." His voice sounded far away, like he was speaking underwater.

The floor swept up toward her and Sabine descended into darkness...

HIS DUTY TO DEFEND

LISA PHILLIPS

2 Thrilling Stories

Double Agent and *Star Witness*

LOVE INSPIRED
INSPIRATIONAL ROMANCE

LOVE INSPIRED®

INSPIRATIONAL ROMANCE

ISBN-13: 978-1-335-43059-5

His Duty to Defend

Copyright © 2022 by Harlequin Enterprises ULC

Double Agent
First published in 2014. This edition published in 2022.
Copyright © 2014 by Lisa Phillips

Star Witness
First published in 2014. This edition published in 2022.
Copyright © 2014 by Lisa Phillips

For questions and comments about the quality of this book, please contact us at CustomerService@Harlequin.com.

Love Inspired
22 Adelaide St. West, 41st Floor
Toronto, Ontario M5H 4E3, Canada
www.LoveInspired.com

Printed in U.S.A.

Recycling programs
for this product may
not exist in your area.

CONTENTS

DOUBLE AGENT   7

STAR WITNESS   231

Lisa Phillips is a British-born, tea-drinking, guitar-playing wife and mom of two. She and her husband lead worship together at their local church. Lisa pens high-stakes stories of mayhem and disaster where you can find made-for-each-other love that always ends in a happily-ever-after. She understands that faith is a work in progress more exciting than any story she can dream up. You can find out more about her books at authorlisaphillips.com.

Books by Lisa Phillips

Love Inspired Suspense

Secret Service Agents

Security Detail
Homefront Defenders
Yuletide Suspect
Witness in Hiding
Defense Breach
Murder Mix-Up

Double Agent
Star Witness
Manhunt
Easy Prey
Sudden Recall
Dead End
Colorado Manhunt
"Wilderness Chase"
Desert Rescue

Visit the Author Profile page at LoveInspired.com for more titles.

DOUBLE AGENT

But now in Christ Jesus you who once were far off
have been brought near by the blood of Christ.
—*Ephesians* 2:13

For my sister Beverley,
who read all fifty-seven thousand versions of
my Speed Date pitch before declaring it was FINE.
I guess it was.

ONE

"What is she doing here?" Army Sergeant Major Doug Richardson hissed out a breath as three guys crowded around him in the commandeered apartment, his Delta Force teammates.

Doug put his eye back to the viewfinder. The glass-fronted bistro across the street was next door to a swanky hotel. The eatery was the current location of their target, who sat at the crowded restaurant bar with his aviator sunglasses on like some kind of hotshot movie star. Doug felt his teammates gather around him—Barker, Hanning and Perkins. The fifth member, Franklin, was positioned in the hotel lobby.

Doug had to be mistaken. Was it really her? Surely there were other women in the world with that stride, with the same dark—almost black—hair that caught the light like that?

But there she was.

She glanced around the restaurant like she was looking for an empty seat. Of course the only one available was the stool beside the target. She had no idea who this guy was. Or that this was a golden opportunity for his team to observe Christophe Parelli conducting business. And there she was, right in the middle of it.

The woman he'd met a handful of times was quiet and well-spoken—not the type to smile like that at the man who had financed her brother's murder.

Their team had hoped Parelli would meet with the person he worked for. In an ideal world, the guy would be here to meet the person known only as the Raven.

Years of team effort would pull together in a result that brought them the mysterious head of the crime syndicate they'd been chasing for what seemed like forever. The idea that Sabine might be Parelli's contact was insane. Doug wasn't even going to entertain the idea that she might be the Raven, because that meant everything he felt was wrong.

At the funeral she'd stood alone beside her brother's grave while the wind had whipped her hair around her face. The weight of her grief had about killed Doug. He'd almost missed the strain when she was handed the folded-up flag, but it had been there. If anyone touched her, it would have broken the tight hold she had on her emotions.

That was two weeks ago now, and Doug hadn't been able to get her out of his head since. Though he'd had an instinct that this mission was going to go wrong, the last thing he thought it might be was her. She was supposed to be at home, grieving the loss of her brother.

Not in the middle of the operation to bring down the man who killed him.

Doug growled, then simply said, "Sabine."

* * *

Sabine Laduca settled herself on the stool and signaled the bartender. Her stomach churned, but she pasted on a smile. "Diet soda, please."

She smoothed down the skirt of her dress and walked her mind through her training. Her whole adult life had prepared her for this moment, and she could not screw it up. Years of instruction with the CIA, coupled with years of missions that took her all over the world and tested her beyond her skills... It all came down to now.

The man beside her was handsome enough, she supposed, if you went for the overly styled Mediterranean-playboy type. That wasn't Sabine's thing. Her type ran more toward a gorgeous Delta Force team leader with almond-colored skin.

The man who seemed to always be on her mind was the perfect mix of a tall African-American army general and a beautiful Caucasian woman. She'd seen a picture of his parents only once and didn't know too much about them, but it was easy to tell he'd been given the best features from both.

Unlike her.

Sabine shifted in her seat and shot the target a cordial smile, like she was perfectly content with her own thoughts.

It really was too bad that life threw a wrench in every single plan she made. Not so much disrupting her dreams, but more like completely obliterating them. Just not this plan—please—because this mission was more important than anything she'd ever done.

Contact with the target wasn't sanctioned, but she needed Parelli's fingerprint to gain access to his hotel room. There were other ways she could have gotten it, but there was no way she was going to pass this up.

This was her chance to look in the eyes of the man who had financed her brother's murder.

Despite being a fully trained agent for years, she'd never killed anyone. It almost seemed fitting for this man to be her first. Except that revenge would be way too easy. Sabine wasn't after quick and painless; her broken heart cried out for the complete destruction of everything this man held dear—which for this guy was money and nothing else.

Retrieving the hard drive from his computer was only the first step of the plan. Her handler's instructions were clear: no bloodshed and no emotions—just get the computer data and get out. The tech guys he passed the hard drive to would do the rest of the work.

She glanced at the target and realized he'd pulled his sunglasses down his nose with one finger and was taking her in. Sabine pursed her mouth and put on her best British accent. "Lovely weather we're having, isn't it?"

He flashed his bleached teeth. "This is the Caribbean. Unless it's hurricane season, it's always lovely weather."

She laughed, trying her best to sound charmed. Her phone rang, stalling what she'd been about to say. It took everything in her to hold back her surprise at the number on screen, but she smiled as though delighted.

"Hello?" How long would it take him to ask why she'd put on a British accent?

"What do you think you are doing?"

She blinked. That was all the reaction she allowed to the fact that he'd roared. "Is everything okay, darling?"

"No, everything is not okay. Get up and leave the restaurant. Now."

He knew where she was. Sabine transferred the phone to her other ear. Hopefully the target hadn't heard Doug shout. She wasn't about to let the Delta Force soldier interfere in her CIA-sanctioned mission. Too bad he was still yelling, which meant she couldn't get a word in. Didn't the army know that an operative was going to be here?

"You have no idea what you're in the middle of."

And he had no idea that she wasn't a banker, but a spy. *Busted.* Or did Doug think she was chasing her brother's killer on her own? Either way, he needed to get off the phone. "Of course, darling, that sounds like a splendid idea. I'll meet you there once I've finished at the shops."

"No delays, Sabine. This better not be what I think it is."

The bartender removed the target's drink and replaced it with a fresh one.

"I go where I want, when I want. As I said, I'll be there when I've finished." She hung up.

"Boyfriend?"

"He wishes." She held out her hand to the target. "I'm Sabine."

He kissed her knuckles. "Christophe Parelli."

Like his name was supposed to mean something to her? Well, it meant something, all right, and none of what she knew was good. It meant the son of a weapons dealer being groomed to take over Daddy's business. It meant too much money and too little sense. In general, trouble with a capital *T*.

"It's a pleasure to meet you, but I must dash. The

day is waning, and there's still plenty of his money to spend."

Across the restaurant she looked back over her shoulder to smile and wave, but his attention was already elsewhere. She skirted the edge of the bar, swiped his empty glass from the tray and strode in the direction of the restrooms. With the glass tucked away in the mammoth purse she'd bought online because it went with her dress, Sabine went down the hall past the ladies' room all the way to the exit door at the end.

Five minutes later Sabine placed the image of Christophe Parelli's fingerprint on the hotel room's door scanner and covered it with the base of her thumb. The reader needed body heat, but she didn't want to confuse it with two overlapping prints. The light on the scanner switched to green, and the lock clicked open.

Doug's team was probably here on the same mission. Too bad for them that she was going to get to Parelli's computer first. She'd always had a problem with sharing.

Her steps were muffled on the plush carpet. Despite the price tag that came with this suite, it was still just a hotel room. Something inside her yearned for home, but she pushed it away. Now wasn't the time for that.

The desktop was bare. The safe in the bedroom closet was shut and locked. Sabine entered the code she'd memorized and held her breath.

She drew out the laptop, flipped it over and pulled a screwdriver from her purse. The hard drive slid out into her hand. She secured the cover again, set the laptop back in the safe and glanced at the watch face on her bracelet.

Still enough time to search the room.

Clothes were strewn over every available surface, and the bathroom counter was cluttered with men's hair-care products. Sabine rolled her eyes. It wasn't like he was a movie star or a male model or anything like that.

Satisfied there was nothing else worth taking, she turned to exit the suite.

The lock on the outer door clicked.

Her breath stuttered and a blue baseball cap appeared between the now open door and the frame. She shoved the hard drive in her purse and blanked her face.

Doug's gaze found her in the middle of the bedroom—dark caramel eyes that gave nothing away. He filled the doorway, so tall that, if he didn't shave his head, his hair could have touched the frame. So wide it was a wonder he didn't get stuck. Sabine was tall herself, but Doug made her feel small in a way that had nothing to do with self-worth and everything to do with comfort.

Her brother had been skinny and baby faced his whole life—even at thirty-one years old, Ben had looked more like a kid playing dress-up in his uniform than an actual soldier. Doug, on the other hand, made that dark green dress uniform look good. Mouthwateringly good.

Today his navy blue T-shirt was damp with the heat of the day, and his cargo shorts and ball cap were every tourist's go-to apparel. Only there was nothing about him that blended in.

Doug closed the door and held up the clear plastic with Christophe's fingerprint on it. She shut her eyes. She'd left it on the scanner. She wanted to reprimand herself over such a simple mistake, but put a hand on her hip instead. "What are you doing here?" Her voice shook more than she'd have liked, but it was too late now.

"What am I— Seriously? That's what you're going with?" He glanced around the room. "Let me guess… CIA?"

She stiffened. He wasn't supposed to get it right the first time.

"Did Ben know about this?"

Her stomach surged like a storm-fueled wave. "You don't get to talk about my brother."

He stepped closer. "This is about him, right? Ben is the reason why we're all after Parelli."

She hated that he pitied her. And that his voice had to go soft. He'd been there when Ben was murdered by a sniper on what was supposed to be a routine mission. As far as she was concerned, that meant Doug was responsible.

"We need to talk but not here. Let's go."

Sabine blinked. "Excuse me? I happen to be working."

Doug looked away. "Copy that, California." He surged forward. "Someone's coming. We have to hide."

Apparently "California" was the handle of the newest member of Doug's team—the electronics expert who had replaced her brother, Ben. She didn't want that thought to touch her, but the knife slipped in, anyway.

She loved Ben's old team: Barker, the big African-American Texan who always smiled; Hanning, who looked like a male model in his designer clothes; Franklin, so ordinary in appearance that she had almost overlooked him, until she got to know him and found out his heart was large.

Doug dragged her to the closet and closed the partition door so they were shrouded in darkness. He pulled on her arm and tried to get her to move deeper into the closet, but she shrugged him off.

"Sabine," he hissed.

Nose to the wood, she studied the suite through the slim gap in the door. "They're here."

Christophe Parelli sauntered in and tossed his sunglasses on the bed. A woman followed him, wearing a red dress similar to Sabine's. She, too, had long, dark hair. In fact, the resemblance was so striking that Sabine sucked in a breath through her nose.

The woman moved to the fridge in the corner and pulled out a glass bottle of amber liquid. She took her time pouring two drinks and then handed one to Christophe. With the limited view Sabine had, she couldn't make out the woman's features. Her bearing was familiar, but Sabine couldn't place where she'd seen her before.

Doug touched Sabine's shoulder. She took another deep breath and expelled it, low and slow. As soon as the woman and Parelli left, then Doug and Sabine would be able to get out of there.

Christophe held up his glass. "A toast, to a beautiful relationship."

"Yes." The woman took a sip of her drink, while she watched Christophe swallow his. "Too bad it cannot continue."

Christophe jerked. The glass fell. It hit the carpet with a dull thud. His hand grasped his throat. "What did you do?" His voice was raspy.

Though the woman laughed, there was no humor in the sound. "You didn't think I could let you live, did you? So naive. You, my dear, are a liability, and liabilities must be eradicated."

"But—"

Christophe dropped to his knees, wheezing. Doug pulled on her arm as he tried again to draw her away from the horrific scene, but she held fast. Something about the woman would help identify her. Anything was better than admitting Sabine was seeing someone take their last breath. Again.

Doug's hand slid from her elbow, and he stilled her fingers with his.

The woman sighed. "I know it pains you to hear it. But you are one small part, an insignificant part that I cannot allow to remain free. So goodbye, my dear. It really was a pleasure."

Christophe collapsed to the floor. Sabine could barely see his chest move. The woman strode from the room, leaving the door wide open.

"She's gone."

Doug opened the closet door. "Copy that, California. Ten minutes."

Sabine forced her gaze away from the dead man. "What?"

"Rendezvous. Let's go."

She didn't move. The woman who had killed Christophe had probably used some kind of fast-acting poison that closed the airways and stopped the heart. Easy enough to get, and who cared if it showed up in an autopsy? The guy wasn't any less dead.

Her red dress had been too much like Sabine's. And that wasn't the only similarity. There was only one logical conclusion.

"I killed him."

TWO

"That woman. She was... It was supposed to look like I did it. Multiple people saw Christophe and me talking at the bar in that restaurant. People would have seen that woman come up here with him. We have the same build. The same long, dark hair. The same red dress." Sabine blinked. "Who knew I'd be here?"

Understanding washed over his features. "We still have to go. More so if you're going to be the number one suspect."

Her breath came faster and faster, and she pressed her fists to the sides of her face. She was going to be framed for this. Sabine stumbled back; her ankle rolled. She hit the floor and cried out.

Doug hauled her to her feet. "We have to go."

"Please." She didn't know what she was asking for.

"You want to stay here with the dead guy?" He half held, half carried her down the hall. "We need to get gone."

Her brain spun until she was hardly able to string two thoughts together. She saw her handler, Neil, at the park under a Saturday-morning sun briefing her on the mission. "She made it look like I killed him."

Doug glanced at her, still pulling her along. "Sabine." His voice was a warning.

She forced away the pain in her ankle to keep up with him. Behind them there was a shout, followed by the rush of feet. Sabine looked back as two men in suits broke into a run.

"Time to go," Doug said.

They sprinted for the exit. Adrenaline pulsed through her. It cleared her mind. Sabine found her own steam and pulled away from him. Doug grabbed her hand again as they closed the distance to the stairwell; he punched open the door and pulled her up instead of down.

"What are you doing? We should go to the lobby. The exit."

He didn't slow, just took each flight of stairs at a punishing pace. Every step shot fire from her twisted ankle up her leg.

"Less talking. More running."

A door slammed below. Dress shoes pounded up the stairwell. The echo bounced off the walls.

"We should split up," she said.

Doug's hand tightened on hers. They rounded the landing on the next floor and continued up. "California, get us out of here."

Sweat ran down her back. Sabine pushed through the strain in her muscles and concentrated on each step. Behind them the two goons raced up the stairs.

"Copy that." Doug yanked her arm and changed direction. Sabine hissed with the pain and trailed him through a door into a hallway where rooms stretched out before them on either side. Doug jerked her again, opened a door that said Maintenance and swept her inside.

The door clicked closed, and they were enveloped in darkness yet again. All she could hear was heavy breathing, though Doug didn't seem to be nearly as winded as she was. It was barely a second before the stairwell door opened.

"Where'd they go?" The voice spoke in Italian.

Sabine held her breath. Christophe was Italian. These were probably the bodyguards Daddy had assigned to him.

A different voice replied, also in Italian. "You search this floor. I'll take the stairs again. Call me if you find them."

The two men dispersed.

Sabine exhaled. "Let's get out of here."

Doug held up one finger, but Sabine wasn't in the mood to be told what to do. He must have seen it on her face because, before she could move, he was between her and the door.

He moved his face an inch from hers and kept his voice low. "Now isn't the time for showmanship."

Everything she'd just seen through the crack in the closet door came back in a rush. The woman had put something in Christophe's drink that made him fall to the floor.

"If this gets out, it'll end my career," she whispered.

Doug shifted. "Quiet."

Where was the Doug who'd been in the hotel room, the one who looked at her with kindness and compassion? Where was the man who had stood by her at her brother's graveside? This guy was the army Special Ops soldier with the permanent callus between his thumb and index finger on his gun hand. Mr. Team Leader was clearly used to giving orders that were obeyed without question.

Sabine had never been good at being told what to do. "So this is your big escape plan, huh? Hiding in a closet?"

He didn't say anything. He didn't need to. In the darkness of the tiny room, frustration came off him in waves. "Copy that, California."

Doug eased the door open and glanced both ways. Sabine took a step to follow. Her ankle gave out and she collapsed, biting back what she really wanted to say. Her right ankle was swollen around the straps of her shoe.

Doug crouched and unbuckled both of them. He lifted her swollen foot and winced. "You need a bandage. Probably some crutches."

She couldn't let herself get distracted by the kindness in his voice. It was normally deep, almost melodic in tone, and she liked listening to him shout instructions when the guys played their extremely intense version of touch football. Now she knew that when he spoke softly in that low voice, it chased away the shivers.

"What I need is to get off the floor."

His mouth thinned, but he helped her up.

Sabine swung her purse on her shoulder and cleared the door so he could close it. "What floor is this?"

"Twelve."

No way was she going to hobble down multiple flights of stairs. She turned and limped for the elevator, not caring if he followed or not. Honest. "My room is only two floors down. I can see myself there. Thanks for your help."

"I don't think so." He kept pace with her, glancing

around. "Copy that, California." He zeroed in on Sabine. "Perkins says you don't have a room."

She smirked. "Amateurs."

"Excuse me?"

They reached the elevators. When Doug didn't press the button, Sabine reached for it herself. "I bet he checked for me under my real name."

"You have another one that we don't know about?"

She smiled. "The things you don't know about me could fill the whole internet."

He folded his arms. "Evidently. For starters, how a professional…whatever you are…manages to be surprised when someone assassinates a target. I thought you guys were all about offing the bad guy."

The whole thing hit way too close to home. Seeing someone killed, despite the difference in circumstances. Well, it didn't matter. Witnessing someone's last breath wasn't something she could forget.

Sabine drew on the only thing she had left: bravado. "Do they teach stereotyping to all army soldiers, or is that just your thing?"

She stepped into the empty elevator and winced at the pain in her foot. That was the only reason she had tears in her eyes. The disappointment on Doug's face didn't have anything to do with it. Who cared what he thought of her, anyway?

"I'm sorry."

She whipped around. "Don't."

"Sabine—"

The elevator doors opened, and they both stayed silent while he walked her to her room. When the door didn't close behind her, she whirled as fast as her ankle would let her. Doug stood there, scanning the room she'd reserved. Of course he'd waltzed in right behind her. Probably thought he was going to personally escort her all the way home.

She looked around at the budget accommodations. It was a far cry from Christophe's suite, but she didn't care what it looked like. This was the room that brought her within reach of the man who was the money behind Ben's death—the man who likely knew who was responsible.

She had to know who'd fired the rifle from that rooftop. She had to know why Ben was gone. Otherwise, what was the point? But how could she find out what had happened when the biggest lead was dead? Not to mention that her retribution plan was now pointless.

She wanted to pray there was something on the hard drive that would point to who had killed Ben, but her emotions were too messed up to deal with the issue of faith just then.

There had to be evidence on there they could use, otherwise all of her investigation into classified government files, running down leads, the days of work she'd put in—everything leading up to this mission— would have been for nothing. And Sabine would be left with only the empty feeling of not being able to make sense of anything.

Doug closed the door with him on the wrong side of it. "We shouldn't stay here too long. Christophe's bodyguards might get lucky and figure out where you're staying."

"The two guys who chased us? Please. I've seen smarter sponges."

Sabine dug through her suitcase for her first-aid kit. She located an elastic bandage, sat on the edge of the bed and started to wrap her ankle. Sharp pain sliced through her foot, and she ducked her head to blow out a breath through pursed lips.

Masculine fingers covered hers. The distinction between his almond-colored skin and her olive-toned flesh made it all the more clear to her that they had little common ground. The loving family he came from was worlds away from her dingy two-bedroom childhood home where everything had gone wrong.

"Let me."

She looked up. The warmth of his fingers on hers registered, along with the look in his eye. Her throat thickened, and she forced herself to nod.

While he made quick work of the bandage, Sabine felt her heart stretch and come awake for the first time. That had never happened any of the other times she'd met Doug—*MacArthur,* as the guys called him. The simple name suited his steady and uncomplicated nature.

At the few backyard barbecues for the team and their families that she'd attended, Sabine had always felt like an outsider. She'd been attracted to Doug, but any time they had talked he steered the conversation through small talk and never lingered for long.

He clearly didn't feel anything special for her. That was when she began to make excuses to her brother and say she had to work—which wasn't a lie. Now that Ben was dead, she wished she hadn't made him look at her that way or feel sorry for her.

Sabine cleared her throat. "So why are you guys here?"

"Why don't you tell me why you're here first?"

"You tell me, and I'll tell you. Otherwise I have nothing to say." It was juvenile, but she wasn't in the mood for a heart-to-heart. Her ankle hurt like nobody's business. Not to mention the weight of a man's life was now on her shoulders.

She didn't know what the recourse of all this would be. No doubt there'd be some kind of investigation into Christophe's death. When her name came up, she hoped she had the strength to stand up for herself. Not to mention that there would be enough evidence to prove it wasn't her who had murdered him.

Doug rubbed his eyes. Was he frustrated this wasn't turning out like he had planned? Good. Immediately she wanted to take that thought back. Despite the imposing size of him, he did look sort of lost.

Sabine had enough to deal with without letting him distract her from her job, so she ignored him. She had the hard drive. It really was time to go before someone identified her. After dumping everything into the rolling carry-on she traveled with, she slipped her feet into silver flats, put her sunglasses on top of her head and turned to the door.

Doug grabbed her elbow, but she kept going. After a tug of war in which she lost her sunglasses and found herself sitting on the desk chair, she finally acknowledged him. He towered over her, his hands on the armrests.

Sabine lifted her chin. "Make this fast. I have a plane to catch."

"I'm coming with you."

Sabine almost swooned with the vulnerability in his tone. Almost. "I don't think so."

"Sabine, this is serious. Right now, where you go, I go. That's how it has to be."

"Why?"

"You're seriously asking me that? We have to figure out what just happened. You want to find Ben's killer? Well, so do I. If we pool our resources together, we have the best chance of that. So we're going to meet up with my team, and you're going to tell me what you're doing here, what you want with that hard drive you hid in your purse and whatever else you know."

She smirked. He thought she was going to spill everything just like that? Yep, amateurs. "Answers, answers. Let's see. Life…the universe…and forty-seven."

"Funny." He wasn't laughing. "I think you know something. Maybe it's a small thing…or maybe you're the key to all of this."

She sighed. "Am I supposed to know what on earth you're talking about?" He should know how it was. They both lived their lives under the radar. That was the whole point of being a spy. He was Special Forces. They only told the people closest to them what they did.

"I guess we'll find out."

Sabine glared. "Even if I could help you, there's no way I would give you even one second of my time. You were there when my brother died—"

"I can't talk to you about that. It's classified."

"Look, MacArthur—"

"Doug."

Sabine rolled her eyes. "The only thing I care about is bringing whoever killed Ben to justice. Whatever association you and I might've had has now ended. Unless you care to share what happened that night."

The muscle at the corner of his eye twitched. "You need my help if you're going to get out of this hotel without getting questioned for Christophe's death."

"You said yourself we don't have much time before those two guys find us, or someone raises the alarm about Christophe being dead and the whole place swarms with cops."

He held out his hand. "Let's go then."

She brushed it aside and stood. "This is where we part. It's been an experience, really. But like I said, I have a plane to catch."

"Look, I know how hard this must be for you."

Was he serious? "You have no idea—"

"Let me finish." He had the decency to look apologetic. "Please. I can help you put this to rest, but I have to know how you fit in."

"You think I had something to do with Ben's death?" She forced the words past a resurgence of the complete and utter desperate, aching solitude that had followed her brother's death. To her horror, a slice of her private grief tracked its way down her cheek.

She swiped away the moisture and shoved past him.

"Try seeing this from my perspective, Sabine. The team is shadowing the man who paid for your brother to be executed—"

"Executed—" The word was a whisper from her mouth.

Doug winced. "We're trying to get to the bottom of it. You can help me find out what happened. If need be, we'll clear your name. We both want justice. Let's work together."

She shook her head. "I can't. Christophe is dead, and I plan on getting as far from this as possible. Unless there's something seriously incriminating on the hard drive that leads to the killer and lays out the whys of it all—which I seriously doubt—then it's over. My brother is dead. Justice is just a vain hope."

"Sabine—"

Her stomach churned. "No. I was wrong to attempt this. A man is dead. Yes, he was a criminal. And most likely responsible for Ben's death. That means in some way justice has already been served. Let's leave it there. Please. I'm going to turn the hard drive over to my handler and walk away."

Doug's eyes were wet. "I can't let you do that. I have to know what happened. I won't beg for your help, but I don't see how you can walk away and let this lie."

The heartbreak on his face nearly did her in. Sabine touched his cheek, feeling the warmth of his skin and the late-day stubble. "We need time to grieve. Both of us."

Something flickered in his eyes, and everything changed. She drew her hand away. Her stomach plunged like an elevator at the thought of exactly what that look might mean. But she couldn't let it penetrate the fortified walls of her heart.

For the first time, Doug was more than her brother's team leader. Despite what had brought them together, he was being a friend to her. Since she had few true friends, it was hard to recognize one or to trust the offer of friendship when it was given.

Ben had reacted…badly, when she had told him what she really did for a living. Granted, he'd been thrown after finally admitting to her what his position was in the army. *Delta Force.*

After he had told her that he was Special Ops, Sabine couldn't let the opportunity pass to open up about her own occupation. How was she to know he would hit the roof when he found out her job was just as dangerous as his—maybe more so, since she didn't have a team to back her up?

She didn't want to know what would have happened if Doug hadn't been there today. She'd needed him to get her out of Parelli's room after she realized she was going to be framed. So much for being a capable agent. Did that mean she couldn't handle this job on her own?

Doug pulled the cap from his head, ran his hand down his face and replaced his ball cap. "I'm sorry. You don't need the weight of my grief, too."

Sabine turned away and swiped up the handle of her suitcase. "Tensions are high. Don't sweat it."

"Sabine—"

"I told you I have a plane to catch."

Sabine was out of her depth. Sure, she was a trained agent. She was just more of an information-gathering, bug-planting, charm-the-bad-guy-into-talking kind of spy. She was about as far from a fully armed Special Ops team as it was possible to be, despite their mutual goal of finding out who had killed Ben.

Doug grabbed her arm. "I can't let you leave, Sabine. You're not going anywhere without me until I get some answers."

THREE

Mistakes. That's what it all boiled down to in Doug's mind. His life could be summed up in a series of mistakes that never should have been made—the most recent of which stood in front of him now. He touched her elbow. It was slender, her skin smooth under his rough fingers callused from a war he had never wanted to reach her shore.

Her head reached his chin, and her hair reflected every shade from auburn to dark chocolate. The red dress flattered her figure in a way that wasn't suggestive. She was pure class. The color looked warm against the almost Mediterranean-rich tan of her skin. Ben had been much lighter. Doug had wondered why the siblings hadn't looked anything alike. On the day he had asked Ben, Doug had been given a *back off* look. He didn't ask again.

Despite the feelings she evoked in him, Doug was on a mission, and emotions had no bearing. At least they weren't supposed to. He'd have to chalk up his earlier outburst to being overcome with grief. After all, who knew the extent of her involvement in Christophe Parelli's life, his business and his death? The quicker Doug got both of them out of here, the quicker he could find out how Sabine figured into Ben's death. CIA or not, she'd be answering a whole lot of questions.

After that she would be free to walk out of his life. He thought of all those get-togethers when he'd had to force himself to be cordial while everything in him hummed just from being near her. The reality of how shallow his attraction to her was hit him like a needle that burst a balloon and deflated his sense of honor.

It seemed like his initial impression had been entirely wrong. Not about her being very good at what she did. He'd believed she was some high-powered financial type at the bank where she worked. Ben had told anyone who would listen that his sister was a big deal, traveling all over the world for her job.

Had Ben even known the truth?

She wasn't the type of woman that Doug wanted to get to know. Even though just looking at her made his brain miss critical steps, Doug couldn't let her affect him. She'd charmed her way close enough to Christophe Parelli to get his fingerprints, and Doug had no interest in a woman who used her looks to get what she wanted. Once this mission was over, they'd both get on with their lives.

"My plane leaves in three hours." She lowered her slim wrist. The gold bracelet didn't look like any watch he'd ever seen. The smallest bit of fear crept on her face, despite the stubborn set to her shoulders.

"You'll be on it. Just as soon as we get to a safe place where you can answer some questions."

A click in his earpiece signaled California had something to say. "You gonna bring her over here, MacArthur?"

Doug caught her eye. How would she react to being crowded by army operatives? She knew each of them, except Ben's replacement. He'd seen her laugh and talk with the boys and their wives and girlfriends. Still, despite her status as a teammate's sister, he doubted any of them would be kind now that there were questions over her involvement.

"We'll be there in five, California."

He hoped the crack in her armor, the one currently giving off waves of fear, was an indication that she'd share what she knew. Doug had no intention of interrogating her. Nor could he hurt her in any way.

Even if it hadn't been Sabine, he wasn't the kind of man who did that. It didn't line up with what he'd been taught, his personal code of ethics or his faith. All in all, that was a lot of rules, but they were good rules. Honest standards he could live by and know he got things right.

Sabine Laduca was the antithesis of everything he stood for—a bolt of lightning. Would God create a woman for the sole purpose of throwing Doug off his game?

Well, he might be thrown, but there was no way she would bring him down.

If that tear she had tried to hide was anything to go by, he'd brought her grief back to the surface. There was no other choice. Doug was tempted to dial down his determination to find the truth. For the sake of this woman's obvious pain, he could take some extra time to soothe her into sharing.

But he wasn't going to.

Could she really be involved? Who even knew what the CIA was up to? In spite of his personal distaste, he had to push her. He couldn't afford to suddenly go soft.

Sabine knew something. Until he found out what, she was going to have to deal with the discomfort. They were together. And she was right. They really shouldn't stay in this room any longer. Parelli's guys could show up again any second.

"You good to go?"

Sabine grabbed her roll-on suitcase again. But this time when she straightened, her face was a blank mask.

He sighed. "Right. Let's move."

He took the suitcase from her. She didn't like it, given the look on her face. Too bad. No man worth his salt made a woman pull her own suitcase when he was perfectly capable.

Doug scanned the hall both ways, gave a short nod and led her out, taking her hand to make sure she stayed with him. He paid no mind to the shimmer of warmth when he touched her slender fingers. He just hadn't held a woman's hand in a long time.

He pressed the button for the elevator. To anyone observing, they were simply a couple on their way down to check out. They could easily be on their honeymoon for all anyone else knew—except for the lack of wedding rings.

And didn't that just prick his heart in a way he wasn't ready to consider? Maybe, after he retired from the army, he could have that kind of relationship with a woman. Whoever she was, the woman he married would understand his driven nature because her heart beat to the same pattern. Family. Loyalty. Trust. Honesty. Those were the lifeblood of any relationship.

It was too bad he could never trust the woman beside him. His dream was just that—a dream. Until then he'd have to rely on God to take care of the future. The years of training that made him the man he was today would cover the here and now.

Six foot four, 250 pounds of muscle, Doug was a weapon honed by the United States Army into one of their best soldiers—a fact that had nothing to do with who his father was. Doug had sent home all the *daddy's boy* naysayers with their tails between their legs. Sure, Doug could have gone the West Point route and earned butter bars, but the gold bars of a lieutenant's rank would have put him behind a desk commanding missions. Not on the ground in the thick of it.

His dad had known exactly how hard Doug would have to work to push himself beyond his limits and earn the position of team leader. The general might have made Doug earn every patch the hard way, but it'd been worth it to feel the achievement of having done it. They understood that about each other, at least.

When the doors opened on the lobby, Doug tensed. Through the crowd of people milling around, he spotted his teammate assigned to the lobby—Franklin. Despite being in his late thirties, Franklin had the air of a middle-aged banker about him that allowed him to blend in anywhere.

Doug shifted his grip on Sabine's hand, and they strode to the front counter where she checked out of the hotel.

After signing *A. Surleski* on the receipt, she looked at him. "It's past lunch. I'm going to need something to eat pretty soon."

Doug looked her up and down. "You seem like a woman way too concerned about her appearance to be worried about something as pesky as eating."

Her eyes narrowed. "They do say that looks can be deceiving."

He doubted that. He knew her type. The expensive clothes said enough, but the way she held herself spoke much louder. He had a nagging feeling this woman was going to prove to be high maintenance when it served her purpose.

"In this case, I can read you loud and clear." He folded his arms across his chest. "But since I'm hungry, too, I guess we can rustle up something." He shot a look at the receptionist. The guy was busy typing into his computer. "After we join the others in our party and finish up our business, of course."

Her dangly gold earrings shook back and forth with the motion of her head. "There's a restaurant next door, remember? We can pick something up there."

"Oh, really?"

"Yes, really. I'm telling you—"

He stopped listening. The two guys who had chased them down the hall stepped off the elevator. "Time to go."

Doug strode to the side door, careful not to rush and draw anyone's attention. Dragged along by his grip, Sabine let out a yelp. He rolled his eyes and looked back. She made a valiant effort to keep up with his long strides. This had better be about her ankle. She'd better not be being difficult just because she wanted to go it alone.

The air outside was like stepping into a sauna. Doug quickened his pace, and heard a stir of noise and movement behind them. He cut right, pulled Sabine along the sidewalk and watched for a place to cross.

"They're coming." Her voice was a hiss. "They're right behind us."

He glanced back, and, sure enough, the men had exited the hotel and spotted them. With a shout, the suits started to run.

"Go. Now," Doug ordered.

A battered sedan pulled in front of them. Doug swerved, skirted the front bumper and glanced back. Franklin was nowhere to be seen, and the men were gaining on them.

"We're not going to make it," Sabine answered, but he was too focused on moving and on the voice in his earpiece to respond.

"Ten feet to your left. Yellow cab."

They climbed in before the driver even stopped.

"Drive." Doug threw a wad of cash onto the front seat, and the driver hit the gas pedal. "Airport."

The radio in his ear clicked. "Copy that. Party's over, friends. MacArthur, we'll see you back at the house."

With that, the team was dispersed to make their own way back to the U.S., where they would rendezvous on base for debrief.

Beside him in the cab, Sabine pulled her hand from his grip and rubbed her wrist. Doug ignored his heavy heart, even as it added to the measure of weight he already carried. What would Sabine say when she found out what he'd done? A woman like her would probably slap him across the face. He deserved it for his part in her brother's death.

He glanced out the back window. The two suited guys stood in the middle of the road outside the hotel. The bigger man formed his fingers into an imaginary gun, which he raised and fired at them.

Sabine flinched.

"We got away," Doug whispered, trying to reassure her. "They won't catch up to us again. I'll make sure of it."

She looked at him. "Because you're so good, you're certain? Wow, you're arrogant."

Doug shrugged, deliberately nonchalant. He needed answers from her. Needed her to talk and not retreat again. "It's true. I'm good at what I do. Once I have what I want, I'll be out of your life for good."

Sabine shifted away from him and kept her voice at a low whisper, too. "Don't make this out to be my fault."

"I stop at nothing to get a job done. It's very important you understand that. And to be doubly sure that we're clear? This is the most important thing I've ever done."

"It's my brother you're talking about."

He dipped his chin and leaned toward her. "Then we're on the same team. Only you want to walk away because your mission went wrong. Well, I don't give up that easily. I want the truth about what happened to Ben."

Sabine's eyes went wide. "I'm not giving you the hard drive."

"You think I care about salvaging your reputation? I couldn't care less about you saving face with your superiors or whoever it is you lone-wolf types report to."

"You just said we're on the same team."

He rolled his eyes again, this time to mask the fact he was impressed with the way she had twisted the conversation around and used his own words against him. "Does that mean you're going to help me find out who killed Ben and why?"

She stared at him for a good minute. "I'll help you."

He looked out the front window. The old man driving the cab alternately looked at the road and glanced back at them, probably straining to hear what they were saying.

"When we're back in the States, I'll tell you whatever I know."

Doug had a valid passport that was part of his government-issue cover identity and a credit card, so he could easily get a ticket on the same flight as Sabine. The problem was, he was suddenly in no hurry to rush back to the lengthy questioning sure to follow. And Sabine was hungry. If he fed her, maybe she would let him in now.

Doug tapped the driver on the shoulder. "We need food. Find us somewhere to eat."

The driver, who looked like the sun had baked him on high for too long, jerked his head up and down. "I take you to my mama's café. Best meal of your life."

"Good." Doug glanced at Sabine, who really shouldn't look that surprised. He was a nice guy. He handed the driver more money. "Make it fast."

Ten minutes later they pulled up outside a bleached building with a sign that read Mama's Café. After some discussion and more money, Sabine convinced the driver they needed to take her bag inside with them.

The ceiling fans did nothing to cut through the cloud of heat. The seats were faded vinyl, the tabletops were cracked and the air was saturated with the combined scents of breakfast and salsa. Doug's mouth watered and his stomach rumbled.

Sabine swept past him, pulling her suitcase, and glanced back over her shoulder. "Order me a burrito.

Extra hot sauce." She disappeared into the women's bathroom.

An older woman with wrinkles, a faded polyester uniform and two missing teeth took his order. Doug slumped into the chair. Rested his forearms on the worn table. Toyed with the salt shaker. All the while he watched the door to the restroom.

He was just about to go searching when Sabine emerged. At least, he thought it was her. The woman who exited the bathroom dragging Sabine's suitcase looked completely different. She'd switched her dress for a white tank top adorned with two long necklaces and jeans tucked inside knee-high white leather boots. Big gold circular earrings hung down, and her hair had been swept up, wrapped in what looked suspiciously like a silk blouse he'd seen her pack in her suitcase.

She settled herself opposite him, pulled up the suitcase and put it on the seat beside her. Her whole demeanor was much more relaxed.

"Nice disguise."

She smirked. "Maybe the six-hundred-dollar dress was the disguise."

She frowned at him, and he noticed the gold watch bracelet was gone.

"It's a shame you don't have any other clothes with you," Sabine said.

"What's wrong with what I'm wearing?"

She grinned. "No offense, but you sort of stick out. Even though that outfit screams 'average-joe tourist.'"

He opened his mouth to object and realized she was probably right. He couldn't answer anyway because the waitress chose that moment to place their food in front of them.

"You could take off the hat," Sabine suggested.

He rubbed his shaved head and tugged the ball cap back on. "The hat stays."

"You don't have enough hair to have a bad hair day."

She picked up her silverware and cut a massive bite of burrito. His eyes widened as she shoved it in and chewed with gusto, then swiped up the bottle of hot sauce and shook a few drops onto her next forkful.

She realized he was staring and straightened. "What?"

He picked up his silverware. "Enjoy your food, don't you?"

"What's it to you?"

Doug shrugged. "It's just…refreshing is all. Women who look like you don't usually eat like, uh…that."

"I'll suffer working it off tomorrow, don't you worry. But it'll be worth the miles. Take a bite and see for yourself. It's really good."

Doug took a bite. She was right, though it was almost too spicy for him. He ate fast, one eye on the time. It would be simplest if they arrived at the airport with enough time for him to get a ticket on the same plane.

"So what's the real reason you don't want to take off your hat?"

He hesitated, unsure how to say it without dredging up a whole bunch of grief neither of them could handle. "It's—"

Sabine's knife stilled and sadness washed over her face. "That's Ben's hat."

Doug nodded.

"He gave it to you?"

"Wanted me to have it."

Sabine swallowed. "And here I only got the joy of

cleaning out his musty, cluttered bedroom." She drew in a long breath, and he saw the quiver in her lower lip. "Not that I've done it yet. I mean, really, you'd think a grown man would be able to keep his room tidy. Especially someone in the military."

"You'd think that, what with all the spot inspections during basic training. Some guys pick up a tendency for order and bring it home with them. Others see their private living space as somewhere else to blow off steam."

"So what are you? A neat freak? Or does your place look like a tornado the way Ben's always did?"

"Does it matter?"

Sabine pulled away, any rapport they might have had now shut down by his tone. Doug had no intention of moving into personal territory with this woman. No matter how much he wanted to.

It was for the best.

He stood. "I'm going to make a pit stop, and then we should get going."

The bathroom looked about as good as it smelled. Doug held his breath and took care of business as fast as possible. What would his superiors say when he turned up with Sabine in tow? CIA operatives and the army didn't exactly mix. Talk about a clash of cultures.

He pushed open the door and glanced around the restaurant. His stomach sank. "You've got to be kidding me."

He rushed out the front door. The cab was gone, too. She'd ditched him.

FOUR

Windshield wipers valiantly swiped the rain away, but more drops continued to pound on the car. Sabine parked her baby—a paid-in-full black Cadillac CTS—in the garage of her Seattle home. Only when the garage door lowered fully did she get out and pull her suitcase from the trunk.

It was late, and every muscle in her body ached, which was good because it distracted her from the throb in her ankle. Sabine had never been able to sleep on planes, and today was no exception. She tried to tell herself it was because she had felt bad for having ditched Doug. His tears had been genuine, the grief he had felt over Ben's death right there in his eyes. He clearly wanted to know what had happened as badly as she did—even if his professional manner left something to be desired.

There was still no way she was going to let him question her. She would need clearance from her handler before she could give him any of the details of her mission or tell him what she knew about Christophe Parelli.

The utter disaster the mission had turned out to be weighed on her. Apart from the fact she had the hard drive, everything that could have gone wrong had. Hiding the hard drive from Doug had been necessary, though apparently pointless since he'd known what she was after.

Now she needed to go through the contents before anything else went awry—like being hauled in for questioning by the army.

Christophe's death played like a movie reel through her mind. Maybe she didn't need to feel bad since the man was responsible for the deaths of so many others. He had acted without remorse or any consideration for national and international laws. But seeing him gasp his last breath had hit Sabine at the very center of who she was.

Her house was dark and quiet, except for the patter of rain against the windows. That wasn't anything new—the Seattle weather or the solitude. Even when she was married, Sabine would come home to an empty house and dinner for one.

What she had thought was her husband's work as an investment banker keeping him busy with "late-night meetings" turned out to be Maxwell having drinks with his twenty-two-year-old secretary. Now Sabine was as alone as ever but with the added bonus of feeling like a chump because her husband had cheated on her with someone younger and prettier. She would think twice about letting anyone else in again.

She punched the first two numbers of her ten-digit code on the panel for the security system and paused. It wasn't armed. That was weird. She'd set it before she left, hadn't she? She never forgot something as im-

portant as security. Sabine set down her suitcase at the
bottom of the stairs and stood still for a moment. The
house was quiet as always.

After a walk-through of the downstairs rooms
yielded nothing, Sabine crept upstairs, keeping to the
side so as not to step on the creaky stair halfway up.
Cold shimmered through her from head to toe. She had
never needed a gun at home before. Her handler's words
from the park came back to her.

*Don't get caught with a gun. Ever. And don't get
caught by the police, not even for a speeding ticket.
You do and you're on your own.*

Careful not to look at the pictures of Ben on the wall,
Sabine rounded the stairs at the top and studied the upstairs hallway. Her ears strained for…a rustle coming
from Ben's bedroom.

The door to her brother's room had been closed since
his last day of leave and his subsequent return to base.
He'd always been sort of juvenile about her going into
his room, a response probably from the lack of privacy
they'd had in foster homes. She'd respected his wishes
and had agreed not to go in there.

Light flashed across the opening, and Sabine crept
forward. She peered into the room and eased the door
open inch by inch.

A black balaclava covered the intruder's face, leaving only his eyes visible. It was definitely a guy, judging by the shape of his wiry body. The efficiency with
which he worked his way through Ben's belongings told
her that he was a professional. This wasn't just some
teenager looking to score.

He slammed the dresser drawer shut and yanked
open the next one. A gun wouldn't scare off this guy

and would likely raise more questions than she was okay with when she had to explain a dead body to the police.

She would have to rely on her CIA training.

Sabine took a deep breath and rushed him. He looked up a split second before she slammed into him with the force of her body and knocked him off balance. The guy twisted so she was the one who hit the floor and the back of her head slammed against the carpet.

Before she could react, his hands were on her neck. She tried to push him off, but his weight and the pressure on her windpipe made her see stars.

The doorbell rang downstairs.

With shaky hands she found his shoulders, then his face, where she applied pressure with her thumbs until he cried out. She kicked off the floor hard enough to dislodge him and dove for the dresser top for something to use as a weapon. Two arms locked around her waist and lifted her off her feet. Sabine cried out and was dragged backward.

A loud thud came from downstairs. "Sabine!"

She struggled against her captor. Strength bled from her like water down the drain but she lifted her legs and slammed until she made contact with the intruder's shins. He let go of her and collapsed to his knees.

Boots pounded up the stairs.

Sabine spun and caught the intruder with a kick to the side of his head. The pain in her twisted ankle nearly buckled her legs, but she followed up with a solid punch. The guy still hadn't gone down. In fact, he was regrouping.

The bedroom door swung open, hit the wall and bounced back. Doug filled the doorway. Despite the fact that she'd left him in the Dominican Republic, something inside her leapt at the thought that he'd come to help her, not interrogate her.

The intruder took one look at Doug and sprinted for the window. The smash was deafening. Sabine ran over and looked out, but he was already up on his feet and running across the lawn. Rain sprayed in through the open window and Sabine backed up from the broken glass.

Doug's phone beeped.

"What are you doing?"

"I'm calling the cops. What do you think I'm doing?"

Sabine tried to grab the phone, but he refused to let go of it. All the warmth she'd felt when he burst in like some kind of knight of yore here to save the princess in distress deflated like a pricked balloon. He was trying to tell her what to do again.

"No cops. There are too many things I don't care to explain about my life or why someone would break into my home." She lost her grip on the phone then, probably because it was soaked, like Doug's leather jacket, jeans and wool hat. "How long were you outside? You're drenched."

"How long does it take to cross the street?" He folded his arms.

Sabine loved the sound of leather crackling.

"Nice weather you guys have here."

"I like it. It discourages lingering."

He grinned. "Kind of antisocial, aren't you?"

"Why are you here?"

Instead of answering, he turned away, and Sabine followed him to the garage where he rummaged around her damp Cadillac and came up with a hammer, some spare pieces of two-by-fours Ben had left and a box of nails.

She stood at the bottom of the stairs, tapping her foot—even though it hurt. Halfway up he looked back over his shoulder. "I don't suppose you'll accept saving you from an intruder as an answer."

"Not likely, since I had it handled." Sort of.

As nice as it would be to believe he'd come here to help, he couldn't have known she'd need saving from an intruder at that very moment. Since Doug was busy fixing her window, Sabine headed into the kitchen for some water and to raid her stash of painkillers. She didn't dare sit. What little strength kept her upright now would dissipate, and she'd be asleep in thirty seconds. While she was incapacitated, Doug would probably throw her over his shoulder and take her to whoever he reported to for that questioning he'd threatened her with.

No, it wouldn't do to let her guard down.

Upstairs she could hear the thud of the hammer. The last time he'd been in this kitchen with her—at Ben's memorial service—he'd been nice. Now he was being nice again, helping her. He probably thought she couldn't have fixed it herself. He'd be right. She was so drained it was tough to think straight.

Was he friend or foe? Doug acted like he cared. Then in her hotel room he had seemed so determined to find out what had happened to Ben that he was like a runaway train. Nothing would keep him from getting what he wanted.

She was a workaholic, but it seemed more like Doug lived and breathed the army. Now that this particular mission had become personal, there was nothing he wouldn't do.

Sticking around was a bad idea.

Sabine had just about summoned up the strength to figure out where her purse was when Doug reappeared, wiping his hands on the leg of his jeans.

"Thinking about running again?"

"I was—" Her voice gave out. Sabine touched her throat. It was tender from the intruder's grip. She sucked in a deep breath. In that moment it was all she had the strength to accomplish.

"Sabine."

His voice sounded far away, like he was speaking underwater.

The floor swept up toward her, and Sabine descended into darkness.

Doug caught her before she hit the floor and lifted her into the cradle of his arms. She weighed more than he thought. Tall and slender, Sabine was lean with muscle. Strong. The woman might have an iron core, but his heart had been in his throat since he'd been on her doorstep and heard her cry out over the sound of wind and rain.

After he had kicked the door in and pounded up the stairs, he'd been scared to death he'd find her dead on the floor. Instead, Sabine had put up a valiant fight against her assailant. Now rather than being outside searching for the guy who'd had the audacity to put his hands on Sabine—Doug had seen the marks on her throat—he carried her upstairs.

Doug set her down on the bed and removed her boots. Her ankle was puffy and swollen, but her breaths were deep and steady. He wrapped her in the comforter, turned on the bedside lamp and left the door ajar in case she cried out.

He sighed and lowered himself to the top step in the dark. He had to get a handle on his emotions. He couldn't freak out like that every time Sabine was in danger.

Pictures lined the wall, all the way down the stairs. He didn't need light to see the images of Ben at Little League or Ben wearing a tux as he walked Sabine down the aisle. She was divorced now. Ben had revealed that much about his sister, though none of the actual details—so long as you didn't count the way his lip curled when he mentioned Sabine's now ex-husband.

All Doug wanted was to find out who had killed Ben and why. After that he wouldn't have to wonder where she was or what she was doing…or if she wondered the same thing about him. Or what that sadness behind her eyes was.

His phone hummed. "Richardson."

"You got her?" The voice was gruff and full of authority, the voice of his commanding officer, Colonel Hiller.

"Found her fighting off an intruder in her house. Soon as she comes around, we'll be on our way."

There was a noncommittal noise. "She okay?"

Doug stood. He stretched out his back and made his way down the stairs. "She took some hits, but mostly she's just exhausted."

"I'm not surprised. That girl's one busy little beaver. Been up to all kinds of things since Sergeant Laduca died."

Doug's heart clenched at the memory of Ben bleeding out in his arms and forced himself to focus instead on his commanding officer's words. "She has?"

"Stuck her nose into classified records, for one thing. Girl's got a lot to answer for. The least of which being who she works for."

Doug found a diet soda in the fridge. It would have to do. "She's CIA."

"Not according to anyone I spoke to. Once upon a time, sure. They hired her, trained her and sent her on missions. A half dozen years ago she went off the grid. Disappeared, and the only thing she left behind was a pool of blood."

"She's some kind of rogue ex-CIA agent? Are you serious?" Then he remembered who he was talking to. "Excuse me, Colonel. I'm just having trouble assimilating this. She was kind of stuck-up about the CIA thing. If she works for someone else, she must be the best actress in the world." He thought for a second. "Did you tell the CIA we found her?"

"They're not stupid. Mostly. They'll figure out why I was asking about her, even though I did my best to keep it to vague questions. Hopefully it'll buy us time."

Doug tapped his finger on the side of the sweating can of soda. He wasn't going to tell Sabine what they'd found out. He'd probe instead with the hope that she would share of her own volition. Had Ben known she was a rogue agent? Doug had to get to the bottom of this before it all broke loose.

If she had betrayed the CIA and gone to work for the enemy six years ago, the CIA would have her on all kinds of watch lists. To have hidden her location and still be going on missions, fooling everyone left, right and center, meant she must be an exceptional spy. That or she worked for some very bad people…with very deep pockets.

A rogue CIA agent?

Doug sighed and ran a hand down his face.

"Get some answers, Sergeant Major. I expect to hear from you bright and early."

"Yes, sir."

"And call your dad."

Doug groaned.

"The old man knows you're back in the States. He's expecting your call."

The line went dead. Colonel Hiller wasn't one for goodbyes or any kind of politeness that could be expected from a fellow human being, but his record as an officer was so impressive; he was already a legend at forty-six. He'd earned his rank the hard way, from the ground up—ground soaked with his own sweat and blood.

Doug found a can of soup in the cupboard and set about heating it up on the stove. He scrolled through his contacts, found "Andrew" and pressed Send, intending to leave a voice mail.

"General Richardson's residence."

Doug smiled at the sound of the housekeeper's voice. "Hey, Jean. I take it he's still up since it's after midnight, yet you're answering the phone."

The fluffy middle-aged lady laughed like Doug's old Sunday school teacher. "How are you, honey?"

"I'm doing fine, Jean. Thank you."

"Well, you know I worry about you. Did you get those cookies I sent?"

"I did, yeah. They were good. The guys loved them."

He'd made sure to set aside some of the two dozen for himself.

"I should think so."

Doug laughed. The lightness in him stretched and grew, even with such a small connection with someone who had nothing to do with the war he seemed to always be fighting.

"My grandmother's secret recipe. Did you know she fought her way out of Nazi Germany with nothing but her recipe card box and her knitting needles?"

Laughter built up in his chest but didn't spill out. "That's a good story. You should stick with it."

"I'll do that. I'll put you through to your dad now, honey."

"Thanks, Jean."

There was a pause, and then a man's voice came over the line. "That you, son?" It was a voice that had both commanded troops and yelled at his teenage boy to straighten his room.

Doug sighed. "Yeah, Dad, it's me."

"It's about time. Did you think I'd settle for you checking in over voice mail forever?"

Doug's chest tightened until it ached. He should pay the old man a visit soon. "It's late. I should probably let you get to bed."

"Don't even try it. This is a momentous occasion. I actually got you on the phone. You think I'm just going to let you say goodbye in two seconds? Besides, isn't there something you want to tell me?"

Doug sighed, loud enough for his dad to hear. Of course he'd make him say it. "Happy birthday."

"You want to make it happy? You show up at my birthday party on Saturday. You wear a tux. You smile.

You tell me that you're letting this whole business go." His voice broke. "I want to see you get on with your life, Douglas. Find a woman. Get married, and make me a grandfather already. I'm getting old."

Before the general was finished, Doug was already shaking his head. "I would if I could, but I can't. Not until I find out who killed Ben."

"It's not just me. You know it's what your mother would have wanted."

"Oh, sure." Doug sighed. "Bring up Mom and how she'd be so disappointed in my behavior." His dad did it because it worked. Doug would never have willingly disappointed his mother.

The general huffed. "Always were too hard on yourself."

"This isn't just about me."

"I get it, son. I do." Fatigue clouded the old man's voice. "You want justice for your friend so your team can go on."

"And for his sister."

"You want to protect her."

"She's strong, but she still seems so…fragile."

There was quiet for a moment and then the general asked, "Is she pretty?"

"Dad."

"Fine, fine. You do what you need to do, son. But when you're done, you come see me, you hear?" The general waited a beat. "I miss you."

Doug pressed End and lowered the phone. "I miss you, too."

FIVE

The first clue that told Sabine something was off was when she woke up in bed fully clothed. Sun streamed through the open curtains and dust danced in the beam. The lamp beside her bed was on, so she switched it off and winced as various twinges made themselves known.

She staggered into the bathroom, dreaming so strongly of coffee she thought she could smell it. Only when she was submerged to her chin in a bath that was more soap bubbles than water did she relax. But she wasn't truly clean until she brushed her teeth, put on yoga pants and a stretchy pink top, and blow-dried her hair.

The soft carpet on the stairs felt nice between her toes. There was something she was supposed to be thinking about. Lots of things, probably; heavy things that made her heart squeeze in her chest. She closed her eyes and turned the corner at the bottom of the stairs, concentrating on the smooth wood of the banister under her fingers.

Until she had coffee she wasn't going to let anything bother her. At least anything more than why it seemed as if the coffee had already been made. Now that she thought about it, it sort of smelled like someone had cooked, too. Under the coffee scent, there was onion and cheese.

Her stomach rumbled.

This must be a dream. No one ever made the coffee except her, and she hadn't had a hot breakfast in years. She always had bland, tasteless cereal. But she wasn't dreaming—there was a dark figure behind the frosted glass of her kitchen door. She tried to inhale but the air got stuck in her throat, and she could feel the press of the intruder's hands around her neck.

"Are you going to get in here or just stand in the hall all day?" Doug opened the door. The smile on his face dropped, and he reached for her. "Sabine—"

She raised both hands. "Don't."

He moved aside for her. She didn't want to decipher the look on his face; it would invite too many questions about why he was in her kitchen. Cooking breakfast. Sabine lifted the lid on the pan and groaned. Sure enough, there was an omelet in there and it was covered in cheese. There hadn't been anything in the fridge last night.

"I went to the store this morning."

She must have spoken aloud. Her cheeks warmed, and Doug smiled like he was indulging her. She narrowed her eyes. "You weren't worried I'd take off while you were gone?"

"Figured it was worth the risk." He poured a cup of coffee and handed it to her. "You want creamer or half-and-half? I wasn't sure how you drank your coffee, so I got both."

Sabine took the cup for the peace offering it seemed to be. Why was he being nice to her? Was it just because he'd seen her when she was vulnerable and unable to take care of herself? Well, he could get over that.

It wasn't going to happen again if she had anything to say about it.

She went to the fridge and got the fat-free milk. "I thought you just wanted answers."

He divided the omelet into two pieces with a spatula, one bigger than the other. "I figured I'd get further if you didn't pass out again."

"I did not pass out."

He looked up. "What do you call it then?"

Sabine turned away and got forks from the drawer. Doug got the message and put their breakfast on two plates.

"It was nothing more than a spontaneous reaction to stress."

She thought he might have snorted. When she was about to give him what for, he held out the plate with the smaller portion. Sabine grabbed the bigger one from his other hand and walked to the table with her prize.

Doug waited until she was finished before he pushed his empty plate aside. He folded his hands together on top of the table.

She frowned. "This looks serious."

"It is serious."

Her shoulders drooped and she sighed. "I guess I have to face the real world eventually. It was nice to forget about it for a while, even if it was fleeting. Thank you for making breakfast."

Did she know she was running her nail along a grain in the tabletop?

"No one's ever done that for me before."

He tried not to look surprised. Her husband hadn't ever cooked her breakfast? "It was my pleasure."

"But now business?"

"Sorry." He wasn't sure why he apologized, as though that would combat any of the guilt. She seemed so small across the table from him, he had to resist the urge to cover her hand with his. "I still think we should work together, Sabine. As I said before, we both want to find out who killed Ben and why. It makes sense to pool our resources and team up. We'll work quicker that way."

"Okay." She didn't lift her gaze from the table.

"That's it? You're not going to fight me on this?"

"Why would I? It makes sense. We do want the same thing. The quicker we get to the bottom of this, the better off we'll both be."

He couldn't disagree with that. The guilt of not being able to save Ben ate at Doug like a stomach ulcer. If he could make enough sense of it to move on, he'd be a lot happier. He'd have peace. Sabine looked like she could use some peace, too.

"So where do we start?"

Doug stood and grabbed both their plates. "The dishes?"

Her eyes narrowed, but she followed him to the sink where he rinsed and she put things in the dishwasher. "Is this some weird way of buttering me up? You come here and play house with me while you try to get me to spill what I know? Is this your attempt at torture?"

He snorted. "If I had decided to torture it out of you, I'd hardly do it by making breakfast. I'd probably withhold food, knowing how much you like it."

"Shame you didn't think of that earlier. It probably would have worked." She waltzed to the door. "Too bad you'll never know what I'd have told you."

"Sabine." He caught up with her at the bottom of the stairs. "We need a plan."

"I'm going to get dressed. That's the plan."

"Then what?"

She looked at him like he didn't have a clue. "When I'm wearing real clothes and I've put on makeup, then we'll look through Ben's things and try to find out why someone was in there snooping."

Doug watched her walk away and tried to figure out how he was going to get out of this without Sabine leaving him twisted in knots. He didn't think she realized the effect she had on him.

It had been hard for him to think straight when she walked in the kitchen. The look on her face when she realized he'd made breakfast almost broke his heart. The loneliness there was the mirror image of how he felt every time he let himself into his apartment and recalled it was just him living there alone.

Too bad relationships were something he'd never had success at. He'd definitely enjoy seeing Sabine dressed up and taking her out to dinner. She needed to smile more; she needed someone to treat her the way she deserved to be treated.

You don't love me. You only love your job.

Tara's voice echoed in his thoughts and reminded him of the reason he couldn't start something with Sabine. Not even considering what she'd say when she found out he was responsible for Ben's death, there was too much going on in the world. Too much evil to fight for Doug to be less than 100 percent committed to his job. Relationships took too much of the energy he needed on missions. He couldn't get distracted thinking about getting home to her, or then his dad would get a call saying Doug had been killed in action.

When Sabine realized he wouldn't give up his job, her heart would get broken and since he couldn't stand to see her hurt, that meant she was off-limits.

She came into view at the top of the stairs wearing pressed black trousers and a blue buttoned-up blouse. Apparently "real clothes" meant she had to look like she worked a regular nine-to-five job in an office.

"We should look at the hard drive you took from Christophe."

She opened her mouth and closed it again. "I'll get it after we go through Ben's room."

Satisfied she might not hold out on him, he looked through the drawers and under Ben's bed while Sabine checked the closet. The shelf above where Ben's clothes hung was a jumble of shoe boxes, canvas bags and blankets that looked like they'd been stuffed up there.

Under the bed was a mess of food wrappers and dirty clothes Doug didn't dare touch. The drawers were disturbed the way you'd think, since someone had broken in and pawed through it all. Then again, when Ben had grabbed his things and left for base the last time, it probably looked much the same.

"Not the neatest person in the world." Doug glanced at Sabine, cross-legged on the floor and rifling through a shoe box filled with old photos. She covered her mouth with her hand, and he realized she was trying not to cry.

He crouched beside her. "What is it?"

She looked up, her eyes wide. "Pictures. Old ones." She handed one to him. Two little kids—Sabine and Ben around elementary school age by the looks of it.

"That your parents?" A good-looking couple had their arms around the kids, and everyone was smiling.

Sabine nodded. "I never even knew he had these."

"You guys look happy."

"I guess. We were in foster care by the end of that year." There was something in her voice, a guardedness which told him that she wasn't convinced there was happiness behind the smiles. "What happened?"

Sabine stuffed the photos back in the box. "It doesn't matter now. Let's keep looking."

"Ben wouldn't tell me what happened, either."

She tried not to let him see her flinch, but he caught it. "I'm surprised he even remembered. He was little, and we never talked about it. They tried to get us to see counselors, but it wasn't anyone else's business. We moved on." Her eyes filled. "And now he's gone."

"It won't always feel like this. It'll ease."

She shook her head. "I don't want it to ease. If the pain goes away, it means I'm forgetting him."

"It's okay to heal, Sabine."

"Sounds like you know."

"I've lost brothers in combat before. It doesn't get easier, but you learn how to deal with it. Some of the guys drink too much. Some blow off the steam of their grief in other ways. You have to, or you'll bottle it up until one day you explode."

She looked up at him. "What do you do?"

"I run. And I pray while I run."

Sabine pulled away from him for the second time. He didn't know where she stood on the whole faith thing, but Ben had been a new Christian before his death. Time and again Doug had caught the younger man eyeing Doug over something he had said or done. One night when they were alone on a mission, Ben had asked Doug why he was different than the other team members.

Two days later Ben had announced to Doug his commitment to follow Jesus.

Two weeks after that, Doug had held Ben's body while Ben took his last breath.

Ben's commitment to the Lord was the one good thing in this whole mess. Sabine had loved her brother. Eventually Doug would have to tell her that it was his fault that Ben was dead, and Doug might as well have pulled the trigger himself.

When she found out, it would kill everything that was between them.

It didn't look to him like she was over any of it. Whatever had happened to her parents was fresh in her mind still. Not that he could talk. He had plenty of issues. "Surely you told your husband about what happened to your parents when you got married?"

She looked at him as if he'd grown two heads. "Don't presume you know anything about me or my marriage. That part of my life is not up for discussion."

Doug wasn't about to back down. "We're not going to get anywhere in this partnership if we can't trust each other."

"That doesn't mean I'm going to share everything with you. All we're doing is finding out who killed Ben. My personal life has nothing to do with it."

"I'm not saying that." Because there was a whole lot he was never going to share. "All I'm saying is there has to be some give and take here."

She folded her arms. "Fine then, you go first."

He sat in the chair at Ben's desk, ready to be grilled. "Fire away."

"Have you ever been married?"

"Almost, a long time ago."

"What happened?"

Doug took a deep breath. "She decided I loved my job more than I loved her."

"Did you?"

"Probably." He didn't feel guilty. It had saved him from getting tied down in a bad situation. He'd have been miserable as Tara's husband. "I do a tough job, one that takes all my attention. There's not a lot left over for a wife."

"That's a total cop-out. Soldiers get married every day. Sure, it's hard to keep a good marriage together, but that goes for everyone. There's added pressure because you're gone so much. I think, if you had wanted it to work, you'd have figured it out."

"Is that what happened to you?"

Sabine flinched. "That was a totally different situation."

"I know, I know." He raised his palms. "Don't presume I know you. But I'd like to. We need to build some trust between us."

He watched her compose herself, like a new recruit facing battle for the first time—trying to hide the fear.

"With Maxwell and me, it was different. There wasn't a lot of affection between us in the first place. That didn't change much after we got married. I mistakenly thought the sense of security that came with being married would make up for it. When he took up with his secretary, I didn't see much point in letting the farce continue."

Doug couldn't believe a man married to Sabine hadn't been totally committed to making their lives together a rich and enjoyable experience. She deserved that much. He wanted to ask why she had settled for a marriage like that, but she cut him off.

"We should take a look at the hard drive I got from Christophe."

Sabine stomped down the stairs. Why had she said all that? She had never talked about her marriage, not even to Ben. He hadn't been under any illusions about it, but he also had never questioned her decision to get married or said anything when she had filed for divorce.

Up until now she would have said she was over the whole experience. The look on Doug's face made her rethink that idea. Compassion, pity—whatever it was—made her uncomfortable. She'd rather walk away and not look back. She'd prefer he hadn't known anything of her bad decision to marry Maxwell. It hadn't really been a matter of her settling for less. A more loving relationship just wasn't something that she deserved.

Now it was so over, the divorce papers had dust on them. She couldn't have the kind of relationships other women seemed to think were so great. It wasn't in Sabine to be so vulnerable that it gave someone else the power to break her heart.

Sabine fished the hard drive from her suitcase and went into her office, proud that Doug would see her sanctuary.

The bookshelves heaved with everything from books on gardening—one day she'd do that—to popular classics. She didn't buy first editions; she bought books she could read again and again, ones that were now frayed. Some had tape on their spines they were so worn out. Just like the armchair. She'd spent many hours in the plush chair by the window, lost in another world.

Even though she'd rather go AWOL in any one of her books, she took the hard drive to the oak desk and slid it in the port that would download the contents to her desktop computer. In minutes they would have everything they needed to bring down the person responsible for Ben's death.

She switched on her computer and tapped her finger

while it booted up. Doug scanned the shelves and made short noises. Was that good or bad?

He looked over at her. "You're pretty good with computers?"

Sabine exhaled. They were out of sensitive waters and back to plain old banter. "Who do you think taught Ben everything he knew?"

Doug looked impressed. Sabine shifted in the leather chair. A few clicks later, she tapped her fingers on the desk while the information downloaded.

"Sabine." Doug hauled her out of the chair, his eyes on the hard drive she'd flown halfway around the world for. Smoke curled up from the bay.

It sparked.

Doug pulled her to the doorway.

A loud boom shook the room. The force of the explosion blew her to the ground, and Doug landed on top of her. His head hit the floor beside her, and she winced at the sound.

Smoke filled the room. Sabine felt the heat of flames but couldn't move. Doug seemed to be unconscious, pinning her to the floor. "Get off me."

She shoved at him. "Get up, Doug." He didn't respond. Heat touched her bare foot. She tried to shift away from the flames, but couldn't move under his weight.

"Come on, soldier. Wake up. I have no intention of burning to death with you lying on top of me."

SIX

"I'm sorry I yelled at you when you were unconscious," Sabine said.

The fire truck pulled away from the house. She was beside him on the front step. Thankfully the blaze had been small and quickly contained, but Doug's head continued to thump from his injury, like he'd been hit with a brick. "I'm sorry I was unconscious."

"It could have been a lot worse." She raised her chin from the cocoon of the blanket the EMTs had given her. "It could still be raining."

Doug shrugged. "I guess."

"You don't really feel guilty about this, do you?" She laid a hand on his arm. "Doug, this wasn't your fault. You didn't know the hard drive would blow up. It's not your fault you were knocked out. We're both barely hurt."

"I know."

"But you should have...what? Done more? Cut yourself some slack. You're not a superhero, so far as I know. Just a regular human like the rest of us."

How was it she could take one look at him and deftly nail his problem? Was it so obvious he was plagued by guilt? He was just trying to do a good job, and things kept getting messed up.

A familiar prickle teased the back of his neck. Doug stood. They shouldn't be out in the open in broad daylight now that emergency services were gone. Too bad it was Saturday. When the front window of her office had blown out, her neighbor had been mowing his lawn. Good that the firefighters had come so fast; bad that many neighbors were home on the weekend and curious about the small explosion.

Doug was just glad he'd come to before the fire spread and thus had saved himself the indignity of being hauled out of the house by a firefighter.

"What is it?" Sabine looked up and down her street.

"It's not safe to stay here."

Her eyes flashed like she was getting ready to argue. "Sabine—"

"I'm not disagreeing with you. I just have to get some things together before I can leave."

He held open the front door for her. "Pack for a few days. And bring anything of Ben's you think might yield information."

Sabine tore her eyes from the charred, waterlogged floor and the ash-covered walls. "Where are we going?"

"When I know, I'll tell you."

She ascended the stairs. Doug pulled out his phone and made a call.

"Colonel Hiller? The hard drive we got from Parelli had some kind of fail-safe. It blew up before we could get anything from it."

Kids screamed and laughed in the background. "I'm going to assume it's you who got the cops to back off with their questions."

"You're welcome, Sergeant Major. What's your plan?"

"Get her somewhere safe. Get some answers."

"Why don't the two of you head to your dad's place?" There was silence for a moment. "You can't tell me the general wouldn't be fine with it. Not to mention he has the most secure residence we know of."

Doug fought the urge to reach through the phone and throttle his superior officer. "You're right, but I don't like it, sir."

"Want me to make it an order?"

Doug sighed. "Is this some kind of conspiracy to get me to his birthday party?"

The colonel barked a laugh and then yelled at his son to stop trying to drown his sister in the pool. "Birthday aside, it wouldn't hurt you to visit the man. He calls just about every day asking after you."

"His clearance is still good?"

"You think I tell him what you're doing?"

"Thank you, sir."

"You're welcome, Sergeant Major. Get yourself on a plane to D.C. Your dad's place will give you the space and the time you need to question Ms. Sabine Laduca. I'll get to tell the CIA that she's in our custody, and they can wait until we're done with her."

Doug wanted to ask all the questions on the tip of his tongue, but Sabine appeared. She hauled two huge suitcases down the stairs. "Yes, sir."

She glanced at him. Doug hung up the phone and she came to him, looking like she expected him to tell her who was on the phone and the content of the conversation.

"Got everything?"

"I'll put these in my car and come back for my purse and lock up the house."

She didn't get his sarcasm, apparently. "Actually, they're going in my rental car." He pointed out front. "The Prius across the street."

Her head cocked to the side. "I would have pegged you more as a big truck kind of guy."

She was right. "It was all they had." He grabbed the first suitcase. "Enough stalling—let's get moving."

By the time he crammed both suitcases alongside his duffel bag in the trunk of the tiny car, Sabine had locked her front door. He scanned the street while she crossed to him, looking good enough he needed to concentrate on something else or he'd get distracted. She might have a smudge of ash on the side of her face, but she was still beautiful.

In the car, Sabine buckled her seat belt. "So where are we going?"

He looked over. She was trying to hide a smirk. The driver's seat was a tight fit for him.

"Want me to drive?"

"No, thank you." He didn't care if his tone was short. "We're going to my dad's place in Washington. Gates, security guards, few people to worry about and plenty of space to sit down and figure all this out."

He drove out of her subdivision, pulled onto the freeway and headed for the airport. "Nothing to say?"

She just stared out the window.

"You're just going to let me take you wherever I want and not do anything about it?" They both knew she could give him the slip whenever she wanted. Doug would have to be on guard. "Sabine?"

She finally looked at him. "Take the next exit. I need something from my storage unit before we leave town."

He couldn't read the look on her face because he had his eyes on the road. Sometime soon they needed to sit down and have this out. There was still way too much he didn't know about Sabine, Ben and this whole business.

But there was something he needed to get clear right then. "Why did you tell me you were with the CIA?"

Sabine blinked and her face creased into a frown. "You think I was lying?"

"Were you?"

"Let me guess. You called to check my story?"

"My commanding officer did."

She nodded. "The CIA is supposed to deny my existence. It's what they do."

"I'm not so sure."

"Tell me what it is."

He glanced at her, and she saw a flash of worry had darkened his eyes. Interesting, since he didn't care about her. The only reason they were together was so he could interrogate her.

"The CIA claims you don't work for them anymore. Since six years ago, you've been a rogue agent."

Six years ago?

Sabine flinched. She could still feel the sting of gunfire from that day. With her cover blown, she'd been given a new handler and now worked in a clandestine department. Well, it was the CIA, so all the departments were clandestine, but hers even more so.

One day she'd either retire or end up as a nameless star on a wall, with only a handful of people who would ever really know what had happened to her.

Of course they would deny her existence. To them she probably didn't exist. That was the nature of the work she did. She didn't need to prove herself to Doug; she knew who she worked for. The fact that she hadn't even stepped foot inside Langley in those six years only proved just how under the radar they wanted her.

Doug pulled up outside a garage-size unit in the far corner of the complex. He could tell the news about who she worked for was a shock, but she seemed to push it away. The closer they drove to her storage area, the tenser she became.

With one foot out the parked car, she turned back. Her mouth was thin. "Stay here."

He watched her walk away. He wanted to go, despite what she said. He gripped the steering wheel so tight he was probably warping it. Sure, she'd ditched him yesterday in the Dominican Republic, but since then they'd fought off an intruder together and had almost been blown up. This was a good time to show her that he would do what she asked. Especially when she said it with that look of total despair on her face—the same look she'd had at Ben's funeral. She'd been ready to lose it to her grief again. What had brought it back to the surface now?

Her family had been happy at one time. At least if the photo in Ben's room was anything to go by. Then something had gone down, and the two of them had ended up in foster care until Sabine had turned eighteen and won custody of her fifteen-year-old brother. Doug had figured their parents were dead, but they could have just as easily been in jail.

Perhaps the loss of her brother was surging up at

the most unexpected moment to blindside her, just as it did to him. Ben was the only family she had and Doug had taken that away from her. As if he had forgotten his culpability.

Doug watched Sabine stride past the unit number she'd given him, the one he would have been able to see directly into. She went three units down, unlocked it and slid up the door. Doug swallowed. He could pretend otherwise, but he had it bad when a woman using all her strength to open a garage door got to him.

He tapped the steering wheel.

Checked his phone.

Sabine reappeared with a briefcase, which she set on the backseat. She clipped her seat belt and looked up. "What?"

"You're not going to tell me what that is?"

"It's a briefcase."

"Sabine—"

"Oh, don't say it like you're so exasperated. I'm tired, Doug. It's been a rough couple of weeks. Can we at least try to be civil to each other for a while?"

"Fine. Only because I'm tired, too. Your couch is not the most comfortable place in the world to sleep. Though, I have bunked down in a lot worse places."

"You didn't use the guest room?"

"You passed out. I wasn't going to snoop around. I figured crashing on the couch was the least imposing way of keeping an eye on you."

"Keeping an eye on—"

"Enough." Doug held up his hand. "Let's go back to the truce. I liked that idea."

Sabine folded her arms. "Truce."

"Good. It won't be long, and then we can rest on

the plane. When we get to my dad's, there might be a little party going on, but we can sneak in through the kitchen."

The *little party,* as Doug had put it, turned out to be a seventieth birthday bash for his father, General Andrew Richardson. Limousines lined the driveway. The entire place was lit up, and swing music from a live band poured out open windows. Doug drove their rental car—a midsize sedan this time—around the side of the house, through a brick archway to a rear courtyard.

Sabine wished she was wearing the green floor-length gown she'd put in her suitcase on a whim. A formal dress could come in handy at any time and packing for any occasion had long been a habit. Then again, anything would be better than showing up in ash-smeared clothes and smelling like she'd run a marathon. At least she'd taken some time at the airport to find a bathroom and clean up a little bit. Though she'd have paid money for a shower.

"Ready?"

She nodded. Doug had valiantly tried to draw her into conversation during the flight, but she hadn't been able to get past the mess of thoughts that had hummed in her head like a swarm of bees. Ben's death, then Christophe's, and the loss of any leads they might have had. It was late, and Sabine was ready for sleep. Maybe one day in the future she'd wake up and not feel just as tired as she had when she had gone to bed. As hard as she had pushed to find out what had happened to Ben, it had taken its toll.

Doug got out the bags and opened her door. "You okay?"

"You mean other than smelling like a gym sock?"

He snorted. "You're so pretty I don't think that would make a difference."

He thought she was pretty?

"Come on." He helped her out.

"I usually don't need this much babying."

"You said it yourself. It's been a rough time for you lately."

"I don't like being helpless."

Doug snorted, pulling her bags by their handles, his duffel hanging over his shoulder. "Whatever you are, Sabine Laduca, it's anything but helpless."

The door opened to an older woman with a stylish bob cut and blond highlights. She was comfortably round in her knit sweater and black slacks, and smiled wide at the sight of them. "I didn't dare believe it until I saw it myself."

Doug dropped the luggage and swept her up into a hug. "Jean." He kissed both her cheeks.

"The prodigal son returns."

Doug laughed. "I haven't been that bad, have I?"

The older lady chuckled. "He's done okay. Don't worry yourself."

"You take good care of him."

"Yes, yes." She ushered them into an extensive galley kitchen. "I'm more concerned with what you've brought with you, or should I say, whom?"

Sabine held out her hand. "Sabine Laduca."

"I know, darling. I'm Jean Pepper." The hand that clasped hers wasn't altogether soft, but it was warm. Sabine imagined the woman was much like a grandmother should be and had to push away a pang of something she didn't want to think about.

"Your brother had nothing but good things to say about you."

Sabine sucked in a breath, not knowing what to say. A lot of Ben's attachment to her had been because of what had happened to their parents. She'd loved Ben, but it was strange to meet someone who knew of her. So much for living a low-key life.

Thankfully Doug came to her rescue. He probably read her discomfort. Why he felt it necessary to put his hand on the small of her back was anyone's guess. Still, it was nice to have him stand shoulder to shoulder with her almost like they were a team. "I'm going to show Sabine upstairs so she can settle in."

Jean glanced between them as though she knew a secret. "Your tux is hanging from the closet door in your room."

"Does he know I'm here?"

"I decided to surprise him. He'd have been disappointed if you hadn't come."

Doug nodded to Jean and grabbed all the bags again. "I'll be back down shortly."

Sabine didn't offer to carry any of the bags. He'd been adamant the few times she had tried to pull even one, giving her some ridiculous spiel about being perfectly capable. Apparently he didn't get that she was just as able.

Doug led her up a wide staircase with rich red carpet, wood paneling and portraits on the walls. The whole place was permeated with the musk of old money, while the bulk of her childhood consisted of mediocre foster homes, some not as nice as others. Sabine liked nice things, but this place made her want to take her shoes off at the door.

They passed a ballroom filled with glitzy people. When Doug cleared his throat, Sabine blinked and hurried to catch up. "Did you grow up here?"

He shook his head as they climbed. "We moved around a lot—you know, military family and all. When my dad got promoted and assigned to the Pentagon, we stayed. I was sixteen."

His voice had cracked. She waited until he was ready to say more.

"That was the summer my mom died." Their eyes met. "Her cancer snuck up on all of us, and it was over almost as fast as it had come."

"I'm sorry." What else could she say?

At least he had a mom for that long. Sabine had neither parent and barely remembered more than the last day they'd all been together, though she'd been nine. That day was still etched into her brain, never to be erased.

Doug left her in a room that was feminine but not over-the-top, with floor-to-ceiling drapes and a four-poster bed. He walked away muttering about simpering crowds and being choked by his own collar.

She smiled. Too antsy to rest, despite being exhausted, Sabine decided Doug might need some moral support downstairs. After all, there was a formal dress in her bag.

She headed for the bathroom.

Fresh from his four-minute shower, Doug walked downstairs still tying the bow tie of his tuxedo. It was an instrument of torture. He really should burn the thing. If his uniform hadn't been in his closet in Texas where he lived on base, he'd have worn that.

He smoothed down the front of the jacket, took a deep breath and pushed open the double doors. The place was loud and bright, full of senators, business-people and high-ranking military personnel. His father held court at the far end of the room, surrounded by eager ears and fat wallets.

Doug would rather be upstairs with Sabine. They could have watched a ball game or a movie. He could have taken his dad for a round of golf in the morning. He wasn't going to tell the old man that, if it hadn't been for Sabine, Doug probably wouldn't even be here.

People turned to look as he crossed the room. Doug refused champagne from more than one waiter with a silver tray, but, despite his size, what probably struck them was the resemblance between father and son. With his dad being a well-known general, it was a wonder Doug didn't get in more trouble on covert missions. The only difference between them, other than age, was the lighter brown of Doug's skin from his Caucasian mother.

He liked that she was still with him, in that way, but he'd rather have her.

The general looked up as he approached. His father's dark green jacket gleamed with buttons and medals. His face crinkled and laugh lines emerged on his chocolate-colored skin. "Douglas!"

The cigar smoke was strong and made his eyes water. Doug smiled while his dad pounded him on the back. "So where is this mystery woman you chased all the way across the country?"

People around them stopped to look at something.

"She's upstairs resting."

The music also stopped, and the general's bushy white eyebrows rose. "Resting, huh?"

Doug turned around. Sabine was in the doorway, and the room grew still and quiet as people turned to get a look at her in a floor-length dark green dress. Her hair cascaded around her shoulders in a riot of waves and curls. She was beautiful.

The general clapped him on the back. "Does she know she's the one?"

SEVEN

It was too late for second thoughts. Sabine pasted on a smile and crossed the room. The music started up again, and she waved off a waiter's offer of champagne. Rarely did she find herself out of her depth, but she felt it here in a roomful of— *Was that the chairman of the Joint Chiefs of Staff?* Sabine was pretty sure she'd seen him on CNN last week.

With a polite nod she made her way to where Doug stood with a bald older African-American man who was a few inches shorter than Doug, but no less wide. General Richardson was a formidable sight with all those medals pinned to his jacket. Sabine raised her chin as he met her eyes and said something to Doug that she was too far away to hear.

Someone grabbed her arm. Before the threat even fully registered, instinct and training made her react with a spin, ready to strike back at her attacker.

"Whoa, take it easy…. Elena Sanders?"

The name brought with it a rush of memory and emotion, and Sabine lowered her hands. An attack in front of a bunch of armed military servicemen and servicewomen wasn't likely.

She blinked at the man in front of her. "Mr. Adams?"

It had been years since she'd seen anyone from the days when she had trained with the CIA, and here she was, face-to-face with the man who'd given her a fail on her weapons proficiency test. She'd retaken it twice. The years had turned Steve Adams's dark hair to silver at the temples and had deepened the lines around his eyes.

A new wariness was there, emphasized when he scanned the area around them and leaned closer. "What are you doing here? You have a lot of explaining to do."

Sabine made a point to glance at his grip on her arm. There would probably be a bruise tomorrow. When he let her go, she backed up, ready to rip into him for man-handling her for no reason. "It's a party. What do you think I'm doing here?"

Doug stepped up beside her. "Everything okay, Sabine?"

"Sabine?" Steve asked.

She ignored the question. "This is Steve Adams, one of my training officers at the CIA."

Doug shook Steve Adams's hand. The quick tightening around Steve's eyes before Doug let go would have been a wince of pain in anyone else.

"Nice to meet you, Steve."

"I'd like to say it's a pleasure."

Sabine didn't want to feel comfort from the touch of Doug's tuxedo sleeve against her bare arm, but she did. It wouldn't take much for one of them to reach out and take the other's hand.

Focus.

"So, Steve…" Sabine cut through the tension between the two men. "What are you up to these days?"

Steve's eyes flickered again, a trace of confusion he

allowed her to see. "I'm a director at Langley now. I have been for the past four years. You?"

"Same old, same old. You know how it goes." She smiled. He would know that she had spent the last few years doing what she did best: gathering intelligence on some of the world's biggest crooks.

"Unfortunately, no, I don't know." Again Steve glanced around the room. He was no doubt as aware as Sabine of the eyes watching them, the ears peeled. "Is there somewhere we can talk in private?"

"I can show you to my father's library."

Sabine trailed behind Doug across the ballroom with Steve beside her. What did this man, a man she at one time considered a mentor, want to talk about? He'd been so surprised to run into her that something strange must be going on. And why did it seem like Doug already knew what Steve was going to tell her? Probably it was CIA business. How had they even known she would be here tonight, at this party? The CIA kept track of its assets, but this was crazy.

Doug opened the door to a room lined with book-shelves. There wasn't a spare space that she could see. It was full, and yet the room didn't feel closed in to her, just warm and open. Sabine would have loved to spend hours in here, lost to worlds of adventure.

The door closed with Doug still in the room. He caught her look and shook his head, like she should've known he would include himself, and turned to Steve. "This room is secure. You don't have to worry about listening devices. You can speak freely."

Steve's eyebrow peaked. "Except that you're here."

If the look on Steve's face was anything to go by, Sabine was going to want Doug to be here for whatever was about to be said. Not that she would tell Steve that Doug was anything more than a regular soldier. "It is okay, Mr. Adams. I trust Sergeant Major Richardson."

Steve's face was blank, a mask of indifference that said enough without saying anything at all. This man felt the need to hide behind nonchalance, which told Sabine of the gravity of the situation.

She chose a dark wood gondola chair that had a green-suede-covered seat. "What is it?"

Steve scanned a bookshelf beside him, then finally came and sat across the cherrywood coffee table in a chair that matched hers. "You have some kind of nerve showing up here, Ms. Sanders. After what you did six years ago, I would think you'd have the good sense to stay away from this part of the country. Either you're incredibly brave or completely reckless."

Doug's mouth opened, and she shot him a look, cutting off whatever he'd been about to say. "I'd love to know what you're talking about, Mr. Adams, but I'm afraid I have no idea. Six years ago, when the Tamaris mission went wrong—"

"Went wrong?" Steve's face flushed. "Three agents, your team, your friends, were all left for dead on that mission. You disappeared. The company spent a considerable amount of time and manpower searching for you to determine if you'd been killed or captured."

"Captured?" Sabine couldn't believe it. "I was left for dead, just like the others. I woke up two days later in a French hospital with three bullet wounds. After I recovered, my new handler told me I had to disappear. He gave me everything I needed to start a new life. It was only after I rebuilt everything from the ground up that I started taking on missions again."

Steve looked her over, as though assessing the truth of her words. "Who is your handler?"

"His name is Neil. That's all I know."

"It would be worth your while to find out more about him." He paused for a beat. "Ms. Sanders, this situation is very serious. For the past six years, everyone at the CIA has wondered who killed the other members of your team on the Tamaris mission. Some even speculated that you killed them yourself and then disappeared."

"I've given my whole life to the CIA. How can they even say that?"

"Because if what you say is true, then those who speculated that you have gone rogue are, in fact, correct."

"Rogue?"

Steve nodded. "Several times over the last few years, agents out on missions claim to have seen you. There was never any hard evidence to prove it. You're quite adept at that which we trained you for."

"This is the most contrived story I've ever heard." Sabine tamped down the urge to rage at the man before her. Instead she tried to remember the respect she once had for him. "You're saying I was duped into being a rogue agent by someone pretending to be a CIA handler?"

"It's not out of the realm of possibility, if you think about it. They convince you the situation was so bad it was necessary for you to go dark, part of some super-secret department. They provide you with a new identity... *Sabine.* Now you work for them, a fully trained CIA operative at their beck and call. It's clever."

"I am not a pawn. I would know if I wasn't working for the CIA anymore."

Steve didn't seem convinced. "Not if they didn't want you to. Whoever you're working for now convinced you that you're still a CIA agent when you've been number one on our list of rogues since the Tamaris mission. They're evidently very good at what they do."

"This whole thing is crazy."

Doug squeezed her shoulder. "You should listen to him."

She turned her frown on him. "Why? How do you know anything about this?"

"After we saw each other in the Dominican Republic, I gave your information to my commanding officer. He said the same thing. I told you the CIA denied all knowledge of you. They've been looking for you. Though how you managed to change your name and Ben's—and stay hidden this whole time—is beyond me."

"We didn't change Ben's name. I never told the CIA that I had a brother. We went our separate ways for a while after he had graduated from high school, and then he joined the army. We had different last names, anyway, so when I needed a new identity, I borrowed his. It wasn't too hard for the government to find they had accidentally lost a few key records of Ben's. The ones that linked us." She shrugged. "It wasn't anyone else's business but mine that I have—had a half brother."

Sabine looked back at Steve and dread settled over her like a storm cloud. "Are you going to have me arrested?"

He worked his mouth. "You should at least come in to Langley so we can get this whole thing sorted out. There's a lot of stuff to unpack, if we're going to figure out what happened and who this handler of yours is… who he works for."

"Not before I figure out what happened to Ben."

Steve frowned. Sabine filled him in on what had happened since her brother's death and her investigation into who was responsible. She left out the part about her intruder and the exploding hard drive.

Steve sighed. "I understand you want justice for your brother, but the army is no doubt conducting an investigation." Steve looked at Doug, who nodded. "While I'm not unsympathetic to your situation, it's of the utmost importance that you yield yourself to us for questioning. We have to get to the bottom of this."

Sabine strode to the far end of the room and stared at a shelf of historical novels. Her eyes refused to focus on the titles printed on the spines. Her brain was far too full, trying to process what Steve had told her. Could she really be a rogue agent?

She picked through her memories and tried to find some indication that her handler, Neil, was anything other than the CIA agent he had claimed to be. Before seeing Christophe Parelli killed by someone who looked exactly like her, she would have said for certain Neil was who he had said he was. Now she couldn't be sure.

There was just no way to predict the outcome. Sabine could end up in prison, disgraced or most likely the victim of an *accident* that brought about her untimely demise. If she really had been duped into working as an agent against the CIA, then she doubted whoever it was would let her live long enough to provide the actual CIA with enough evidence to discover their identity.

Sabine had been a victim once, long ago. After that she had vowed never to return to such a helpless state. The truth about Ben's death would stay hidden unless she was able to help Doug figure out who had killed her brother and why. There was no way she could turn herself in to the CIA for questioning when they would most likely detain her indefinitely.

She turned back and found both men watching her. "I will help you find out who it is I've been working for."

"Good—"

Sabine cut him off. "But not until after Doug and I find the person who killed my brother. You need to keep this to yourself, Mr. Adams. Do not tell anyone you've seen or spoken to me. In return for your promise, as soon as this is over, I'll turn myself in to the CIA. You can do whatever you want with me."

"Sabine…" Doug's voice was guarded. He was probably right to be worried.

"I'll even work out a meeting with my handler. You can set up surveillance. I'll wear a wire. You can use me however you want to find out who it is I've been working for. But I do what I need to do first."

Steve shook his head. "I don't know about this."

"I don't need you to agree, Mr. Adams. I can walk away right now. I can disappear again, and you'll never find me. I'll still get what I want—time enough to hunt for Ben's killer—while you get nothing."

A thought occurred to her. "If my handler really is working against you, they're no doubt keeping tabs on their asset…me. If they think I've given you anything, they're going to close up shop as fast as possible and go so far underground that you'll never figure it out. It's what I would do."

Doug nodded slowly. "Not before they get rid of all the evidence."

Sabine caught his gaze and knew he'd reached the

same conclusion as her. "They'll kill me. Which is not part of my five-year plan."

Steve rubbed a hand down his face. "You want me to pretend I never saw you when a roomful of government staffers just witnessed the two of us meet and leave the room together?"

"There's no reason to believe they'll say anything. Or that they won't. It's a risk, but a calculated one that I can live with. I think I can trust General Richardson's taste in friends."

Doug folded his arms. "You can."

"You want me to sit on this until you decide to turn yourself in? You've been gone for six years as far as anyone at the Agency is concerned." Steve blew out a breath. "You want me to let you leave on good faith?"

"You know me, Mr. Adams. Or at least you did. If what you say is true, I was duped. As far as I'm concerned, I've been nothing but an upright agent of the intelligence community my whole working life. That means, despite being deceived, I'm still as trustworthy as I ever was."

Steve studied her for a moment and then nodded. "Give me some insurance, and I'll trust you."

Sabine snorted. "Typical. You'll trust me, but not without something to hold over me? That's hardly trust, but I don't suppose I expected differently from a CIA agent."

"I could detain you right now."

Doug put himself between her and Steve. "You could try it, but you wouldn't get two feet from my father's house with her."

Steve's eyes widened. "I see. It's like that, is it? You're willing to go to bat for a loose cannon?"

Sabine was as surprised as Steve that Doug put himself between her and the complete destruction of her career and her reputation. Any way she looked at it, this was bad. Was he really willing to jeopardize his life, as well? She stared at Doug's back. In most ways, they were polar opposites. Not to mention that he didn't even trust her. Why was he doing this?

After everything they'd been through, Sabine had come to admire him. She could even admit she was attracted to him, but there was too much grief over Ben between them for anything to develop romantically.

"Being a loose cannon is part of her charm."

Sabine wasn't sure how she felt about that. Was Doug trying to compliment her in a roundabout way? If she was a loose cannon, he was about as impulsive as a piece of plywood. Talk about opposites attracting.

Steve looked around Doug. His eyes zeroed in on her. "You have one week."

"A week!"

"That's all I'm giving you. Seven days from now I expect to get a call from the security guards at Langley asking if I'll authorize your admittance."

Sabine nodded. That was the best offer she was likely to get. "Done."

She reached up and clasped the flower on her necklace, one of the last gifts she'd received from Ben. A peace offering for the way he had blown up after he'd found out she was a CIA agent. Now that might not even be true.

"You have something to give me?"

Sabine found a notepad and pen in the top drawer of the desk, scribbled on it, tore off the page and handed it to Steve. "I'll see you in a week."

Steve Adams pocketed the paper and closed the library door behind him.

She turned to Doug. "You didn't seem too surprised about what Steve had to say. You want to tell me what you knew about all this?"

"You want to tell me what was on that piece of paper?"

"No."

Doug smiled, completely disarming her. "Good, because I'd rather dance with you anyway."

"But—"

"Sabine." He came around the desk to her. "Let's go back to the party. We both need time to let this settle in."

"But—"

He lifted her hand to his mouth and kissed the back of it. "Have I told you how beautiful you are in this dress?"

EIGHT

Doug held his arms loose, when everything in him wanted to clasp Sabine to him as tight as possible as they swayed slowly in the middle of the dance floor. Couples all around them moved to the rhythm of an old love song, caught up in the moment.

The comment his dad had made when she entered the ballroom ran through his mind. Was she the one? He could hardly see there being a time in either of their lives when they might be free to begin a relationship. No matter how appealing the thought was.

And yet it felt so natural to hold her in his arms. He wanted to keep her there as long as possible, but circumstances seemed to conspire against them. A cloud of foreboding settled on him—like if he let her go he'd lose something he would never get back.

Doug wanted to go to Langley with her when she turned herself in. He wanted to be her line of defense. Mostly he wanted to stick with her and see where this might lead, and there was little time to lose if they wanted to find out what had happened to Ben.

But Sabine was wound so tight, she needed to take her mind off what was going on.

He was still floored by everything he'd learned about her from Adams. The CIA guy had been genuinely surprised to see her. When Adams had said she'd been AWOL for the past six years, Doug had discovered why. Watching her process the news that she'd been so thoroughly deceived into being a rogue agent and then come up with a solid plan that Adams had agreed with had been impressive, to say the least.

Doug had a huge amount of respect for the woman in his arms. She possessed strength few people would even be able to understand. Even so, there was hardness in her that he didn't know if he'd ever be able to penetrate, no matter how close they grew. There was little that was soft and sweet about her, despite how good at dancing she was.

"You're a great dancer," Sabine said.

Doug chuckled.

She tipped her head back. "What?"

"I was just thinking the same about you."

"Oh…well." She glanced around everywhere but at him. "This is a wonderful room."

Warmth moved through him, and his stomach unclenched. "It is. My mom and dad used to dance in here late at night when they were all alone. They'd put a record on, dim the lights. I would sneak in past curfew, and they'd be in here, totally oblivious to anything except each other. It was kind of frustrating. And also gross to a teenage boy."

Sabine laughed and then seemed to realize they had stopped dancing, and yet he still held her.

"You should do that more often."

"What?"

"Laugh like that. It's a pretty sound."

"Thank you. You're sweet."

Doug rolled his eyes. "I don't think I've ever been called sweet before."

"It's true."

"Do me a favor and don't tell anyone, okay? I've got a reputation to maintain."

Sabine looked at the floor and then back up at him, her eyes a shade darker. "I'm scared."

"I couldn't tell."

"That's because I'm good at my job. Which is probably what got me in this mess in the first place."

"Sabine—" He was going to tell her to leave all the worry for tomorrow, but she cut him off.

"You are sweet." Her eyes held his.

Doug shifted his weight.

"You loved seeing your mom and dad dance."

"Yeah, I did. I loved how in love they were, but they also made it clear I was a part of what was between them, so I didn't mind too much when it felt like I was overlooked. When my mom was diagnosed, it was like the light went out of my dad's eyes. He kept it together for her, though. Then she died, and he threw himself into his work like never before. I left for basic training, and when I came back it wasn't to the father I'd known. He was never the same after she died."

"Is that why you let your fiancée break up with you? You wanted the same thing your parents had, and you knew it wasn't her."

"You're saying I let Tara walk away because I was just biding my time with her?" Doug didn't know whether to be offended at her presumption or impressed at how astute she was. "I've always assumed no woman would be able to handle the stress of my job, but I probably did hold myself back. After Tara broke our engagement, it was easier to date women who were just friends, or friends of friends. Romantic feelings make things more complicated."

"I agree with you."

"That doesn't mean I don't dream of having what my mom and dad had. Someone to share my home with, to have children with and to see the kind of people they grow up to be."

"I thought that once." She shrugged her slender shoulders. "What little girl doesn't dream of happily ever after with her handsome prince? But life isn't like that. Perfect relationships are the stuff of fiction."

"So you just stopped dreaming?" He studied her. What had happened to her and Ben? "What made you so hard?"

She stepped out of his arms. "When you witness something as horrific as what Ben and I were forced to endure, it changes you."

Doug took her hand and wove them through the crowd to the open French doors that led to the patio. At the stone ledge he turned and laid his hands on her shoulders. "Tell me what happened."

Sabine took a deep breath. "You're going to regret asking me that."

"I don't think so." She was fighting tears. "I need you to trust me. This secret of yours is tearing you up. No matter how badly you refuse to believe that, I can see it in your eyes."

She turned away to look out across the manicured lawn. "I was nine, and Ben was five the day my mom shot my dad."

"You can't be—"

"You asked." Her chest heaved. "If you want to know so badly, then be quiet while I tell you."

Doug closed his mouth.

"He was actually my stepdad. Ben's dad. He was good to both of us, and I loved him. We were playing cards, when Mom walked in with this look on her face."

Sabine wrapped her arms around her waist. "She had a gun. I pulled Ben across the room as far away as I could. She yelled for us to stop. Said something to Dad about betrayal and then shot him. There was so much blood. When she turned to us, she still had that look on her face. She said, 'I should have done this a long time ago' and pointed the gun at me and Ben. We ran out the back door and through this gap in the fence while she shot at us. We just kept running until we couldn't run anymore."

She took another deep breath. "Some cops found us in an alley behind a Dumpster a couple of miles away. I remember the smell and how freezing it was. I've hated cold places ever since."

"Your mom is in prison?"

Sabine shook her head. "They never caught her."

"What?"

"She got away. No one has seen her since. I guess disappearing runs in the family, because I seem to have the knack for it, too."

"You're nothing like her."

"You don't know that, Doug. I'm good at my job. So good everyone at the CIA apparently thinks I killed my whole team six years ago. Maybe I'm more like her than I want to admit."

"I don't believe that." He took a chance, reached out and touched her cheek, thumbed away a tear. "Thank you for telling me. You took a chance trusting me, and I won't let you down."

She smiled a sweet, sad smile. One that brought him closer, made him want to express his gratitude that she had shared her darkest moment with him. He leaned in and—

"There you are."

Sabine stepped back. Her face was probably beet red, since they'd been seconds away from what promised to be a memorable encounter. At least it would have been, if the look in Doug's eyes was anything to go by.

The general stood in the doorway with a wide smile on his face, like he knew exactly what they'd been about to do. "I was wondering where you two got to."

Doug grabbed her hand and pulled her back to his side. She sucked in a breath and tried not to look as guilty as she felt. Their almost-kiss wasn't something she would ever regret, but getting caught by his dad made her feel like she was acting out against that dream parent she used to wish for.

She'd long ago given up on the childhood fantasy of having good, healthy parents. Real life was much harder. There was little space left over for wishes. When she looked at Doug, it was like the petals of a flower unfolding to the summer sun. The man beside her made her want to dream again.

Sabine refocused. They were both waiting for her to say something. "I'm sorry, what?"

They laughed, though Doug's laughter sounded more embarrassed. When she looked at him, she realized he was as nervous as she was.

The general stepped forward. "I asked if you wanted

to dance, my dear. It would be my great honor to spend time with the woman my son brought home. I thought you might indulge me, being as it is my birthday."

Sabine couldn't help but accept. "Certainly, General. I would love to."

He held out his arm. "Please, call me Andrew."

He led her to the dance floor where the crowd had thinned out, leaving only the late-night die-hard partiers. Wrung out, she tried not to lean too heavily on Andrew...until he shifted closer to her and absorbed the bulk of her weight.

"I won't keep you long."

He knew.

"My son should have better sense than keeping you up when you're exhausted."

"I appreciate your concern, Gen—Andrew. The past few weeks have been some of the hardest of my life, and your son has been an invaluable help. I can see where he gets it. You should be very proud."

"Thank you. I am." Andrew frowned. "I'm selfish enough to admit I would have liked to see him ascend through the ranks and follow more in the way my career progressed, but Doug has always made his own way in life. I encouraged that."

"I know he's Spec Op—"

"He's a clerk, dear."

Sabine blinked. A clerk?

"That's how we refer to it. The men of their field like to keep their occupation on the 'down low,' as the kids like to say."

"Of course." Sabine smiled. "You know my brother worked with Doug?"

Andrew nodded. "I'm very sorry for your loss."

"Thank you. Even though his duties as a...clerk kept him busy, my brother was still a huge part of my life. I miss him."

The general nodded. His eyes were shadowed with the same grief she felt. Then he seemed to shake it off, and pulled her into an elaborate turn that took her breath away and made her laugh.

"May I ask how you've managed to keep going, since you also suffered grief in your life?" Maybe she was being too forward, but Sabine hoped he would answer.

"That I have. Many men under my command, as well as my wife, Doug's mother."

Sabine nodded. "He told me."

The general smiled, small and wistful. "She was a gem of a woman. Much like you."

"How do you go on?"

"Have I? I'm not sure I've really moved on from that day. It seems to have stayed with me and not a day goes by that I don't remember. That's what happens when you lose a part of your heart. After that, you just do the best you can with the bit you have left."

Sabine wanted to cry for him but held the rush of emotion back. He wouldn't want her pity. "Was it worth it? I mean, if you knew how it was going to end, would you still let yourself fall for her?"

The general's arms fell to his sides. Sabine was about to apologize when he spoke. "Yes. Absolutely, unequivocally yes. Even for the simple fact of having Doug with me still. It is hard to lose the person you were supposed to grow old with, but you cherish what time you have together. No one knows the future, Elena. So you live life to the fullest. You take the risk. Because if you don't, how do you know you're really alive?"

The general kissed her cheek and walked away.

It was tempting to want to live life to the fullest. She wouldn't be able to hold back anymore. If she wanted a relationship between her and Doug to be worth anything at all, then she'd have to give it everything she had. But a man like Doug would never accept a strong woman inclined to take care of herself. He'd want to be the hero.

She wanted a man who would be her equal partner in life. Someone to stand beside her, instead of in front trying to protect her from things she had plenty of experience with. If she hadn't learned how to take care of herself by now, she wouldn't have the job she loved so much.

Doug no doubt wanted a woman who was the stay-at-home type. His wife would be with their kids while he went all over the world on missions. Missions he couldn't tell her about. At one time Sabine had dreamed of a real family that was all her own, but life had stolen those dreams. Still, it was a tempting thought, if only to see how different it might be from Maxwell's coldness.

The memory of her ex-husband crested over her like a wave of ice water. It wasn't worth going there, even in comparison. That time in her life was over. He had a new wife now, one he was free to ignore unless he was in the mood to criticize everything about her.

She would have liked to think she was strong enough to fight the past and go for it with Doug. But if it didn't work, it would destroy her. Could she take the risk?

Considering her abysmal history, staying alone was a whole lot simpler. She should probably look into getting a cat or something. Cats were friendly, right?

Then Sabine realized something else.

The general had called her Elena.

* * *

Doug sipped his drink and watched Sabine leave the ballroom. He could see how tired she was; she hadn't really needed to make her excuses to him. On the way out, she said something to his father that made the old man smile.

"Sergeant Major."

Doug turned and came face-to-face with his boss's boss's boss's… He lost track after a while. "Major General, sir."

They shook hands. Major General Robert Taylor was his father's golf buddy and also bore a striking resemblance to Bruce Willis. Doug would have saluted, but they were both out of uniform, and this was the room he used to slide around in his socks with his friends after they ate too much candy.

"I read your report."

Doug could see the major general didn't believe Sabine's theory about being set up for Parelli's death. "Any idea what the repercussions will be?"

"Depends. The army certainly has no problem that a weapons dealer is dead. Outside of us, things get more complicated."

Doug snorted. "That's a fact. Why do you think I'm content being a noncommissioned officer?"

"It does create a certain distance between you and all the bureaucracy, doesn't it?" The major general's eyes gleamed. "Good move. Wish I'd had the same foresight as you."

"Feeling the pressure of command?"

The major general huffed. "Nothing I can't handle."

"Of course." Something hard emerged in the older man's eyes, and Doug wasn't sure he would like where the conversation was about to go.

"Word to the wise, son. This girl could spell big trouble for you. I'm not sure you want to get tangled up where she's heading. Could be the end of your career. Just a little friendly advice, since you've been like a nephew to me for a long time, Doug. Women like that are never good for us." The old man laughed. "Trust me. I've been married three times. All of them were strong…you could even say dangerous women. I know it feels exciting and new right now, but if you let yourself get sucked in, when she walks away—which she will— there won't be much of you that she leaves behind."

"I appreciate the warning, sir."

"But you're not going to listen to me. No, don't argue. I can see it in your eyes, kid. Take it or leave it. When this girl's troubles all descend on her, you won't want to be in the middle of it."

The major general sucked down the remnants of his drink and left.

Did he really believe Sabine would do that? Her job was the kind that forced her to give it all and rarely let anyone else walk away with anything to show for it— aside from bruises. She could absolutely take care of herself. Fiercely independent, that's what she was. Or was it that life had taught her to guard her heart above all else to keep from risking it being broken…again? It would take a lot to get through that shell of hers.

Could she let someone in enough to be comfortable including them in her inner circle? Ben had lived there. Now that Doug knew what the two of them had been through, he could see how saving her little brother's life meant that they stuck with each other from then on.

Would she ever let Doug in like that?

NINE

"Richardson." Doug rubbed the sleep from his eyes and listened to the voice bark instructions through the phone. "Understood."

He pushed away the urge to mourn for what would have been his first full night of sleep in days and got up. It was 4:00 a.m. After he splashed cold water on his face, Doug put the few things he'd got out of his duffel back in and zipped it closed.

He tapped on Sabine's door and waited, but she didn't appear. Sleeping that deeply wasn't good in her line of work. At the same time he was glad she felt safe enough at his dad's house to get the rest she needed. He peered in to check on her.

The bed was empty.

The sheets and blanket were rumpled like they'd gotten twisted up while she had tossed around trying to fall asleep. He didn't want to be going on a mission when she was like this, but it couldn't be helped. Work called. He'd have to trust her to stay here and wait.

The Raven, or someone who worked for him—or her, he supposed, since they had no idea—had withdrawn money from a bank in the Cayman Islands. The team was off on a treasure hunt that could lead who-knew-where. He'd get the full details at the briefing, which would likely happen on the plane since the team was spread all over the place.

Downtime was a bit of a misnomer when you were still effectively "on call." That was the nature of his work, and he wouldn't have it any other way. Being a nine-to-fiver with weekends off had never been his thing.

Sabine's bathroom was empty. The major general's words came back to Doug, and he had to push away the distrust. Just because she wasn't where he could find her didn't mean she had betrayed him. She was Ben's sister. That fact alone was enough for him to know he could trust her. Ben would never have spoken so highly of her if she was their enemy. Sure, she'd been deceived into working for someone other than the CIA. That didn't mean she was working against the U.S. It wasn't like she was an agent for the Raven.

Sabine wasn't in the kitchen, TV room or the library. A low light shone from under the door to his dad's office, so he went in to ask the general if he knew where Sabine was.

Sabine's fingers froze on the keyboard. Doug was in the doorway, and his mouth hung open. She slid the chair back from the computer. "It's not what you think."

He folded his arms across his chest. "Is that right?"

She wasn't going to be able to talk her way out of this. If she did, it would destroy the small bit of progress they had made toward trusting each other. "I was looking for something."

"There are a lot of things to find in here. You know,

I was just thinking to myself, no, there's no way Sabine would ever betray me because Ben trusted her. I guess you deceived him, too."

She gasped.

"Good thing all the sensitive information is secured."

He thought she was capable of that? She would never, ever have betrayed her brother. "Is that your way of warning me away from betraying the very country I've been working for this whole time? You think I'm some kind of spy against America?"

Except that was exactly what people thought of her.

He crossed the room. "You have to admit it looks pretty suspicious. Charm the general's son. Blow up a hard drive so I have no choice but to bring you to the safest place I know, the general's own house. Break into his office in the middle of the night to steal secrets."

"You forget that your dead teammate was my little brother, whose killer I will find."

"By breaking in here?"

"The door was unlocked."

"Sabine."

"Your dad called me *Elena,* okay?"

Surprise flickered on his face before he quashed it.

She blew out a breath. "I need to know what he knows. If there's information going around about me, I have to know what it says. I'm so twisted around, worried about what's going to happen to me."

His lips thinned. "Most people would just say, 'Hey, General, why'd you call me that?'"

"I guess I'm not most people."

"I guess not." He sighed. "Did you find anything?"

"You want to know what dirty secrets I'm privy to?" She narrowed her eyes. "Sorry, but I didn't get through the security features on his computer yet." He smirked, which she took as a challenge. "Come back in ten minutes, then I'll tell you something juicy."

"Not going to happen." He studied her. "You couldn't have come to me? You felt you had to sneak in here—"

"I couldn't sleep. It seemed like a good time, and I didn't want to wake you." She closed her eyes. "I don't know why I feel like I have to justify myself to you."

"And yet you'll betray our trust because you couldn't tell us the truth?"

She stood up, to put them on more level ground instead of having him tower over her. "Would you have?"

"What have I said or done that gave you the feeling you couldn't trust me?"

"That's not what this is about." Besides, his whole job was secrets. Why hadn't she seen that before? This could never work. There was no way they'd ever be able to completely trust each other, forever wondering if the other one was holding out.

His eyes darkened. "As much as I'd love to stay and work this out with you, Sabine, I have to go."

"You're leaving?" She walked around the desk. She needed to get by him with a sliver of her self-respect still intact. "I guess I should have known better, should never have told you about my parents. Ben never did. Maybe he was right not to trust you with it."

He grabbed her arm as she passed.

She looked at him but didn't let the look of pain on his face penetrate her mask. "Time will tell."

"What's that supposed to mean? Sabine, I got a call. The team moves out first thing this morning. I have to go. It's my job."

"Ah, yes, the almighty job. Greatest above all things."

"Sabine—"

She shook her head. "Maybe I can trust you, maybe not. Maybe I'm the bad guy. I guess we'll see, since I'm obviously stupid enough to stick around right under the noses of everyone who wants me out of commission, just to find out. Boy, do I wish attraction didn't make me an idiot."

He caught up to her at the door. "You seriously like me?"

"That's not what I meant." At least, she didn't want it to be. She wanted to forget she'd said it. Why had that slipped out? She had to change the subject. "How long will you be gone? You know, so I can be waiting by the phone."

He sighed. "Honestly? I have no idea. I could be a day or it could be weeks."

"Weeks?"

"You know how it is, Sabine."

She did. Ben's schedule of being overseas versus being in the States had been erratic to say the least. "I'll be sure to stay here like a good girl and wait for the big, strong man to come home."

He sighed. "Just promise me you won't disappear. Or do anything dangerous."

She didn't want it to affect her, but it did. "I don't invite these things, you know. And I don't like being a victim."

"When I look at you, a victim is the last thing I see."

Sabine was floored, but managed to keep her jaw from dropping. A few more of those petals opened to the sun.

"This house is safe for you. My dad and I aren't hiding anything."

"You can't believe that. Not when you both have enough secrets to fill the Library of Congress."

"I promise you, Sabine, we aren't hiding anything that could harm you. We're trying to help you, and I need you to let me do that."

She studied his face. "Okay, I believe you."

"Will you promise me something else?"

She nodded.

"Don't do anything to hurt my dad."

"I would never—"

He sighed. "Just say you won't, so I can believe you and trust you while I'm gone."

It grated that he felt he had to make her promise not to hurt his dad. As if she really would. But since he'd found her searching his dad's computer, she relented. "I promise."

As he walked away, Sabine realized he took a little piece of her heart with him. She watched from the office as the general appeared at the bottom of the stairs in blue-and-white striped pajamas and a pair of slippers. Doug hugged his dad and looked back at her, but she didn't know what that look meant.

Then he was gone.

Andrew turned and saw her in the doorway to his office. His eyes widened. "Find anything interesting?"

Her cheeks heated, and she knew that—even in the dim light of predawn—he saw her embarrassment.

"Come." He waved toward the kitchen. "We can have tea, and you can tell me. I doubt either of us is going to sleep any more tonight."

The light above the stove was already on when they entered, the curtains pulled tight across the window. The effect was privacy and a sense of detachment from the outside world that helped her forget what was going on. Even if it was fleeting, it was still nice.

Sabine sat at the table while Andrew filled the kettle. He turned back, folded his arms across his chest and gave her a look she'd seen on Doug's face several times. She looked at the table's surface. The refrigerator hummed. Deeply ingrained traits that had been cemented by her CIA training gave her a sick feeling in her stomach. But with any luck, if she trusted him, he'd reciprocate and tell her why he'd called her Elena.

She sucked in a deep breath, pushed away the discomfort of opening up and launched into the whole story of her parents, the CIA, Ben's death and how she met Doug. The general smiled when she told him how she'd ditched Doug in the café and how he'd come after her in Seattle, bursting into her house to save her.

"Sounds like the two of you have been good for each other."

"I'm not sure Doug sees it that way."

Andrew's wrinkled face brightened. "I think he needs someone exactly like you, Sabine. You're a firecracker."

She laughed. "Was that even a compliment?"

"Honey, it's the highest one I know. Doug's mama was a firecracker. There was never a dull moment with that woman." His gaze took on a wistful air.

"I'm not sure we'll ever get to that place. There's a lot that could go wrong if we're not careful."

He squeezed her fingers. "If there was nothing to overcome, how would you know it was worth fighting for? You have to ask yourself if he's worth it."

"I suppose you're going to tell me that he is. After all, he's your son."

Andrew shook his head. "My opinion shouldn't play into it. You're the only one who can answer the questions of your heart."

Sabine was quiet for a moment. "Thank you."

"You're wondering why I called you Elena last night."

"Yes."

"A lot of paperwork has crossed my desk in the last week. Mission reports and the like. It was nothing but an old man's slip of the tongue." He studied her. "Do you wish to be called that, or should we stick with your cover, *Sabine?*"

The name Elena brought back a lot of memories of her mother and stepfather, of years spent in the fight to survive foster care. Then again, she had been accepted into the CIA under her real name—Elena Sanders.

"I prefer Sabine." She smiled. "Sabine is the firecracker."

Andrew laughed.

"Elena wasn't nearly so tough, even if she did make it through CIA training. She feels like who I used to be, while Sabine is who I am now." She remembered Doug's parting words. "She's a survivor."

"I have to ask. You changed your name and used Ben's last name?"

"I had covered my tracks well enough that it seemed to be okay and for him to have a room there, being as the house was under my cover name and he wasn't listed on anything. He needed a home base when he wasn't working, and it'd been long enough that my new identity was established, but some part of me still can't help thinking maybe someone found me—or Ben discovered something—and that's what got him killed."

"He was killed on a mission."

"I know that."

"You still worry it had something to do with the job you chose?" Andrew shook his head. Behind him, the kettle had begun to boil. "Trust my son."

"I do."

"If Doug thought Ben's death was because of you and not the Raven, he would have told you."

"The Raven?"

"The reason your brother was killed. Doug's team found evidence that links the Raven to the man who funded the hired gun."

"Christophe Parelli."

Andrew nodded.

"So Parelli hired the guy who killed Ben, but Parelli really worked for this Raven guy?"

"That's as much as I know."

"And now Parelli's dead, too."

The kettle began to whistle. Andrew stood to make the tea.

There was a crack, like breaking glass, and the curtain billowed up as something flew in the window. Shards of glass sprayed the room, and Sabine didn't have time to react. The projectile dented the fridge and hit the floor. Andrew grabbed his chest.

Before she could reach him, he fell.

TEN

Sabine had to fight not to roll her eyes at the cop. "No, I don't know who could have done this. Or why. How many times do I have to say it?"

"Until I'm satisfied, I'm afraid."

She bit back a retort and adjusted her perch on the rock-solid hospital waiting-room chair. The police detective's eyes had dark circles that overshadowed the fine lines on his face. After she adjusted her estimate of his age for the fact that he had a tough job, Sabine still guessed somewhere over fifty. Bald with a soft middle, he looked more mobster than cop.

"I know you're tired, Ms. Surleski, and I appreciate your answering these questions. It's important we get to the bottom of…"

Doug pushed through the doors at the end of the hall.

"Ms. Surleski—"

She ignored the cop, already out of her chair, and ran toward Doug. She wanted a hug. The force of the need to be held made her stop short. Why was the instinct to seek him out for comfort so strong? Doug must have seen the look on her face, the war between what she wanted and what was appropriate. He shook his head and gathered her in his arms.

Sabine sighed, not wanting to think too much about how nice it felt to be surrounded by his warmth. "I can't believe you're here."

"I hadn't left yet. My colonel gave me permission to come, and the team went without me, but—" He shook his head. "Let's just say they'll be fine. Not sure how I feel about being expendable, though."

Sabine nodded, thankful beyond words that he was here. That she could support him. "I'm still waiting for word."

"Uh, excuse me. Ms. Surleski?"

Sabine ignored the look on Doug's face at the mention of the name she used on missions. The use of that identity was risky, but she was too tired and too overwhelmed with worry about Andrew to figure out which was safer—the name of the woman who killed Christophe Parelli or the name she usually went by.

The one the CIA now knew.

She turned back to the cop. "This is General Richardson's son."

"Of course." The two men shook hands, and the detective turned to her. "If we can continue with our questions?"

She nodded and they walked back. Doug sat beside her.

"You said a rock flew through the window?"

"That's right."

"And that led to the heart attack?"

Doug flinched, but she ignored it. Instead she tried to smile and hoped it looked pleasant.

She hadn't planned on mentioning the note attached

to the rock. Not that she wanted to lie to the police.
She'd just spent too many years taking care of her
own problems. The police, the Feds, whoever got their
hands on the note to test it for fingerprints or whatever
wouldn't have the first clue what it meant. Plus Doug
would want to see it, anyway. Plenty of reasons to slip
it in her pocket.

Tread carefully.

Sabine couldn't have said how she knew, but it was
meant for her, and it was about their investigation into
Ben's death. It was a waste of ink as far as she was concerned. Nothing was going to stop her from finding out
who had killed her brother.

The detective sipped his coffee. Rude, since she
didn't have anything to drink and he hadn't offered. She
could dearly use some caffeine. The adrenaline surge
from seeing Andrew fall down had long since worn off,
and she was still waiting for news about his condition.

"You have no idea who could have done this?"

"No, I have no idea. Just like I told everyone else
who has interviewed me since I got here. All I want is
to find out if Andrew is okay. Not sit here answering
questions from everyone who thinks this is their business to investigate."

Doug shot her a look, his eyebrow raised, but she
wasn't going to back down.

Apparently when a high-ranking military official
was attacked at home, everyone wanted to know what
the deal was. This cop was the fourth person to interview her in the last two hours.

Every agency in existence had been through the waiting room where she sat—the FBI, the Secret Service, federal agents with the military. She'd seen less people in the center of London on a Saturday night.

Still Sabine was impressed by the attention the general was getting. Most likely it was the result of how much respect he'd earned and how many friends he'd made over the years. Friends who cared enough to move heaven and earth to make sure he was okay.

That was why she humored them all by answering their questions. Not too long ago Sabine would have taken off the minute Andrew was in the hands of EMTs. Tonight she had stuck around. Maybe because, even though they had only met the day before, Andrew meant a lot to her. Maybe it was the shared connection they had in Doug. Either way she wanted him to know she was here for him.

The detective didn't look too impressed. In fact he looked downright insulted. "This is clearly the jurisdiction of local police."

Sabine stood. "Look, I've answered your questions, but I will not be dragged into a tug-of-war between you and the FBI and everyone else. If you'll excuse me, I'm going to get an update on the general's status."

She crossed to the desk where a nurse sat. The young woman had pink hair and a bored expression on her face. "Help you?"

"I'd like an update on General Richardson. It's been two hours, and no one's told me anything."

The nurse sniffed.

Sabine realized her tone could have been nicer but, under the circumstances, couldn't bring herself to feel guilty.

"Are you a relative?"

"I am." Doug appeared beside her. "His son."

The double doors at the end of the waiting room swished open. A good-looking middle-aged man in a white coat came in, talking with the general's housekeeper. Jean's sleek hair was disheveled, and she grasped a balled-up tissue in one hand.

Sabine rushed over. "What is it? Andrew's okay, right?"

Jean sucked in a shaky breath, and the doctor turned to Doug, probably seeing the resemblance between father and son. "The general had a heart attack. He's stable now, but we'll be keeping him here and running tests later today, after he's had a chance to rest."

Jean motioned to Sabine, and they stepped aside while Doug asked the doctor questions.

"Will I be able to see him?" Sabine asked.

Jean's eyes hardened. "I don't think that's a good idea. It's been a long night and Andrew is sleeping. Besides, Doug is here now."

"Oh…of course."

Sabine tried not to be disappointed that they'd left her out in the waiting room tied up being interviewed until the general was asleep and she couldn't see him. "I'll stay until he wakes up then."

Jean smiled but it didn't reach her eyes. "That's really not necessary. Don't feel like you have to stick around."

"I don't really have anywhere else to go." She was supposed to be under the radar. Where better than a hospital full of staff…and security guards? She'd promised Doug she would stay safe, though. And she wanted to be near him.

"I'm sure you'll think of something."

Sabine flinched. She turned too fast and nearly stumbled, but held herself together long enough to get to the hall with some kind of dignity. It had been a long time since she'd been dismissed so thoroughly. To her surprise, it stung in a way she hadn't felt since Maxwell's infidelity had come to light.

More than that, it hurt to realize the pain was so familiar. It had stuck with her all this time without her knowledge.

In a lot of ways the divorce had been a relief. After all the stress and pain of dividing one life back into two she had resolved not to enter into another relationship that left her vulnerable. Now she was free to live. She'd been happy, on her own terms.

Or so she thought.

Sabine swiped a tear from her cheek and pushed away the old feeling of inadequacy. She just wasn't the kind of person who inspired love in other people.

After her mom killed Ben's dad and tried to kill them she'd resolved with a child's understanding that there was something missing in her. Ben's love had filled a lot of the gaps and helped her to heal a great deal—both before and after the disaster that was her marriage to Maxwell. But despite Ben's acceptance of her, that old feeling somehow never went away.

A young woman stepped out of a side room and almost collided with her. Sabine offered a quick apology. The girl's face was the picture of peace, though her eyes were red and puffy like she'd been crying. She smiled and stepped past Sabine, who looked up at the door. It was the hospital's chapel.

Crying in a hospital could mean anything—a loved one in an accident or suffering a terminal illness. Maybe the crying girl had recently lost someone close to her, or she could be worrying about a friend. And yet the look on her face had been radiant.

Ben had looked the same way the last time Sabine had seen him. When she had asked him what was different, she got a wide smile for an answer. He'd said Doug had "led him to the Lord," whatever that meant. Ben had become a Christian, but she didn't really understand it.

What good had it done her brother, anyway? He'd found religion and it got him killed. In reality that probably wasn't what happened, but she couldn't ignore the timing. Within two weeks of becoming a Christian, Ben was dead. Not exactly a good advertisement.

Her phone buzzed. She drew it from her pocket and looked around to make sure she wasn't going to get in trouble for using her cell in a hospital.

We need to meet.

Her body tensed, readied for battle. Not with the enemy, but with her own handler.

This was her first contact with Neil since she'd found out that he had lied about her working for the CIA the past six years. If she was going to get to the bottom of things, she had to meet with him…and play things very carefully.

She sent a text back.

Where and when?

Doug hadn't been in a hospital since his mom had died.

His dad lay wrapped in a white blanket, asleep to the steady beep of machines. Doug decided he wasn't going to lose another parent to illness. He laid his hand on his dad's weathered one, and the old man's eyes flickered open.

"I wasn't sleeping. I was just resting my eyes."

"Sleep is good, Dad." The last thing Doug wanted was for him to downplay all this and wind up hurt worse.

"I'll rest if you go to your girl. Sabine needs you more than I do right now."

"I know."

"And what are you going to do, anyway? Just stand there all night staring at me?"

Doug snorted. He put his hand on the old man's head, leaned down and touched his forehead to it. "I'll be back tomorrow."

The general shifted and dislodged the blanket. "Not if you have better things to do, you won't."

Doug would come back the next day. Nothing would be going on that was more important than checking on his dad. He reached down and straightened the blankets. "We'll see."

It wouldn't do to have the old man think he meant to come and visit no matter what. The dance of their relationship was a delicate one, despite the manner in which they spoke to each other. He couldn't let on how much he needed his dad. Nor would his dad ever let on how much he wanted Doug there.

His mom was the one who had brought the two of them together. Would there ever be a day when they could just say what they meant? Doug looked back at his dad lying in the bed, and his heart squeezed. His mom had gone into the hospital and had never come out.

A heart attack was a far cry from terminal pancreatic cancer, but, to Doug's little-boy heart, it felt the same.

Lord, don't let my dad die.

He turned away from the sight of the slow rise and fall of his dad's chest, then walked until the door closed on the beeping.

Out in the waiting room Jean paced, wringing her fingers together.

"Hey, you okay?"

She shook her head, tears in her eyes.

"What is it? Where's Sabine?"

"I'm so sorry, Doug. I was really mean to her. And after she did so much to help Andrew. She was right there. She even got him an aspirin before the paramedics arrived. Probably saved his life. I'm afraid it was my fault."

She needed to finish her story so he could go to Sabine. "What happened?"

"I was just so mad. I only found out what happened when the hospital called to say Andrew was asking for me. I thought your Sabine purposely didn't tell me. I froze her out. Then when she walked away I saw the look on her face. She was just trying to be here for us and be supportive. I feel so guilty."

Doug tried to muster up some sympathy, but he was exhausted. It was almost dawn. He had no doubt Sabine really was hurt when Jean rebuffed her. "Jean—"

"I know, I know, but I can't apologize because she hasn't come back in."

"I'll find her. I'll tell her you're sorry."

"Please, Doug."

He took a step back, ready to alert hospital security to start a search for Sabine. "I'll find her."

He headed for the elevator. There was no reason to suspect Sabine was in immediate danger, but something about her being alone—even in a busy hospital—put him on alert. Add to that her being upset and he figured he better find her fast. His finger hammered the down button, and he had to remind himself yet again that she was a trained CIA agent who was absolutely capable of taking care of herself. Now he just had to convince his heart not to worry about her.

Was this their future, constantly fretting about each other's well-being?

If that was the case, Doug wasn't so fired up to let things between him and Ben's sister get any deeper than they already were. Doug really didn't know what kind of woman she was. They'd had limited contact before Ben's death, only small talk at team barbecues when everyone brought their families. Because Doug hadn't let it be more.

Now they were thrown in this situation together and struggling to figure out each other plus what was going on.

He got off the elevator on the first floor and made for the front entrance. He didn't know why he was going outside, only that the instinct of flight usually made people head for the nearest exit.

Sure enough, she was at the curb about to get in a taxi.

"Sabine." He ran to catch up. "Where are you going?"

She straightened and stood in the gap between the open cab door and the body of the car. "I have to go."

"I know what Jean said. She's sorry. She was upset about my dad and she didn't mean to freeze you out."

He touched her elbow. "I thought you would go and see my dad with me."

She shook her head, and he didn't like the lack of emotion on her face. "I didn't want to get in the middle of a family thing. You needed time with him."

"No, I needed a buffer against the fear that was about to drown me seeing him lying there just like my mom." Doug's throat hitched. He hadn't meant to say that much, to lay the weight of it on her. He prayed she wouldn't get scared away. "Don't go."

"I have a meeting, Doug. There's too much that needs to be resolved."

So that's what it was. Sabine had switched to work mode. "What happened? Did your handler contact you?"

She nodded. "I have to find out if the last six years were a lie."

"Let me help you. If we can get an ID on your handler, we'll know more about who we're dealing with."

"I have to know who wanted me out of the CIA and why that woman looked like me." She bit her lip and looked down.

"What is it?"

Her eyes lifted. "Will you come with me? I know it's a lot to ask with your dad and all, but—"

"Wouldn't miss it."

However much he had tried to convince himself that things were still developing between them, the fact was that he was already in deep with this woman. He'd been attracted for a long time. His heart just saw the woman, not the problems that could emerge.

Especially when she found out Ben's death was his fault.

ELEVEN

"Remember to breathe. This is just like any other meeting you've had with your handler."

Sabine tucked the listening device in her ear. "I have done this before, you know. I'm aware of the procedure and the risks."

Doug had parked in a crowded lot at the mall in Boise. It had been a long plane flight, considering they'd gone from Seattle to D.C. only the day before. She'd never flown so much in such a short space of time. If only she could have done it using her real ID, then she could use all these Air Miles she was earning. A vacation sounded good.

His hand rested on her shoulder and jolted her from her thoughts. "It's never been this personal before."

"Ben would probably have a fit if he thought we were making this much fuss over his death." She smiled to herself, lost in memories. "Then again, he'd probably do the exact same thing if it were one of us."

"He knew you were CIA?"

She laughed, though it wasn't too funny considering how angry he'd been. "About threw a fit over the whole thing. Told me he was Delta Force. What was I supposed to do, but reciprocate? How was I to know he'd hit the roof? Just because he has a team to back him up and I don't."

Sabine pushed away the ache in her chest. She needed this meeting with her handler, Neil. She had to focus on something that would demand every skill she had, something that would push her to draw deep from her strengths in order to succeed.

She looked at Doug. His eyes were hard, like he didn't want to admit how he felt.

"You agree with Ben?"

He took a deep breath and blew it out. "Can't say the thought of you running around on your own with no support doesn't scare me, because I'd be lying. No…let me finish. I know you're trained. So am I. And they're different businesses, but you can't deny there's an element of danger in our jobs. Both high risk, both requiring intense skill. Can you honestly tell me that you never worried about Ben?"

"No. Of course I worried about him." Sabine tensed. "And with good reason, since he died."

She slammed the door behind her and marched between cars until Doug grabbed her hand and turned her to him. He didn't need to apologize. The look in his eyes took her breath away.

His hand went to her cheek, and then he touched his forehead to hers. "I worry about you. You worry about me. Where do we go from here?"

Sabine leaned her head back. "I'm still going to do my job."

"And so will I."

"To the best of my ability. Yes, there's risk, but I don't put myself in danger more than is necessary. I'm not some kind of maverick just because I don't have a team with me. I follow procedure. I trust the people I work with—" Her voice broke. "I trusted Neil." She shuddered and drew in a breath. "What if Steve Adams was telling the truth? What if I betrayed my country?"

"Did you kill your team?"

"No."

"Did it ever cross your mind that Neil might be lying?"

"That's not a good thing." She stepped away. "If I never considered I was being duped, what kind of agent does that make me?"

"Human?"

"That's unacceptable."

"Seriously? You give me grief for feeling guilty about not doing more when the hard drive exploded, and you think it makes you less of a person to believe that someone's telling the truth?"

"I should have known."

"Sabine—"

"If it's true, this man has destroyed my life. And who do I work for, if not the CIA? The Russians? A terrorist organization? The CIA is going to put me in jail for the rest of my life, Doug. I'm done. It's over."

He grabbed her elbow only enough to get her attention. "This isn't the end. Get it out now, and then go in there and meet with Neil. Look him in the eye and give the performance of your life. Yes, we need to know who you've been passing information to. We also need to know what they know about Parelli's death. But you're not done. You still have some fight left, and I don't believe God would bring you into my life and give me the best shot I've had so far at finding out why Ben was killed and then rip it all away. I can't believe that."

"I need that, Doug. I need one of us to believe, to be completely sure."

"It's not too late. It's never too late."

Not for the first time, Doug wished he could simply will someone else to believe. Just as Ben had been resistant to the truth, Sabine didn't see God the way Doug did. He understood it. Little in their lives pointed to the fact that God was on their side. Witnessing their mom kill their dad and then try to kill them was beyond heavy. Doug wasn't surprised it was difficult for her to trust anyone.

He tucked his hands in his jacket pockets and watched her walk into the entrance closest to the food court.

Ben had done it.

Doug had no doubts that Sabine could come to believe, just like her brother. Ben had seen Doug's life and the way he lived out the things he stood for, even though he wasn't perfect. When Doug had laid out what Jesus had done, dying on the cross, Ben had been blown away. It had been a short jump from there to giving his life to the Lord.

At least his friend had become a Christian in time. It hadn't been too late. Doug could only pray Sabine wouldn't leave it too late, either.

"Excuse me."

Her voice came through his earpiece as she stepped aside for a young mom pushing a stroller. He pulled out his phone and sent Sabine a text.

Got you loud and clear.

Doug checked his watch. He waited for the five-minute mark and then made his own way inside. After buying a corn dog, he chose a spot across the busy food court where he settled at a table with a side view of Sabine drinking a soda.

Two minutes before the cutoff time when Sabine would have stood up and walked away, a man approached. The khaki pants, golf shirt and loafers made him look relaxed, like a retired old man out for eighteen holes of conversation with a buddy. The tweed cap shadowed his face, but Sabine clearly recognized him since she offered him the seat across from her.

His bearing was familiar.

Doug couldn't place where he knew this guy from and didn't know why he'd expected a younger man. He'd been geared up to instantly dislike the smooth talker who had convinced Sabine that he was a CIA handler. This man was more grandpa than sophisticated deceiver. It was clever, really. Since most people were inclined to trust a harmless old man.

If only Doug could see the guy's face.

"I read your report. I'm concerned about this woman you think was pretending to be you."

Sabine put her elbows on the table and leaned close as he talked in a low voice. "Do you have any idea who she was?"

Neil shook his head. Doug was having trouble reading the man's body language. If he was lying, he was incredibly skilled at it.

"Security cameras from the hotel are grainy, so we haven't been able to figure out who she was. Unfortunately that makes it more likely that the authorities will suspect you, I'm afraid."

Sabine scratched her hairline. "So I was right. They're pinning it on me."

"So what if they do? You're a ghost. If you need to

lie low for a while, then stay out of the Dominican Republic. That's not too hard to do. There's plenty of work elsewhere in the world, so we just leave this Parelli thing alone and focus on something different."

"You want me to let this go?"

Doug tensed. Any effort on this Neil's part to push Sabine away from searching for her brother's killer had to be viewed as suspicious.

"I know you want to trace the money from Parelli to whoever originally paid for the hit on your brother, but the hard drive was destroyed. I'm not saying do nothing while the person who killed your brother goes free. I want you to let me work on it. There's a team back at Langley whose only job is to trace that money. As soon as we know something, I'll pass it on. But it's not always possible to get a win, Sabine. You know that. Sometimes you have to cut your losses and move on."

The corn dog didn't settle well. What a pack of lies this guy was spewing. How could they find the person who was behind Neil? When Doug's team got back, he'd have to task the new computer guy to do some checking into the handler.

The kid had navigated them through the hotel to escape those two Italian bodyguards and the police, and he could also unearth information on anyone. California was an exceptional hacker. They needed to trace Neil's phone, get into his email, that kind of thing. Neil was entirely too much of an unknown component for Doug's liking.

"I have a new assignment for you."

Sabine sighed. Doug could see the fatigue wasn't faked. She was genuinely tired. His phone vibrated in his pocket.

"I need some time off, Neil. I've got to get my head straight. I shouldn't have gone on that mission so soon after Ben's death."

Neil patted her hand. "Ben wouldn't want you to push yourself, but neither of us is willing to let his killer just walk."

Doug hated that this guy even thought he was good enough to say Ben's name when Neil had being lying to Sabine for years. Doug could see just how hard this was for her, in the set of her shoulders and the way her fingers were laced.

The woman was trained to project what she wasn't feeling and make it look authentic. If she was giving off tells like that without knowing it, she needed some serious rest.

She sucked in a breath. "What does it matter? Parelli is dead. The hard drive blew up. We might never get to the bottom of what happened. The army isn't going to just hand over the information."

Except that she would likely know before Neil if the army did find out, since Doug would share with her. They needed to know the extent to which Neil was keeping tabs on her. Did Neil know that she'd been with Doug, or even that she had stayed at the general's house?

Neil cocked his head, like he was so innocent. "The soldier you've been spending time with, your brother's teammate. Richardson, isn't it? He hasn't told you anything?"

Neil knew every move she made.

"I think he just feels sorry for me."

Neil nodded. "Stands to reason. If he feels responsible, he might want to help because he feels guilty about what happened. Have you considered that?"

Doug held still. His phone vibrated again, but he didn't pull it out. He caught the eye of an older woman at the next table and nodded politely when inside he wanted to rage that this man had the audacity to question Doug's motives.

"We can get to the bottom of this." Neil put his hand over Sabine's once more. "There are other leads. When you're ready, I'll put you back to work and we'll finish this. It's what you're good at, Sabine."

Tread carefully.

That was what the note had said—the one Sabine had shown Doug on the plane. It seemed that was becoming a familiar refrain.

Sabine held still while the old man kissed her on the head, and then she said goodbye to her mentor. She was valuable enough they didn't want to lose her as an asset, which unfortunately was too bad, since she'd most likely end up in jail for the murder of her team and of Christophe Parelli.

She wasn't sure she'd object to that if it came down to it. After all, she was the one stupid enough to have been duped all these years. She figured she deserved it. Her handler had been convincing, but something should have told her that Neil was deceiving her.

It was so obvious now.

As soon as he had gone down the escalator, she made her way through the mall and bought a coffee, trying to get the bitter taste out of her mouth. She sipped and stared in a store window at a particularly nice blue dress. A shadow darkened the window beside her.

"He's keeping tabs on you."

"Knows every move I make. Probably knew you

were here today." She looked over. Doug's eyes were soft. "What do you think?"

"Ditch your phone. Get another that's untraceable. We need to find out everything we can about Neil and who he talks to."

"I'll go over Ben's computer. I haven't had the chance yet, but there could be something on there that might lead us to why someone would go through his room. There has to be a connection."

He nodded. "Agreed."

Sabine turned and leaned back against the store window and took another sip of her coffee. "Did you check on your dad?"

Doug turned and did the same so they were shoulder to shoulder. "On the way over here from the food court. He's awake. The tests were uneventful. He should be released tomorrow, provided he takes it easy and follows up with a cardiologist."

She didn't have the energy to comment, so she smiled. Doug nudged her shoulder with his. "What now?"

"Please, no more airplanes."

He laughed. "Let's go see a movie."

"That sounds amazing."

"Then dinner. After that we'll find somewhere to rest. When you don't look like you're about to fall asleep on your feet, we'll figure out our next move."

And maybe after that, Sabine would have the necessary brain power to figure out why, after years of not bothering, Neil had chosen today of all days to start disguising his appearance.

Later that evening Doug drove back toward the airport. There were decent hotels there, and when they checked in he asked for rooms across the hall from one another. He set Sabine's suitcase down at the end of the bed in her room and watched her take her coat off.

"You look like you might fall asleep if you try to take a bath."

She brushed the hair back from her face. "I'll probably just crash. Thank you for this afternoon. I really needed that break from everything."

"You're welcome."

"Not to mention I might not have the opportunity to go on many dates after I get incarcerated."

"Sabine—"

She shook her head. "It's okay, Doug."

"Seriously? You think it's okay you've lost the will to fight for your life?"

She blew out a breath. "I can't help it if it's inevitable. I'm not giving up. I'm just saying the likelihood of me being free to live my life after the CIA picks apart the last six years is seriously depressing. I told you that I need you to believe for me."

"That won't sustain you. It'll drag us both down. There has to be hope."

"It's slim."

"Slim is okay. It means there's still a chance. And from where I'm standing, there's more than a small chance."

"Truly?"

He rested his hands on her shoulders. "Look, I know you're exhausted, and it's been a good day, so let's not end it on a bad note. I'm just saying impossible things happen all the time. Did you think Ben would ever become a Christian?"

"Never."

"And yet he did."

She nodded. "Okay."

"Text me if you need anything?"

She nodded again.

"Can I kiss you good-night?"

Sabine tilted her face. Doug touched his hands to her cheeks and placed a kiss on her forehead. Her eyes drifted closed.

"Good night, Sabine."

TWELVE

Despite how tired she was, Sabine woke early. After a shower and a cup of bad hotel-room coffee, she decided to look at Ben's computer. When she found the file, she shot up to rush across the hall but saw the clock. She should probably wait until six before she sent him a text.

Within seconds, she got a reply.

Hallway. Breakfast.

They rode in silence to the basement level where the restaurant was. It was quiet since it was so early, which was good because what she had to tell him was important. The laptop loaded while Doug poured and doctored two cups of coffee.

He sat, a frown creasing his forehead. "Isn't that…?"

Sabine nodded. "I got Ben's laptop from the storage unit when we left Seattle."

"Did you get any sleep?"

She shrugged. "I got to thinking about the guy in my house and what he might have been looking for."

"Good thing this was in the storage unit."

"That was Ben. He didn't like being vulnerable." Sabine sighed. She hadn't meant to blurt that out.

Thankfully Doug chose not to pick up on it, instead motioning to the computer. "I'm assuming you found something."

Sabine tugged the small netbook around so they could both see the screen. "He has files of newspaper articles and police reports from the night—" Her voice gave out.

"The night your mom killed your dad."

Sabine nodded. "It's like he was looking for her before he died…for months. He has pictures that look like surveillance photos."

She clicked on a picture of a woman older than Sabine remembered, but still much the same. Dark hair, thick and completely straight, cut to her chin so it framed her face. Sunglasses were pushed to the top of her head, and she had one foot in the back of a limousine like she was getting in or out.

"She looks like you."

Sabine's whole body froze. "What?"

"Or you look like her, however that works."

"I'm nothing like her." She pointed to the screen. "That woman killed the only father I've ever known. For all we know she's responsible for Ben's death, too."

"I'm sorry. I should have thought before I spoke. If there's any resemblance, it's purely genetic." Doug rubbed his eyes. "Is there something here that makes you think your mom killed Ben?"

Sabine's energy deflated. "Strictly speaking, no, but I can't ignore the past. She did try once already. Then there's the fact that he was investigating her when he was killed, digging up buried history. I guess now that

I've thought about it, the idea that she's involved in all this won't leave me alone."

"Then we should check it out. Is there anything that will lead us to her?"

"Just the places she's been. Ben didn't know what name she'd been using all these years, so it would be hard to track her electronically." Sabine leaned back in her chair. "I can't believe he never told me that he was looking for her. I can't even ask him what he was thinking. Maybe he didn't remember what happened the same way I did. He was four years younger."

"It's possible he was trying to find her out of curiosity. Maybe he wanted to get some closure. He never said anything to me about her or what had happened back then. He kept a lot of things close to his body armor."

Doug scrolled through files while Sabine sipped her coffee. Her stomach rumbled, and he squeezed her hand, though his eyes didn't stray from the screen. "Get some breakfast."

Sabine walked to the buffet, picked out cereal and yogurt, mixing the two together with a spoonful of strawberries while Doug studied the photos and muttered.

She sat next to him. "What is it?"

"That's Spain, three years ago. Two days before Sheikh Amad Fashti was murdered in his hotel room. Two Delta Force operators were killed that day." Another picture flicked onto the screen. "This is January of the following year."

"Where is that?"

"Prague. The week before a hotel was bombed, killing more than a hundred people."

Sabine frowned. "That means something to you."

"It shouldn't fit. Maybe it's nothing." He scrolled through more photos. "I wonder if Ben realized."

"Realized what?"

"The Raven was behind all of these incidents. And your mom was apparently right there."

Sabine was about to eat another bite, but paused. "That terrorist you're trying to find?"

"More like international criminal. We're not sure where the Raven's allegiances are. It's easy to call bad guys *terrorists,* but it's not always accurate. Life isn't usually that cut-and-dried."

"What does the Raven have to do with my mom?"

"Maybe it's nothing."

Sabine leaned forward. "Or…"

"Maybe your mom is the Raven."

His words were like being slapped. Sabine jumped out of her seat, ready to defend her mom's honor, and then remembered what she'd seen her mom do all those years ago. She closed her eyes and squeezed the bridge of her nose. There must be something in every person that made them think the best of the people they came from, regardless of whether it made sense or not.

Doug laid his hands gently on her shoulders. She opened her eyes and said, "For her sake, I hope she isn't."

He pulled out his phone. "We'll figure this out."

Doug walked a few paces away. "Yes, sir, I do." He paused a second and then barked out a laugh. "Thanks for the vote of confidence."

He listened for a while and then nodded. "Understood."

When he came back over, he was smiling, like a

thousand pounds of weight had been lifted from his chest. "They're already here."

"Who?"

Four guys came in. They were all different body types and had different styles, a fact that had caught her eye before. This wasn't a team cut from the same mold. Each of them was an individual with different skills. The team all scanned the room as they entered. Ben had done the same thing. It didn't matter if they were at a restaurant or walking a street after dark. Safety in the face of constant threat was paramount.

Three of the men she'd met before—Barker, the big Texan; Hanning, the lady's man; and Franklin, whose mom had the best potato salad recipe ever. The fourth was new to her, which meant he was likely "California," the man Doug had spoken to during their escape from the hotel in the Dominican. All of them had bruises on their faces and hands.

They'd been in a fight.

Doug felt like he'd been punched. His team had gone without him, and they came back looking like this? Not that he'd have been able to change the outcome of the mission. It didn't matter that he would have come back looking the same way; it just mattered that he hadn't been with them.

He swallowed the feeling and crossed the room to meet them with a lot of handshaking and some gentle back-slapping.

The new kid, Perkins, who they all called "California" because he dressed like a surfer, looked like he'd been knocked around in a school-yard fight. Barker's breathing was shallow, probably because the Texan had tight bindings on his broken rib. For once Hanning didn't look like he was ready for a photo shoot for a male clothing magazine, and Franklin's inconspicuous-banker look was disturbed by the white bandage over his broken nose.

His team was back. That could be said at least. They were in one piece, which meant the night could have gone a whole lot worse.

"Sit down, all of you. Before you fall down."

No one sat.

Beside him, Sabine shook her head. "You boys look like you need a nap."

"No way." Hanning's chin lifted. "The team is ready and raring to go."

Doug snorted. "Good for you, but you're in luck. It's downtime for the lot of you."

"Downtime?"

Doug nodded. "As of right now, all of us—me included—are officially off the search for the Raven."

Barker moved and Doug braced for it. "I don't believe—"

"Sergeant Barker." Doug moved until his face was an inch from his teammate. "You will sit down before you fall down and you will hold all questions and comments until I have finished what I am saying. Do you understand me?"

"Yes, Sergeant Major."

"Good." Doug gestured to the table and they all sat. Sabine moved away and pulled out enough cups for the men. His heart swelled that she thought to take care of them. "As far as the Raven is concerned, the attempt to dispose of the team was so much of a success and you were all injured so badly that we've been forced to call off missions for the time being. It's vacation for the lot of us. In the meantime, we're switching to alternate identities and we're going to finish this."

"You want the Raven to think we're out of commission."

Doug looked at Barker, who took a steaming mug from Sabine. "I'll give you a moment to catch up, since you have a concussion, but yes."

"Why? We're just now getting close. We're actually onto something if the Raven has resorted to trying to get rid of us. So why stop the progress we're making?"

"Because if the Raven thinks he's bested us to the point that we're giving up, that makes for him to feel added confidence. And confidence makes you cocky. We leak it that we're all recovering from injuries, and once that happens it's only a matter of time before he makes a mistake. One that we will monopolize to the fullest extent of our capabilities. The decision has already been made.

"In the meantime, the CIA knows Sabine has resurfaced. They can't wait to get their hands on her. We all want to find out what the Raven has to do with Ben's death. With what Sabine has found on Ben's computer, we're now closer than ever. Our job is to keep Sabine safe until we can unravel what's going on. Then we can finally get the Raven."

Sabine felt the tap on her shoulder and turned from putting her cereal away. It had taken everything she had not to shout at Doug for making it sound like she couldn't take care of herself. Then she saw he was trying to hold the team together with the sheer force of their respect for him.

Still, she couldn't help saying, "You do know I'm standing right here."

The four of them grinned at her and she smiled back. "Are we done with business now? Can I say 'hello'?"

Despite the fact that Doug had limited his interactions with her to small talk when they had met at team barbecues, the team's acceptance of her had been swift and complete. They didn't hesitate to joke around and make her feel like part of their makeshift family.

Barker swept her up in a bone-crushing hug that lifted her feet off the floor. The Texan's arms were like hams.

Sabine grimaced. "Can't breathe."

He set her down. "Sorry. It's been a long night, but it's good to see you."

"All right, all right, give the woman some room," Hanning cut in. He kissed her hand. "Mademoiselle."

"Aaron." She nodded, mostly to appease him so he would let go of her hand. Hanning always wore designer clothes and could have doubled for a movie star with his blond hair and blue eyes.

Doug was suddenly there, his shoulder in front of hers. "Let go, Hanning. Give her some space."

Franklin adjusted his glasses, the middle-aged banker look firmly in place, despite the broken nose. "So good to see you, my dear."

"You, too. How's your mom?"

He shrugged. "The same."

The fourth man hung back.

Doug waved him over. "This is Perkins. He's—"

She nodded. "Ben's replacement."

"We don't make replacements. California's our newest team member."

The name fit. He really did look like a California surfer. "But he fills what was Ben's role, right?"

"Technically, yes," Doug answered. "He's a good kid."

Perkins shot his team leader a look. "Not a kid."

The kid really was adorable. She had to remind herself he was likely at least thirty, so not more than five years younger than she was. She shook his hand and then turned to Doug. "So what's the plan?"

"The guys eat while we fill them in on what you found on Ben's computer and figure out where to go from here."

Sabine waited until the whole team heaped plates with food and sat back down. "How'd you guys get here so fast, anyway?"

Barker grinned around a mouthful of pancakes. "Our commanding officer made the recommendation that we join you."

Hanning smiled. "Not to mention that following Doug would probably be more interesting than going on vacation, anyway."

Perkins pouted. "I still think we should have gone surfing."

"No, you don't." Hanning cuffed him over the back of the head.

Sabine shook her head over their antics. How did they manage to get anything done? Doug caught them up on the contents of Ben's computer. Hearing the evidence again, she didn't know what she'd do if the Raven turned out to be her mother. Or maybe her mother was just an unwilling pawn in all this. And what about the woman she'd seen kill Christophe Parelli? Sickness roiled in her stomach. She could have been watching her own mother kill someone—again.

If her mother really was an international criminal who discovered that Ben was tracking her, she might have thought he was about to expose her. Perhaps Ben was killed because he had revealed himself, and it meant their mom was finally able to finish what she had started all those years ago, the night she had killed their dad. If that was true, Sabine was left with a truck-load of incentive to find her mom and get justice for her brother.

Whether her mom was the Raven or not.

The idea that Ben kept secrets tainted her memory of him in a way she hated. The need to settle this was like a rock in her stomach that wouldn't go away. Surely justice for her brother would get rid of it. And yet there was something in all this that made Sabine think she might never find peace.

Her life was far too mixed up to ever be all the way straight again. She would continually be looking over her shoulder, watching for that moment when everything crashed down again. She would always and for-ever hesitate before trusting her own judgment.

Doug pushed his chair back and stood. "Let's hit the road."

Sabine grabbed the laptop. "We're leaving?"

"The team is going after the Raven. I have a place you can be safe in the meantime."

"You're going to stick me with your dad while you take down Ben's killer? Doug—"

He came close, his eyes dark and hard. "You're not coming with us."

THIRTEEN

When Sabine pulled out her cell phone before the plane to Washington, D.C., took off, there was a new message.

I have an assignment for you.

She powered down her cell with heavy fingers. "He knows I don't want to work right now."

Doug had his Bible open and balanced on his knee. The volume was no bigger than a CD case, dog-eared and bent like it lived permanently in his back pocket. When he had pulled it out, she'd seen strips of tape across the spine.

He looked up. "What's that?"

She sighed. "You were there. You heard me tell Neil that I wasn't working right now. I can't even consider him or the CIA or my future. I have to put my worry aside until we find the Raven."

"I thought you were going to contact that CIA guy, Steve-something, after you met with Neil. When we met with him you were all about doing surveillance on Neil and finding out who he was, passing it on."

"I know. I just…" Sabine barely had it together enough to focus on justice for her brother. Now that her mom was involved, Sabine was stuck in some kind of self-defense mode, like she was back behind that Dumpster, crouched beside her brother. Trying to convince him everything would be okay, when she knew full well it never would be.

"You gave your word to him, Sabine."

Her heart sank. She had also promised Ben that she would always look after him.

Doug squeezed her arm. "Steve gave us seven days until the CIA launches a manhunt for you. I know it's only been three days, but I won't let us go back on that promise."

At that moment she felt further from Doug than ever before. He didn't understand her at all. He thought she was strong, when in truth she was barely hanging on to the morsel of determination she had left.

Ever since he had dropped the bomb about her not going with his team, there had been a wall between them. She was determined to change his mind. The discussion at the departure lounge of the airport had been awkward to say the least. Every member of his team had seen the tension between them, but no one spoke of it.

Once they were on the plane—which, if you counted all the layovers and detours, totaled nine flights this week—he'd pulled out his Bible. Another reminder of how different they were. Differences that felt somehow insurmountable, since faith was a whole side of him Sabine didn't begin to understand. Nor did she particularly want to know. Not about a God who pointed his finger down from lofty heights and smote people for messing up. The last thing she needed was for someone else to tell her that she wasn't good enough.

She glanced up. There was a question in his eyes. "What?"

"Nothing."

Sabine turned and stared at the carpet of clouds outside her window. They were at cruising altitude now, where the whole world looked like an ant farm. How could God know each and every one of those tiny beings, let alone care about them all?

"He does care about you."

She'd said that out loud? Sabine shut her eyes. How convenient. Doug might not love her, but God did.

Doug looked away so the team didn't think he was crazy, staring at the back of Sabine's head while she looked out the window. He studied the page again. The words blurred.

God, she's so broken, I don't know how to help. Sabine needs You in her life so badly. Show her Your love.

It had been weeks since Doug had prayed with any regularity. Somehow he'd lost the rhythm of daily Bible study and prayer, and it left him off his game more than he had realized. Since the day she had walked into the restaurant where his target was, Doug had been reacting first and going to God second—if at all.

I'm sorry, Lord. I've been trying to figure all this out on my own. If You don't help, this will all go sideways fast. Sabine could get hurt.

The idea of her injured was unthinkable. He was falling for her. He could admit that to himself now, though he hadn't wanted to. And he hadn't needed his dad to say it. Why else would it feel so right to have her beside him? If she wasn't the woman for him, why did he keep having that dream where she was his wife?

God, I want that. I want her in my life. Marriage, kids, the whole package. Only You can figure all this out. I'm trusting You to do that, because she's way too important to me to leave to chance. Help us get the Raven, without Sabine being destroyed in the process.

Doug couldn't begin to imagine a nightmare from his past coming back like that. The horror she'd seen as a child was still with her now. He could see it in her eyes. After years of looking out for her younger brother, Sabine might have lost him to their mother after all. It was a wonder she had managed to hold herself together so well, especially when she didn't know the peace of being able to trust God.

Beside him Sabine shifted in the narrow airplane seat and stretched her neck left and right. It was now or never. She had a right to know what had happened to her brother. To be given the chance to put her fears to rest, even if he would never be able to.

"Sabine?" He cleared his throat. "Honey?"

She turned, and he saw the loneliness in her eyes. Part of him hated that he was about to destroy all the trust she had in him. Once this was done, she would know why they could never be together. Despite how he felt, it was doomed.

It was going to take everything he had for this all to come out the way he dreamed it might, and he didn't have everything to lose. Once she knew he was responsible for Ben's death, it would kill everything she felt for him. She would walk away, and he'd let her, because he wasn't going to be responsible for the death of someone else he cared for. Mistakes cost too much, and he couldn't risk her being another one.

This thing between them couldn't get any deeper; he had to cut if off now.

"There's something I have to tell you."

Sabine listened as Doug told her of a dusty scorcher of a day in some Middle East desert country only weeks ago.

"I was supposed to be the one on point, but something didn't feel right. Ben took charge like I was incapacitated and led the team right into the line of fire."

The anguish in his voice was like a knife to her heart. To see this strong, capable man, whom she cared for, so broken.

"I shouldn't have let him do that. The mission was my responsibility. It was my operation, and it should have been me who went first. One second we're half a klick from the helo, coming up on the end fast, looking forward to going home. The next second we're all diving for cover. Ben was hit in the neck. It was over in seconds."

He sucked in a shaky breath. "It should have been me."

She reached out and gripped his arm. "You can't think that. Ben knew what he was doing. If he disobeyed you and went against protocol, that's on him. It's so hard for me to say that. My baby brother should have been looked after, but that's just the sister in me talking. He was a Special Forces soldier. The best of the best. He was trained, just like you were. He knew the risks."

"But it was my fault."

"Did you fire the gun that killed him?"

Doug looked up from staring at his clenched fists, tears in his eyes. Sabine's chest ached.

"Did you pay the shooter to be there that day?" She laid her hand on his big shoulder and squeezed. "Let's go get the person responsible for it."

"What if it's your mother?"

Sabine shrugged. "She stopped being my mother the day she pointed a gun in my face. There's nothing between us anymore, and I don't want there to be. If she did kill Ben, she's going to answer for it."

Doug took a deep breath and nodded. "I promise you, she will. I'm going to make sure of it."

"So will I. When we face her together."

He shook his head. "I'm sorry. Like you said, we're trained soldiers."

"And my training and ability is tainted because I've been deceived for the last six years?"

"I didn't say that."

"You didn't have to. I can see it all over your face, Doug. You think I'm not up to par because I was tricked. Well, I can match you step for step any day."

"That might be so, but you can prove it another time. You're not coming with us. I have to know you're safe, Sabine. I promised Ben I'd take care of you, and there's no way I'm going to let him down again. I couldn't live with myself."

"So you're tying my hands because of your guilt."

Doug's mouth thinned. "And you're disregarding the way I feel because you don't agree. A bunch of nice words don't erase the fact that Ben's death is on me. There's no way I'm going to let you get hurt, too."

"What about Barker, Hanning, Franklin and Perkins? Aren't they important, too?"

"Of course they are—"

"Then by your own logic, they should stay behind with me. Why don't you just go and bring the Raven in all by yourself, if you're so worried about letting everyone down? Go be a one-man army and bring Ben's killer to justice."

"You know that's not how it works."

"So you'll risk them but not me."

"Because I care about you."

Sabine's heart leapt, despite the fact he'd shouted it at her. She laid her hand over his. "That's good. Because I care about you, too. But caring about someone means you put aside your fear and let them do what they're trained to do. You give them wings. You don't tie them down."

He shook his head. "I can't do it. I won't."

Sabine strode down the gangway into the departure lounge of yet another airport. After a while, destinations and layovers all bled together so she had a general sort of recognition regardless of what country she was in, or what time of day or night it was. She gave a cursory glance to the pack of people sitting around waiting to be shipped all over the world like a crate of apples, each one trying not to bruise the one beside it. She wound her way between exasperated parents and bored business types way too concerned with their smartphones and kept walking.

She barely recognized her life. Everything had changed since Ben's death, and it seemed as if that one phone call had been the catalyst for her whole world to turn inside out. She'd gone from solo covert agent to being shadowed 24/7 by a team of Delta Force operators. Granted, they were hanging back unnoticed, but she still couldn't help feeling smothered by an over-protective detail.

Any other day she might have been able to cover the feeling with the strength of her training. Today it bled into her walk and the painful grip she had on the handle of her rolling suitcase, proving exactly how much of a toll the past weeks had taken.

What was Doug's problem anyway? He thought she was incapable of being any help to their team. If it was her mom they were after, there was no way Doug could justify Sabine's absence.

She had a right to be there.

A flash of color, high and to the right, caught her attention. The widescreen television was on the channel for CNN, and the older man in the picture was one she knew well. She stumbled, and Doug was immediately at her side.

"What is it?" He looked at the TV and sucked in a breath. "That's Major General Taylor."

The anchorman spoke. "The body of this United States Army officer was discovered this morning, washed ashore on the northwestern coast of the French island of Corsica. His family has provided no explanation as to what Taylor might have been doing on the Mediterranean coast, and the army has declined to comment at this time.

"An investigation into the major general's death is forthcoming, and details will be released then. So far the military seems to be keeping a tight lid on exactly what happened."

Neil.

Sabine pushed back the disbelief. The revelation that her handler was in fact a major general with the army was a complete surprise. Of all the coincidences to happen today, her handler found dead wasn't one she'd prepared for.

Doug blew out a breath. "That's crazy. I spoke to him at my dad's birthday."

"He was at the party?" A shudder moved through her. She'd seen Neil—Major General Taylor—less than thirty-six hours ago, in disguise. He'd been at Doug's father's birthday?

Doug looked over at her, his face wistful. "You probably didn't notice him because Taylor would have blended in and looked like any of the other officers there. He was a great soldier and a good friend. Even said he thought of me like a nephew, probably because we've known each other for so long."

At their meeting in the mall food court, he'd made extra effort to disguise his appearance. Had he known Doug was there and needed to keep his betrayal a secret?

She wrestled away the reaction that would have broadcast her surprise. Doug knew her handler, a man who was a traitor to this country? Sabine would deal with this herself. Neil—Major General Taylor—was dead now, so what did it matter if Doug never found out his trust was misplaced?

Doug frowned. "It's kind of funny, though. He actually warned me away from you. Said you would be trouble, that you'd walk away when you were done and I'd have to pick up the pieces. Guess he thought you were some kind of heartbreaker I had to watch out for."

Neil had warned Doug away from her? Had he also thrown that brick through the kitchen window, triggering Andrew's heart attack?

Sabine raised her chin. "I'm sure he didn't know what he was talking about. After all, I've done nothing but conveniently supply you with fresh leads since this began."

His face softened. "I know that, honey. You've been invaluable."

"Then why won't you let me come with you? I won't get hurt. I can take care of myself."

He sighed. "It's not just about your safety. The team's safety is at stake, too. We've trained and gone on operations together for years. Perkins might be new, but he's one of us. You're an unknown component."

"That's unfair! It's—"

"The truth." Doug laid his hand on her shoulder, but she shook him off. "Sabine, each one of the guys has had the exact training I have had. I know every nuance of how they do what they do. In the middle of an op, I can tell you exactly what action they will take and probably what they're thinking. They'll tell you the same about me. Our training exhausts every contingency, every possible outcome. I'm not trying to shut you out. I'm trying to protect you. You're a live wire, and I love that about you."

She jerked back and he snorted. "Don't give me that look. There are plenty of things about you that could make someone fall in love with you. But you're not one of us. I can't put you in the middle of an operation that could change direction at any second and be able to trust that everyone will get out in one piece. As much as I can control what will happen, I am able to say that about my team."

Sabine looked down, understanding what he was saying but not liking it one bit. It wasn't like she was going to jump in the middle and mess up everything. If they laid out a plan, she would stick to it.

"Sabine." He lifted her chin with his fist. "I need you to be safe."

The shame in his eyes melted her heart. She could see the guilt he felt over her brother's death and his promise to Ben that he'd take care of her. She had no desire to put the team in danger but couldn't help how she felt.

"And if you're talking about my mom?"

"The woman tried to kill you. You want to kill her before she gets the chance to finish what she started all those years ago? You want revenge for Ben?"

"I want justice."

"I'll get it for you."

Sabine sighed. "This isn't right."

"Maybe not, but it's the way it's going to be."

Her stomach churned. "So that's it? Your way or no way at all? I can't live like that, Doug. I need give and take. I need a partner, not a dictator always telling me what to do. I need someone who'll stick beside me through everything. Not someone who's one step ahead pointing the way he thinks I should go. I can find my own way."

Doug's hand moved until his palm warmed the side of her neck. She felt herself being tugged toward him, into the shelter of his embrace, and pulled back. "Don't."

He didn't listen. "I don't know if I can be anything other than who I am."

Her heart sank. "So I have to be the one to change? Because I don't believe the same things you do, I'm not good enough?"

"I never said that."

"Well, it's coming across loud and clear." She pulled away.

"Don't do this, Sabine. I'm just trying to keep you safe." Disappointment was plain on his face, but she ignored it.

"What chance is there for us? We can't agree on anything, so what's the point?" She swiped away the wetness on her cheek and walked away.

FOURTEEN

Sabine hoofed it through the airport terminal. While she walked, she pulled out her phone and turned it back on as she weaved in and out of people meandering. It immediately buzzed with a new message from Neil.

Terminal B. Gate 32 at 2:35 p.m.

Neil was dead. Who was sending text messages from his phone? Apparently that person knew exactly where she was. She glanced around to find the walkway that would take her to Terminal B and looked for anyone who might be watching her.

She hadn't told Doug about her connection to the dead major general. She probably should have told him she knew his death was tied to what was happening with them—between them.

Doug was determined to protect her. Even now he followed a few paces behind with a heartbroken look on his face that she refused to think about. There was no way she wasn't going to be part of what was about to happen. If it had been her who had died, Ben would have done everything possible to bring her murderer to justice. And her own mother?

Ben loved her and he was dead because of it. Her mom tried to kill her. Maxwell cheated on her and declared he never loved her in the first place. She'd been a convenient wife for him, present in his life but not enough to be a nuisance. Doug had said he was falling for her, but showed it by taking away the only power she had left. If he thought she would stay out of it, he didn't understand the first thing about her. She would have to figure out on her own how to get in on this mission.

Now she had a meeting to attend and less than ten minutes to make it there. She clasped her flower necklace she wore—a peace offering from Ben—and tried to draw some strength from his memory.

Task number one: ditch the protection detail.

Doug folded his arms across his chest and stared at the door to the ladies' bathroom. He couldn't fault Sabine for hiding in there. She didn't like the way he had pushed her out of this op. He didn't, either. But, if the unthinkable happened to her, he would never forgive himself.

Hanning strolled by and raised his wrist, indicating his watch. Doug gave him an *I know* nod. There was no time to hang around. They needed to get moving if they were going to drop off Sabine and get to the meeting they had scheduled with Colonel Hiller.

A plan had already begun to formulate in Doug's mind. Using the photos and the information Ben had gathered, the team would draw the Raven out. Once they had a location, they'd be able to move in and detain him—or her, if it really was Sabine's mom.

Major General Taylor's death was connected. If it wasn't, then the timing was entirely too coincidental for Doug's liking. In his experience, there were no such things as coincidences.

Something hovered just outside his consciousness, as if he were trying to grasp a cloud between his fingers. There was some detail about this whole thing that he was missing—something that connected Sabine's handler with CIA agent Steve Adams and the dead major general.

God, help us find the Raven. Let Taylor's death mean something.

Doug kicked away from the wall and tried to look nonchalant instead of on alert. He strolled to the door of the restroom, his mind flashing back to the Dominican Republic. That time he'd been the one in the bathroom, and Sabine had made an effective getaway.

And she was really good at disguises.

He announced his frustration out loud, turning several heads. The cell phone in his hand rang. "Richardson."

"What is it?" It was Barker.

Doug sighed. "Sabine ditched us."

"Girls take a long time in there, doing whatever they do. What makes you think she split?"

He gripped the phone. "Who knows? But I intend to find out. When I get my hands on her, I'll—"

"You were going to leave her anyway. Weren't you?"

"That's not the point." Doug was done arguing about it. "You and Perkins find security and get a look at the recording. She'll be in a disguise. I want to know when she left and where she went."

A young woman with pink streaks in her blond hair

exited the bathroom pulling Sabine's suitcase. "I'm out."
He ended the call. He jogged over to the girl and swung
around so he could cut her off. "Excuse me, ma'am?"

She jerked to a stop, her eyes wide.

"Where'd you get the suitcase?"

The ring in her lip jutted out. "What're you talkin'
about?"

Doug folded his arms. "My friend went into the bathroom pulling that suitcase, and you came out with it. I
know it's hers. It has her name tag on it."

A. Surleski.

She sighed like Doug was imposing on her. "Fine,
some chick gave it to me. What's it to you, anyway?"

"It's important that I find her."

"I get it." She nodded. "You're the stalker boyfriend."

"What? No, she's in danger. She's freaked out, but if
I don't find her, she could get really hurt."

The young woman with the pink hair narrowed her
eyes. Doug tried not to let his impatience show. Finally
the girl found him worthy. "She paid me a hundred
bucks to trade bags, but I ain't givin' you the money."

"Which way did she go?"

"I was in the bathroom. How should I know?" She
walked away, shaking her head.

Doug called out. "Hey!" The girl looked back. "What
color was your bag?"

"Pink tote."

Doug moved. The nearest exit was off the food court
that connected the string of gates that branched off from
it. He passed the kids' play center and was almost to the
gathering of restaurants when his phone rang.

"Richardson."

"Security tapes came up dry."

"Look for a pink tote bag."

Barker sighed. "The image is black and white."

"Assume she's in disguise."

"I thought you were kidding. Fine, we'll check for totes, and a woman with her build."

"Let me know what you find. I'm heading for the exit. Maybe she's leaving the airport and not planning on getting a ticket on another flight."

"Benny's sister really got to you, didn't she?"

Doug hung up. She'd been in black slacks and a red sweater before, hadn't had much time to change, maybe added a jacket and pulled up her hair. She could be wearing a hat.

A woman with Sabine's build and a wide-brimmed hat strode by on high-heeled black boots. Doug grabbed her arm and succeeded in freaking her out, but didn't find Sabine.

God, help me find her. Keep her safe.

Worry churned the remnants of the sandwich in his stomach. It was hard to believe that God might choose to keep her safe by keeping her away from Doug, but he would accept it. He scanned the crowd again.

His phone rang. "Tell me you found her."

"Dark jacket. Hair tied back with what looks like a bandanna, but it's definitely her. She went west, looked like she was with two guys in suits. Tracked her all the way to the exit. She looked in a hurry, but you might be able to catch her on the curb."

"I'm right there."

Doug ducked out the doors and through the crowd that waited for arriving passengers. Now that he knew she'd left the terminal, he could head out there. If he'd risked it, he might have had to come back through the security line when they found her still inside.

He weaved through families, skidded so as to not collide with an old man and had to wait a second for the automatic doors to let him out. The curb was lined with vehicles being loaded. A cop leaned against his squad car with a paper coffee cup.

The fact that she thought she would be better off alone instead of with him freaked him out big-time. There was no way he'd be able to concentrate on apprehending the Raven if he didn't know she was safe.

A hotel shuttle bus pulled away from the curb where they made pickups. Doug scanned the windows for a woman with a cloth over her hair. Beyond where the bus had been was a black Escalade in the far lane. Two men in suits—Christophe Parelli's bodyguards—had their hands on Sabine.

Doug was halfway across the street when shouts erupted and a car horn screamed by behind him. A truck sped into the edge of his vision, and he sidestepped as fast as he could. It screeched to a halt inches from his hip. The cop yelled for him to stop running.

Sabine was almost in the car, being shoved with a hand on her back. Her head hit the door frame. She cried out and turned, and her eyes flew open.

"Doug!" She swung the pink tote at the two men. One of the men grabbed the bag, threw it aside and punched her in the head.

Sabine slumped into the man's arms. Doug was spurred on, narrowly missing another car. He barreled at full speed while they loaded her into the car. The last man climbed in, and the car pulled away before he got the door closed.

Doug braced, prayed and leapt for the open door. His momentum pushed the guy in, creating a tangle of limbs. The car swerved, and Doug gripped the door-frame to keep from falling out. Something pressed into his side and crackled. Just before everything went dark, a heavy accent spoke.

"Maybe we'll get paid double for two of them."

FIFTEEN

The road twisted and turned as it climbed the mountain. Trees lined the edge of the gravel, at least the side that Sabine could see. Her forehead was pressed against the window. Her head pounded from the slam of that fist, and she was about ready to throw up. The press of a large body smashed her against the door. How many people were in the back of this car anyway?

She kept her eyelashes low and hoped they didn't realize she had regained consciousness. She had no idea how long they'd been driving, or where they were headed.

All she could do was watch as her mind replayed the image of Doug running toward her in high definition. That was followed by violent images of them killing her and dumping her body. She tried to remember him in her kitchen, instead. The way his lips moved into a smile and the light of it shone in his eyes.

How would he find her? Did he even want to? She'd hardly been nice to him. The last words spoken between them had been full of frustration over the life she wanted with him, but could never have.

The car slowed and finally pulled to a stop. The landscape was still all trees and the orange glow of sunset. If they'd been driving all afternoon while she was passed out, they could be hundreds of miles from the airport by now. Way out here there was little hope for escape and no one to call for help.

Deep breaths.

She scoured her memory for a time when she'd been in a worse situation, but the pain in her head was too much. Still she hadn't survived being a covert agent for this long without developing some skills.

Think.

A door slammed. Footsteps on gravel rounded the car to her door. When it opened, she started to slide, but football-size hands hoisted her up and out of the car. She was flipped over him fireman-style and her stomach hit his shoulder with every step. She swallowed hard against the nausea as he carried her across the clearing up the wooden steps of a structure.

She couldn't let him get her in the house.

Sabine locked on to his torso with her legs, levered herself up and dove sideways to pull him off balance. They slammed down on the hard wood of the porch. His weight knocked the breath from her lungs. She flipped over as soon as she could move and found herself face-to-face with a .357 Magnum, silver with a black grip.

She swallowed. "Nice gun."

Beyond the barrel of the pistol, the big Italian smirked. "'Tis my favorite."

Sabine stretched out her muscles as she clambered to her feet. Her head still thumped, but a brisk five-mile run through wooded terrain would take care of that. Sadly she didn't get her wish just then, because he poked her in the back with his weapon. She stepped ahead into a small hunting cabin, and the two men crowded in behind her. She turned to glare at them... and froze.

The other Italian hefted a body from his shoulder, flipped it over and dumped the unconscious man on the floor.

"Doug."

She tried to run to him but thick arms banded around her like a vise. Sabine kicked and squirmed. "I'll kill you. If you hurt him, I'll kill you."

A woman walked up the cabin steps. The urge to fight dissipated from Sabine, and her knees gave out.

The woman's snug black dress outlined a figure that was the blueprint for Sabine's own body. Chocolate-colored hair fell past her shoulders, and her eyes were dark and hard, heavy with smoky eye makeup.

There was no trace of the mother Sabine had known. All that was left now was a woman who had killed her own son.

"Hello, darling. Long time no see."

The Italian bodyguard set Sabine down. She stumbled but forced her shoes to stay planted on the bare wood. She couldn't look at Doug. She couldn't react at all, so she kept any sign of emotion from her face, determined not to let weakness show. The daughter couldn't do anything but react emotionally to what was happening. The covert agent could fight...and win.

"Nothing to say?"

Sabine shrugged, as if reuniting with the long-lost mother who had once tried to kill her was no big deal. She reached up and sought solace from the necklace Ben had given her.

Her mother raised an eyebrow at the sight of Doug unconscious on the floor. "What is that?"

The bodyguard by the door replied in Italian. "He decided to join us."

Her mother huffed and replied in English. "Interesting, since I was under the impression he was recently rendered out of commission in a nasty accident. He looks relatively uninjured to me. I'll have to note that tactic for the future."

Sabine cleared her throat. "Can we get on with... whatever this is?"

A perfectly shaped eyebrow rose. "You have somewhere to be?"

Sabine could name a hundred places she'd rather be. Somehow she'd known this day was coming. The day she would finally face her mother again and have to try to survive when neither her stepdad nor her brother had been able to. Now that it had arrived she felt seriously unprepared to handle what was happening. She had to get herself and Doug out of there.

She swallowed, giving herself a moment to tamp down her emotions. "What's it to you? I doubt you suddenly started to care about my life just now."

Her mom sighed. "I had hoped for the chance to explain a few things to you."

"At gunpoint?" Sabine held back the laugh that wanted to spill out. "Wow, that's one warped sense of atonement you have. You want to make amends so you can have a clear conscience when you kill me?"

"Why on earth would I want to kill you? You're my best agent."

Sabine took a step back. She'd known it, but it was still a shock to hear it confirmed.

Her mother's smile emerged, like a feral tiger. "You've been working for me for years now. You're really very good at your job, Elena."

"It's Sabine."

Her mom waved away the correction. "Details. Anyway, your handler, Neil—"

"The dead major general."

"Very good, and yes, he's dead. Pity, really. He had his uses."

Sabine felt sick. "And my team, six years ago when they were all killed?"

Her mother shrugged. "It was necessary—to make your transition easier."

"It was necessary to ruin my career? The CIA thinks I killed them and went rogue. They're looking for me. I've been under the impression I was an American agent all these years, and now I find out I'm a criminal? How dare you."

Her mom sat on the couch and crossed one leg over the other knee. She motioned to the armchair. "Have a seat, darling, before you blow a gasket."

"I don't want to sit down."

First they had her in the car, now the cabin. If she sat down it would be like taking another step on the plank toward the murky water of her death. The bodyguards both took a step closer, each of their guns pointed at her. Sabine wasn't ready to get shot so she sat and folded her arms. "You expect me to be happy that you did what you wanted with my life?"

Arrogance shone in the older woman's eyes. "You love your job, don't you?"

"I'm supposed to be grateful?" Sabine shook her head, unable to comprehend this woman's audacity.

"I'll probably end up in jail for the rest of my life because of what you've done. It was you, wasn't it? You killed Christophe Parelli and made it look like I did it."

Her mother's eyes narrowed. "I hardly think you'll end up in jail."

"How can you be so sure about that? I can't just pick up where I left off and start running missions again. Am I supposed to be some kind of covert agent for hire, doing jobs for whoever will pay the most and living my life with cash and no identity? You may think you have power over me, but you don't." Something clicked in her mind. "I won't turn into you."

Her mother jerked as though Sabine had slapped her.

A tempting thought.

The older woman studied Sabine. "Who said anything about your future?"

"So you *are* going to kill me."

"You said it yourself—the CIA is after you. If you're not going to join me, I can't really afford to let you go. There's no way I can leave loose ends like that." Her surgically perfect nose wrinkled. "Bad for business."

It wasn't a surprise that her mom wanted to kill her. She'd tried it once before. Her mother had no conscience whatsoever. The thought skittered over Sabine like a thousand ants. Once she'd dreamed of home and a family, and while Sabine hadn't been born into the life she wanted, it now looked like she wouldn't be able to make that life for herself, either.

"Is that what Major General Robert Taylor was? A loose end?"

"Your Neil's death was an unfortunate accident. The old man had his charms. I'll miss him."

Sabine saw the first glimpse of humanity then, in

her mother's eyes. Would her mom really miss Neil? That would mean she actually had a heart. While Neil might have been lying to her, he had also supported her for years. The man had been both a sounding board and a mentor to her.

Sabine leaned toward her mom. "I'm sorry for your loss."

The woman glared at Sabine. "I don't need your sympathy."

"Good, because I was just being polite. That man betrayed his country because of you."

"Pshaw." Her mom waved her hand. "People will do a lot of things for the right amount of money...and a little added pressure."

Sabine was nearly sick. "Why?" The word was a whisper.

Her mother blinked, and all trace of emotion vanished from her face.

"Why did you kill Ben...and Dad?" Sabine had to know, since she figured she was as good as dead. Her mom had won, and Sabine didn't care what was going to happen to her, so long as Doug got out of there alive. She just wanted to know why the woman—who was supposed to have kept her and Ben safe, and to have loved their father—could have turned on her own family.

"Life rarely gives a satisfactory answer. You should get used to being disappointed." Her mom stood, then strutted on her spike heels to the door.

"I'm well acquainted with disappointment. I had you as a mother."

The older woman actually laughed. The sound cut off when the front door slammed behind her.

Sabine studied the room. It was a typical cabin, one room with one door at the front. Yellowed single-pane windows, high and small, dotted the walls, but not so tiny she wouldn't be able to dive through one if she got enough of a head start. First she had to get past the two goons with guns.

Not getting shot would be the hard part. After that, her mother would be easy pickings given the rage that burned inside Sabine. All the deaths her mom was responsible for—it was so senseless.

Doug lay motionless on the floor. If he was still unconscious, he must be really hurt. She'd already shown them how much she cared for him by exploding when they had dumped him on the floor. This was going to be even more difficult if she had to protect him, fight two big Italian thugs and drag Doug's prone body out of the cabin.

Sabine refused to admit defeat when she was perfectly able-bodied, in full possession of her faculties and had the skill that was borne of her training plus the brain God had given her. She refused to be just another statistic on her mom's vast résumé of crimes.

God, I want to live.

She wasn't even sure how it would help. Not to mention that a sudden conversion when the end loomed near seemed a little too cliché. She always mulled things over—to death, if you'd asked Ben. She wasn't one to make rash decisions on something as important as devoting her life to a religion.

Then again, the track record of her decision making so far wasn't all that great. Her marriage to Maxwell had been an unmitigated disaster, and she'd held him off for months before she had agreed to get engaged. Weeks later they'd been married. He had probably sped up the timetable so she didn't have time to change her mind.

If she prayed to God to get her out of this, she'd have to keep her end of the bargain when He did. Was she ready to change her whole life just on the off chance that Doug was right? Would everything really be better if she gave it to God?

She looked at the two bodyguards. Any idiot could pull a trigger and kill someone. It didn't matter if they had good aim or not, these guys could end her life. How could God make this situation any different? Her mom would either kill her now or make her suffer first. Either way she was still dead. Doug had to get out alive. That was a promise she made to herself.

God, I don't care what I have to do. I believe in You. That's not the problem. Doug says You love me, but I don't understand how You could or why. I don't expect You to get me out of this, but help me save Doug.

Maybe it was even more of a cliché to give her life to a God she didn't know and didn't understand only because she needed help, but she would have done anything just then. Although if she could have a minute when he was conscious to say sorry for walking away and trying to ditch him again, she'd take it.

Doug probably thought she was a horrible person, duping him for a second time. If it had been her, she would have left him after being given the slip twice. She wasn't one for taking chances and trusting people. Hopefully Doug was more forgiving than she was.

Sabine reached up once again and gripped her flower necklace. The petals were warm from her body heat, and she felt a surge of reassurance. She felt Ben's presence in her memories like the phantom pain of a limb that had been amputated.

God, help me.

Footsteps crunched the gravel outside as her mom moved around the exterior of the cabin doing…something. The guard by the door let his attention flick to the window.

Sabine seized the opportunity. She kicked him and grabbed his gun as he fell. The other gun fired as she spun. The bullet sliced through the muscle of her left shoulder, and she gritted her teeth but held on. Two shots from her gun and he dropped to the floor, groaning.

The first guy's arms wrapped around her from behind. "You'll pay for that."

He squeezed the breath from her lungs and lifted her off her feet. The pain in her shoulder brought black spots to the edge of her vision. He should be permanently down, but Sabine didn't have time to figure out how her aim had been off.

There was a rush of movement behind her and the guy went limp. They both fell to the floor. She slammed into him, and her breath whooshed out.

A hand was stretched out in front of her face. Beyond it, Doug smiled. Sabine shoved the guard's arms from around her middle and let Doug haul her to her feet.

There was the unmistakable sound of a gun being cocked. All sign of life bled from Doug's face, and his eyes turned to the eyes of a warrior. Something small and unyielding touched the back of her head, and she froze.

"You move and she dies."

SIXTEEN

"Hello, Raven." Doug stared at the woman who had destroyed Sabine's family, most likely had killed a respected major general and was either a conspirator or accessory to so many other crimes that it would take all day to list them. It wasn't his life that flashed before his eyes in that moment; it was the life he might have had with Sabine. It was the *maybe*.

The older version of Sabine snarled. "Clever boy."

Doug stepped back and put one foot of space between him and the two women. The Raven had been outside. Doug had been so intent on saving Sabine that he'd let his guard down, and now she was going to pay for it.

Sabine's eyes flashed, but Doug simply couldn't stand to lose the promise that he saw when he looked at her. There was no way he was going to let her die. His entire world had been thrown upside down by a beautiful woman. Ben's sister. She had become more to him than he'd ever imagined, a vital part of his life.

"Now—" the Raven's eyes tracked his retreat "— my daughter and I are going to walk out of here. You don't follow us, and I don't catch even a scent of you, or she's dead. Understand me?"

Doug nodded.

Tears streamed down Sabine's face and blood soaked the fabric of her shirt on her upper arm. Doug shook his head, tried to communicate to her that everything was going to be fine. He would find her. He loved her.

Anything other than her safety was unacceptable. And it would destroy him.

God, go with her.

It took everything he had not to run down the cabin steps and tackle the Raven, but he couldn't put Sabine in that kind of risk. He had to wait. He'd thought the Raven intended to kill Sabine. From their conversation, it had sounded like the older woman planned to kill both him and Sabine. So why take her now? It made no sense. Far worse than a cold and calculating enemy was one who acted irrationally and without logic.

Doug stood immobilized while Sabine's mom marched her from the cabin to the SUV parked outside. As part of his heart got farther and farther away, he reached for every ounce of training he'd ever had. He needed his team if he was going to pull off the biggest mission of his life. If he was going to have any hope of getting her back.

The Raven, her gun still at Sabine's temple, pulled out a cell phone. Doug's brain spun, like wheels that suddenly found traction. She'd been outside doing something.

There was a shimmer in the air. Wind rushed through the open door, and he started to run for the back of the cabin. He launched himself through a window, over the rear porch, with a wall of hot air behind him, and hit the grass with a grunt.

* * *

Wind whipped Sabine's hair as a roar launched from the space behind her. The cabin exploded into a fireball that launched flames and smoke into the air. Her mother spurred her to the car.

"Maybe you do have your uses. After all, you saved me the trouble of having to plant the evidence you killed those two Italian idiots and your boyfriend. I'd already set the explosive charges when you decided to play hero-spy-escapes-the-evil-abductors. Even if you did ruin the plan that you die in there with them." She shrugged. "Oh, well."

Hands gripped Sabine under the arms. "In we go."

She cried aloud and almost passed out as the pain radiated from the gunshot wound in her shoulder. She stumbled but her mom held her weight, hauled Sabine's limbs onto the front passenger seat and slammed the door.

"No." Sabine's voice was barely a whisper. She tried to grab the door handle, but her fingers wouldn't cooperate. Nothing was working. Where were they going? What was her mom going to do with her?

Her mom slammed the driver's door and started the engine. A feral noise emerged from Sabine's throat. Doug had been in the cabin. He was dead. She squeezed her eyes shut and willed away the rush of tears.

Her mom grabbed her around the shoulders. Her hand pressed directly on the bullet wound on Sabine's upper arm. "Don't worry, darling. We're together now."

Sabine didn't have time to cry out before the world went black.

Hours later Doug sat on a crate in a Baltimore warehouse. He wanted to pace out his frustration, but the team was all giving him the same look—the one that said, *Sit down already. You're making us crazy.*

He exhaled, but it didn't help to dissipate the pain in his limbs. His head still throbbed from when he hit the ground after jumping through the back window of the cabin. He didn't even want to think about the glass cuts on his hands.

Colonel Hiller sat across from Doug, his pressed suit and combed hair a contrast against the dust and grime of the warehouse. "Perkins's job is to get everything he can from Ben's computer. Everyone else knows what to do. And regardless of what some people think—" he shot Doug a look "—I'm not giving you the runaround. We will find her."

Doug tried to believe that. He had to believe it, because he was scared to death that, if he didn't, there wouldn't be anything left for him.

Father, I need Your help.

He loved her, more than anything. More than his job even. She'd walked away at the airport because of it. Now, after he'd found her, she was gone again. Like sand falling between his fingertips. The missions his team undertook might be important work, but her life meant so much more to him than any of it. Sabine was everything. And it was tearing him apart that he'd realized it too late.

Please don't let it be too late.

Colonel Hiller was still talking. Doug tuned in to what he was saying.

"—can't forget this woman is a trained agent. She can take care of herself. We want to save her for Ben's sake, because she's his sister. It's tempting for us to think we're the only ones who can get her out of this because of who we are. We know what we're capable of, but Sabine is good. I read her CIA file. Even six years ago she showed excellent promise."

Doug had fallen back on his training. He'd tracked her across the airport and still hadn't been able to save her from being taken by those two Italian bodyguards. Guys he'd last seen working for Christophe Parelli; guys who'd died, unconscious, in the cabin fire.

Another puzzle piece in the mystery of the Raven had fallen into place.

The two Italians had become reemployed entirely too fast not to have had close ties with the Raven even before Parelli's death. A good lead, one that could prove useful, but it didn't wash away the sting of Sabine being taken…again.

Mistakes piled on top of mistakes. He hadn't thought he could take any more failure, and here it was again. All that reliance on his training had been useless. Doug's instincts were of no help. Sabine was gone, and the way it sliced at him left him wide open, tasting bitter defeat.

A piece of paper was shoved into his hands. Doug looked up. Hanning's movie-star looks held a distinct shadow. "This wasn't your fault."

Doug saw differently in his friend's eyes. "That doesn't get her back."

"You know what will?" Colonel Hiller stepped into view beside Hanning. "We run this down like any kidnap victim we're going after. Stop moping around, and let's get to work."

Doug looked at the paper in his hand. "Wasting our time with phone records?" He stood up and got in the colonel's face. "And pep talks? Like a motivational speech is going to help. Sabine could be dead already, and you think we're going to find her by sitting here?"

"We know you love her." The colonel's voice was measured, as if he held back what he really wanted to say—probably a reprimand for talking that way to a superior.

Doug sat down. There was a time when he had lived to run down the target and save the life of the innocent person stuck in the middle. But no more. The love he had for his life disappeared around the same time as Sabine. Now he had a new dream, one that featured that very same woman as a key player. He needed to find her so he could tell her. So he could apologize for failing and promise it would never happen again.

He put his face in his hands, vaguely aware of the team and the colonel discussing repeated numbers on Major General Taylor's phone records.

"I got an interesting delivery this morning. From Steve Adams."

Doug lifted his head. "CIA agent Adams?"

The colonel nodded. "Disappeared three days ago. Flew to the south of France and vanished."

"The south of France again. What was in the package?"

"It was one of those 'in the event something has happened to me' deals. Full of records, such as a copy of a passport for Neil Larson with Taylor's picture."

Doug's eyes widened. "Larson?"

"Major General Taylor's wife's maiden name, of all things. Not very original, if you ask me, but there you have it."

"What else?"

The colonel held up a grainy photograph. "Copies of

call records for Neil Larson's cell phone, listing some very interesting numbers, including your girl and a Brenda Sanders."

Doug's breath caught. "The Raven. Sabine's mom."

"One and the same."

"I told you all this already! How does this help us find her? The woman killed her husband and Ben. Who's to say she won't just shoot Sabine and disappear?"

Colonel Hiller's mouth pressed into a hard line. "She's had plenty of opportunity. We're banking on the fact that, since Sabine has worked for the Raven all these years, Sabine will either be valuable to the woman or she'll be given enough freedom that she's able to get away to a phone to call for help."

"If she wants to."

Everyone turned, and Perkins found himself suddenly the center of attention. Ben's laptop was perched on his knees.

Barker smacked Perkins on the back of the head. "Why would you say something like that?"

Perkins winced. "The colonel said it. She's worked for the Raven for six years. Maybe all this is a ploy to go and work for her for real, but she's making it look like she's being forced. Do we know for sure she's legit? All the evidence says Sabine killed her whole team six years ago. Maybe she really did go rogue."

Doug surged forward. "How can you say that?"

Hanning and the colonel grabbed Doug's arms.

Perkins shrugged it off. "I'm saying we don't know for sure. She could be one of them now. I don't think we should ignore the possibility."

"We can." Doug clenched his jaw shut. "And we will.

There's no way Ben's sister has gone to work for the Raven."

Perkins put the laptop aside and stood. "Your opinion of Ben is clouding your judgment of this woman."

"You think I don't know her? You think I'm not capable of knowing whether someone is being honest or if they're just stringing me along?"

"She's a woman. You're telling me that you've never let—"

Doug was ready to explode. "You'd better stop right there, California."

Perkins was about to shoot something back, but Colonel Hiller got between them. "Perkins, thank you for your incredible distrust of all women everywhere. We will take it under advisement, but your job is that computer and nothing else." Perkins sat back down.

Barker slapped him on the back of the head again. "Hey!"

Barker scoffed. "Get back to work."

"I already found something."

Doug, the colonel and Hanning all surged forward. "Well?" Doug was about to wring it out of him. "What is it?"

Perkins turned the laptop around on the crate so they could see the screen. "Ben had a whole folder labeled *Sabine*."

"And?"

"You see this?" Perkins pointed to a program icon on screen.

"What is it?" Colonel Hiller looked about ready to lose it.

"A GPS program."

Doug frowned. "Ben had his sister bugged?"

Perkins nodded.

"The flower necklace. It was a gift from him."

"If it's active, then we can find her." Perkins clicked on the program, and they all stood silent while it loaded.

A map of North America popped up on the screen, a satellite image. A red dot hovered over West Virginia. Doug held his breath while the map zoomed in, closer and closer.

The screen went black.

"What just happened?"

Perkins didn't answer. He started tapping buttons in what looked to Doug like a frantic panic to get the map back. Nothing happened. A cursor appeared on the screen. It flashed a couple times and words started appearing, like someone typing on the keyboard.

You'll never find her.

"Perkins—"

"It's not me. Someone hacked this computer or the GPS program. When we activated the search on Sabine, we tipped them off."

Doug turned to the colonel. "The Raven."

"Seems like it." There was no hope in his senior officer's eyes. "She's gone."

Doug strode from the warehouse to the vehicle he'd rented. He climbed in, slammed the truck door and hung his head until his forehead touched the steering wheel.

His phone rang. "What?"

"Everything okay, son?"

He sighed. "Not really, Dad. I'm kind of busy."

"I wouldn't be asking if it wasn't important. Major General Taylor's body is arriving tonight. You know he was a friend of mine. I'd be there to greet him myself, but, if I leave the hospital, I'll never hear the end of it from Jean."

"You're not well enough to put yourself under that much stress." Doug frowned. "Wait…what do you mean the hospital?"

"I might have…sort of…"

"Dad—"

"Had a little issue earlier. But it's nothing. They're just adjusting my medication."

"Don't go anywhere. I'll meet Taylor's body for you."

Despite everything that was happening, Doug would do this favor for his dad. He didn't want to think about the old man being anything other than the energetic father he'd always been. The general needed rest so he could get back to being his old self…. Doug couldn't let his dad find out Dad's old friend and colleague had been involved with the Raven.

The sun gave way to the black of night before Sabine allowed herself to comprehend what had happened. She flexed her bound hands and drew her knees up to her chest. The nasty motel headboard wasn't pleasant to lean against, but that was the least of her worries.

Her shoulder throbbed under the tight bandage. Her mother had threatened to sew the wound together herself. But she'd backed away fast when Sabine had screamed loud enough to alert all their motel neighbors. With no anesthetic and a lack of sterilized utensils, Sabine wasn't about to let anyone near her arm, least of all a crazy woman.

"That should hold them off for the time being."

Sabine could admit to a certain curiosity about what her mom was talking about, but wasn't going to let her know that. Instead, Sabine turned her head and stared at the curtain that blocked the view outside.

"Your man's team. Did you know they tried to convince me that they were all incapacitated?" Her laugh was high and piercing. "Now he's gone, and they'll never find you. I've made sure of it."

Sabine should have let her mother sew up her arm. Dying from an infection would probably be more pleasant than having to listen to this.

Sabine looked back at her, not caring that all the despair she was feeling was probably right there on her face. "What do you want from me?"

The gleam in her mother's eyes made her look like an unhinged lunatic. She crossed the room and yanked the necklace from Sabine's neck, tossed it to the ground and stomped on it with the heel of her shoe.

"We're a team, you and I. From now on it's us against the world. We're going to finish what I started. There won't be anywhere in the world where people won't know what you and I have done." She grinned. "It's going to be incredible."

"You were going to kill me."

"Please." Her mother rolled her eyes. "That was never the plan. We're going to make a name for ourselves."

The woman was crazy, flip-flopping back and forth. Did she even know what she was saying? Now instead of dying, Sabine was supposed to be a terrorist? Or some kind of traitor to her country? The idea tore apart what was left of her heart. The CIA already thought she was guilty of multiple murders and betraying her country. After this they would have irrefutable proof. They would never believe she was innocent now.

She forced herself to push back the panic and breathe easy. "What have you done?"

"We haven't done it yet, silly. We're going to do it tonight. The clock's already ticking." Her mother cocked her head, looking at Sabine like she was a small child. "We're going to bomb the CIA, of course. And those military snobs, who think they're so perfect. At the exact same time. That's the beauty of it. I finally figured out that selling weapons was only part of my destiny. I'm going to finish my enemies once and for all so they never find us."

"From a motel room?"

"Why not? No one will expect it. They'll just be all boo hoo, so sad they're dead. Poor Taylor. Poor Agent Adams."

Sabine jerked. "Steve Adams?"

Her mom nodded. "Don't you know? You killed him, too."

Three hours later

Uniformed soldiers flanked the aircraft as the body of Major General Robert Taylor was carried from the plane. The casket was covered with a flag, the white stripes gleaming under the harsh glare of the lit runway. Doug stood beside his teammates as the procession emerged from under cover of the plane's tail.

With a blinding flash and a deafening crack of thunder, the world went black.

SEVENTEEN

"What happened here?"

Doug didn't have to know the guy; his whole manner screamed CIA. After being blown back by the force of yet another explosion, Doug's hands were still shaking. The dissipation of adrenaline left him antsy and itching for a fight. "The casket of Major General Robert Taylor was the source of the explosion."

Dressed in a dark suit and plain red tie with his hair gelled back, the CIA guy's eyes widened. "Fire marshal went through here already?"

Doug took a cleansing breath. "No. I saw it myself." The shock of the explosion had blown them off their feet. Perkins had a concussion from hitting the tarmac, and Doug's head still hadn't stopped pounding. Again. "Most likely they'll find a bomb was planted in the casket. Whether or not the major general's body was also in there remains to be seen."

The CIA agent pulled a cell phone from the inside pocket of his jacket and turned away.

The whole tarmac was a flurry of activity. Firefighters, police and military personnel walked back and forth, trying to make sense of what had happened.

The injured had all been taken away in ambulances. This was the last thing Doug expected when he was only here as a favor for his dad. He could hardly believe what he'd seen, and his army life so far had been a long one.

The thought of retirement entered his mind, not entirely unwelcome. Being a team leader had been an exhilarating experience where every minute was different from the last. Years of training had left him with calluses on his hands and his mind from the repetitive action of attack and defend.

And he would give it all up if it meant finding Sabine. If it gave them a shot at the something wonderful he already knew existed between them.

"Confirmed. Did we figure out the source of the other explosion yet?" The agent listened for a minute. "I'm on my way. Tell everyone. No one goes home until we find the Raven. Both of them."

Doug had been about to walk away but turned back. "What was that?"

The guy slid his phone into the inside pocket of his jacket. "Classified CIA business. We don't share, especially not with people who associate with known enemies."

Everyone seemed so intent on thinking Sabine was the bad guy. Someone had to be on her side. "You're gonna share with me."

She was used to being alone. Doug didn't know why he couldn't trust her self-sufficiency. There was too much about her that made him want to protect her. She might not like that she brought out his hero-of-the-hour instincts, but that was the nature of what he felt for her. She wasn't just a kidnap victim.… She was his.

She was strong, fierce and brave. He couldn't help loving her. She held his heart in the palm of her hand, and all Doug wanted was the chance to tell her that.

"We know all about your relationship with Elena Sanders." The CIA agent got in Doug's face. "Given the suspicion she's under, you have to know the position that puts you in. Someone who consorts with the Raven surely has bad judgment. I'd watch yourself, Sergeant Major Richardson, before all the hard work you've put in over the years gets thrown away because of a woman."

"Sabine isn't the Raven. Her mom is."

The agent's eyes gleamed like he'd won a prize. "Not according to an email sent to every news agency in the country an hour ago. The Raven, a mother and daughter team, have claimed responsibility for both attacks."

"Both—"

"If you see or hear from Elena Sanders, this woman you call Sabine, you are to contact the CIA immediately or you will be aiding and abetting a fugitive. It was her work that caused the carnage you see around you, the loss of American lives. Honorable men and women who serve their country. You ought to know something about that. The son of a general, a Special Forces soldier—"

"How do you—"

"We will find Ms. Sanders and bring her in. Dead or alive. Rogue agents cannot be left to run loose. They must be dealt with swiftly and precisely, regardless of your feelings for her. Your obligation to this country means that, if you see her first, it's up to you to take care of the matter."

He strode away, and Doug wished he could let go and pummel something until he collapsed. It wouldn't help.

Everything he wanted was being ripped away. Sabine's reputation was trashed. Even if they could prove her innocence, she would never be free to live her life. She would always and forever be under suspicion.

Hanning trotted up beside him. "Now we know why the colonel got that package from Steve Adams."

"Why?"

"His body arrived at Langley the same time that Taylor's got here. Adams's casket blew up the delivery guy, his truck and the security guards the same time the bomb here in the major general's casket went off."

Doug hissed.

"There's more. Colonel Hiller found something. He wants us on a plane to France. Now."

Sabine sat on the bedroom floor aboard the yacht. The carpet was thin, and the plastic wire on her wrists cut into her skin. She had no idea where her mother was. After tying Sabine up, the Raven had piloted the boat out into open water and lowered the anchor. Who knew what she was doing now? Across the room a small TV was tuned to news coverage.

The TV show was broadcast in French so she had to piece the story together from what words she understood, along with pictures of the wreckage and the look on everyone's faces.

Two pictures came on screen—her own and an old shot of her mom from years ago. This was it. She was actually being associated with her mother. And for something she had no knowledge of. It looked like a couple of pretty big explosions. That much carnage surely meant innocent people were dead.

God...

Sabine let the tears come. Tears for Ben and everything he hadn't felt he could share with her, for him looking into their past and trying to move on. If she hadn't known it already, the huge step he'd taken in dealing with the past would have convinced her how strong he was.

More tears came. For everything she should have had. Things she'd lost. Things that had been taken from her. For Doug and the relationship they would never get to have. For not having had the courage to trust him, to love him sooner. Before it was too late.

Sabine cried for the kind of love Doug would have showered on her. He'd have made her feel accepted for the first time by a man other than her brother.

And she cried for the loss of a life full of love and laughter…marriage and kids.

It didn't matter now that they would have had to fight to stay together and manage to overcome the obstacles life had put between them. All that mattered now was the dream of what could have been.

God…

She didn't know what to pray, or what she could possibly ask God to do that would make this all go away. Everything honest and upright in her wanted to scream at the injustice of it. She had lived so long in the shadows. Now that everything about her was being called into question, there was no one to vouch for her.

Maybe it was the pain in her shoulder, or the wooziness of being drugged and flown halfway across the world until she didn't know if it was day or night. Not to mention she hadn't eaten anything in more than a day. All of it made her brain come up with some pretty crazy thoughts.

Sabine blinked and tried to focus on something else.

It was that or go around and around again. It was all over for her. No one would ever trust her now. She couldn't even trust herself after being duped so completely. Her last act should be one of honor if she was ever going to repair her reputation, not to mention the side effect it would have on Ben's reputation. Even though he was dead, she still couldn't stand for people to think badly about him. And Doug—his judgment would be called into question for believing in her.

There it was.

Rid the world of a woman bent on evil and destruction. It was the one good thing Sabine could do. She wasn't going to be able to fight much longer before her mom snapped, frustrated because Sabine wouldn't do what she wanted her to.

Better to kill her first.

She thought she could pull a trigger on the woman who'd destroyed her life. After all, Brenda Sanders had never really been a mother to her. Not to mention the countless others her mom had killed or people whose lives she had destroyed.

The world would be a better place without the Raven in it.

God would forgive her. Wouldn't He? There had to be some justification for murder, some time when it could be right. Otherwise Doug would never have become a soldier. His honesty and high morals would never lead him into a job that was at odds with what he believed.

A rustle at the door brought her head up.

Brenda came in, her body vibrating and glee in her eyes. Sabine wanted to throw up. She had to get her hands on a weapon, but there was little she could do tied up. She would have to make this believable. She swallowed and made her voice quiet. Hollow. "What have you done?"

Her mom blinked. "We, dear. We killed a bunch of military people and CIA types."

Sabine's stomach clenched. She had to convince the woman she was just as crazy. "There's nothing left for me." Tears spilled onto her cheeks and her heart ripped out all over again as she remembered the cabin exploding. "It's all over."

Her mom had to believe she'd joined the cause because it was the only thing left. She had to think Sabine had no intention of retaliating. Sabine lifted her bound hands. Raw, they sliced with pain at the movement. "Cut me free. I want to die."

Her mom crouched in front of her and touched her hands. "You don't want that, darling."

"Yes, I do. I have nothing to live for. My reputation is in ruins. Everyone I love is gone. Let me die."

"I'll take care of you." She stroked Sabine's fingers. "Everything will be better. You'll see. We can go somewhere sunny, and you can work on your tan."

Sabine wanted to slap her. Instead she held still while her mom produced a knife.

Her mom hesitated. She shifted the knife in her fingers and then pulled back. "I think I'll wait. I don't want you to harm yourself. We'll leave you tied up a little longer."

Sabine sighed aloud. "Whatever you think is best." She could tell her mom was surprised, so she kept her eyes lowered. "Could I get some water?"

"Sure, darling."

Bingo. Her mom went to get her a drink.

And left the knife on the floor.

* * *

Doug adjusted the binoculars to focus better on the yacht. Prayer hadn't been far from his lips during the whole plane ride. Or the time it had taken them to flash the Raven's picture around at the harbor and find out which boat was hers.

Now they were a mile offshore, hidden by the dark, cloudy night. Watching.

"Let's move in."

"MacArthur—"

He ignored Perkins. "The debate is over. It's time to execute. I want Sabine out of there and the Raven in custody before the CIA gets anywhere near here."

None of the guys said anything; they just nodded and gathered up their stuff. The small boat barely held all their gear and weapons. It bobbed around, dangerously low in the water. He prayed they would continue to go unnoticed in the middle of the Mediterranean with their engine silent.

Doug was the first to slip into the water. The swim was swift and silent. Hanning appeared beside him at the yacht where he gave Doug a boost that launched him up and over the side of the boat. He immediately crouched to make sure no one had been alerted to their presence and then pulled the next man up until the five of them were on deck.

Someone screamed.

Five weapons were suddenly more than ready to take care of whatever situation was in front of them. No words, no instruction was needed. Each man simply turned to his task, the procedure already firmly laid out in their minds.

Doug met no resistance, not a soul between him and

the closed door to the bedroom. There was a thud, and the scream rang out again. This time he was certain it was Sabine.

Hanning appeared behind him. Doug stepped back, his weapon trained on the door while he reached in his pocket. His teammate kicked the door in. Doug threw a flash-bang. A split second later, he entered the room.

Sabine wrestled with the Raven. Both of them gripped the knife as they fought for ownership of it.

"Down!" Doug yelled.

Sabine reacted instantly to his command. She hit the floor, arms curled over her head. The Raven launched at him from the far side of the bed, her eyes wild, and the knife in one hand. He didn't have to think to aim his weapon. He just flexed his trigger finger and the Raven was no more.

Doug crouched beside Sabine and drew her arms down. She had deep gashes on her wrists and a bruise on the side of her face. Her left shoulder was bound with a thick bandage soaked with red. Eyes, wide and full of tears, looked up at him, and the sight of it broke his heart.

"Sabine."

He got his weapon out of the way before she wrapped her arms around him and burrowed her face in his chest. "Thank You, God. Oh, thank You, God."

Her words were a prayer. Her breath came in great heaving sobs. Doug's heart felt like it grew wings, knowing she had placed her trust in God. Doug would give anything to never have to leave her again. "Sabine, it's me. I'm okay."

"The cabin…"

Doug leaned back and held her face in his hands.

Tears streamed down her cheeks and wet his palms. "Honey, I'm so sorry." He swiped away a tear. "I'm so sorry."

She sniffed, brokenness written on her face. "You were dead."

His stomach flipped over. "I'm sorry."

"I realized I loved you."

"We'll take it from here." Suited agents surrounded them the minute they stepped off the plane. Behind them stood other suits with dark blue jackets as well as regular police officers, all with their weapons drawn. Doug had known his time with her would be limited, but he'd vainly hoped for more than this before Sabine was whisked away for questioning.

In a last-ditch effort, Doug had pleaded with her not to get on the plane but to disappear into the world with him. They could live their lives together. She had stubbornly refused to run, telling him in no uncertain terms, "I have to answer for what I've done."

He loved her more in that moment than he already did.

Faced with the reality of it now, Doug felt her shake beside him. Being careful of her freshly bandaged arm, he brought her against him. His lips touched her forehead, the softness of her hair.

I loved you.

He would get her to admit she loved him now, and not just when she'd thought he was dead.

Tears filled his eyes, but he didn't care. "I'll see you soon."

She sucked in a breath. It probably would have been

a sob, but for the sea of people surrounding them. She pulled away and looked up at him. Her eyes were dry.

"Sabine—"

She brushed back a lock of her hair and stepped away. "Goodbye, Doug."

Doug forced himself to stay put while she walked to the agents. What if he never saw her again? It was useless to believe she would ever be a free woman. The CIA would lock her away for her connection to the Raven. For being unable to prove she hadn't been in league with the woman all these years.

God, help us. There has to be hope, and it can only come from You.

In Doug's own strength he would just fail. Only God had the power to bring it all in line so that Doug and Sabine could be together. And he had to believe that they would. Why else would he keep having that dream—the one where he walked in their house, and she took him into her arms? The dream where his ring was on her finger and her tummy was round with his child?

Please, Lord.

"Murderer!"

Doug rushed to Sabine before it registered in his mind that the middle-aged man in the trench coat had burst from the crowd.

Who was he?

A clatter of gunfire erupted from the man's AK-47. Doug had Sabine shielded with his body when the stab of fire hit his chest, and she screamed.

EIGHTEEN

Sabine lifted her head from the cold metal of the table. "I understand how it looks, but what I'm telling you is the truth. My mother—the Raven—who I hadn't seen in over twenty-five years before a couple of days ago, she orchestrated this whole thing."

The room was bare. Plain walls, fluorescent lights and a single window that only reflected back the picture of her and the agent performing the interrogation. She had no idea where she was being held. The agent looked calm and collected, while Sabine sat there, dirty and sweaty, wearing the same clothes she'd been in for two days now. She probably stank to high heaven, but she couldn't smell it anymore.

"Then you understand my dilemma, Ms. Sanders—"

"It's Ms. Laduca. Sabine."

It might be a small thing, to quibble over the name she'd been given by her mother versus the name she had chosen for herself. Ben's last name. She had to hold on to the things she could control. She had to grasp the thing that gave her peace. Especially when she couldn't stop reliving the moment when the man she loved had shoved her out of the way and had taken a bullet for her—in his chest.

His chest.

She still couldn't help thinking about what she'd seen in his eyes as he lay there, bleeding out on the carpet of the departure lounge while she was pulled away from him. At least she knew now that he loved her. Though, had she been given the choice, she'd have picked better circumstances than his mouthing the words as she was dragged away by armed government agents.

She had no idea if he was dead or alive. No one would tell her. Her only comfort was the fact that Doug was a trained soldier. He faced situations like this all the time, although she didn't want to think about the implications of that. He was strong. He knew what he was doing.

Worry for Doug had torn her heart apart, but she couldn't show even a hint of weakness to these people. They held the reins on her future, whether that meant a lifetime in jail or worse.

God, help me.

She looked at the agent across the table—a nameless, faceless suit and tie. The man studied her, as though trying to figure out why someone who had just bombed two different government facilities and killed at least a half-dozen people looked like she was about to cry.

"Ms. Laduca, I'm trying to help you. But I can't do that if you're not willing to give me anything."

"What's to give? The Raven is dead. I had nothing to do with her, except that she duped me for six years into running missions. All I did during that time was collect intelligence."

"Then explain this." The agent laid a picture of Christophe Parelli on the table between them.

Sabine sighed. "That wasn't me."

Her interrogator barked a laugh. "You're telling me you weren't there?" He laid down a surveillance photo of her in the hotel.

"I broke into the hotel suite. I got Parelli's hard drive. When Doug—Sergeant Major Richardson… When he interrupted me, someone else was already coming. Parelli and my mother came in behind us. We hid in the closet, and I saw her poison Parelli."

The agent tapped the table. His mouth worked back and forth. "Christophe Parelli was an informant for the U.S. government."

Sabine's stomach dropped. "I didn't know that."

"Evidently." The agent's jaw clenched. "What with you working for the Raven and all."

"I was duped."

"So you've said. And what kind of an agent does that make you, do you think? That you can't tell when the wool is being so completely pulled over your eyes."

Sabine swallowed. "Not a very good one."

She had thought her facade of a marriage to Maxwell was the end of it. She'd been so sure that she would never let herself be fooled again. But she had. Sabine had trusted someone and, like an idiot, had allowed herself to believe a lie. Again.

A shadow crossed over her heart. Was the love in Doug's eyes for real? Finally she'd found something—someone—who was worth believing in, and she found herself unable to let go.

Sabine felt arms wrap around her, despite the fact no one was near. It hit her deep inside, where she felt comfort at the thought of seeing Ben again. Where she knew Doug would be okay even if the worst had happened to him, God was reaching out to her.

With no movement or spoken word, Sabine reached back and found the solid foundation of a God who loved her without reservation. Not dependent on anything she had done. Love that defied explanation.

I believe, God. Help me trust You. No matter what happens.

Sabine felt like the tender new bud of a flower, fragile but with the deepest roots. Whatever happened to her, to Doug, she would be okay, because God was with her.

"Ms. Laduca, you're facing serious charges. Perhaps you should be more worried about what will happen to you."

More worried? She was clearly a better covert agent than she thought if he couldn't tell she was completely freaked out. Then again, perhaps this new warmth of peace in her chest had made its way to her face.

The agent collected up his papers. "I'll give you some time to think. But your options are pretty limited unless you can give us something that will sway us from putting you in jail for life." He stood. "It's up to you, Sabine."

The agent reached for the door handle.

"Wait."

He turned back. Sabine took a deep breath and pushed away the voices that said this was crazy. "I'll tell you everything I know. Everything I've done and learned over the last six years."

"You think that's good enough?"

"It's all I have."

The agent's eyebrows rose.

"Except—" Sabine lifted her chin. "Except…me."

The agent straightened. "I'm listening."

"What good is telling you what I know if you don't trust me?"

She was innocent. It could be argued that none of this was her fault, provided she ignored the fact that she should have known she was being duped. Should she even have to prove herself? Or was that just her pride telling her to be stubborn and refuse to start on the bottom rung of the ladder and earn her way back up?

It all boiled down to how badly she wanted to be an agent again. At one time it had been everything, her whole life. Just like Doug and the army. Then it had been about getting justice for Ben.

She had to know if she could trust herself, and right now that was seriously in doubt. She should ask them to put her in a teaching position, training new recruits. But could she mold new agents when she had failed so massively?

Could she do it? Could she earn back their trust? It was a crazy idea, but one that meant she would be free, at least to an extent. The CIA would have to be willing to work out a deal with her. One that meant she would go back to work for them, slowly working her way back to active status. She would never be the full agent she had once been. But she could still be an asset to them. Let them set whatever stipulations they wanted.

Because, if it meant she might get to see Doug, it didn't matter what the cost. *If he's still alive.*

The agent cocked his head to one side. "What is it you want, Agent Laduca?"

Sabine opened her mouth but couldn't say it. Going back into covert intelligence wouldn't make her happy. She was bone tired. What she really wanted was to walk away, to find a cottage on a beach somewhere and get started on the pile of books she'd bought but hadn't read yet.

"I want out."

The agent nodded. He walked back to the table and sat down. "This will be a long process, but I'm confident that with your cooperation we can work something out."

"Just like that, after threatening me with life in prison?"

"Make no mistake, Ms. Laduca, this won't be easy. You give us everything you know. And I mean every single thing you have from the last six years. Everywhere you went. Every person you talked to, every bug you planted and every computer file you stole. Then we'll talk about your being released. Completely under the radar, you live quiet as a mouse, and, if we ever call you…for anything, you do it. No questions."

"So I'm going to be your puppet forever?" Sabine shook her head. "Prison is starting to look appealing."

"The choice is entirely yours."

The constant pain left him breathless and, although he didn't want to admit it, very cranky. Between Jean and his father, Doug was never alone for a second. At that moment, Jean was straightening his blanket. He brushed her hands away and gave her a look.

The general was at the door, his arms folded.

Doug shook his head. "You look mad. What gives?"

"What gives?" The general stepped into the room. He walked carefully, and there were dark circles under his eyes, but Doug didn't think that was from the heart attack. "This isn't some joke, son. You've been hurt before, but never like this. You nearly died, and days later I find you putting your shoes on."

"You know why I have to find her, Dad. I'm going crazy not knowing where she is or what's happening."

She was in God's hands, but he was still going crazy not knowing.

The general sighed. "That's why I made some calls."

Doug's eyes widened. "And?"

"No one knows where she is. Colonel Hiller said they're refusing to even confirm that they have her."

"That's crazy. We all know she went with them. Where did they take her?"

"I'll find her, Doug, but I need time. And you need to rest up so you can get back to active duty."

He surged up from the bed. Pain lanced through his chest. "Sabine might not have time. I can't care about my job right now."

"Calm down." Tears filled his dad's eyes. "Please. You can't go get her if you're immobilized, and if you keep pushing it you're going to set yourself back. You're not invincible."

Doug forced himself to take slower breaths. He ducked his chin and immediately felt his dad's hand on the side of his neck.

"I don't want to lose you, too, son."

"I'm sorry."

"You have to trust me."

Doug nodded. He would trust his dad. They had never been this close, never in his whole life. All the strength he needed to lie back and let himself heal was there in his dad's touch.

Doug sucked in a lungful of air and blew out the need to dissolve into tears.

"Find her."

* * *

Eight days later Sabine was finally wrapping things up with the CIA when there was a knock on the door. She'd been in that same interrogation room from dawn until dinner every day and had lain awake nights in the glorified prison cell where her bed was. No contact with the outside world had left her bereft. She couldn't relax until she knew if Doug was okay.

The agent, the same one who'd interrogated her every day, glanced up. A familiar old man strode in wearing his dress army uniform with stars on his shoulders.

"Am I early?" His face split into a wide smile.

"Andrew," she whispered.

"My dear."

Sabine shot across the room and burrowed into his arms. She was taller than him, but it didn't matter. Doug's father folded her in his embrace. "How is he?"

The general nodded slowly, his eyes wet.

"How is he?" she repeated.

"He's worried about you, fighting everyone, refusing to listen to reason. Says he wants to leave the army."

"That's crazy. He loves being a soldier."

The general shrugged. "Says he's done. No one can get the why out of him. He's refusing to talk about it, demanding we find you. So I did. I can't have him rip out his stitches again, struggling and not listening to reason."

Sabine squeezed her eyes shut.

"Excuse me." The agent stood beside them. "Ms. Laduca is in our custody—"

"Not anymore."

Her face jerked back around and zeroed in on the general.

"You can't just waltz in here and yank this woman out—"

"I absolutely can, son." Andrew pulled out a trifolded paper and handed it to the agent. The agent studied it. His eyes widened. Andrew glanced at Sabine and winked.

She smiled back, reached up and touched his face. "Thank you."

He nodded.

The agent grunted. "This is highly irregular."

Sabine turned to him. "Our agreement stands. You know how to reach me."

She hooked her arm through the general's. She didn't care how it looked for a military officer to be outwardly affectionate. Apparently neither did he.

Out in the hall Andrew leaned in. "Agreement?"

Sabine shook her head. "A small price to pay for my freedom. If they decide to abuse the hold they have over me, I'll just disappear again." She ignored the look of worry in his eye. "Is Doug really leaving the army?"

"Seems so. We're all worried about him. It is so uncharacteristic to suddenly throw everything away."

Sabine sighed. "It's because of me, isn't it?"

He opened a door for her. "Would that be bad?"

"He loves being a soldier. It's everything to him."

Andrew's eyes darkened. "I don't think it's everything anymore."

"Are you sure?"

"Do you really have to ask that?"

"I know." She looked away as they walked. "He got shot protecting me. He nearly died, and now he's a mess.

I can't help feeling guilty, like he would be better off if I had never come into his life. I can't help thinking that I failed at marriage before and I failed at my job now. I have nothing left, nothing to give him. And in return he's giving up everything he ever wanted."

She stopped and turned to his father. "I have to live a simple life now, and I'm okay with that. But how could Doug be happy with that? He needs action and a purpose. My life won't give him that. He'll be bored of me within a month."

The general's eyes were dark. "You sound like you're talking yourself into walking away."

Sabine hardened her heart against disappointing him. "I don't want Doug to be hurting. I can't stand hearing he's all worked up, worried about me and setting his recovery back." She waited for the affirmation. "He is, isn't he?"

"He's not doing himself any favors. How could he? He has no idea where his woman is. He's scared, Sabine."

"I was, too, not knowing if he was dead—" Her voice caught on the word.

Andrew touched her shoulders. "You love him."

Sabine nodded. She sniffed, wiped away a tear. "I'm not supposed to show emotion."

Andrew huffed. "Because bottling it up inside is so much better? You love my son. You tell him. Give him that, at least. When he's better, you see where things are at. Can you do that?"

She wasn't sure. It would mean being with Doug while he recovered, knowing she was going to walk away as soon as he was well again.

When she finally left this time, it would be so much

harder for her. Doug could go back to his life physically recovered, and have the opportunity to be the career soldier he was meant to be. He might regret the loss of their relationship for a while, but eventually he'd find someone new.

Her heart tore open.

She shut her eyes. No more than a couple of weeks. Just long enough to make sure he was okay. In the meantime she would put her feelings aside and focus on helping him get better.

Sabine raised her eyes and looked at Andrew, hoping he didn't see the truth. "I can do that. I can give him time."

It didn't matter how much she loved him; he couldn't know. Not if it meant he was going to throw his life away.

NINETEEN

Andrew put the car in Park outside his home, and Sabine got out. Doug stepped carefully down the stone steps of the porch, his face lined with pain. She had hoped for more time to prepare before she saw him, time to get her thoughts and her heart on board with the plan. Too bad that wasn't going to happen.

She would be here for however long it took him to get back to full strength and see that the right decision for him was to stay with the army. It would take everything she had to keep her heart in one piece.

Doug stopped at the bottom step, and she didn't wait for him to come to her. Andrew passed by him and squeezed his shoulder, but Doug's eyes never left her. She remembered the way he'd shaken his head at her in the hospital, and this time she went straight into his arms. Sabine encircled his chest lightly, so as not to hurt him, and burrowed into him with her face in his neck.

"I love you."

Sabine burst into tears. She loved him, too, but she was going to walk away. There was no doubt in her mind that, despite the fact they loved each other, she wasn't the woman for him. The woman he married would support him, not get him shot and tear his life apart. It was better to cut the ties as soon as he was recovered, instead of getting in any deeper than she already was.

Sabine sucked in a breath. The CIA might have let her go, but it wouldn't be long before they considered her too much of a risk to be walking around. And there was no way she would let Doug get caught up in that.

She pulled away, wiped her cheeks and forced herself to let go of him. "You should be resting."

His eyes narrowed, but he didn't say anything about the distance she put between them. "Don't start. I have enough babysitters. I don't need one more."

"Too bad, because that's exactly what you've got." Sabine linked her arm with his and turned them to the door, but Doug held still.

She looked at him. "What is it?"

He studied her for a moment and then shook his head. "I was about to ask you the same thing."

"Doug—" She hated that she was playing this game. "I've had enough interrogation to last me the next ten years."

"So I'm not allowed to ask you anything?"

She let go of him. "I don't want to fight with you. That's not why I came here."

He looked at his sneakers for a moment and then back up at her. "I've been dreaming about this moment since I woke up in the hospital. I have to admit, I had a different picture of what our reunion was going to be like."

"Sorry I disappointed you."

"Are you really? I just told you that I loved you. Is there anything you'd like to say to me?"

Sabine swallowed. Apparently when she thought she could do this, she hadn't realized it would be the hardest thing she'd ever done in her life.

It's just another mission.

That didn't help. It was impossible to convince her heart not to break a little more every time she looked at him. They could never be together.

"I do love you."

It took everything she had to admit that out loud.

"Then why do you look so sad about it? What happened to you, Sabine? What did they do to you?"

He was right. Something had happened to her. Sitting in that interrogation room recounting everything she'd ever done as a spy, Sabine had realized that nothing about her was real.

For too long she'd played a part, never genuinely opening up and certainly not living life to the fullest. The missions she went on amounted to lying to get what she wanted. When she came home, there was little that was different. She'd lived a role with Maxwell, too, trying to be the perfect wife…at least until it all fell apart.

She kept herself removed from everything and everyone, got lost in books because it was a way to escape the pressure of trying to be…normal. Which was something she wanted more than anything else.

The only person who'd ever seen the truth was her brother, and he was gone. She hadn't thought it possible, but this man in front of her made her want to be real—to live.

God, give me the strength to do the right thing.

Doug touched her cheek, his hand sliding back into her hair. Sabine closed her eyes, felt the tickle on her cheek and realized she was crying again.

His lips touched one cheek and then the other, but the tears kept coming.

"Sabine—"

She shook her head. "Don't."

He kissed her—so softly—on the lips. "Tell me." His forehead touched hers. "Tell me."

She should have known he would never let her get away with it. Doug was the last person in the world she wanted to know how she really felt, the one person she wanted to guard herself from. He was the only person who could see the truth she hid behind her eyes.

She sucked in a breath. "Please don't make me do this."

She knew how he would feel when she walked away, because it was the same way she would feel—completely and utterly torn apart. They both needed to be strong.

Doug stepped back, and Sabine opened her eyes to the disappointment on his face. That hurt, too, but the only thing that was important was his recovery.

"I'll give you time. You can tell me when you're ready, but you will tell me."

She nodded.

Doug turned away and walked inside, taking her heart with him.

The movie credits rolled, and Doug looked over at Sabine, beside him on the couch. Lamplight illuminated the lines of her face, her closed eyes, the slow rise and fall of her breath as she slept. He stretched; the pain in his chest was a sharp ache but he didn't want a cloudy head from the medication.

Why was she was so hesitant to accept what was happening between them? What had the CIA told her? She was holding back everything, but why? Doug ached to make her tell him what the problem was, but she had to work it through in her mind before she could come back to him.

Her eyes flickered open. "I honestly thought you were dead, you know."

He sighed. "I'm sorry."

"Not half as sorry as I am. This was all my fault. If it wasn't for me, you'd never have been shot."

The look in her eyes broke his heart. "Like you could get rid of me that easily?"

She got up. Doug followed her into the kitchen. "Sabine—"

"Don't." She filled a kettle with water and set it on the stove. "It doesn't matter."

He laughed. She didn't mean that. Not when everything in her stance said she wanted to touch him, have him hold her again. "Because I'm not dead?"

"Yes."

Doug put his hands on her waist and turned her to him. "I'm sorry I joked about dying. You said you love me. You'll have to forgive me, because I'm going to be very happy about that."

"I said it doesn't matter."

"You can try to convince yourself of that all you want, Sabine, but it matters to me. It matters a lot."

"Why? There's no point. This can't go anywhere."

He knew she believed that, but he also didn't care anymore. "The fact that you think it can't go anywhere means you're acknowledging that there is something between us. I can work with that. All I have to do is convince you it'll be worth it."

Sabine didn't speak, so Doug gave her a small smile. "When you know what I see when I look at you, and what I feel when I touch you—" he took her hand "—then you'll be as convinced as I am that, while this might not be easy, it can be great. It doesn't matter how long it takes, Sabine. I've got all the time in the world to wait for you." He waited a beat. "What do you say?"

"I say okay."

His smile stretched. "Okay?"

She nodded. "I'm willing to let you convince me."

He leaned in to kiss her, but she sidestepped him and smiled. "Not like that."

"Why not?"

She dropped her hand, but he held it, not ready to let her go. She had the cutest look on her face, like she was trying hard to be serious.

"A kiss is not *convincing* me, it's swaying me to your way of thinking." She frowned. "When you kiss me I can't think straight. It's too easy to forget—why are you smiling?"

"Because I like hearing you say that." He squeezed her hand. "You make me happy. I like knowing I have an effect on you, too."

"There's a lot we have to work through, but I don't think there will ever be a lack of feeling between us."

"I'm glad to hear that, Sabine."

Doug settled for a kiss on her cheek. He didn't want to push her but still felt like he needed to stake a claim—a claim that would hopefully pay off with a relationship. The more time they spent getting to know each other, the stronger the foundation of their relationship would be later.

Her shoulders slumped and she frowned over the tea

pot. When she yawned, his heart felt like it would burst. The woman was wrung out, physically and emotionally.

"Where'd your dad go?"

Doug leaned against the counter. "He took Jean to dinner. He wanted to give us some space—"

There was a short hum, and the power went out.

Sabine gasped. He reached out, found her shoulder and gave it a pat. "There's a flashlight in the cupboard beside the trash. Stay here, I'm going to go check the breaker."

Sabine found the flashlight where he said it would be and scanned the kitchen. The light illuminated a figure clad all in black, wearing a matching balaclava, who must have breached the general's security system. He was across the room by the back door. He looked like the same tall, wiry guy who'd been searching through Ben's room.

He raised a handgun and pointed it straight at her.

Of course the CIA would send someone to silence her. She just hadn't thought it would be this fast.

Before he fired, Sabine clicked off the flashlight and dropped to the floor. The gunshot illuminated the room around her. Surrounded by dark again, she crossed to the intruder. Retreat might be the gut reaction of the average civilian, but she had been trained to go toward danger instead of away from it—however unwise that might be.

She followed the sound of his footsteps and came up behind him. This needed to be finished before Doug came back from wherever the breaker switches were located.

She went for his head. An elbow flew back and connected with her temple. The pain was blinding, but she forced it away and kept a lock on the senses that told her where he was.

He slammed into her.

Sabine deflected blow after blow and managed to knock the gun to the floor, but this man was well trained and stronger than her. A brutal punch made her fall to her knees, and she fought away the instinct to panic. How had she ever managed to convince herself that dying was no big deal?

The intruder tackled her. Sabine shoved at him, but his hands grasped her neck and squeezed her throat shut. She groped for anything to use to defend herself... her fingers closed around the warm metal of the gun. She whipped it around and aimed dead center, but he knocked her arms away.

Then he was pulled off her.

Doug kicked and punched the man, his face bathed in rage.

Sabine grabbed his arm. "Stop!"

Doug froze.

"He's out cold."

The intruder was slumped at the bottom of the wall, unconscious.

"I'm okay." Sabine touched the sides of Doug's neck. His pulse was racing. "I'm okay."

Doug touched his forehead to hers and blew out a long breath. "This time we're calling the cops."

Sabine smiled.

"I'll give you some time." Colonel Hiller stood with his back to the railing, facing Doug. "You shouldn't rush into a decision like this. Retirement isn't easy. I've seen guys make that mistake. They wind up wasting time, and then they sign up again, but it's never the same."

Doug shifted on his seat and winced at the shard of pain but tried not to be obvious about it. He was saved when Sabine came out and laid a tray on the table with two steaming cups of coffee and a plate of cookies.

She didn't meet his eyes, just set it down and walked away.

Colonel Hiller said, "Are you sure this is what you want?"

Sabine hadn't spoken a word to him in the two days since he subdued the intruder in his dad's kitchen. That had been a fun conversation with the police. This whole thing was driving him crazy. Right when they were getting somewhere, some guy had broken in, and she had withdrawn into herself again.

Doug sighed. "Yes, I'm sure."

Was he?

Despite the distance she'd established between them, he was still certain she was the one for him. More certain than ever, even when he saw the conflict in her eyes. Beside him every minute, she was there to help with whatever he needed—except when what he needed was her. Then Sabine shuttered herself behind defenses he couldn't penetrate.

He could get past any obstacle he was faced with. Why not this? His training should count for something. Yet when he needed some hint of what she was feeling, she refused to give anything away.

Doug looked out over the lawns of his father's expansive yard. Doug had wanted to believe he could have his current way of life…and Sabine. The dream had to be possible, or else what had he been fighting for all these years? But something told him that his tenure with the army had come to an end.

What if God had a whole other plan for Doug?

TWENTY

He was going back to work.

Sabine tried to listen to the sermon, surrounded by a crowd of people all dressed in their Sunday clothes. Doug sat beside her, his focus on the open pages of his Bible. He glanced over at her, so she shot him a small smile and then looked back at the pastor. She would have trouble recounting what the man was talking about. Her Bible was flipped to the middle of Deuteronomy, but she couldn't focus.

She had to face the fact that Doug was going back to work. Soon he'd be flying off to his base in Texas, back to missions and a life that she wasn't meant to be a part of. It was time for Sabine to leave. She'd known it for three days now, since Colonel Hiller paid Doug a visit and she heard them talking.

Time to go. So why was she still here?

She had tried to guard her heart. It wasn't working. If she left now, it would hurt worse than ever, but eventually she would heal.

He leaned in and whispered in her ear. "Are you okay?"

She looked at him. Okay? Of course she wasn't okay.

Doug wanted forever with her; he'd told her as much. Told her that he would wait until she sorted out...whatever it was that he thought was wrong with her.

Leaving was going to break both their hearts. She should just get it over with, like ripping off a Band-Aid, because being here was slow and painful torture. She saw it every time she looked in his eyes. He wanted to comfort her, to tell her every dream he was hiding in his heart.

Like the ones she hid in hers.

Sabine grabbed her purse and coat and stumbled to the aisle, past rows of congregants. People stared at her, but she ignored them and kept going. She pushed open the heavy double doors. The sky was low and gray and steady rain streamed down.

She trudged across the parking lot in the direction of Doug's truck and heard the sound of his shoes following behind her.

She turned...and squeezed her eyes shut. This was hard enough without seeing the pain of heartbreak in his eyes, too. "I have to go."

"I'll drive you. Wherever it is, we can go together."

Sabine shook her head. She felt his touch on her elbow. Her eyes flew open, and she stepped back. "I mean I have to *go*."

His eyes hardened. "Don't do this, Sabine. Don't walk out on us without even giving it a chance."

Sabine blinked against the sting of tears. She shouldn't have stayed for so long just because she couldn't find it in her to leave him. This was smart; it was the right thing. And it was going to be worse because she'd drawn it out.

"You were going to do this all along, weren't you?

Ever since you showed up at the estate, this was your plan."

She winced as the roar built in his voice. "I—"

"Taking care of me but not really 'being' here. What was the point, if you weren't going to stick around?"

"Doug—"

"Don't lie to me. Tell me the truth. You were always going to walk away, weren't you?"

"Yes."

His face was damp. Rain soaked both of them, but she didn't know if he might be crying, too. "Why?"

"It's never going to work between us. I'm not the woman for you—"

"So you get to decide for both of us that this isn't going to work? I don't get a say at all?"

She shook her head. "It's not like that. This is for the best. You need to get on with your life without me…"

"Without you, what? Tell me why you're not the one when all I can think about is how right it feels having you here with me. Tell me. What?"

"You deserve better than me."

He blinked. "How can you say—"

"Because it's true." Sabine's world was crumbling, but she had to do this. "You need to be with someone who doesn't have a cloud of doubt over her head. I might have been officially cleared, but plenty of people still think I killed my team and betrayed this country. What would the army think if we got married? They'll be forever suspicious that you're feeding me information, or that I might turn you against this country."

She sniffed. "No one in charge is ever going to trust me. And if us being together means they won't trust you, either, then what's the point? I can't even ping on their radar or they'll haul me in for another round of interrogation—"

His eyes shut. "You should have told me."

"That you'll lose your job because you're too close to me? That everything you've worked for will be over because of me? Yeah, what a fun conversation that was going to be. So now you know. I won't be the one who ruins your life, okay? That's not what love is."

"God brought us together for a reason, Sabine."

"I know that. I believe that. I do. And it's been wonderful. I've never known anyone like you, Doug. But this is it. It has to be. God has someone for you, someone honorable who doesn't come with a classified past. Someone with a good life who comes from a good family. Someone who isn't me."

She turned away and ran. Her feet pounded the cement, splashed puddles and soaked the legs of her dress pants. *Never look back.* She ran until she couldn't run anymore, and then collapsed on a bus bench and sobbed.

Two days later Sabine parked the rental car she'd picked up at the airport in the driveway of a ranch-style house at the north end of Boise, where the oldest houses were. To get there she'd driven by the alley where the police had found her and Ben huddled behind the Dumpster all those years ago.

She looked out the windshield at a house shrouded in night and memories.

She steeled herself against the rush of the past and rummaged through her purse. The key had been among Ben's things. Why had she even chosen to come here? The place was probably full of spiders and woodland creatures trying to escape the wind and rain.

This was the only home she'd had until that horrible day she still couldn't seem to erase from her mind. A psychiatrist would probably have a field day with her inability to let go of the past. Or maybe it was normal that she'd never, ever forgotten, no matter how hard she tried. Who knew? She could only hope that being here now would somehow help her to make sense of the mess that was her life.

Inside the house she glanced around, her eyes wide. It looked the same. It hadn't degraded or deteriorated, nor was anything covered in dust. Someone had regularly cleaned the place…for years. Ben had done this. And he hadn't told her.

Sabine made her way to the kitchen. There she found a note on the table.

I don't know when, or even if, you'll read this, but here you are. I'm glad you came back. I'm proud of you for taking this step to get some closure on the past. I hope it helps you as much as it helped me. I love you, big sister.
Ben

Her sobs echoed around the place where she had once had a family, while she grieved for the family she could have had with Doug—the family of her heart.

Doug sat at the kitchen table in his father's house with the newspaper and stared at the black ink, not seeing any of the words.

"This is ridiculous, son."

Doug sighed. He knew the picture he made wasn't pretty. The week's growth of beard itched, and his eyes were probably bloodshot. His sweatpants and T-shirt were sort of clean.

"I didn't get that girl out of CIA custody for you to let her walk away."

"She wanted to go." Doug rubbed a hand down his face. "It was her idea."

His dad pulled out a chair and sat. "You think I don't know that? You think I didn't know she came here with every intention of hiding exactly what she felt for you and how much she loves you?"

"You're wrong."

"That she loves you? I don't think so. Your mother did the same thing, son. Told me there was no way that a diner waitress who lived in a trailer and hadn't even graduated high school was going to marry an officer. Said I should forget about her and get on with my life."

Doug rolled his eyes. "Mom was not a diner waitress."

"She was when I met her."

"You said you guys met in a restaurant."

Andrew smiled and shrugged. "Thereabouts."

Doug looked up. "Why are you telling me this now, anyway? What's the point of this pep talk?"

His dad leaned closer. "Because you apparently need me to explain something to you that any fool can see. That girl loves you so much it scares her, because she's watching her life fall apart and looking to you for safety, only to find you throwing away yours."

"I'm not going back to the army."

"Since when?"

"Since her. There's something out there for us to do together, something better."

"You never explained that to her. You just let her

walk away because it wasn't going the way you thought it was supposed to go." His dad paused. "I made that mistake, too, and I almost lost the best thing that ever happened to me. Until I realized I'd give it all up to have your mother, even the army."

"But you didn't. I did."

"Very nearly did, son. Had the papers and everything. Your mother hit the roof." His dad chuckled. "Finally she said she'd marry me just so I didn't throw my life away."

Doug frowned at him. "Mom married you so you wouldn't leave the army?"

"That's exactly right." He patted Doug's shoulder.

"Maybe leaving to go be with your woman is right for you, son. If that's what you did, I'm certain when you tell her, she'll make sure you never regret it for one minute of the rest of your life. That's the kind of woman she is."

"I don't want her indebted to me."

"Tell her that." His dad drew a small velvet box from his pocket and laid it on the table between them. "And give her this. It's what your mother would have wanted."

TWENTY-ONE

One month later
Barcelona, Spain

"Bye. Thank you. See you all tomorrow!"

Sabine received hugs and kisses from each of the children and ushered them out of her classroom to where their mothers waited. They were all adorable and so eager to learn English that it made her job easier than anything she'd ever done.

Her Spanish had been a little rusty at first. Within days of being saturated with the Spanish culture and such a beautiful language, she had rediscovered the nuances of it.

Blanca entered the back of the classroom. In a matter of weeks the older woman had become so dear to Sabine—something that had surprised her. After all, she'd never had a healthy relationship with an older woman in her whole life.

Together they cleaned up the school supplies, and Sabine swept the floor. When Blanca didn't set down the dust pan for her, Sabine looked up. "What is it?"

"You know you can tell me anything, child." Blanca's eyes were bright, even surrounded by fine lines.

The strands of silver in her dark hair made her more beautiful, and Sabine could tell that as a young woman Blanca had been breathtakingly gorgeous.

"I know. It's just—"

The old woman nodded slowly. "Heartbreak is not an easy thing to heal."

"How did you know?"

"The Good Lord, He tells me things."

Sabine hadn't told any of the staff at the school. Or anyone she had met at the small church up the hill that had been started by missionaries. It was an outreach to the local children, kids from poor families who came to school in ill-fitting clothes and worn sandals. None of them knew where she came from, or why she'd just shown up one day, willing to help out. They'd given up asking.

Apparently they didn't need to ask.

Sabine smiled. "Did He tell you anything else?"

The old woman's mouth curled up, and her eyes sparkled. "I'll finish tidying up. Why don't you take a walk along the cliff top? I've seen you eyeing that book reader thing sticking out of your purse."

The e-reader had been a gift Sabine had bought to console herself. Aside from the time she spent teaching, she was practically attached to the thing. She gave Blanca a kiss on the cheek and surprise lit up the old woman's face.

Sabine walked the path along the cliff that overlooked the ocean. The sun permeated everything until it was impossible to believe it was anything but a beautiful summer anywhere in the world. It just seemed as if, since it was so nice here, it should be this nice everywhere.

Ocean breezes fluttered the skirt of her knee-length

flowery summer dress as she walked. When she reached
the bench, she sat carefully so the splintered wood
didn't catch on the fabric and pulled out her e-reader.

A seagull swooped a wide arc that drew her eyes
from the screen. She watched it twist and rise, much
like the journey Sabine's heart had taken the past few
months. Rising from the depths of grief, she had found
peace and hope in Jesus. His love filled her to overflowing, washing over her like the waves on the shore.

Everything seemed so right. She had what she
wanted—freedom, peace and the chance to live the
life she had always dreamed of.

So why did it feel like there was still something...
missing?

Footsteps ascended the path up the cliff, the gait
heavy. Sabine turned. The old instinct to flee pulled
her to her feet. She skirted the bench and backed away.

He stopped and frowned. "Come here, Sabine." It
was the first word of English she'd heard outside of
her classroom in a month, and it sounded beautiful.
His khaki slacks and light blue button-down shirt made
him look like a businessman on vacation. A very good-
looking businessman who seemed interested in a holi-
day romance.

Tears blurred her vision. "Why did you come?"

"You mean why have I been searching the whole
world for the last month? Or why did I leave the army?
Because the answer to both is the same. You."

"I— You can't just—"

He closed the gap between them. "I did."

She shook her head and stepped back. "I won't go
through this again. There's no point in rehashing all of

this just because you came here. You shouldn't have...
You need to go."

She brushed past him and fled down the hillside. Not
a hundred yards from the bench, he caught up to her.

"Stop running away from me."

She turned back. "Nothing has changed. I don't know
why you came, or why you want to bring it all back up
again. Are you trying to hurt me on purpose? Is that it?
You want to get back at me."

"I would never do that to you, Sabine."

She ignored the way his eyes softened, the light touch
of his fingers on her elbow. "Why did you come here?
What's different now? There's still no way we can be
together, so why are you prolonging it? It hurts too
much, Doug. I'm trying to heal. I'm trying to get on
with my life."

Doug touched her cheek. There were tears in his
eyes now. "I won't let you go again. You're only seeing
the obstacles and letting what you assume I want cloud
your judgment. Don't you think that I want to be with
you? I mean, seriously... I could get a job as a plumber,
and I'd not only be happy, but I'd get down on my knees
every single day and thank God that you believed in us
enough to let me love you. That you believed in what
we could be together enough to love me."

"Those are nice words, Doug. But I can't imagine
that you'd be happy without dangerous missions to go
on, plus the greater good and the impact your job has on
the world." She bit her lip and shook her head. "That's a
huge part of who you are, and now it's just gone? How
can you be okay with that?"

"How are *you* okay with it? Rogue or not, you had

missions, and you believed the work you did was important. Was it just a job, or was it something more?"

"It was everything."

His eyes were soft. "And now that you've lost it all?"

She looked out over the valley. "I don't need a mission. But since I've been here, I've loved teaching these kids. To know I'm making a difference with just one of them… It feels good."

"Because you want to do something that matters."

She nodded.

"Do you want some help?" He shrugged, and a smile curled the corners of his mouth. "I like kids. What if we did something together, like an outreach or a drop-in center? Fostering. Mentoring. There's a whole world of options, Sabine. We could do anything."

Sabine took a deep breath.

He frowned. "Do you believe in us enough for that?"

"I'm scared. I love you so much, but what if it isn't enough?"

He reached up and wiped the tears from her cheeks. "Just promise me one thing. Promise me you'll always fight for us. That you'll take all that passion and strength you have in you and put it into building something with me."

He really saw her that way? Sabine's heart swelled until she thought it would burst from her chest. "I promise. I'm sorry I ran away."

He touched his forehead to hers. "I'm sorry I let you go."

Sabine opened her mouth. He covered it with his fingers. "The time for talking is over."

Doug drew her into his arms. His mouth covered hers, and he kissed her in a way she'd never been kissed before. It was full of passion and the promise of a rich life. She smiled against his lips as the sun wrapped them in a cocoon of warmth.

From a distance, someone clapped. It turned into more people clapping, and then someone cheered. When Doug released her, she glanced around, dazed to find the entire staff on the hillside watching them.

She looked back at Doug.

"I love you. Do you love me?" There was so much worry written on his face. Was he wondering if he had made a mistake?

"How can you even ask me that?"

He stayed still. "Is that a yes?"

She nodded. "Of course I love you."

"Then you'll marry me?"

"Where will we live? What will you do?"

He rolled his eyes, but there was a smile there. "Can you just answer the question, please?"

"Yes, of course I will, but—"

He cut her off again, his fingers on her lips. "We'll figure it out, honey. But honestly, so long as we're together, I don't really care."

"Oh." She smiled. "That's a good answer."

He pulled her to him again and wrapped his arms around her. Sabine buried her face in his neck. She laughed and felt his chest shake with his own laughter.

At long last she had found a place to belong. She'd thought it would be a home or a family to love her, and she would have those things now, too. But at the center of it all, she had a Father in Heaven who loved her and had blessed her life beyond what she thought possible.

Because He'd given her Doug.

* * * * *

STAR WITNESS

And he came and preached peace to you
who were far off and peace to those who were near.
—*Ephesians* 2:17

This book was written during NaNoWriMo,
and massively rewritten later.

Huge thanks goes to Heather Woodhaven,
who talked me off the ledge many times.

ONE

Mackenzie Winters didn't need her years in witness protection to know someone was targeting her. She was looking at the evidence.

All four tires on her old, nondescript car had been slashed.

Mackenzie glanced up at the dark sky. After the day she'd had, all she wanted was to go home and crash. But that wasn't going to happen anytime soon.

She looked back at the dark building, the center that she managed for at-risk teens. Locked up for the night, it looked almost menacing, but that was crazy. It was only bricks and mortar.

The broken streetlight at the far end of the parking lot cast long shadows on the pitted cement. Mackenzie gripped the strap of her purse and strode around the building to the street, where there was a pay phone that seemed to have been long forgotten.

Downtown Phoenix was busy even at this time of night, and there wasn't much time before the last bus of the day. Mackenzie dropped some coins in the slot and dialed her WITSEC handler's number. Eric would know what should be done about her slashed tires. He'd do what he called a "threat assessment" to determine if she needed to be *really* worried—as opposed to just regular worried.

All because of one night: the night Mackenzie had walked into the hotel suite her entourage shared and saw a man holding a gun to her manager's head. Seconds later, he'd pulled the trigger, and Mackenzie, her manager and her head of security, who'd been with her that night, were all on the floor bleeding. She was the only one who'd survived—the one who had testified against the shooter and crippled a drug cartel in the process.

The call to her handler went to voice mail, so Mackenzie left a message and started walking again.

She scanned the street in front and behind her. The hairs on the back of her neck stood on end. Whoever had slashed her tires could be watching right now, waiting for the right moment to strike. Why else would they make sure her car was undrivable, instead of just slashing one tire and making her change it? They must want her out of her normal routine. But for what?

Paranoia came with the territory, even though it had been sixteen years since the day she'd testified against the shooter. The adrenaline never really left. Not when at any moment you could be recognized, gunned down…or kidnapped and left for dead in the middle of the desert.

Okay, so she needed to watch a romantic comedy tonight instead of a movie about vengeful mobsters.

A car slowed beside where she was walking on the sidewalk, but she didn't look. Traffic was backed up, so it could be nothing. Mackenzie walked faster. It was better to be safe than dead. She should call her WIT-SEC handler again as soon as she got home. It had been years since she'd needed protection, and months since she'd even talked to Eric on the phone, but if there was a threat, then he should know.

She flicked her gaze to the street. The car was still there, tracking with her every step.

This was her life. It had been ever since her manager had made a deal with the wrong people. It wasn't enough that he'd spent all the money she made him as a musician on his habit; no, he'd needed more money to sustain that habit. And when he'd neglected to pay the money back, the cartel had come looking for him.

Hello, witness protection.

Now for the past two weeks she'd had a funny feeling—nothing more than that, not until the tires. It could be simple vandalism, nothing more. Maybe someone with a grudge against the arts center she'd founded. Since she was still alive, she didn't think it was about her former life. If Carosa found her, he would simply kill her.

Mackenzie knew what it felt like to be watched, and to have her whole life dissected for everyone to read about in the tabloids. But no one would even recognize her now. Mackenzie's WITSEC persona was more of a spinster librarian than a famous musician. To her surprise, she'd found being unassuming felt more natural than all the makeup and sparkly clothes in the world.

The car slowed to a crawl and a window whirred down. Mackenzie's foot hit a crack in the sidewalk. She stumbled and broke into a run. There was only one more block to the restaurant where she sometimes got dinner before she went home. The car engine revved to catch up.

A door opened ahead, and a man stepped out, blowing across the top of his white paper cup. It was Eric, her handler. Mackenzie tried to stop, but she slammed into him. Eric's coffee went flying. She grabbed his arms to steady herself and his eyes flashed wide.

"Someone's after me."

The rapport of gunfire shot toward them like fireworks. The window of the coffee shop shattered, and concrete chips flew up from the sidewalk, stinging her legs. Mackenzie's head spun. She was being turned; Eric had his arms around her. He hit the concrete first, grunting when she slammed into him. They rolled toward the car parked by the curb. Gunshots flew over their heads and people screamed.

When they reached the spot between the parked car and the curb, out of the line of fire, Eric hauled her up on her hands and knees. "Crawl. Go!"

With him right beside her, they scrambled away. The sidewalk cut through her tights, so she got to her feet. Eric's grip on her elbow held her down, lower than the cars parked on the side of the street.

The gunfire stopped, but he still didn't let her straighten fully. Thank God he was here. What would she have done if Eric hadn't walked out of that coffee shop at exactly the right moment? She'd probably be dead, and she owed the U.S. Marshals Service so much already. They'd given her a new life when she desperately needed one. How could she possibly thank him for this?

The engine revved, and the car sped away.

"Okay, I think we're good." His voice was deep, deeper than she remembered, and his proximity warmed her chilled skin. His denim-blue eyes scanned the area and then focused on her. "You can get up now."

He stood first and winced when he touched his left shoulder.

"You're bleeding." Mackenzie gasped. "You've been shot!"

"It isn't from this. I just ripped my stitches is all. Don't worry about it."

"We should call an ambulance."

He checked the street and finally looked at her, his blue eyes almost gray. "What we should do is get off the street."

Mackenzie glanced around. The sound of sirens was getting closer. Probably someone in the coffee shop had called 911. "Do you think whoever shot at me will come back and try again?"

Eric shrugged, as though being shot at was no big deal. "I wouldn't rule it out."

"Are you going to make me leave Phoenix? I like it here."

His forehead crinkled in confusion. It was a nice forehead. What was wrong with her? Eric was her handler; she wasn't supposed to think he was good-looking.

He motioned to the coffee shop. "We should at least go inside."

"Right. People might need help."

Mackenzie needed something to focus on aside from the weirdness that seemed to resonate between her and Eric. That had never happened before.

Eric usually wore a suit and tie. Maybe it was the jeans and a black T-shirt he was wearing that made him different. He seemed relaxed...and tired.

"Is there a reason you're staring at me?"

Mackenzie turned away, praying he didn't see the awkwardness. *So unprofessional.* She spoke over her shoulder as she walked. "I'm going to see if they have a first-aid kit."

Inside the coffee shop, broken glass crunched under her feet. The two baristas and half-dozen customers looked shaken, but no one seemed to be injured.

Eric entered right behind her, probably intent on protecting his charge. He'd always been efficient. It was probably why they gave him the responsibility of working in witness protection.

Mackenzie went to the barista, crouched by an older man who seemed to be having trouble breathing. "Do you have any medical supplies? My friend is bleeding."

The woman who'd made Aaron's Americano jumped up and ran behind the counter. He stepped away from the crazy lady who'd launched herself at him—that part hadn't been all bad—and tried to ignore the sting in his shoulder.

He crouched in front of the old man clutching at his chest. "Take a breath. Blow it out slow and try to relax."

Outside, the sirens grew to deafening proportions. Aaron turned just as two police cars and an ambulance parked on the street outside. He looked back at the old man again. "Medics are here."

The man's brow flickered. "Army?" His voice was barely audible.

"Yes, sir. Good guess." He wondered what the old man would say if Aaron told him he wasn't just army, but Delta Force. But that wasn't something anyone but close relatives could know.

Aaron glanced around. The crazy lady stared intently at the door the barista had disappeared behind. She looked shell-shocked, which he didn't blame her

for, since she'd just been shot at on the street. He'd never seen anything like that stateside, except in the news. It was usually contained to the war zones his team was dropped into, not downtown Phoenix.

Some trip to come and see his brother this was turning out to be. First Aaron's twin was too busy to see him, and then he suddenly had to fly to D.C. for whatever reason a U.S. marshal needed to be somewhere. A federal court case was the obvious guess. Why didn't he know more about what Eric did?

He'd figured they could spend some time together, reconnect. That wasn't going to happen now. Aaron had been bouncing around his hotel room earlier before he ran out for coffee just for the sake of something to do. Anything was better than staring at the ceiling trying to sleep.

EMTs raced in, carrying their bulky bags. Aaron got up and out of the way. He looked at the woman he'd collided with. She dressed kind of dowdy, but she had nice eyes. It was a shame she was loopy, and paranoid. Just because someone had been shooting in her direction didn't mean they were out to get her.

Her arms were folded, the sleeves of her wool cardigan pulled down over her hands. She clutched her elbows, making herself look small. Vulnerable.

Aaron stepped closer to her. "Are you okay?"

She really did look shaken. Maybe all this was for real. He'd have to make sure the cops looked out for her if she really was in some kind of trouble. But what trouble could a harmless-looking woman be in?

Her eyes locked with his. Beyond her, three cops stood huddled on the sidewalk and she motioned to them with a tilt of her head. "What do I tell them?"

"The truth is probably a good plan."

Her face paled. "I guess. Someone did just try to kill me."

She looked as though she believed it. So was she a great actress, or was she really onto something? "The police can help. You can't hold back anything from them."

"Okay. I can do this." She gave him a short nod. "I can tell them I'm in witness protection, if you think it's for the best."

"You're…what?" Aaron sucked in a breath and choked. "Do not tell them that."

A uniformed police officer strode in, all business as though this was an everyday occurrence, and maybe it was. Maybe she hadn't just told him what he thought she had. *Witness protection?* Surely that wasn't something you just blurted out.

Mackenzie's face jerked from the cop to him and her eyes widened, as though she wanted to latch on to him for safety. Why was she looking at him that way?

The cop looked between them. "You folks all right?"

She shifted up on her toes, as though she was anxious to leave. "My name is Mackenzie Winters and someone just tried to kill me."

The cop's eyes widened. "I'm Officer Parkwell. Maybe you should tell me what happened."

Mackenzie. It wasn't the name of a woman you overlooked—it was too special for that. Aaron liked it. She looked at him, as if she was asking for permission. He shook his head.

She should definitely not tell the cop she was in witness protection. Why had she told him? They didn't even know each other. There was probably a procedure to these things. If this Mackenzie woman really was part of that, shouldn't she know what the rules were?

She turned to the cop. "Okay, well, someone tried to kill me. I think they've been stalking me, whoever they are, because they slashed my tires tonight so I couldn't drive home. While I was walking to the bus stop a car pulled up by me, and someone started shooting."

She looked at Aaron and relief washed over her features. "Thank God you were there. I'd be dead if you hadn't acted so quickly."

Aaron shifted his feet. "No problem, ma'am."

It wasn't a big deal. Why was she making it such a big deal? Anyone else would have done the same thing. Just because he'd got them both out of harm's way didn't mean Aaron was someone special.

He knew he wasn't a hero, because heroes didn't ruin missions and get their teammate hurt. His shoulder injury was inconsequential compared with the fact Franklin wasn't ever going to see again. And it was Aaron's fault.

His first time as leader of their now four-man Delta Force team, and he'd led them right into a trap. The package had been retrieved—eventually—and the information brought home to whoever needed the intelligence, but the success of the mission on paper didn't make the reality any better. Not when Aaron had been shot and Franklin blinded by shrapnel. Sure, they couldn't have known there would be that level of resistance at the plant they'd infiltrated, but they were trained to be prepared for anything.

The truth was that while Aaron had been a spotless Delta Force solider for years, when the responsibility of leading the team was on him, he'd frozen. And the cost of that hesitation, that moment of trying to decide whether to continue on or abort had been high. Too high.

The cop looked up from his little pad at Mackenzie. Her eyes were on the EMTs carrying the old man out on a backboard. "I'm sorry people got hurt. I didn't know." She looked at Aaron, tears in her eyes. "What do I do now?"

"How should I know?" Why did she persist in looking to him for help? Did Mackenzie really think he knew how to help someone in witness protection? He was on vacation, not some kind of hero for hire.

"You're not going to help me? You're just going to abandon me? What if they come for me again, what if they...kill me?"

Aaron motioned to the officer. "That's what the cops are for. They'll be able to keep you safe. I've got a life to get back to." Not to mention a career to rebuild, and a whole lot of reparations to make.

She blinked and a tear fell down her cheek. He didn't want it to prick his heart, but it did. The last thing he needed was a vulnerable woman looking up at him with brown eyes that really were too big for her face.

Aaron cleared his throat and turned to the cop. "You have someone who can look out for her?"

The officer nodded. "Of course. If you'll wait here, I'll inform my sergeant that Ms. Winters feels that this wasn't a random shooting and that her life is in danger."

He walked away and Aaron looked at Mackenzie again. "We'll get you squared away, don't worry about it. No one's going to hurt you."

"You're really not going to help?"

This again? Why did she think it had to be him who

kept her safe just because he'd thrown her to the ground while bullets were flying? That was nothing but a reflex.

He couldn't let the hurt on her face get to him. He sighed. "Look, you seem nice and all, but I think you've got the wrong end of the stick here. I'm not your hero."

She swiped away tears that were still falling. "Of course you are, Eric. You're the only one who can help me."

TWO

Mackenzie watched the realization wash over his face.

"You think I'm Eric."

She didn't know what to say. This *was* Eric. Had he hit his head when he pulled her down onto the sidewalk?

"I'm not Eric."

This was bizarre. "Well, if you're not Eric, then who are you?"

The man's lips curled up into a smile, and he stuck out his hand. "Sergeant Aaron Hanning, U.S. Army. I'm Eric's twin brother."

She stared at his hand. What was there to smile about? "I just told you I'm in witness protection."

"How was I supposed to know you were going to say that?"

"I thought you were Eric!"

"That's apparent now, but I didn't know it then."

"This is awful. Eric's going to make me move for sure. I don't want to leave. I like it here. I've lived in Phoenix for years." Mackenzie sucked in a breath to try to get control, but Sergeant Aaron Hanning, U.S. Army, just stood there smiling at her. She put her hands on her hips. "There is nothing funny about any of this."

"You just told me my brother works in WITSEC. I thought he worked at the courthouse, or ferrying prisoners around and whatnot. This is cool."

"Cool? It's going to get out. I'll be exposed. My life is over because of you."

"Me?" He glanced around the room, and then sighed and looked back at her. "Look, I'll call Eric. We'll get this figured out. Get your name removed from the witness statement or something so you're not in danger."

"You'd better."

"Excuse me?"

"This is your fault. I'm already in danger, I didn't need this."

His eyes widened. "I didn't shoot at you. I saved your life. Maybe you should say thank-you instead of yelling at me because you blew your cover to me."

Mackenzie gasped. "It's not a cover, it's my *life*."

"Okay, okay, calm down already."

"Calm—"

Sergeant Aaron Hanning, U.S. Army, put his hand over her mouth. "I'm going to call Eric, okay? He'll tell us what to do, and we'll get you squared away."

She took a breath and nodded. The frustration bled away a little, leaving a sick feeling its place. His eyes flickered, but he didn't look away. He just kept staring into her eyes until Mackenzie reached up and pulled his hand away from her mouth. "Please call Eric."

He blinked and whatever connection they had dissipated. Aaron pulled out his phone and stepped away. He stuck the phone between his ear and shoulder and pulled open the first-aid kit that was on the counter.

Officer Parkwell strode back in, his mouth set in a thin line. "We have a witness that identified the plates of the car your shooter was driving. It belongs to a local gang member. At this point we think it's highly unlikely this was anything but a random shooting. Unless you can think of a reason someone might want to harm you?"

"It could be about the arts center where I work. In fact, I think it is about the center. Someone slashed my tires before they shot at me."

It wasn't a happy thought to consider that she was the cause of someone being hurt. Or that she had grieved someone enough they felt they needed to retaliate and slash her tires. But tensions often ran high at the center. Especially when a person took into account the tough background each of the kids had.

"The performing arts center down the street?" The cop scribbled on his notepad. "Is that where your car is?"

"Yes, in the center's parking lot, around back."

"We'll get someone over there to check it out."

The cop strode out again.

The shooter had followed her before they fired. Was that to confirm she was their target? Nothing about this felt like coincidence. Even if it wasn't related to her testimony all those years ago, it was still about her.

Aaron came back over. "I got voice mail. Eric's been in D.C. the past couple of days. He could be on a plane coming home."

Mackenzie hoped that was it. Because in the meantime, she was stuck with the injured, sarcastic twin brother of the all-American U.S. marshal who was *supposed* to be the one helping her. Why couldn't Eric be here now?

Mackenzie wrapped her arms around herself. It was

like being eighteen again, having her whole life end because she'd been in the wrong place at the wrong time. The sound of gunshots from the car had frozen her. Again. She rubbed a hand on her collar, over the place the bullets had entered. She wanted the comfort of a hug, but she'd already gushed over Aaron enough when she'd thought he was Eric.

He'd acted quickly, saving her life. Another "she'd have been dead, if not for…" to add to the long list already in her WITSEC file. But she had to keep her distance, because not only was he a stranger to her, but he didn't seem like the kind of man who appreciated a woman who couldn't stand on her own two feet.

"Are you okay?"

Mackenzie tried to smile. "Sure, I'm fine." It wasn't as if her whole life might be over or anything. "It's just late and it's been a really long day. I didn't need this drama with you on top of it." She looked at the front window. "I hope that man's going to be okay."

He moved close to her side, and then he said, "Me, too. So, listen, if you're going to be fine, then I'm going to head out—"

She whipped around to look at him.

"I'll talk to Eric, and when the police have what they need, they'll probably let you leave."

She was supposed to just go home? Mackenzie swallowed. "Uh, sure. That's fine, I guess. You need to get to the hospital anyway, right?" There was blood all down his sleeve.

He nodded. "Right."

But he didn't leave. Mackenzie's cheeks burned under his stare, so she lifted her chin and stared right back. "You said you and Eric are twins?"

He nodded.

"Uh…that's nice." Probably identical twins—they looked similar enough that she'd mistaken Aaron for Eric. But now that she looked closely, she could see slight differences in the nose, where Aaron's looked as if it had been broken. Her cheeks heated. "I thought you were leaving."

"So did I." His lips curled up, his eyes on her. "And yet I don't seem to have gone yet."

He might think this was amusing, but Mackenzie did not. He was nice enough looking—okay, so he was downright gorgeous—but that didn't mean she wanted him to stare at her. He might get the idea that she actually wanted a relationship.

His phone rang.

Aaron reached for his back pocket and hissed. *Ouch.* His medical leave was only supposed to be two weeks, but given how hard he'd hit the sidewalk and rolled, he guessed the recovery was going to be longer.

He stepped away from Mackenzie. "Hanning." The background noise was a steady rush of people and movement.

"You called?" Eric's breathing was labored. Was he in a hurry?

Aaron perched on a circular table in the corner. "So…you work witness protection, huh?"

There was a short pause. A door shut and Eric said, "Who told you that?"

"Met a friend of yours tonight. Mackenzie Winters. She thought I was you, but that was after she and I nearly got shot in a drive-by." Aaron rubbed his eyes with his free hand. It was a shame his coffee had spilled all over the sidewalk.

"I got her voice mail, but it didn't say anything about a shooting. I take it you saved her?"

"A gun went off. After I reached for the weapon I wasn't carrying, I just moved us. It was a reflex, nothing more."

What was it with everyone assuming he was some kind of hero? He still hadn't told Eric he was on medical leave or why he'd instinctively fled from anything army related.

Reconnecting with his brother was long overdue, there was no doubt about that. But the real reason he'd come to Phoenix to see Eric was more about what he was going to face when he returned to work. About the fact his teammates wouldn't even let him see Franklin. They'd expected him to apologize before he left, but how did you say sorry when you'd blinded someone? It just wasn't good enough. "I'm not a hero."

Eric sighed. "I'm boarding another flight right now, I'll be back ASAP. Can you stay with Mackenzie?"

"Why? She's fine. The cops are taking care of her. I didn't think this had anything to do with her being in witness protection. She said something to the cop about the center where she worked."

"The likelihood is that it isn't connected with her being in WITSEC. But I'd still like someone watching out for her until I can get there to assess the situation." Eric sighed. "Please do this, Aaron. I really need your help."

Eric wanted him to stick around with Mackenzie longer, when his last failure had cost someone their sight—and their future? "I'm not your guy for this one.

Don't you have resources? Surely there's a plan when things like this happen."

"Of course there is, but that was before I spent two days in D.C. trying to get to the bottom of a potential leak in my office."

"No offense, but I'm on leave with an injury. This doesn't really concern me."

"You saved her. She'll trust you, and she needs someone to keep her safe until I can find out if this is related to her past. And find the traitor in my office."

Aaron blew out a breath. "You think a U.S. marshal is responsible?"

"All I have is supposition right now. We can't rule anyone out until the FBI determines who caused the leak of a number of files. It could have come from inside or outside of the office—at this point we still have no idea. We had the FBI warn the witnesses whose names were leaked, and those with active threats have been moved."

"So why was Mackenzie still in Phoenix?"

"Her file was not one of the ones that were leaked."

"So the shooting is unrelated."

Eric's footsteps stopped. "We still have to keep your involvement in this under wraps. If Mackenzie is being targeted for anything, then she should be kept safe. The leak could be a diversion. I can't go through normal channels because everything is balanced on the edge right now. I can't disrupt anything or the FBI case unravels. If there's a mole, whoever it is will bury themselves so deep we'll never find them."

Aaron got to his feet, his eyes on Mackenzie. He might not be a true hero, but there was no way he was going to leave a woman unprotected if he could help it. "What do you want me to do?"

"You'll help?"

"I'm not going to leave you hanging." Maybe this was the chance he'd wanted to connect with his brother. If the cost was reopening the wound in his shoulder, Aaron would gladly pay it. Eric was all the family he had, and at least his brother didn't think he was a failure like his team did. They wouldn't even let him in Franklin's hospital room. "What do I do with her?"

"Keep an eye on her until I get this whole situation figured out. The FBI thinks it should only take a couple of days to track the source of the virus that copied the files. Have Mackenzie stick to her normal routine, but keep your eye out. The cops will do their own investigation to find out if there's a threat against Mackenzie, and I'll be there tomorrow."

Mackenzie turned. Her eyes widened and her cheeks flushed at whatever was on his face. So she wasn't used to direct attention. And why not? She was a pleasant-looking woman; she just downplayed her looks, unlike pretty much every woman Aaron had ever dated.

He hung up and crossed the room to her. "Eric asked me to keep an eye out for you. In case someone is after you, I can make sure you're safe."

"So you believe me?"

Aaron shrugged his good shoulder. "Does it matter? Someone may or may not be trying to harm you, and in the meantime I'm going to make sure they don't succeed. The truth will come out in time."

"Oh." She glanced around the café.

Aaron took gentle hold of her elbow. She was the

protectee now, and he would maintain a professional distance.

"Let's walk to my truck." His shoulder needed looking at, but he'd have to find supplies somewhere. He did have extra gauze and bandages in his hotel room, plus no one would know she was there.

He looked around the parking lot as they walked but didn't spot anything suspicious. Eric wanted her safe, and the best option for that was a hotel he already knew was secure. But that was probably the last thing Mackenzie wanted.

"We can stay at your house."

Her eyes widened. "I don't have a guest room."

"I'll sleep in the truck."

"You can't do that. You're injured."

"I've slept in worse places. Believe me." Aaron got the feeling he was going to have to do a lot of reassuring with this woman.

When she'd settled herself into the passenger seat of his truck, Aaron turned to her. "Okay, here's the deal. You do exactly as I say and you don't ask questions. If something happens, we're not going to stop in order for me to explain it to you, we're just going to run."

THREE

By the next morning, Mackenzie had almost managed to forget that someone tried to kill her the night before. But when Eric walked into the Downtown Performing Arts Center, it all flooded back.

Aaron was around somewhere, supposedly protecting her, although she hadn't seen much of him. She hadn't told him anything the night before, but she had convinced him to stop by the E.R. and get stitched up. Mackenzie had driven back to her house and in the end she'd convinced him to spend the night on the couch instead of in his truck. He'd said it was so he could see her front door, but she'd seen the pain in his eyes. Especially considering he'd refused a prescription for pain pills.

"Who is that?"

Mackenzie turned to Eva, who taught classes at the center while Mackenzie ran the office. They were standing at the entrance to the hallway that led to the classrooms. "An old friend of mine."

"What kind of old friend?" Eva grinned. Mackenzie blinked. She hadn't even thought of Eric in those terms before. She supposed he was handsome enough, though Aaron was the better-looking brother. Both of them could be movie stars. The idea that either one would ever look twice at someone like Mackenzie was laughable. "Thank you, Eva. I needed that."

Eva blinked. "What did I do?"

"You reminded me that life isn't all doom and gloom." Mackenzie wrapped her arm around Eva's shoulders. "And that the best things don't ever change."

"You're welcome. I think." Eva stepped back from their huddle, smiling. "I should get to my next class. The natives will be getting restless."

Mackenzie nodded.

"Are we still on for dinner later?"

"Absolutely." Mackenzie smiled, excited to have been invited. Which was good, since anticipation covered the feeling of being a complete ninny because she was all worked up over one dinner. Eva probably went out with her friends all the time while Mackenzie couldn't remember the last time she got invited to hang with someone. Plus it had the added benefit of taking her mind off the fact that someone had shot at her and she now had a permanent shadow in the form of Sergeant Aaron Hanning, U.S. Army.

Eva was one of their best teachers, able to easily relate to the street kids who populated the center. Her application two months ago, after the previous teacher had suddenly quit, turned out to be a blessing Mackenzie never expected.

Mackenzie studied her WITSEC handler as he approached; his suit was still crisp though it was after lunch. But the look on his face said he was about to apologize for something.

"Hi, Eric."

He nodded. "Mackenzie. How are you?"

She motioned behind her. "Let's go to my office."

He followed her in and sat in one of two chairs in front of the desk. Castoffs from a doctor's office. The whole room was smaller than the closet she used to have before she became a federally protected witness.

The brothers weren't much older than her, she didn't think. Eric wore the air of authority that came with the marshal's star badge with ease, while his predecessor had been a burly guy with a gray goatee and a thing for barbecue ribs.

Eric shifted in his chair. "How are you?"

Mackenzie poured Eric a cup of coffee. "Do you think Carosa still wants to kill me, even after all these years?"

He took the cup from her. "If you weren't in danger anymore, you'd have been released from the witness protection program. Carosa is still out to kill you for testifying against his brother." He took a sip and sighed. "I don't want you to be unaware of the reality of the situation. But I did run a check with immigration this morning, and to the best of our knowledge, he's still in Colombia."

"So he didn't shoot at me." Why wouldn't the nausea in her stomach ease? This wasn't about her past. "It was someone else."

"The police think your slashed tires and the attempt on your life were both the work of a local gang. Maybe someone with a grudge against the work the center does with teens, getting them off the streets." He gave her a small smile. "Apparently the car belongs to the brother of Hector Sanchez."

Hector was a regular visitor to the center. "So I might be in danger, but not from Carosa."

"Unless your identity is revealed. If anyone discovers who you really are, or your picture gets in the media, you'll be pulled out of Phoenix." Eric sighed. "We don't want to jump the gun, but the Marshals Service is dealing with an internal investigation right now. It doesn't directly relate to your case, but it's why I asked Aaron to keep an eye on you."

Mackenzie squared her shoulders. "I could leave on my own."

"If you do that, I can't protect you. You'll be leaving the cover of WITSEC and effectively opting out of the witness protection program. That's why Aaron is here."

She squeezed the bridge of her nose. Hadn't she atoned enough already for the person she used to be? For years she'd been so careful to adhere to every rule for life and living. It was as though it didn't even matter.

Eric's mouth curled up into a sad smile. "I really am sorry you're caught up in this, Mackenzie. I know it's the last thing you need. But I'm sure the police will resolve it quickly, and Aaron will make sure you're safe in the meantime."

He shouldn't be sorry. She was the one who'd gotten herself in this mess in the first place. It might have been a case of wrong place/wrong time that caused her to witness a double homicide. But she'd only been there because she'd thought being famous was the ultimate life. Now that the man she testified against had been killed in prison, she should have been able to get on with her life.

Would she ever be free?

Mackenzie squeezed her eyes shut. It was as though God wasn't done punishing her for her selfishness. She read her Bible every day, and when she had made up for what she'd done in her former life, then she would allow herself to fully accept what Jesus had done for her.

"You can trust him, Mackenzie. Aaron won't let anything happen to you."

"He's right. I won't."

Aaron filled the doorway. Mackenzie stared at him, trying to figure out what it was that made him so much more compelling than his brother. It couldn't be physical. She chuckled. "You really look a lot alike."

Aaron glanced at Eric, and they both shook their heads. He'd never seen what people meant when they said that. Apart from the blond hair and blue eyes, their similar features, they were completely different. Aaron's nose had been broken more times than he could remember since he first went skydiving on his eighteenth birthday, whereas Eric liked to *read*.

Aaron turned to his brother. "You have the picture of the guy after Mackenzie?"

Eric nodded and handed Aaron a file. Clearly he hadn't liked the idea of showing Aaron a picture of the brother of the man she put in jail, but Aaron didn't want the guy walking up to Mackenzie on the street and pulling a gun before he even recognized the threat. "You know I don't like going in blind. Ever."

Eric shrugged, as though Aaron's discomfort didn't much bother him. "And you know I can't tell you anything. If Mackenzie wants to share, that's up to her. But legally I can't divulge the details of her case. We don't even know for sure the shooting is related. In fact, I'm with the police on this one. I don't think this is anything more than someone with a grudge against the center. Albeit a dangerous grudge."

Mackenzie came around the desk. "So I can tell Aaron about me if I want, but I don't have to and you're not going to?"

Eric nodded. "In this instance, it would be okay for you to tell him. And, honestly, he can better protect you if he knows."

Great. Aaron wanted the details. How was he supposed to protect her when he didn't even know what the threat was? And she wanted to keep her secrets? That had the potential to kill both of them.

Aaron glared at her and then said to Eric, "I need to know."

Only Eric didn't look as if he was going to give it up. He said, "I can't even confirm whether or not the woman in this room is, in fact, in the witness protection program. As far as you know, she's a friend of mine who has a man in her life who wants to do her harm."

"Right." Aaron studied the photo in the file. Middle-aged man, Hispanic, his hair sprinkled with gray. Aaron committed the image to memory the way he'd done with so many photos of targets before, and then passed the file back to Eric.

"You need anything else?"

"Can't think of anything." If Mackenzie wasn't going to tell him, Aaron would have to get the information some other way.

Although he would settle for a shoulder that didn't scream with fire every time he moved it the wrong way.

Eric frowned. "I'm sorry I can't tell you how long this will take. I have to go on as if nothing is wrong until we find the leak, but if we hit the point when you have to go back on base, we'll have to deal with that when it comes."

"I called my C.O. this morning, so he knows that for the time being I'm involved in something." And hadn't that been a fun conversation? His commanding officer was known for his brevity, but at least Aaron now knew that Franklin wasn't doing any better than he'd been before Aaron went on leave.

"My lunch break is almost over." Eric turned to Mackenzie. "Be safe, okay? Listen to Aaron. He knows what he's talking about."

The door shut. Silence stretched out into a minute as Mackenzie and Aaron stared at each other. He looked as though he was expecting something, but she didn't know what. Or she just didn't want to admit she might know what he wanted her to say.

There was a light knock at the door.

"Kenzie?" Eva stuck her head in and glanced between Mackenzie and Aaron. Her full lips tipped up on one side in a half smile. Mackenzie's friend was probably more than confused about the second of two strange men she'd seen with Mackenzie today. "You okay, girl?"

Blood raced through Mackenzie's veins, and her cheeks warmed. "Sure."

Eva's eyes gleamed. She'd be digging later to find out who Mackenzie's male visitors were. Why couldn't her life be boring? Instead Mackenzie had been dragged into this strange play where she didn't know her lines.

"What's up?"

"We're a teacher short. Chris had to rush out. The day care called, and his son, Tim, is puking everywhere. The kids in the blue room are waiting for their voice lesson. I need you to cover."

"No. I can't do it." Paperwork, yes. Answering

phones, yes. Fund-raising, no problem. Sing in front of people again? No way. That could get her killed.

Eva's lips thinned. "There's no one else."

Mackenzie glanced at Aaron, but he was pressing buttons on his phone and hadn't seen Eva's face. She looked back at her friend. Eva was the opposite of everything Mackenzie tried to be—sparkly and loud. But right then Mackenzie's closest friend—which wasn't saying much, since they usually only saw each other at work—wasn't happy, to say the least.

"I can't do it."

"Kenzie, do you think I don't know what you're hiding? Do you think I haven't figured it out?"

"I—" It wasn't possible. Mackenzie had worked too hard for too long for her secret to get out now. "I don't know what you're talking about."

"Girl... I heard you sing."

"What?" Mackenzie sucked in a breath. "When?"

"Do you think I'm stupid?"

"Of course not." How could Eva think that?

The other woman's eyes softened. "About a month ago I left my phone here. It was late when I came back to get it. I heard you, playing piano and singing to yourself."

Mackenzie didn't know what to say. It didn't spell total disaster, but her voice was distinctive. She had assumed she'd be safe just working in the office. After all, she'd set the center up. Wasn't that enough to balance the scales? She'd come to terms with the fact that music couldn't be part of her life anymore, except in secret. Now she wouldn't be able to sing at all, not even when she thought everyone was gone.

Why did that hurt?

Eva's head tipped to the side. "You know, you kind of sound like—"

Please don't say it. "I know."

"They're already in the blue room waiting. Please. There's no one else."

Mackenzie sighed. "There's a ton of work to do in here."

It was an excuse, but she had no interest in being the person she used to be. Not again. And she would do everything she could not to fall back into that trap of selfish, wild living. The only thing those days of youth had done was set her on a collision course with this life of hiding and secrets.

"Kenzie—"

She bit her lip. "Okay. I'll go and oversee things. They can practice, and I'll just make sure it doesn't get out of control."

But there was no way she was going to sing in front of the kids. No way on earth.

Eva beamed as if it was Christmas morning. "Great."

Mackenzie rolled her eyes, but Eva didn't see because she'd already breezed out the door. It was only one class. Surely disaster couldn't happen that fast.

"Hold up a second."

Aaron stopped her with a hand on her arm. Mackenzie looked down at his fingers on the sleeve of her sweater. She could feel his heat through the material and it struck her that she'd never felt anything so warm. His hands were strong, his nails trimmed short, and his little finger was bent as though it'd been broken and not quite set straight.

She looked up at his face. "The kids are waiting."

"We still need to have a conversation. I know what

Eric said, but if I'm going to have the best shot at protecting you, then I need to know what happened."

"Fine." Even though Mackenzie had no intention of telling him anything about who she used to be.

He apparently didn't buy it, because he said, "If you don't, I will absolutely walk. I have to know what I'm up against." The hint of a smile gleamed in his eyes. "Who knows, I might surprise you."

"I don't like surprises."

FOUR

Aaron leaned back against the wall, listening to a teen girl singing. There really was no other way to keep an eye on Mackenzie without it looking as if he was doing exactly that. Diligence was the only thing that paid off. Faith in a higher being to solve all his problems was nothing but a childish dream. Not when in one split second everything could go wrong and no matter how hard he tried to fix it, someone still got hurt.

He rubbed a hand down his face, dismissing the memories of heat and sand…and blood.

He loved the spontaneity of being Delta Force, though there was a shelf life to the career. Retreating just didn't sit well with him, but when it was that or put his teammates in danger because he couldn't admit he was slowing down…there wasn't anything to it. When the time came, Aaron would just finish up his days and move on with the confidence he'd done his duty to Uncle Sam.

Aaron was almost to his mid-thirties, so it was past time to start thinking about fallback options. Especially considering the fact his team hated him at this point. When he got back, there wasn't going to be much of a working relationship between them all if they didn't trust Aaron anymore.

They'd banded together around Franklin, which was the right thing. Aaron didn't fault them for giving their support to their blind teammate. Franklin would need it. But did they have to reject Aaron in the process? Hadn't it just been a mistake? A horrific one, sure, but he was only human. Didn't they know that?

"What do ya say?"

Aaron glanced down the hall where a teen boy in a white T-shirt and saggy jeans crowded a younger girl against the wall.

"I'm not sure." The girl's voice was a nervous murmur. "I don't think—"

The boy's face hardened. "Not the right answer, babe."

Aaron sauntered over. "Hey, what's up, guys?" They both turned to him. The boy's face hardened and the girl's eyes went wide. "Is there a vending machine around here? I'm really craving a soda."

The girl's face washed with relief, even though the boy hadn't stepped back. She pointed down the hall behind Aaron. "In the kitchen. They're a dollar, but if you hit the top three buttons on the left and the bottom right one at the same time, an orange soda will drop out."

The boy looked at her. "Why would you tell him that?"

"He's Ms. Winters's new boyfriend. I saw them together earlier."

The boy looked back at Aaron. "For real? You're Ms. Winters's new boyfriend?"

Aaron nearly rolled his eyes at the third degree from a kid who apparently thought his teenage self was something everyone needed to take note of. Was that what he had looked like at that age? Aaron must have seemed ridiculous. It was a wonder his foster parents hadn't laughed at him.

Aaron looked at the girl, admittedly a little intrigued. "Does Ms. Winters have a lot of boyfriends?"

"I think you're the first."

"How long have you been coming here?"

"Like, four years."

That was interesting. So as far as the kids knew, Mackenzie didn't date. At all. Maybe it wasn't just him who noticed the air of "I'm hiding something" that she wore. Or he only saw it because he knew she was in witness protection.

Aaron lifted his chin to the boy. "You might want to back up a step there, champ. Give the girl some breathing space."

The teen's eyes narrowed and he moved forward. Aaron's body tightened in readiness.

"Is everything okay?" Mackenzie appeared beside Aaron, bringing with her the scent of cotton candy. She looked at the girl. "Megan?"

"Everything's fine, Ms. Winters."

Aaron watched the boy step back and wondered how Mackenzie managed to generate that level of respect just by smiling.

"Class is over, so your sister is waiting for you."

The girl scurried around their huddle and disappeared around the corner into the room where Mackenzie had been teaching. Aaron turned back to see Mackenzie had closed in on the boy. "You take care, Hector."

Hector? This was the kid whose brother had shot at them on the street?

"I don't need advice from you." Hector stepped back, motioning with his fingers.

Aaron moved to shut down whatever the kid was about to do, but Mackenzie stopped him with a hand on his chest. "Let him go. He's dealing with enough."

"Like an older brother who tried to kill you yesterday? I'm surprised he even showed up." Aaron blew out a breath. "You shouldn't let him disrespect you that way."

Mackenzie frowned. "You don't think these kids understand love, or kindness?"

"Trust me, they have one currency and that's respect. Nothing else gets through to them."

"You sound as though you know what you're talking about."

Aaron shrugged. "Same world, different city."

"Maybe you could tell me about it later."

"Why? So you can feel as if you know me?" He shook his head. "I'm not one of those kids."

"I know that. Aaron, I just—"

"Thought we should be friends? Is that what you want? Or do you want me to keep you safe from the guy who wants you dead? Because you can't have it both ways. That's not how this works."

Mackenzie stepped back and her face blanked. "I'll be in my office. Try not to start any more fights, okay? I'm only going to grab my purse."

He followed her, unwilling to mess up the only thing that would keep Eric's respect when he found out Aaron was responsible for the failed mission and his teammate's medical discharge. He watched her switch off her computer and shut out the lights. The other woman who worked there—Eva—met them in the lobby.

"So I'll meet you at the restaurant? Or are you going home to change first?"

Aaron glanced between them. "What's this?"

Mackenzie sighed. "I forgot to mention it. I'm really sorry, Eva."

She thought Aaron wasn't going to let her go?

Eva glanced between them before her attention settled on Mackenzie. "But you have to come out. You promised. It'll be fun, I'm telling you. All-you-can-eat appetizers and we'll splurge on something chocolate for dessert even though we don't need it. Come on, what do you say?"

Mackenzie clearly wanted to go. Did she not want him tagging along and putting a crimp in girl's night out? Well, too bad.

Aaron smiled. "Sounds great. I'm in."

Eva's eyes flickered, but she recovered quickly. "Sure, why not."

Aaron stuck his hand out. "Aaron Hanning, nice to meet you."

She shook his hand. "Eva Partez."

"Mackenzie and I'll meet you there. All right?"

Mackenzie swallowed. "Sure."

He grabbed her elbow and led her out before she could change her mind. Mackenzie locked the front doors as Eva sped off in a black Mustang with the top down. The sun had turned the sky pink and Aaron had to sidestep so he could see Mackenzie's face without the glare.

"All-you-can-eat appetizers?"

Mackenzie sighed. "She's been asking me to hang out with her for weeks and I finally broke down yesterday and agreed. I actually thought it would be fun, but now that Carosa might have sent someone to kill me…"

"Carosa? As in the Colombian drug cartel?"

She hesitated for a minute, and then nodded.

"So that's who the guy in the picture was." He whistled. "You don't mess around, do you? But don't worry. I'll be there to keep you safe, whatever this is. That's why Eric asked me to stay."

"Why would you? I mean, it's kind of clear that you don't really like me. Why would you give up your time to protect someone who basically means nothing more to you than some stranger on the street?"

"What I'm protecting is Eric's witness. It's his career on the line because of your safety. And I never said I didn't like you."

"Seemed kind of obvious to me."

"Well, I'm—" he swallowed "—sorry for that. In the future, I'll try to be…nicer."

Mackenzie laughed. "That was hard for you to say, wasn't it? Big tough guy like you. It must be rough, having to be pleasant."

Aaron didn't like one bit that she was laughing at him. "Let's just get going, okay?" He grabbed her elbow again and headed down the street toward where he'd parked his truck.

"Why do you do that?"

"What?"

"Haul me around like a sack of potatoes."

He loosened his grip but didn't let go. "Guess I need to be nicer about that, too. I don't usually work with people who are willing to cooperate. I normally have to push a lot harder to get the result I want."

"Then maybe you should just try asking nicely."

"Is it going to be as uncomfortable as apologizing?"

Mackenzie laughed. "Probably."

Okay, when her face brightened like that he didn't much mind that she was teasing him. Maybe it wouldn't be so bad having to be around her for a couple of weeks. He could get used to sparring with Mackenzie Winters.

Aaron opened the passenger door for her, like a gentleman was supposed to. Unfortunately that meant they both got a look at the interior. Last night he hadn't been in any shape to apologize for the state of his truck. He'd just shoved everything into the middle to make a space for her. But now he saw exactly how bad it was. The foot well had a bunch of fast-food wrappers tossed there, and the passenger seat was under his jacket, a duffel bag and two gel packs that weren't frozen anymore.

Aaron tossed the duffel and jacket behind the bench seat and motioned to the seat. "Your chariot, my lady."

"Why, thank you, kind sir."

When he pulled out, he scanned the street while Mackenzie stared at him again.

"So what are we going to tell Eva about you? I mean, you did just show up out of the blue, so we can't pretend you're my new boyfriend. What about my cousin?"

He glanced at her and then back at the road. "Why do we need to have a story?"

"Isn't that what people do in these situations? Develop a cover story. Perhaps you could be my cousin from out of town, recently laid off from your job of hunting down rogue skunks in the Alaskan wilderness."

"Rogue skunks?"

"Or something."

He smiled. "Judging by the contents of the bookshelves in your living room, it doesn't surprise me you have a vivid imagination."

Mackenzie folded her arms. "What's wrong with what I read?"

Aaron waved away her question. "I'm not even going to get started on what's wrong with your taste in books. You really don't want to know."

"Well, what have you read lately?"

She probably thought he didn't know how. He smiled. "Dr. Seuss."

"Like when you were six?"

He nearly laughed. "No, a couple of weeks ago. There was this kid in the hospital who had burned his hands, so he couldn't hold the book. I hung out with him a while before I got discharged. Sweet kid."

"Seriously?"

"What? It was a nice thing to do."

"It was."

He pulled across an intersection, about a mile from the restaurant. "And you're the only one who can help kids?"

"I didn't say that. It's just contrary to what I've seen from you before. You were a little…gruff earlier."

"I apologized then."

"And I accepted. I'm just saying—" Mackenzie froze.

A black van came at the front left corner of the truck. Another van came from the right, boxing them in. The two vehicles moved closer together, tightening the noose. Aaron gripped the wheel, fighting to keep them from bouncing off the side of one van into the other.

The vans screeched to a halt, stopping Aaron's truck with them. The door on one van slid back, and Mackenzie gasped as hooded men in black fatigues with big guns poured out. More appeared behind them, cocooning them in the truck. All the weapons were lifted and pointed at Aaron.

"Let the girl out!"

Aaron gripped the wheel with both hands but didn't move or speak.

"Um… Aaron?"

One of the men in all black moved toward her door.

"Put it in Reverse." Aaron spoke, but his lips barely moved.

"What?"

"They can see both my hands. Reach over and put it in Reverse." He pushed out a breath. "Now."

He moved his foot to the clutch. Mackenzie ground the gearshift, wincing at the sound. Before she was barely done, Aaron's foot hit the gas and they flew backward. She screamed and gripped the dash. The truck spun in an arc, Aaron changed gears again and they sped forward. She looked back. "They're right behind us. They're chasing us."

"I know."

"They didn't shoot, though."

Aaron glanced at her and then took a corner so fast they almost went up on two wheels. "You want to talk about this now? Fine. I'm guessing they don't want you harmed. They don't get paid for delivering damaged goods."

"Carosa wants to kill me himself. I know. He yelled it across the courtroom the day I testified against his brother." She took a deep breath and pushed it out slowly as they raced down the street. "This isn't about Hector's brother now. Maybe someone hired him just like they hired these guys."

"Good thing for us Carosa seems to only know semi-competent thugs."

Every few streets she glanced back until finally she said, "They're not there anymore."

"They must have backed off." He pulled into a gas station and out the other side, cutting off a Buick. "That means they're confident they'll get another shot."

FIVE

Aaron drove for the sake of driving, not worrying about where he was going. He reached over and squeezed Mackenzie's hand. "You okay?"

Mackenzie's fingers were chilled, as though the courage had been drained out of her. He let her hand go, wondering what he was supposed to say now that all of this was officially a whole lot bigger than just someone with a grudge against the center. Carosa had sent men for her.

Aaron pulled up at a stoplight. Mackenzie's big eyes made her look more like a scared girl than a woman who dressed like a grandma librarian—except for the black high-heeled boots that started directly under her knee-length skirt. Her hair was still pulled tight in that ugly bun she'd been wearing all day. It was as if it was some kind of uniform she used to protect her identity. Had she been a recognizable person before? He looked at her again, trying to think if there was someone she resembled.

Eric should have pressed the local P.D. harder. Clearly Mackenzie's name had been leaked somehow, given that it had taken no time at all for hired mercenaries to find her. And for what? Aaron didn't even want to think about what Carosa would have done with her. Or how her current identity had been connected to the person she used to be.

Mackenzie looked out the side window. Her fingers gripped the straps of the backpack that sat between her knees. They were on the run from Carosa, but Aaron had no idea what the deal was. What had happened to her?

Ignorance wasn't bliss—it got you killed.

When the danger was hypothetical, that was fine. He'd had the time to wait for her to share. But now that it was real, he didn't like not knowing the people involved, or the fact Eric couldn't give him all the information about Mackenzie and the guy after her without breaking WITSEC rules.

Some favor.

He needed to get Mackenzie someplace safe until Eric called to say it was all clear for her to come home... probably only to be relocated again. Who knew what the fallout from this mess would be? Especially when the Marshals Service realized Mackenzie had disappeared.

He studied her while the light was red, trying to guess who this woman really was and why she was hiding.

"I need to know." He clenched his jaw, willing her to talk to him. "Do you know any of the men who tried to stop us?"

"I've never seen them before."

He sighed. "I'm sorry, I had to ask."

"Now you're in danger, too. Because of me."

And that seemed to concern her a great deal. Why, he had no idea. She didn't know him from any guy on the street, just like she'd said of him. Mackenzie cared way too much about a bunch of kids most people would write off—even him, before he'd seen how they opened up to her.

Aaron squeezed her fingers again. "It makes no difference if I'm in their sights, too—the play is still the same. We stick together." He followed the line of cars that clogged the city's streets. "My shoulder's still healing. Eric didn't know who else he could trust, and we'd already met."

"What are you healing from?"

"You don't have to worry about that. I'm perfectly capable of keeping you safe until we meet up with Eric and get the next move all figured out." He hung a right, one eye on the traffic behind them, watching for a tail.

"Are you sure you're okay with being involved? I mean, drop me at the next corner if you want. I won't be responsible for dragging someone else down with me." She glanced away, out the window. "Not again."

Now, why did she have to go and say that? "I might not be a hero, but at least I'm not a jerk. I'm in this with you, and I have no intention of ditching just because things got hot. The threat is real now."

"I know."

"Mackenzie, you don't have to worry. I'm going to stick with you until we know you're safe. Either Eric will figure out what's going on or we'll get you a place to stay. Then you can go back to your life."

Back to the Downtown Performing Arts Center, a building filled with kids and laughter from the moment school got out until well after dark. Music had permeated the whole place today—everything from the most somber classical piece to the latest radio hit song. What was it about Mackenzie that she could take a broken-down building and a bunch of kids everyone had written off and infuse them with so much life?

Aaron needed to know more about why Carosa was after her so he could wrap up this favor and get back to his life. But first he had to lose any possible pursuers, just in case there was someone behind them he hadn't seen.

"Why now?"

Aaron didn't know if she was talking to him, or if she had even heard what he said. He took a sharp right down an alley and hit the gas. They came out the far side onto another busy main street, and he flipped a quick U-turn to the sound of multiple beeping horns.

It was as if she didn't even notice.

"Why couldn't this have happened years ago, before I made a life for myself? He shouldn't have been able to find me. This shouldn't be happening."

Aaron's chest got tight. "I get that this is a shock, Mackenzie, but it can't be unprecedented. Can it?"

She finally looked at him. "Being ready for what is a remote possibility is one thing. Thinking you're actually going to have to leave the life you love because a group of soldiers is trying to abduct you is something entirely different. I'm done, I won't ever be safe. He found me this time, he'll find me again."

"So that's it? You're going to give yourself up to die?"

She huffed. "What do you expect me to do? I'm going up against a man who'll kill me without a second thought. What do I do in the face of that? Hit him with a guitar? Sing him to death?"

Aaron made a turn onto a major street lined with stores and restaurants. "As entertaining as that would be, you don't have to worry. It's why I'm here."

"And I get to be the helpless female while the big strong man protects me? Sorry, that doesn't work for me."

He pulled up behind a sky-blue Cadillac at a stoplight. The air conditioning took that moment to stop working, and hot Arizona air filled the cab instead. Great.

He turned to her. "If you're going to fight me all the way, maybe you should get out at the next corner. Or you could trust me and I can teach you how to survive."

"Like how to shoot a gun?" She shuddered. "I don't think so."

"Then you seriously need my help. Eric wouldn't have asked me to stick around if he thought you should just give up and die."

"It's his job to make sure I'm safe."

The light was still red. Aaron studied her profile, folded in and wound tight again. "You don't have to be scared."

"I'm not worried about dying, but I'm also too much of a realist. Survival is pretty much a pipe dream at this point. This guy will never, ever give up."

Something dark flashed in his eyes. "You're not going to let me help you?"

She reached for the door handle. Aaron was blocked in, cars behind and in front of him in his lane and the light hadn't changed.

"I'm not letting anyone else get killed because of me. I'm doing this alone."

Mackenzie slammed the door. Aaron jumped out and called her name, but there were no footsteps that followed her. He wasn't the kind of man who abandoned his truck on the street—even if it was a dump on the inside. It had been torture sitting there chatting as though she was going along with the whole thing while she waited for the right time to make her move.

She couldn't trust anyone; that was the bottom line. And there was no way she would put anyone else in danger. Nothing good could come from spending time in an intense situation with a good-looking man who didn't seem like a bad guy, even if he was occasionally a jerk.

Mackenzie needed to save her energy for staying alive instead of falling back into her old ways. Sparks, smiles, then a brief touch of the hand, a light kiss…it might as well be a whirlpool that sucked her under, or a riptide that took her back to the kind of person she had no intention of becoming again.

Mackenzie started down the sidewalk. Traffic streamed past in both directions. It took her a second to get her bearings, but she headed for a bus stop, watching every vehicle that passed for the vans the mercenaries had been driving. When she finally slumped into a seat on a bus, Mackenzie would be able to close her eyes and let herself relax. Buses were anonymous. People left each other alone for the most part, and she would be able to just stare out the window and not think about what her life had become.

Sometimes she rode the bus all day—through the city, out to the desert, tourist bus trips to the Grand Canyon—wondering what would happen if she never got off. The bus would stop eventually, done for the day. She could disembark and hop another bus…anywhere.

If you leave, I can't protect you.

And yet she had left, which meant WITSEC was going to kick her out of the program for breaking the rules. She was off on her own now, no Eric, no Aaron. Fear churned her stomach, reminding her she hadn't eaten since lunch. There was no way she'd be able to stomach anything now. Her life was over and she was as good as dead. Staying with Aaron only meant prolonging the inevitable.

At least this way he would be safe.

A young mom pushing a toddler in a stroller passed her. Mackenzie returned the woman's smile. That could never be her. She'd done too much to ever be free of the chains of her past. She would be forever bound by the consequences of the girl she'd been.

A new life meant leaving behind everything and everyone she had come to love. She should have kept emotion out of it, done her job and gone home at the end of the day to her empty house. Too bad everything about the center kids made her fall in love the minute she looked in their eyes. They might be rough at the corners and some even hard, but they were so full of life and promise.

Something she didn't have left.

Not since she'd testified against the son of a drug lord in a trial that ended with him getting life without parole for double homicide and attempted murder. Then it had all ended four years later in a prison riot. She should have been free because Pedro Carosa was dead. Problem over, except it wasn't. In the years since then, his older brother, Alonzo, apparently hadn't given up the idea of revenge. It seemed he was just as committed as ever to making Mackenzie pay for tearing his family apart.

And there was no way she was going to let anyone else get caught in her cross fire.

The car engine revved, but she didn't turn. It was happening all over again, and this time there was no Aaron to dive with her out of the line of fire.

The vehicle slowed, but she wasn't about to turn that way and allow whoever it was to get a look at her. Mackenzie sped up her pace, her eyes on the road ahead.

How could she get out of here? A side street? Into a café and out the back entrance? Would a bus come along just in time? Maybe a cab.

But what was the point? Carosa had found her.

The vehicle's brakes squealed as it stopped and the driver's door slammed.

She started running.

SIX

"Mackenzie." He didn't like the look on her face when she spun, eyes wide and stark with fear. "You're exposed out here. We have to get somewhere safe."

Her spine straightened. "I told you, I can't go with you."

"So you walk along the street out here, late at night, where anyone can pick you off and make you just another tragic statistic? The guy after you gets exactly what he wants, and your life is over. Great plan."

She flinched, and he knew he'd hit the mark he was aiming for. "If it sounds as if I'm trying to scare you, that's because I am. We can't give this guy the chance to succeed. You said yourself you want to be free of this." He held out his hand to her. "I'm giving you a shot at living the rest of your life, Mackenzie. I know I'm practically a stranger to you, but you can trust me."

Someone brushed past them on the sidewalk, close enough to jostle her. "Can I? How do I know that?"

Aaron studied her. Something didn't jibe with what she said. She inferred it was an issue of trust, but he didn't see fear in her eyes...he saw pain. What had happened to this woman that made her so hesitant to trust someone that she willfully put her own safety in jeopardy? She pushed him away in order to protect herself and wound up with the opposite outcome.

He was going to be here for her, but he couldn't let himself get close, even if she was an intriguing puzzle. Because he didn't want to know what she would think when she learned the kind of man he really was. A crusader like her would never approve of a guy who didn't measure up.

Mackenzie lifted her chin. "He'll kill you, too."

"You don't know that anything is going to happen to me. You barely know me, which means you can't judge what I'm capable of."

"I've seen you in action. But I'm not going to trust you, not yet. I don't do blind faith in people." She sighed, and a little of the fight in her deflated. "I'll come with you, but my eyes are wide-open."

Aaron studied her. Brown eyes, dull and lonely. Pink lips that should be tipped up in a smile, not dampened with reality. "I can live with that."

Just as long as she didn't see too much, because Aaron would come up short. That was what the women he'd tried to get close to always said. Since the last "it's not you, it's me" conversation, he'd given up. That was three years ago, not that he let the guys on the team know.

Aaron held out his hand, and Mackenzie gave him the first true smile since he'd saved her life yesterday. Why did it feel like so much longer?

He used his grip on her hand to steer her to the truck. It figured that doing Eric a favor meant he had to spend time with a woman who wasn't content with what he was doing for her. No, she had to make it personal, too, and force him to convince her to trust him. She wanted to save him from the danger she posed. He shut the passenger door and rounded the front of the truck, shaking his head.

The sound of engine revs cut through the general hum of traffic. Aaron looked back in time to see a now-familiar van cut across two lanes of traffic. It was closing in on them fast, ready to ram his truck.

A big engine roared behind them, and Mackenzie turned. It was the van the soldiers had been in. The headlights bore down on them like some macabre scene where a group of kids in a movie watched certain death head straight for them. *So this is how it ends.*

Aaron shoved the key in the ignition. The engine turned over...and over, but didn't catch. The van slammed into the back corner of the truck.

"Go!" Aaron reached past her and flung the door open.

The truck was slammed again until the tires bumped up onto the curb. Aaron shoved her out and followed her, crowding her onto the sidewalk and away from the truck. People screamed and fled in every direction in a haze of panic. Aaron's hand closed around hers as they ran. It was warmer and bigger and imbued her with some of his strength so that she ran faster, harder.

Mackenzie prayed they would be lost in the dispersing crowd. She was dragged along in his wake as he tugged her around the corner, down a back alley.

When she couldn't run anymore she yanked on his hand and bent over. She gasped and sucked in air while Aaron rubbed a firm hand up and down her back.

"Breathe."

"I'm trying." She straightened and took him in. Of course, he wasn't even winded. That must be from his soldier training. "I think I need to work out more. I seriously thought I was in good shape, but apparently that DVD was lying."

He didn't react. Didn't even crack a smile.

"We should get moving."

Mackenzie looked up and down the alley. The Dumpster was overflowing, and the smell of old garbage filled her nose. She took the hand he held out and followed him to where the alley broke onto a busy street, bright with light from restaurants and neon signs.

She sucked in breaths. "Don't you want to know how they found us again so fast? Do you think they're tracking us?"

"I think I'm not going to stand around here and risk catching a disease from all this garbage while we wait for those mercenaries or your Colombian friend to find us." Aaron let go of her hand to curl his arm around her shoulders in a protective gesture.

"He was *never* my friend."

His eyes settled on her. "My mistake."

"Yeah, it is. I didn't ask for this, okay?"

"Wrong place at the wrong time?"

She nodded, because that was essentially true. He watched for a moment at the mouth of the street before he stepped out in time to flag down a cab.

That was it? He had nothing to say? If they'd known for sure Carosa was here, then she could have had a detail of marshals instead of being saddled with Mr. U.S. Army.

Was it too much to ask for a simple conversation? They could get to know each other without her having

to tell him everything about Carosa. Aaron had said he
wanted to know what happened, but that was only so he
could protect her as a favor to his brother. If he didn't
have such an obvious devotion to his sibling, Mackenzie
would have wondered if he felt anything at all.

Aaron pulled out his phone and hit a bunch of buttons.

Forty-five minutes later, the cab exited the freeway
into a residential neighborhood she wouldn't have chosen to be in at this time of night, although to be fair it
wasn't much worse than her own street. Small houses.
Cars parked on driveways and in the street, bland vehicles that didn't cost much.

Aaron spoke to the driver. "Right here's fine."

They pulled up at a playground covered with graf-
fiti. One of the swings was broken off, leaving two
chains dangling. Mackenzie climbed out while he paid
the driver and stretched her arms up above her head,
trying to relieve the cramp in her muscles. Her legs
were shaky and her fingers wouldn't stop trembling.
Seriously, she needed a gym membership.

"Jittery?"

She looked over at Aaron.

"It's adrenaline. It'll wear off, but you'll be amped
up for a while and then you'll crash as though someone
gave you a sleeping pill."

He said it as if that was normal life for him, an everyday occurrence. Had he been on the front lines? Was
that how he got injured?

"What is that you do for the army, exactly?" For all
she knew, he could be a medic or a cook.

Something flickered in his eyes. "Soldier."

"That's it? That's all you're going to tell me?"

"I'm not allowed to give out specifics, so yeah, that's all I'm going to tell you."

Well, at least he wasn't being curt because it was part of his personality, but that he was actually required to keep it confidential. It seemed as though there was a lot of that going around. They both had enough secrets to fill Madison Square Garden. Would she ever meet anyone who wasn't a federal agent and be able to be completely open with them for a reason other than because it was required of her?

Mackenzie paced a few steps away, trying to burn some nervous energy, and watched him out the corner of her eye. Did they teach that posture in basic training? His feet were hip-width apart, and his torso was completely still, as though he was waiting for something. The only way she could think to describe it was…ready.

The jitters in her stomach eased. "What are we doing here?"

Aaron folded his arms, the material of his jacket stretched tight. "Waiting for Eric."

"Why is your brother coming here?"

"Because I texted him and asked him to." He sniffed but didn't move otherwise. "The sooner I have all the information about Carosa, the quicker we can get this resolved and I can be done with this vacation. No offense."

That wasn't a problem for her, so long as she wasn't the one who had to say it all out loud. She had no desire to relive any of it.

"Why would I be offended? You just saved my life. Again. And you've agreed to protect me for the time being, right?" He didn't argue. "I wouldn't be standing here if it wasn't for you."

The corner of his mouth twitched. "Uh, you're welcome. I think."

"Doesn't it bother you that you risk your life for your country and you can't even tell anyone about it?"

He shrugged. "Comes with the territory."

"I'm not trying to be mean, or make a judgment about the way you live your life or anything. I'm just trying to figure you out."

Maybe then she could settle herself, find peace with this life of going back and forth between the person she was and the better person she was trying to be. She felt more comfortable in her skin now, but was this truly who she was always supposed to have been?

Aaron frowned. "What's the point? It's not as if we're actually going to be friends."

Mackenzie turned away to hide the flinch. She held back the surge of emotion that felt a lot like right before you burst into tears. Her eyes were hot and her sinuses were about to burst. She might not be ready to trust him fully with her life, but did her concession mean nothing to him? Everything she had—her life, her future—was dependent on him.

She glanced at him now. If she were to allow herself to daydream about what her life could have been, she imagined it might feature someone like him. Strong and courageous, but probably a bit nicer. She could admit that, if only to herself. He was movie-star handsome and probably way out of her league.

If she wasn't in hiding, she could have struck up a conversation that might lead to him asking her out to coffee or dinner and a movie. If she was free to live her life without watching over her shoulder all the time and not wanting to get close to anyone for fear they'd get sucked into this just like—

Don't think about that.

Aaron might be a soldier, but the man she'd thought she was in love with—even if he'd never reciprocated— had been her head of security. And now he was dead.

The man who occupied her thoughts now scanned the road that stretched up the street from where they stood. He ran a hand through his hair, rubbing his head as though he was just as jittery as she was but more familiar with the feeling and better able to dispel it through such a small gesture.

It was a good thing her life wasn't conducive to starting a relationship, because she'd have been hurt by his dismissal. Now she could concentrate on protecting her heart instead of trying to figure out if there was something behind his insistence on keeping her at arm's length until the favor was done. That was fine. So long as she was alive at the end of this. Sure, it would hurt to watch him walk away, wondering what could have been.

But at least she would be alive to feel it.

SEVEN

Headlights cut a wide arc through the darkness, and then a car pulled up beside them. Mackenzie's breath caught in her throat. When the engine shut off and the driver climbed out, Aaron moved in front of her in a protective gesture. "Eric."

Mackenzie let go of the knot in her stomach and looked at her handler. Eric moved as if he was exhausted. A lot different than the last time she saw him. Was it really just that morning? Now his gray suit was rumpled and his hair looked a month past needing a cut.

When he came within arm's reach, Aaron grabbed Eric by his shirt collar and pulled him so there was an inch of space between their faces. "You seriously look awful."

Eric's lips thinned. "It's been a long day." He gave Mackenzie a small smile. "Was it really just this morning that I was in your office?"

Aaron released him. "I suppose you're not going to tell me what this is, either?"

Eric's blue eyes were a match for Aaron's, except there was something immensely sad there. Apparently satisfied with what he saw, he looked back at Aaron. "Did you get a look at the guys Carosa sent?"

"Mercenaries, probably ex-military. Eight of them. They caught up to us twice."

Mackenzie froze again with the reality that she was being hunted. Even after seeing those guys surround the truck, she was blindsided enough to close her eyes in a futile effort to shut out what was happening. This was her life. Why did it sound so much worse when they said it out loud? The past played like a movie reel in her mind. The burn of pain that felt like ice and fire at the same time, knowing she'd been shot and watching Daniel take his last breath.

Mackenzie stiffened behind him, but he couldn't do anything about it. Eric just stared, while Aaron finally understood why this meant so much to his brother. Why Mackenzie's safety was so important to him, more than just any other witness he was assigned to protect. "Man, I'm so sorry. I'm really sorry, but this doesn't have anything to do with Sarah, does it?"

She shifted again, but Aaron kept still. Eric's fiancée had been tragically injured a year ago, and was now paralyzed from the waist down. Ever since then, Eric seemed to not be able to let go of the need to see Sarah in every woman he met.

Eric shook his head. "It's not like that."

"So you're going to put your job at risk and protect Mackenzie at all costs because you can't let your fiancée go?"

"You think I want to watch Carosa swagger around after exactly the same kind of person who hurt Sarah and killed her family? I won't let anyone else become a victim of selfish people who think they're above the law." Eric's eyes blazed. "I didn't ask you to stay because I can't get over what happened. I asked you to stay because I have to focus on the hunt for the leak, and I don't want to see another woman suffer the way Sarah has."

Eric's fiancée hadn't wanted anything to do with him after the accident. Eric had tried to get her to let him back into her life, but the pain was too great for both of them. In the end he'd had to accept the reality that Sarah wanted it to be over, and move on.

"Um, sorry...but who is Sarah?" Mackenzie's voice was small and more than a little concerned.

Aaron found Mackenzie's hand and gave it a squeeze. "Eric—"

His brother pulled his gaze from Mackenzie back to Aaron. "Outside of you, I don't know who I can trust."

Aaron gave his brother a short nod. Eric needed him, and Aaron wouldn't let anything happen to his brother, his brother's job or anyone else who was innocent and couldn't defend themselves.

He looked at Mackenzie. Her eyes were wide as she took it all in.

"So what now?" Mackenzie asked.

Eric squeezed his eyes shut. "Nothing's changed. Aaron keeps you safe while I find the leak."

Aaron frowned. "Shouldn't you be getting her a new identity and flying her somewhere undisclosed? That's what you guys do, isn't it?"

"If Carosa discovered her location once already, there's nothing to say he can't do it again. And I have to let this internal investigation play out if we're going to find the leak. That's the most likely explanation for what's happening. Regardless of what the police think, it's more likely Carosa hired someone to slash your tires and shoot at you. The mercenaries were probably hired, too, to take you to him so he can get his revenge."

Mackenzie swallowed, her face pale with fear.

Eric continued, "I will get to the bottom of this. It's the only way to keep your identity safe…not to mention anyone else Carosa or the leak decides they want found. This could turn into a bidding war that puts everyone in witness protection in Phoenix in danger."

Mackenzie moved around him to step closer to Eric. "I can help." They both turned to her. "Look, I'm not going to sit around waiting for Carosa to find us again when we could be doing something. I'm not going anywhere and I don't want him hurting anyone else."

Aaron sighed. *So much for giving up.* He kept his eyes on his brother. "We can help you find out who you work with that has a connection to the Carosa cartel. No offense, but you look as if you could use a few extra pairs of hands, and we don't have anything more pressing going on right now."

"The guy's name is Schweitzer." Eric started to shake his head. "But I—"

"Have a team ready to help you?" Aaron studied his brother. "Have a clue who is doing this and a plan to catch them in the act? Have a way to get irrefutable evidence so you can close the file on this quickly and cleanly?" He waited a beat and saw the defeat in his brother's eyes. "Didn't think so."

"Good." Mackenzie squeezed his hand. "Let's make a plan."

Aaron glanced at the woman beside him. Every moment he spent with Mackenzie peeled back another layer of who she was. She might be scared, but she was also dedicated, hardworking, compassionate, wise and unabashedly tenacious.

He needed to keep this about business, take care of things and move on. Between work and his family, Aaron didn't have any room for someone who would sneak into his heart and take up residence before he even realized she was there.

Back when he was dating, it was usually casual, friendly and light enough he could walk away at the end of the evening having had a good time. He'd had no intention of getting involved any deeper, though occasionally it happened naturally.

Mackenzie wasn't like any woman he'd ever spent time with before, which was exactly why he couldn't let her in. Aaron had seen what Sarah's injury did to Eric, what their dad's incarceration had done to his mom. There was no way he was going there. Not when his own mistakes had cost his team so much. His first shot at being team leader, and he was left with an injury while his teammate was forced to retire.

Aaron put his hand on the side of Eric's neck. "Go home and get some sleep. In the morning go to work and do your job. Get us what you can, and I'll take care of this. You have my word I won't let anything happen to Mackenzie."

Because if a good woman was killed, then Aaron would have to right the wrong—a wrong the justice system should have taken care of long before now. And Aaron didn't know if he could take another black mark on his life.

The sound of automatic gunfire rang out across the

park. Aaron grabbed Mackenzie with one hand and Eric with the other and hit the sidewalk.

He would really like to know how these guys kept finding them.

"What do we do?"

Mackenzie glanced around from her prone position on the sidewalk. Gravel dug into her hip, but she didn't dare move. The gunfire had stopped. What were they waiting for? Did they really want to take her alive and undamaged like Aaron had said? It seemed more as if they were toying with her so she would freak out. But why would they need her to be unhinged, unless that was part of Carosa's twisted revenge plan?

Nothing about this made any sense.

Eric whipped out his gun. "Mackenzie, get to my car."

Aaron's face was tight, his lips pressed into a thin line. In the yellow light of the streetlamp there was something dark in his eyes. "Both of you, start crawling." He had a gun out, too, and his voice didn't invite any discussion.

Eric's lips thinned. "You go with Mackenzie. I'll take care of the mercenaries."

"No, you go with Mackenzie." Aaron's face invited no argument. "Since I'm the one they're trying to kill, I'm the one who gets to be the diversion."

When Aaron reached the car, he leaned over and spoke to Eric. "On my word, you're going to cover me."

By the look of it, Eric didn't like that idea. "You need to get in the car, too. Get Mackenzie to safety."

"Now. Rendezvous on the north side, but only if it's clear."

Eric fired his gun in rapid succession into the trees. Mackenzie covered her ears. Aaron rushed away and she ducked. Faster gunshots spurted back at them. Eric ducked down also, and shots pinged off the car. "If the mercenaries don't kill him, I will!"

Aaron disappeared behind a bush on the far side of the park, away from the gunfire. That was something, at least. Was it a diversion? She prayed it would work, even if Eric wasn't happy Aaron had made the decision. Minutes later there was a group of gunshots, and then silence.

Mackenzie stuck her elbows out and kept her body to the ground as she moved, like one of those military movies where they crawled through the mud. The asphalt was hot from the day's sun and Eric grunted beside her.

"Shouldn't we call for help?"

"We have to get you to safety first, or we'll be dead before the cops could get here."

She kept moving until she reached the car door, lifted up a fraction and reached for the handle.

"No. Not yet."

She turned to Eric and whispered, "I thought we were going to get out of here."

"We are. But let's give Aaron enough time to draw their attention away."

He watched for a moment. Waited.

"Okay, in the car." Eric opened the door and she crawled across the seat.

"What's happening? Is Aaron dead?"

"No. He's keeping them busy so we can escape. Now get down in the foot well and stay down."

Mackenzie's breath came in snatches. "How do you know he isn't dead?"

"Because those shots we heard were his."

"What now? Are we supposed to pick him up or something?"

"That's what he meant by rendezvous. But only if it doesn't put us in more danger."

Eric started the engine, his body shifted low in the seat. Mackenzie curled up, her body cramped in the small space below the glove box. Aaron had put himself in harm's way so they could escape? She focused on Eric's face as he shot out of the parking lot.

He scanned the area and the rearview mirror and finally said, "Okay, it's clear. You can get up."

Mackenzie crawled onto the seat, feeling the grime of the day and everything that had happened.

Eric motioned behind them. "Your go bag is on the backseat. I stopped by your house and grabbed it for you."

"Thank you." Mackenzie pulled it forward and held it on her knees. She had clean clothes now. Was it selfish to want a shower, too?

She looked around, watching for his return. Aaron was trained for battle, but maybe that didn't work when it was a regular neighborhood.

"Why did he do that?"

Eric glanced at her. "Stay behind?"

She nodded.

"It's what he does."

"As a soldier?" Her brain was spinning with all of it. She wanted to tell him to go back so she could find out if Aaron was okay. They were just going to leave him there?

"Yeah, that, too. But since we were kids he was always that way." Eric flipped on his turn signal and slowed for a stoplight. "Always getting into fights and claiming he slipped. One day he came home covered in mud with a black eye. I was sick with mono or something like that. He said I was faking it just so I could stay home and read comics, but I wasn't. Our foster mom was good, you know? Way better than our real mom."

Mackenzie looked at him. "You were in foster care?"

Eric nodded. "Dad was in jail for armed robbery back then. He's out now, but neither of us are about to make the trip to California just to see him. Mom left us with the neighbor so she could go get high. Couple days later the neighbor called child protective services, and we were placed with Bill and Frankie."

"Wow."

"He's always been the one who took care of…everything. I might have resented it for a while, but that was my issue. I couldn't ask for a better brother than Aaron, even if he might take it too far sometimes. But I'm making peace with that."

Too far? Eric seemed to think Aaron had done something that he didn't think was a good thing. Both of them seemed so cautious that instead of trusting themselves to others, they retreated to each other every time.

Was it familial love that bound them together? Mackenzie had never known family to be that way. Her parents had walked away the day she joined WITSEC, too enamored with their high-society lifestyle to bother following their daughter into witness protection.

It was a powerful love these two brothers had. Mackenzie could only hope that in her life she'd find someone who would love her that way.

She glanced at Eric. "Thank you for sharing that with me."

Eric gave her a small smile. "There's nothing Aaron wants more in the world than to protect the people he loves."

Mackenzie wanted to know what would happen if feelings were to develop between them. She'd like to think he could feel that way about her, but he held himself back so much she couldn't be sure it was even possible. As soon as Carosa was stopped, Aaron would return to his job with the army and she would go back to her life. They would never see each other again.

In the short time they had left, she wanted to press Aaron and make him open up to her. Not because she liked him, but because the world would be a poorer place if he never loved anyone but his family. Still, if she pushed too far he would likely retreat even further.

Eric turned left and then left again. He stopped at a corner that looked like a different end of the park from where Mackenzie and Aaron had arrived. He tapped his foot, flipping his cell phone over and over in his hand. Then he froze. "There he is."

A figure stepped out of the trees, looked both ways and ran toward them. Aaron slid into the backseat just as two men in black fatigues ran out of the park, pointed their guns at the car and started shooting.

Mackenzie screamed.

Eric gunned the engine and they sped away.

EIGHT

Eric dropped them at a motel just before two o'clock in the morning. It was the kind of place where you paid in cash and no one asked for ID, but at least there was a connecting door between their two rooms that Aaron kept unlocked. As it was, Mackenzie spent most of the night staring at the ceiling. The minute she closed her eyes, she would descend into the world of memory. It happened over and over. Her body would relax enough that she dozed, and shortly after she would wake with a jerk, tangled in the sheets.

She could still hear the gunshots from the park. They had reminded her of that night years ago and the horrible things she'd witnessed. For years after it happened, she had nightmares. The anniversary of that night was always the worst. She would wake up and have to run to the bathroom. Sweating on the floor beside the toilet got old really fast, but thankfully her night hadn't been that bad.

Still, she didn't get any sleep, either.

When sunrise hit the back of the curtains, she got up. Instead of her usual as-fast-as-possible shower, Mackenzie took her time and let the hot water wake her. Her go bag that Eric had brought to the park for her was packed with two spare changes of clothes, extra underwear and shoes. But it was nothing like her WITSEC persona would normally wear. When she opened it, she was filled with a sudden rush of nerves. What if she looked like an idiot?

High fashion might not be her thing now, but it had been once. She couldn't remember the last time she wore jeans with rhinestones—even fake ones. Would she look good, or like a country music wannabe? And who cared anyway, since the only person who was going to see her was Aaron?

She dumped the contents on the bed in a spill of clothes. The jeans had come from a resale store and were prefaded, and the pink top was admittedly cute, but she hadn't had anything that bright in her closet in years. It reminded her of Eva. Was she mad they'd missed dinner?

Hopefully her friend wasn't singlehandedly running the center. But who knew how she was doing? Mackenzie couldn't even call and check. Maybe Chris—the teacher Mackenzie had covered for the first day Aaron was there—was still out with his sick son.

Eva always commented on how she dressed. But Eva just didn't get that, when she was younger, Mackenzie had dressed for the express purpose of drawing attention to herself. Her life now wasn't just about staying below the radar, it was also about not being the person she used to be.

She would probably never be able to tell Eva her story. In fact, something made Mackenzie think she might never see her friend again. Eric would set her up with a new identity in some half-empty state where she could live in the mountains in seclusion, hiding from Carosa for the rest of her life. Aaron was no doubt a skilled soldier, but would he be able to go up against a drug cartel?

Mackenzie wanted to scream. Just walk outside, look up at the sky and shriek until she had no breath left. She would surely be alone and hiding for the rest of her life. But she would still do it, because it was the small bit of power she had left.

She wanted to hold on to what she could control for a little bit longer—long enough to balance the scales.

When his friend's sedan pulled up outside, Aaron stepped out of his motel room into the dry heat of eight o'clock in the morning. Hours had passed since they'd been shot at, but he could still hear it ringing in his ears. He needed reinforcements and was glad he'd been able to reach Sabine Laduca last night. His former team leader's fiancée was a former CIA agent. If anyone could help, it was Sabine.

Sabine's smile was wide as she stepped out of the car, and if he'd been able to see her eyes behind the huge sunglasses she wore, there would probably be a gleam of mischief there.

"You look a little rough this morning."

He snorted. "I'm thinking that's an understatement."

"Bad night?"

"You could call it that, yeah. I liked the automatic weapons especially."

Sabine pushed her sunglasses to the top of her head, her eyes wide. It hadn't been that long since she'd been branded a rogue CIA agent and became the subject of a manhunt while she searched for her brother's killer.

Ben—Sabine's brother and Aaron's former teammate—had been killed in action, but it was a hit that was paid for. Ben had been murdered by Sabine's mom.

It had taken the whole team working, and especially Aaron's former team leader, Doug, to get her out of that fix. But now her mom was dead, and Sabine had Doug's ring on her finger.

"Enough of that, though." Aaron grinned. "Mademoiselle."

Sabine laughed and gave him a quick one-armed hug. "Yeah, yeah. Cut it out, I'm an engaged woman."

"Doesn't make you any less beautiful." Aaron said it without thinking, but it hit home. She looked happy. And the way she looked at Doug? Aaron's former team leader was a fortunate guy. But Doug would say it was God's blessing.

As a kid, Aaron had gone to church. After all, it was part of the deal he'd struck with his foster parents. Still, he didn't see how God had done anything much for him, let alone bless him. That was why he'd left faith behind when he went into the army. And he'd done fine without it, so why change things now, simply because his friend had some kind of revelation?

Aaron motioned to the car. "What do you have for me?"

"One staid, boring, completely unnoticeable car bought with cash. The plates are still registered to the dealership until we do the paperwork."

"Great, thanks."

Sabine's gaze flicked to the motel room beside his. "So what's she like, this Mackenzie Winters?"

Aaron narrowed his eyes. "What do you think you know?"

"Nothing. I didn't even do a full computer search or anything. You should be proud of me."

He wanted to roll his eyes, but let her have her moment. She could find out just about anything if she wanted to. Maybe not that Mackenzie was in WITSEC, but Sabine could likely make a good guess if she uncovered enough evidence that suggested Mackenzie's identity had been constructed instead of lived. She had been trained by the CIA after all.

Sabine smiled. "It's a great thing she's doing, with those kids at the center. Only… I'm just curious why she needs protecting? I can guess since you told me your brother, the U.S. Marshal is involved, but I wouldn't want to assume."

"Good. Let's keep it that way." Of course she would figure it out. He should never have told her this had to do with Eric. "We'll be fine, Sabine. I've got this covered."

"I know you do. It's just…with Doug in Tampa talking to that guy about a job—" Aaron had talked to Doug before he left town about the interview. His former team leader was still looking for work that would suit him as well as the army had.

"I'm kind of—" she came close and whispered, as if it was a secret "—bored."

"Wedding planning isn't turning out to be as exciting as you thought?"

Sabine laughed. "No, it's not that at all. I mean, it's going to be great getting married and then being married. But this seems interesting, too." She waved her hand, encompassing him and the motel rooms. "It could be fun."

"Sure, running for your life when people are shooting at you is great fun."

Sabine rolled her eyes. "You don't have to say it like that."

"And if I let you get shot at while Doug was out of town, what then?"

She sighed. "Fine. I'll go back to tulle and sequins and vol-au-vents."

A cab pulled up in the parking lot and Sabine held up one finger to the driver. "But if you need anything, and I mean *anything,* you give me a call, okay?"

Aaron held on to the laughter that wanted to spill out. "Sure, Sabine. I'll do that."

At the knock, Mackenzie stood up from the bed with her shoes tied but didn't cross the room. "Who is it?" As if she didn't know. She'd seen Aaron out front talking to a glamorously beautiful woman fifteen minutes ago, before the shower went on in his room. Of course he was in a relationship. Aaron was a good-looking man, and he could be nice enough…when he wanted.

Mackenzie pushed away the ridiculous feeling of disappointment and looked through the peephole.

"It's me."

She rolled her eyes and opened the door. Aaron stood there with one hand high on the door frame looking more casual than she'd ever felt in her life. He wore designer jeans and a collared T-shirt with three buttons. How did he manage to look like a movie star when his hair was still mussed from sleep? She probably had bags under her eyes.

He smiled. "Ready to go?"

"Where did you get a change of clothes from?"

"I ordered them."

"From that woman who was here?" Mackenzie's

sleep-deprived brain made her mouth blurt it out before she could catch it. "Never mind. It's none of my business."

"Her name is Sabine."

So she had a cool name. That didn't mean Mackenzie had to like her, or the way she smiled at Aaron as if they were best pals. "Are we coming back? Should I bring my bag?"

"Pack it and carry it with you. I'm not sure if we're coming back, so it's better to hold on to everything since it's not much anyway."

Mackenzie crammed her things in her bag and zipped it closed. "Where are we headed?"

He was frowning at her. "I figured breakfast, for starters."

She ignored his obvious need for her to explain why she was in a bad mood and said, "Great, I'm starving. Is there somewhere within walking distance?"

He motioned over his shoulder. "Made a call last night and procured us a new ride that Sabine brought, along with clothes. The car is untraceable, so we'll be able to stay off the radar of anyone trying to find us." His eyes studied her. "But a walk actually sounds good. There's a diner around the corner."

Mackenzie hesitated. "Am I supposed to know what that means, you 'procured us a ride' or should I just not ask?"

He shrugged. "Means what it means. I didn't want to leave you unprotected, so I needed the stuff brought to me. I made a call and got it done."

Mackenzie couldn't help it. She had to ask, even if that made her weak and needy. "So who is Sabine? Other than someone who will drop everything just be-

cause you called and show up before breakfast with a
car that no one can trace and some clothes."

And didn't that just burn a little. Mackenzie was a
nice person, wasn't she? There must be some other reason she didn't have friends like that. Perhaps she had
been such an awful person in the past that it showed
through now. Or this was yet more punishment.

Maybe everyone in WITSEC felt this alone, a pa-
riah who couldn't seem to make friends. Mackenzie
had to hide every single thing she was actually good
at, holding it at arm's length while she pushed papers
and tried to convince herself she was doing something
worthwhile.

"You really want to know about Sabine?"

"Am I not allowed? Is that something we're not supposed to talk about?"

He sighed. "Mackenzie. You're making this a bigger
deal than it needs to be. She's just a friend, who is actually more the fiancée of a friend of mine. Sabine had
some troubles a while back. I worked with her brother
when he was killed, and my team leader then, Doug,
helped her with her problem and they fell in love."

"Right." Mackenzie slung the bag over one shoulder.
"Lead the way, then."

So she wasn't his girlfriend, but he still probably had
someone special in his life. There was no way a guy
who looked like he did was available. Unless there was
something wrong with him.

She'd met enough good-looking people in her former life to know they often didn't have character to
match. And while he didn't seem completely as though
he thought the world revolved around him, he definitely

possessed an air of authority—the kind that assumed you'd either hop along for the ride or leave.

Aaron grabbed her backpack and they walked by the faded gray car parked in front of their motel rooms. He glanced at her. "You look great, by the way."

Maybe that was his idea of an apology. She looked down at the clothes she had packed. "Not exactly my style." She might actually blend in with women her age for once, instead of looking like a librarian spinster.

"Still." Aaron held the door to the diner open for her. "You look nice."

The chain diner was one she only went to every few months when the need for carbs overwhelmed the desire not to eat a thousand calories in one sitting. They found an open booth, and she studied the options, trying to convince herself she was going to be strong and get the fruit and oatmeal. She let the plastic menu drop. Maybe it was best to accept the inevitable.

A voluptuous waitress poured coffee for them, and Mackenzie shot her a smile. "I need biscuits and gravy."

Aaron nodded. "What the lady wants, she shall have."

The waitress leaned in toward Mackenzie. "You've got to love a man with that attitude."

Aaron laughed, and the waitress walked away smiling.

Mackenzie squinted at him and crossed her arms on the table. "Why are you in such a good mood all of a sudden?"

"I can't be happy?"

"It's just weird. You bump into my life—literally—and all of a sudden you're a mainstay. You never really talk to me except to tell me what to do. You're in my business and being my protector. Not that I'm not grateful. And now I'm supposed to share all my secrets?"

A smile played on his lips. "You might want to take a breath."

She sighed. "Now what? You want to be friends or something?"

Aaron's eyes widened, and he took a sip of his coffee. When he replaced his cup on the table, he looked up at her. "There's nothing wrong with making this whole thing more enjoyable by being pleasant to one another."

Mackenzie stared at him. "Who are you?"

Aaron tipped his head back and laughed. Mackenzie just sat there. It was as though the stress of the past two days had been wiped away and they were just two people sharing breakfast.

It was great for him that he could push it aside, but she wasn't wired that way. Nor was she convinced this would ever be over for her or that she'd come to a point when she wasn't running from Carosa. Or a bunch of mercenaries who seemed to be able to show up everywhere they went.

He cleared his throat. "Seriously, though, this will be a whole lot more pleasant if we get along."

"So tell me about yourself, then. What is your job like? Did you get injured on a mission? Is that what you're recovering from?"

"Yeah, it was a work injury." He didn't say any more, just reached for his cup and took another sip.

Mackenzie took a chance on a different but not less sensitive subject. "Who was Sarah?"

He blinked. "Eric's Sarah?"

"He mentioned her last night. It sounded as if something happened to her. Was she killed?" Mackenzie swallowed. "Will you tell me what happened?"

NINE

Aaron would have much rather gone back to the light-hearted banter, or Mackenzie trying to discern whether or not he was in a relationship—which was interesting in itself.

The waitress delivered his skillet with everything and Mackenzie's biscuits and gravy.

The woman across the table was a pretty good distraction with those different clothes on, but she still had her hair in that awful bun that made her face look pinched. Whatever it took to convince him that he wasn't drawn to her, he had to focus on that.

When this was done, she would find someone else, and Aaron would go back to being single and trying to repair the damage he'd done to his career. And his friend's life.

He set his fork down. He should probably get on with the story.

"Sarah was... Sarah. Beautiful. Smart, like crazy smart. She was an accountant when she met Eric and they started dating, but after they got engaged she fell in with the wrong people before he could stop it. Then they had her trapped with threats to her mom and dad.

Eric had her contact the FBI, but they couldn't get the evidence for more than surveillance and definitely not enough to get her, or her parents, in witness protection.

"Eric set her parents up so they could disappear, and she went back to work, under cover of the FBI. She handed the feds everything she could about how her employers forced her to launder money for them. Eric didn't like it, but figured the FBI would keep her safe. Aside from them running, too, there wasn't much else they could do."

Aaron glanced at the room of diners but didn't really see any of them. "Sarah discovered that what she knew was just the tip of things. You could make a case that she got cocky and pushed it too far so they made a move to kill her, but the fact is both she and her parents were gunned down in a supposedly random drive-by. As if no one would see the correlation. Sarah was paralyzed and her parents were killed. Eric is convinced someone at the FBI leaked the fact that she was working for them and her employers retaliated. It's just too big of a coincidence to be anything else."

"That must have taken a lot of guts, for her to do that."

"What it was is stupid."

Mackenzie gasped. "How can you say that? She did the right thing, trying to bring criminals to justice."

"Might have been right, but it wasn't smart. Now her parents are dead, and my brother doesn't trust anyone because she pushed him away."

Mackenzie frowned. "You don't think there's a mole?"

He shrugged. "Maybe there is, maybe there isn't. It doesn't mean it has anything to do with you. I'm not big on coincidences, but it doesn't totally fit. Unless it's a smoke screen to cover someone helping Carosa. Either way, if it puts you in danger then we have a problem, because there's more than just Carosa and his mercenaries to worry about, and that's enough by itself."

"What if we could find out?"

Aaron studied her. "Eric got to you."

"So what if he did? He lost the relationship he had with the woman he loved and I feel for him, which means I have a heart. He might be barking up the wrong tree—"

"Let's just call it what it is. Paranoia."

"Still, even if he's just grieving the loss of his relationship and—"

"Unhinged?"

"You really think that? Explain to me what's wrong about helping him make sense of all this."

Aaron swallowed the last bite of his eggs and tossed his fork on the plate with a clatter. "Those kids at that center of yours aren't enough of a crusade—you have to take up Eric's cause, too?"

Why did she need to save everyone? He didn't even understand it. She was practically an alien species. It was a good thing he didn't have his own crusade, or she'd probably take that on, as well.

Mackenzie flinched. "Since when did helping people become a bad thing?"

"I didn't say it was. But if it consumes your whole life because all you're doing is using up your energy fighting for other people's causes, then how is that good?"

"Because they need me."

Aaron covered her hand with his. "I'm just saying

you might not be doing them a favor if all you're doing is killing yourself in the process."

"That's my choice."

"But why would you choose that?"

She pulled her hand out from under his. "That's none of your business."

"Maybe I'm making it my business."

Her eyes went wide. "What does that mean?"

"I'm not going to protect you so you can go kill yourself trying to save everyone else. If we're going to help Eric, we do it my way, because you seriously have no idea what you're getting into."

"Wow, thanks. That's so flattering." Her mouth flattened into a sneer. "You need my help, oh, poor defenseless female, because you don't know how to do anything except teach people how to sing, and you don't even do that because you hide in the office all day."

Aaron ran his hand through his hair. "I didn't mean it like that, okay? You have plenty of skills. Unfortunately, none of them have anything to do with covert investigation into a federal agency. Which the FBI is already doing, I might add."

Her head cocked to one side. "And you do?"

"Actually, yeah."

She didn't relax, still energized with anger. "What do you do?"

He really wasn't supposed to tell her. But if a woman in WITSEC couldn't keep a secret, who could? And she needed to know he could do this. "I already told you I'm a sergeant in the army. My unit is small and specializes in missions that require stealth and finesse."

"Like James Bond?"

"That would be espionage. We're talking about soldiers."

"Special soldiers."

He grinned. "I like to think so."

"Like Special Forces?"

"I'm not going to lie, it is specialized work. For the purposes of protecting you, you can know at least that much. We train constantly when we're not on missions just so that we stay sharp. Each of my team knows the other's movements like their own. They have to, or one of us could misjudge something and end up getting killed."

"And do they all have big egos like you do?"

He laughed. "Definitely. We work extremely hard to be the best. You can't afford to be average. That's how people get dead."

Aaron waited while she processed this information. She'd known him as a bodyguard and soldier, an average guy. Not to mention there was a disconnect between sitting in a diner and what she likely knew of covert ops from movies and TV.

After a minute or so of her opening her mouth but saying nothing, he smiled. "Feel better now that you know?"

There might be more to the story, since he'd have to fight to regain his standing within the team. But, his disastrous debut as leader notwithstanding, Mackenzie needed to know he was capable of protecting her from Carosa. He might have messed everything up, but he wasn't going to let anything happen to her.

Mackenzie frowned. "I guess. I mean, there are worse people to have protecting you than a Special Forces soldier, I suppose."

"Uh, thanks." Apparently she didn't get the significance of what he'd just told her. It was a huge thing in his world for someone to know what they did for a living. Delta Force wasn't just a job, it was their lives. And keeping it a secret meant everything.

Together they walked to the front door of the restaurant, where he held the door open for her.

"Do we have somewhere to be now?"

Aaron saw the fatigue in her eyes. "No. I think we both need a breather for the rest of today. After we check ourselves out, we can drive and find a new motel, get some rest, hole up for a few days somewhere quiet."

Long enough for him to look into Eric's coworkers, specifically the man he'd mentioned, Schweitzer. And maybe long enough for Aaron to find out how Carosa's mercenaries had found them twice now. Long enough to get some distance from a woman who smelled like whipped cream and sunshine.

She frowned. "Didn't we push it by hanging out here and getting breakfast?"

And miss the most important meal of the day? "Gotta eat somewhere. But it's probably a good idea to keep moving rather than risk being found. They do seem to have a knack for locating us."

She looked around.

"Everything's going to be fine, okay?"

"Sure," she said. But she didn't sound as if she believed him.

He waited while she let herself into her room. She strode to the bathroom, pulled back the shower curtain and then came out and looked under the bed.

"Checking for bad guys? I thought that was my job."

Mackenzie straightened. "No, I was just making sure

I hadn't forgotten my shampoo, or a sock, or something."

Aaron smiled. "Gotcha."

Wheels screeched to a halt outside. Aaron pulled back the curtain an inch. A now-familiar black van was parked out front. "Time to go."

"How do we get out of here?"

A fist pounded on the door. "We know you're in there. Come out, or we let ourselves in!"

Aaron pulled out his sidearm. "Bathroom window. Now."

Mackenzie swung her backpack over her shoulder and strode to the bathroom. He crowded in behind her and shut the door.

Mackenzie turned back, wide-eyed. "I don't think it opens."

"It will." He moved her aside and shielded her with his body while he used the butt of the gun to shatter the frosted glass of the tiny bathroom window. Then he knocked out the remaining shards.

He heard the front door hit the wall and hauled Mackenzie toward the window, ignoring her shriek. "Go!"

The bathroom door flew open and a small canister rolled into the room. Aaron spun Mackenzie and stuck her face in his shoulder, covering her head with his arms while he squeezed his eyes shut as the flash bang went off.

He went for the window again to the sound of boots stomping through the room and calls of "Clear!"

Mackenzie gripped his arm, her other hand grasping a handful of Aaron's shirt. She was ready to move, but a surge of men wearing black fatigues and carrying AR-

15s stormed in. All the weapons were pointed at Aaron. He forced his fingers to still and not reach for his gun.

One of the men spoke. "Lani Anders, you need to come with us."

Lani Anders? The image of a teenage star dressed to look like an adult flashed in his mind, but Aaron didn't have time to process the name and what that meant about Mackenzie and the girl she'd been so many years ago.

How was he supposed to get them out of this? He only had a handgun and Mackenzie gripping the back of his shirt, trusting him not to let her down. Fear was a foreign feeling and one he wasn't sure he liked at all.

Aaron stared them down, four men from the park. Guns for hire—that was never good. Although the fact they only worked for the money they made might be his doorway in.

He focused on the point man. "Whatever you're being paid, I'll give you double to walk out the door right now."

The mercenary's eyes flicked to Aaron. "Think not, dude."

Another of the hired guns pulled on Mackenzie's arm. "Walk or we kill you both."

TEN

Mackenzie whimpered, not taking her eyes from him—as though pleading with him to do something. Was he supposed to burst into motion and save them, against four guys with automatic weapons? No one was that good in real life, just in movies.

The fear in her eyes churned his stomach. They were mercenaries; they wouldn't get paid if she wasn't delivered—intact.

She was pulled away. A tear rolled down her face. He wanted to reach for her, and not just because he was there to protect her and failure would be awkward to explain to his brother. He'd spent breakfast looking at her across the table, seeing her smile. And now he really didn't want to lose her.

"Aaron..." His name was a low, keening cry. But he couldn't do anything.

Didn't she know any move he made would lead to him being killed and maybe even her, too? He didn't mind taking risks with his own life, but he wasn't about to lose her. That would be a lousy end to his vacation.

"Move, woman. Now."

Aaron gritted his teeth at the steroid-induced soldier

talk. What was with this Neanderthal? Mackenzie didn't release her grip on Aaron's arm. He moved an inch. A gun muzzle swung to him and stopped a hairsbreadth from the end of his nose. "I've warned you already. You wanna get dead?"

Aaron shook his head a fraction. "You've got no problem from me."

His hands curled into fists. They weren't going to kill her. They were going to take her to Carosa, and Aaron was going to run them down and get Mackenzie back—if she would just let go of his arm.

The mercenary turned to her. "You get to walking or I make a hole in your man's head."

She released Aaron's arm immediately. It was the right thing. He couldn't lose her. And maybe in the process of getting her back he could get a lead on Carosa, or find out if there really was a leak in the Marshals Service.

The minute they were out the door he'd be after them, jumping in his car and gunning the engine in pursuit. One last flash of hurt in Mackenzie's eyes and she was out the door, surrounded by three mercenaries like a Secret Service detail. Aaron stood fast, waiting for his chance to go after her.

The gun butt came out of nowhere. Pain drummed through his temple and everything went black.

Mackenzie clenched her jaw to keep her teeth from chattering. The plastic tie she was bound with was thin and cut into her wrists. Her arms were pulled back, making her shoulders feel as if they were on fire. Tears filled her eyes, but she held them at bay, not wanting four macho men to see her break down.

He'd just stood there and let her go.

Now she knew what kind of man Aaron was—the kind who didn't come through for you when it really counted. He'd let the soldiers take her to Carosa to die. What a fool she'd been to trust him, to believe that he would keep her safe when he only cared about protecting his brother's reputation. Had this been his plan all along? Wait for the first opportunity and then hand her over and walk away?

Mackenzie shuddered as icy tendrils of fear crept through her.

The van raced west along Interstate 10. What if he was just a car or two behind them? Maybe he really did care about her safety. That was possible, right? Maybe he'd wanted her to get caught so he could find Carosa. But then what? She squeezed her eyes shut. There was no one else in the world she wanted to rescue her. Just Aaron.

They turned left and she saw a sign for a small municipal airport.

Mackenzie looked back, but no one took the turn to the gate behind them. Aaron's car was nowhere in sight. He'd let her go, and if there was any hope for her, she was going to have to make it herself.

The van was waved through security and drove between two hangars onto the tarmac where a small plane was waiting. Tears ran down her cheeks. Here, little more than one hundred and fifty miles from the Mexican border, Mackenzie faced the fact she would never have the chance to say goodbye to any of the center kids or Eva.

She would be in Carosa's hands, dead in a fit of revenge. Killed by a man who thought saving face for his family—killing the woman he thought had brought the cartel low—was more important than life.

Aaron came around on the carpet of the motel. His arms were bound behind him, so he arched his back and slipped his feet between his elbows, bringing his arms to the front and almost kneeing himself in the face in the process. *Ouch.* Then he lay back on the floor and sucked in air, trying not to black out while his shoulder screamed with pain.

Lani Anders.

It was almost unreal. It didn't make any sense at all that Mackenzie was the same girl who danced and sung in packed arenas all those years ago. Aaron had been in the early days of basic training then, and after that came his first posting—to Georgia. Lani had been all over the magazines and radio, her songs heard everywhere.

He pulled out his phone and made a call from the motel floor.

Eric answered on the second ring. "What's up, brother?"

Aaron sniffed, pushing away the throb. "Well, I'm tied up for starters. They got Mackenzie. Or, I should say, former teen superstar *Lani Anders.*"

Eric muttered something Aaron didn't catch and then said, "Where are you?"

"Lying on the floor in—"

"Well, get up. Go after her."

"The guy clocked me with his weapon. Give me a second, and quit shouting." Aaron sat up and focused on his boot laces. "Four mercenaries in a black van. It's really starting to make me angry how they seem to be able to find us everywhere we go."

"What? How?"

"Exactly. On the way to the restaurant, at the park and now at the motel. It's been barely twelve hours since the last attack and they show up. *Again.* They have to be tracking us. There's no other explanation."

Aaron got to his feet and swayed a little. Once he was sitting in his car he'd be okay. If he could find his knife and cut the ties on his hands. "I have to get going. Any idea how to track a van without letting anyone know we're tracking it?"

Eric sighed. "Why don't you call Sabine?"

"I can't, man. Doug will kill me if I involve her more than I already have."

It was true. His former team leader wouldn't want Sabine involved, even if she was an ex-spy. And for a teen pop star who'd used her looks to get what she wanted? The mental picture of Lani Anders juxtaposed with Mackenzie's face, scared and being taken away… Aaron couldn't get it to fit. No wonder she hadn't wanted to tell him.

Eric said, "Never mind Doug, I'll kill you if you let Mackenzie get hurt, and Sabine will kill you if she finds out you're in trouble and didn't call her. Didn't she help you get that car?"

Aaron found his backpack and pulled out the multitool his brother had sent him for Christmas. It took some doing, but he got the knife out and sawed through his bonds. "I'll give her a call."

Mackenzie was shuffled out of the van by the combined motion of two big men, which was sort of helpful since her hands were tied in front of her. They just moved and she got caught up in the wave. She stumbled finding her feet, her hands slamming on the ground. Her knee hit the asphalt and pain shot to her hip, but no one came to her assistance. One of the soldiers in front turned to see what was happening and waited while she stood up.

Apparently it didn't matter if she was a little damaged upon delivery.

They walked her across the tarmac toward the plane. The horizon was a haze of heat coming up from the runway. An aircraft took off behind them in a rush of engine noise and wind that whipped her hair across her face.

Mackenzie shuffled along, dragging it out, trying to make it take as long as possible to get to the plane. Once she was on board, they would be gone and Aaron would have to search longer and harder for her.

If he even intended to.

She scanned the area. It was too open to run. They would either shoot her or chase her down in no time. But what other choice did she have? She'd been pretty good at track before she quit high school to go on the road full time. Maybe sneakers and none of that heavy stuff they carried on their belts—and the fact they didn't seem interested in killing her right here—meant she might have a chance to get away.

The front end of a gun poked at her back and she continued her steady forward shuffle pretending she didn't feel well. Good thing she didn't have to feign anything. The knee she'd fallen on stung and her jeans were starting to stick. Was she bleeding?

Aaron wasn't coming. He knew who he'd been protecting. Maybe that was why he wasn't coming. Maybe he'd decided she wasn't worth it.

Quit feeling sorry for yourself. You need to get away from these guys.

Car tires screeched as a vehicle wound a semicircle in front of them, cutting off their forward progress. Mackenzie shrieked and the men dived out of the way. She pushed away the question of whether it was smart or not and tore across the stretch of runway to the nearest building. She pumped her legs over and over, ignoring the sting in her knee and thinking only of safety and freedom. Her bound hands were no help, so she tucked her elbows close to her body and kept going.

Gunfire erupted, followed by the ping of metal hitting metal. Had someone called her name? She crossed the threshold of a hangar and plunged into darkness. Her footsteps faltered, and she slowed down enough so she could hear her pursuers.

They were gaining on her.

Mackenzie picked her way deeper into the hangar, angling toward the outside wall so she could get her bearings. Should she have stopped by the door and ducked to one side? Should she just freeze in the dark in the hope they wouldn't be able to find her? Why was she no good at this?

Flashlight beams swept the room.

Mackenzie ran for the door at the back.

"There she is. Two o'clock."

Bullets whizzed past her. Apparently when someone ran, they were fair game to be shot.

A thump was followed by the spurt of more bullets, but these weren't directed at her. Another thump. Mackenzie twisted the handle and barreled through the door. It was an office with a metal desk, a file cabinet and absolutely no exit. She closed herself in, heart pounding in her chest and her lungs screaming for air.

The blood in her hands throbbed. She needed to cut them lose, so she felt her way backward to the desk drawer and found a pair of scissors. She nearly dislocated her thumb, but she cut the tie and her hands were finally free.

Flexing her fingers and shoulders, she ignored the pins and needles rushing through her skin and went for the window. She pushed and shoved at the frame, waiting for someone to come in. Waiting for gunfire.

For death.

ELEVEN

The window wouldn't open. Again, Mackenzie sank to the floor. Tears filled her eyes. Someone had caused a diversion, subdued her captors and then…left. What kind of person did that? But honestly, she shouldn't expect more. She'd been alone forever. There were hundreds, if not thousands of people in witness protection.

Sarah had been hurt simply because she did the right thing, while Mackenzie worked a job she adored and got to feel every day as though she was making a difference. Until it all fell apart. If Eric's fiancée hadn't been saved from harm, what made Mackenzie think she was good enough to be rescued?

Salty tears touched her lips. She swiped away the wetness from her cheeks, tucked her chin to her knees and squeezed herself as tight as possible. She hadn't asked for this. It was a high price to pay for being self-absorbed—too high. Daniel, her head of security, was dead. Her manager was dead, too, and she was all alone in the dark waiting for Carosa to kill her. Other people got to live their lives, but she was being punished for the way she'd been.

Why, Lord? This is too hard. I can't do it. Take it away, please.

She sobbed into her hands, sucking in breaths and trying to get air. The doorknob rattled, and Aaron was there. "Mackenzie. Thank God I found you."

She burst into tears again.

Aaron crossed the room and gathered her in his arms. "They're gone. You're okay."

She squeezed her eyes shut and soaked in the feel of him holding her. "I don't think that's true. I don't think I'm okay." He was really here? "You're here. You came."

"Of course I came. You think I'd let Carosa get you?"

"You let them take me from the motel."

"I couldn't incapacitate four of them all by myself. I had to turn the situation in my favor if I had any hope of getting you back."

"By letting me walk away?"

His hands moved to the sides of her face and his thumbs wiped the tears from her face. Even in the dark she could see the softness in his eyes. "I came, didn't I? Can't that be enough?"

Mackenzie bit her lip. "You don't hate me because I didn't tell you…about me being Lani?"

"Of course not. It threw me, but I get that you didn't want to cloud my judgment of who you are."

Mackenzie closed her eyes and sucked in a breath. She didn't deserve what he was doing for her. Not when she was a liar. Despite the look of concern in his eyes, a look that said he was sorry for the pain he'd caused her, it didn't matter who she was now.

Part of her would always be that selfish girl who had thought she ruled the world. She didn't deserve someone who could brush aside all the wrong she'd done as though it was no big deal. It was too big to pass off as forgivable.

Aaron's warm hands moved down to gently squeeze her shoulders. Mackenzie opened her eyes in time to see him tilt his head to the side, and she knew what was coming…

Until he stood and backed away, and then ran a hand through his hair.

Had he actually been about to kiss her? Mackenzie tried to tell herself that wasn't what she wanted. She needed time—time to get herself together and figure out why all this was happening. Why did her past have to come back now? Why couldn't she still be at the center, doing the good that she was supposed to be doing? There was no way she could make up for any of it if she was alone with Aaron, running from Carosa.

Always running.

The air between them was cold, so she wrapped her arms tight around herself, not willing to give in to the shudders. He might say he understood, but eventually he would see Lani when he looked at her. It was inevitable.

"Are you two going to stay there all day, or can we get out of here?"

Mackenzie looked beyond Aaron to the door of the warehouse office. The glamorous woman from the motel stood there with one hand on her hip.

"You're telling me I was only in there for ten minutes?"

Sabine turned back from the front passenger seat of her rental car and squeezed Mackenzie's hand. "Felt like much longer, didn't it?"

Mackenzie nodded, unable to believe she spent such

a short time alone in the hangar's office. It seemed like so much longer before Aaron walked her out and introduced the woman as Sabine, his former team leader's fiancée.

Sabine had laughed and added, "Ex-CIA. For a while now, since my mom—who was an international arms dealer and all-around criminal—duped me into running missions for her. Until she killed my brother and tried to kill me, too. Doug helped me. My mom didn't survive, but we did. Now Doug and I are getting married."

Mackenzie liked her. "How did you find me?"

"Uh…well, I had the cab drop me at the rental place and doubled back to the motel. I saw you guys return from breakfast. When the mercenaries took you but not Aaron, I followed."

Mackenzie laughed. "Why did you say that as though you've done something you shouldn't have? You saved me." She seemed so perfect, while Mackenzie was the kid who got picked on in P.E.

"Aaron told me to leave it alone." Sabine rolled her eyes. "He should know me better than that."

"Have you been friends long?"

Sabine nodded and some of the levity disappeared from her eyes. "My brother was on the team with Doug and Aaron. I've hung out with all of them when they were home a bunch of times, but only really got to know the rest of the guys since Doug, even though he's no longer on the team." Her smile turned wistful.

"I'm sorry you lost your brother."

Sabine gave her a small smile. "Thank you, Mackenzie."

Mackenzie kept her eyes on Sabine so she wasn't tempted to look out the front window of the car, at

Aaron. Again. Sabine hadn't asked, she'd just handed him her keys and he drove them, since he didn't want to keep the other car any longer. Sabine had tried to get Mackenzie to ride up front, but it would've been too weird.

After he parked them behind a warehouse in an industrial district he excused himself and got out to use his phone. It might make her feel better if he'd even looked her in the eye once since he hadn't almost tried to kiss her in the warehouse.

Why was he being so weird about it? So she'd jumped to the wrong conclusion about why he was getting close and he didn't feel anything romantic for her. Couldn't they just forget about her monumental dorkiness thinking he really was about to kiss her and move past this awkwardness?

Mackenzie sighed. "So you were the one driving the car? You provided the distraction so I could run away from those men?"

"Except you were supposed to get in, not run away."

Mackenzie's stomach churned with a combination of lingering adrenaline and embarrassment.

"That was when Aaron showed up in the car I left you guys." Sabine smiled. "Time seems to stretch itself out when you're hiding, overwhelmed by fear."

Mackenzie rolled her eyes. She didn't want to be that weak woman, but there was just so much to be afraid of. "That makes me sound stupid." She glanced out the window where Aaron paced back and forth by the building, talking on his phone with big hand motions and a tight face. "I don't like being overcome by fear. Helpless."

"We've all been there. Me, plenty of times. No one thinks any less of you, least of all Aaron."

Mackenzie frowned. "He's a soldier. I doubt he understands hiding in the dark and crying because you're scared someone's going to kill you."

"On the contrary." Sabine's face gentled. "Soldiers probably understand fear better than any of us, but the job they do means they have to channel that fear into completing the mission. Fear is good. It keeps you sharp."

"That sounds a lot like personal experience."

Sabine's nose crinkled. "It is. The CIA thought I was a traitor and my mom, of all people, was trying to kill me. But haven't you had to overcome your fair share of fear? Performing in front of thousands of screaming fans can't have been easy. How did you overcome your nerves then?" She bit her lip. "I hope you don't mind, but Aaron told me."

She shrugged one shoulder. Mackenzie had never even thought of fame like that. "It's true. I did get really nervous, especially before those big shows. I don't think you ever get used to it, and the attention was just part of what made up that lifestyle."

"So how did you deal with it?"

"You just push it aside and get on with it, I guess." Mackenzie laughed. "Boy, I never would have thought fighting stage fright would apply to running for your life from men with guns."

"You have the tools already, Mackenzie. Almost as though God knew one day you might need them."

She glanced out the window again but couldn't see Aaron. "What about Aaron…and your fiancé? What makes them put themselves in harm's way on purpose?"

"It's the kind of men they are, I suppose. Highly specialized skills and a personality that means they can risk their lives on a daily basis and never get any credit for it because no one even knows that's what they do for a living. And they'll get up and do it all again tomorrow."

Aaron was so relaxed about his life. Everything except for Eric seemed as if it wasn't a big deal to him, even being Special Forces. She was sure it was his job that showed him what was really important. After all, he had given up his time to help Eric, even though he was injured.

How would it feel if he turned that commitment and loyalty to her? There was no doubt that whomever he fell for would be a blessed woman. Maybe it would be her, maybe not. And why did that make her want to kick something?

She didn't even know if Mackenzie Winters was the kind of girl who fell in love. Her WITSEC persona might feel more real, but even after all these years sometimes she still had to think what the girl she was now would do. Besides, she was too busy with the center for romance. Or, that was what she'd always thought.

But then, maybe there was more to her that she hadn't let grow because she'd been so busy trying to be the best Christian she could be. Her life the past sixteen years had been so narrow, her world so isolated, that it was hard to believe she could ever be truly normal.

How could a romantic relationship help balance the scales of the person she'd been? When would she feel like she'd finally atoned for being a shallow, self-centered role model?

"You look lost in thought."

Sabine's face was bright and open, with the happy

look of a woman who knew down to her soul that she was loved by a good man. She was planning a wedding and setting up her life. Sabine juggled everything because her husband-to-be was off on a job interview.

Mackenzie would never be half the woman this lady was. "I was just thinking about the kind of person it takes to be supportive to a man who's gone so much."

Sabine did that nose-crinkling thing again. It made her look more like a young woman than a sophisticated lady. "I spent a lot of years being alone—I suppose I got used to it. Now that I have Doug, I know he's thinking about me as much as I'm thinking about him. Apart from that, you just keep busy with your life. When they get home, you make the most of the days you do have together. I'll say one thing for this life. It makes you take nothing for granted."

"I'm sure."

"You could do a lot worse than Aaron."

Mackenzie laughed and pushed back a wayward strand of hair that had escaped her bun. "I don't know if that kind of life is for me. Who knows what'll happen to me before all this is over? I don't see much point in false hope. Even if I thought Aaron was thinking about the future, I'm not. I can't."

"Doug's father told me that you have to let your heart answer the question. If it's what you both want, then God will make a way."

"I used to think that. But the reality is we have two completely different lives. Even if I did want a relationship, it looks impossible." Mackenzie sighed.

"It looked impossible to me, too." Sabine waved the fingers on her left hand. "And look where I'm at now."

That was nice for Sabine, being on the giddy-with-love side of things. It was easy to tout the blessings of a solid relationship and marriage when you already had it.

Being single was much harder.

Aaron growled. "Yes, I'd like to leave a message."

Why couldn't the Marshals Service office just say where Eric was? His brother hadn't answered his cell any of the times Aaron had called to tell him Mackenzie was fine. Something had to be going on if he wasn't sitting by his phone waiting to hear word on whether or not Aaron had gotten Mackenzie back.

Something serious.

At least that would explain why the office was giving him the runaround. But what was going on? Hopefully it meant that whoever leaked information had been found.

"Oh," another voice spoke in the background, and then the lady came back on the phone. "Marshal Harper, the marshal in charge of our office—"

"I know Steve is Eric's boss."

"Oh, well, he said if you let us know where you are, then we'll send a car to you and you can be here when he gets back. How does that sound? Eric shouldn't be long anyway. He just had something to see to."

A niggle of doubt scratched at Aaron's spine. "You can have Eric call me."

"Are you sure you don't want me to have us come to you?"

It was as if she was stalling him.

TWELVE

Aaron hung up the phone and ran a hand through his hair. If the marshals wanted to know his location, that couldn't mean anything good for Eric. He climbed back in the driver's seat but didn't shut the door.

"Something wrong?"

He didn't look back, instead dismissing Mackenzie's question with a jerk of one shoulder.

Out the corner of his eye, Sabine glanced between them. But she would have to deal with not knowing why he was being like this. He wasn't going to embarrass Mackenzie by explaining that he hadn't been about to kiss her. Even if—for just a moment—he'd really wanted to.

She was a good woman with a big heart; she just wasn't the kind who would put up with someone like him. Eventually he would disappoint her, and then there would be pain and heartbreak.

But that didn't mean he needed to be a jerk. "I'm worried about Eric. And I don't want to stick around here so those mercenaries can find us again. We need to be more careful." He turned back. There was hurt in her eyes. "In fact, give me your phone."

Mackenzie blinked. "My phone?"

"Yes. We don't need anyone tracking us." He shook his own cell in front of her so she'd know that was what he meant. "So we're going to get rid of them."

"I don't have a phone."

Aaron exhaled. "Seriously? Everyone has a phone." Why was she being so difficult?

Sabine shifted in her seat. "She really doesn't have a phone." She was frowning. Why? He wasn't Doug. Aaron was used to disappointing people. "At least tell us what you know, Aaron. What's going on?"

"I think the marshals were trying to find out where we are. They're probably tracking my phone."

He cracked open the back of his phone, took out the SIM card because he'd need it later when this was all over and tossed the phone out the car. It bounced on the concrete and broke into pieces. Aaron slammed the door shut and fired up the engine.

Now Eric wouldn't be able to get hold of him; Aaron had just officially severed all contact. If he was a praying man, he'd ask for protection for Eric and Mackenzie. He didn't deserve any consideration for himself, but Eric and Mackenzie were two of the best people he knew. If anyone should have peace and happiness, it was them.

Aaron pulled onto the road. Two black SUVs sped up the street behind them, along with three police cars. Their lights were flashing, but sirens were quiet. He held his breath until they turned into the complex he'd parked in, then pressed on the gas and sped away.

Aaron glanced at Sabine. She'd seen the team coming for them. She gave him a short shake of her head. He wasn't sure if it meant that she didn't want Mackenzie to worry, or that she was disappointed in him. His charge had been kidnapped earlier, but he wasn't sure he wanted to start keeping stuff from her. But how was he supposed to keep her safe when their pursuers were so close behind?

How much more of this could Mackenzie take before she broke? She'd been pretty strong so far, and even given how scared she'd been in the warehouse she'd still recovered quickly. But how long would it last?

"Uh-oh."

Aaron took a left and headed for the freeway. He glanced at Sabine. "What?"

She hit a button on her smartphone and held it up.

A news reporter's voice spoke over a picture of Eric. "Deputy U.S. Marshal Eric Hanning was arrested just a short time ago. He is suspected of selling information that put specific persons who are part of the witness protection program in danger."

Aaron pulled over to the side of the road.

He grabbed the phone, aware Mackenzie had leaned forward to watch over his shoulder.

"A source inside the Marshals Service office informed us that Hanning has worked for the Marshals Service for eight years, the past six serving as a WITSEC inspector. And now he has allegedly betrayed the very people he was supposed to be protecting."

Mackenzie gasped. "No one's supposed to know."

"Someone just threw Eric under the bus."

"Law enforcement is also looking for two other people, a man and a woman, in connection with Marshal Hanning's arrest."

A picture of Aaron beside Mackenzie flashed on the phone's screen.

"The identity of the woman is as yet unknown, but the man is U.S. Army Sergeant Aaron Hanning. He is the brother of the arrested marshal and is suspected of colluding with him in this leak of highly classified information. He is also suspected of kidnapping the unidentified woman."

The news reporter flashed a smug smile of perfect white teeth. "If you see either of these people, there is a number on-screen to call and report their whereabouts. We will provide more information as it comes to us."

"We're being set up." Aaron wanted to throw the phone or punch something. Sabine grabbed it out of his hand, probably not wanting to spend a few hundred bucks on a new phone right before her wedding.

"They think you kidnapped me?" Aaron turned back in time to see Mackenzie shake her head, her face pale. "This is unreal. What on earth is going on, Aaron? How could they think Eric is the mole in the office? He would never do that…to either of us. It's just not possible."

"I know that. You know that." Aaron sighed. "Someone is setting him up."

Sabine gritted her teeth. "They probably planted the evidence to make it look as if he was the mole. Get everyone's focus off the real mole and on looking for Mackenzie instead."

"And destroy all our lives in the process."

Sabine said, "Which makes sense if the mole is now helping Carosa. Because if they think Mackenzie's in danger, the police will be looking for her, and the marshals who know who she is will be trying to contain the leak. That means Carosa has even more of a chance of someone finding her and revealing her location."

Aaron frowned at Sabine. "Okay, seriously? You're supposed to be planning a wedding."

"Not anymore." Sabine looked smug. As though she knew he needed her and they both knew the help of a former CIA agent would be invaluable.

He did, but that didn't mean Doug wouldn't skin him if he got her hurt. "Sabine—"

"I think she should help us."

Aaron opened his mouth to tell Mackenzie it didn't matter what she thought, because he was the one who was going to keep her safe. He sighed. She'd had a rough day as it was. "Sabine is not even supposed to be here. Doug's going to knock me flat when he finds out I let her hang around when we've been repeatedly in danger."

Mackenzie pressed her lips together and nodded. "I don't want to run. I've done enough of that already."

"Carosa is going to be that much closer to finding you now."

"Then we have even less time than we did before to help Eric. And it's all the more important now."

"It's risky." But Aaron liked that she would put herself on the line for his brother. It was irrational, but emotions had never made sense to him.

She lifted her chin. "I can handle it. Can you?"

"Okay, we go after Eric's partner first. It's a good place to start. We'll snoop around and see if we can get something that will point to him as the mole so we can get Eric cleared. If it's not Schweitzer, we'll move on to the next guy, and the next. I'm not stopping. Eric will need all the help he can get." Aaron pinched the bridge of his nose. "He's pretty much done now that the reporter told everyone he works for WITSEC, but who knows? If we can get Eric out from under suspicion, maybe he can salvage his career."

Sabine's eyes were on him. "I'll give you all the info I have on the people he works with."

"And then you'll get lost."

She huffed. "Fine. But I'm calling Doug. If you get in even one sliver of trouble, he'll be expecting a call."

"Sabine—"

"You know he's going to be mad that you didn't call him in the first place."

Aaron figured that was probably about right. He started up the engine again. "Okay, let's get on with this."

Mackenzie could hardly believe what had happened. As familiar streets rolled by, she tried to assimilate the fact that Eric had been arrested, Aaron was suspected of kidnapping her and she was supposed to be the unwitting victim in all this.

Everyone would be looking for them. Carosa would find her even faster now, aided by ordinary people who called the hotline, thinking they were helping her. Did that reporter have any clue what she'd done? Apart from ruining Eric's career as a WITSEC inspector, provided he could get clear of whatever charges were against him and didn't end up in jail, the reporter had smeared the reputation of both brothers.

It was only a matter of time before someone who'd known her personally years ago—an old fan or acquaintance—saw the newscast and recognized her as Lani, and the fact that she used to be a pop star was made public.

Her heart broke for what Eric must be going through. She really liked him. Not romantically, but he seemed like such a caring guy.

A tear rolled down her face, and she wiped it away. Aaron glanced back at her and frowned. "You okay?"

"I'm just worried about Eric."

Sabine was talking on her cell phone, filling Doug in on what had happened. It seemed as though they had the kind of close relationship where they told each other everything. Mackenzie didn't even know how to be that vulnerable with someone. It would have to come with a whole lot of love and trust.

She wanted that with Aaron. Despite the fact that it would likely never happen, she couldn't help the jump of hope in her heart. Someday he might turn that intense devotion he felt for his family and friends toward someone else.

"I know that." Sabine sighed. "I know—"

She sighed and held out the phone to Aaron. "He wants to talk to you."

Aaron nodded. "Put it on speaker."

Sabine motioned toward Mackenzie. "Are you sure?"

"Just put it on speaker."

Mackenzie had too much buzzing around her head. She couldn't get mad that there might be things they wanted to keep from her. The three of them were close; it was obvious to anyone watching that Aaron had a huge amount of respect for his friend, which now extended to Sabine.

Aaron raised his voice. "Hey, man, what's up?"

"What's up?" The voice through the phone was low and tough, and crackled a bit. "You bring my fiancée along for the ride when you have mercenaries and cops after you? Are you crazy?"

"I didn't know the cops would be there."

"Sabine can't show up on anyone's radar. Ever. You know that."

Mackenzie studied the two of them in the front seats. Sabine held out the phone, her cheeks an endearing shade of pink as she said, "I kept a low profile. This isn't Aaron's fault."

Aaron sighed. "Mackenzie was kidnapped and Eric couldn't get away. There was no one else, and it turned out Sabine was on the case already."

"Yeah, she and I already talked about that. Maybe you guys should start a business, make all the car chases and gunfights official. I'll be your secretary."

Aaron snorted. Mackenzie couldn't imagine what a guy with a voice this gruff would look like making coffee and typing up invoices.

"Were you just bored, was that it, Aaron? Looking for another thrill since you're on medical leave?"

Sabine sighed. "Doug—"

"Listen—" Aaron hit the turn signal so hard Mackenzie thought it might break. "Sabine saved Mackenzie's life. We needed help. More now, since Eric's been arrested. Mackenzie and I are going after the leak."

There was a big sigh over the line. "Sabine, stay in Phoenix. My flight leaves in an hour, so I'll be there tonight. I'll call my lawyer, too. We'll do everything we can for Eric. Aaron, just keep Mackenzie safe, and we'll talk later, okay?"

"Nothing like having cops on your tail to keep the mercenaries at bay."

Doug laughed. "No doubt, brother. Now drop my fiancée off."

The line went dead.

"I'm really sorry." Except it sounded as if Sabine was laughing.

Aaron smiled at Sabine. "He was like that before you. He's just worried, that's all."

Mackenzie watched Sabine smirk. "What is with this new and improved Aaron, who's all understanding and compassionate? I don't get it. Where'd you go? Where's the smooth-talking designer-clothes-wearing guy who used to be so shallow?"

"Ouch, Sabine."

"I know it was bad. I know—well, I'd need longer than this to check the pulse of how you're doing and where you're at, but I think maybe this time off might have done you good."

"Seriously?" His brow had crinkled and he didn't look pleased. "There was nothing good about what happened. Now I just want to forget it and try to salvage what's left of my career."

Sabine sat back in her seat. "I'm sorry. I shouldn't have said anything."

Aaron blew out a breath and pulled into a supermarket parking lot. "Where are you going to go now?"

Sabine was silent for a minute and then sighed. "Don't worry about me. Like Doug said, we'll help Eric any way we can until this clears."

Aaron nodded.

Then Sabine said, "And don't worry about the colonel, either. He knows what happened wasn't your fault. Franklin is alive, and the guys will come around."

Aaron's jaw flexed as though he was grinding his teeth. Mackenzie watched the byplay between them. She'd had hints before now that something had happened to Aaron. This wasn't just about his shoulder injury; it seemed as though something more had gone on. And Sabine knew what it was.

If she pressed him, would he open up to her? He'd inferred she didn't need to know all the details of his life to trust him, but she couldn't help wanting to see if she might be able to make it better. Only that would make Aaron a project, just like all the kids in the center. Did she want that to define their friendship?

Being his counselor was not a good idea. She might forever define their relationship as something she didn't want it to be. She might have a degree, but she wasn't a licensed therapist.

Something had to change for him. He seemed so torn up about whatever it was that he lashed out when anyone tried to tend the wound that was inside him. And now he was channeling the anger, the pain of...whatever it was, into fighting for his brother. She could see it in his eyes, in the way he held back, protecting himself. If the wound was too fresh, it explained why he hadn't told her.

Mackenzie got out when Sabine did and gave her a hug. Sabine squeezed her as though they were long-lost friends, and Mackenzie prayed that when this was over they could become that.

"Take care of him."

Mackenzie pulled back. Sabine was serious. "He needs taking care of?"

"More than he knows or would be willing to admit, ever. But he needs someone like you, Mackenzie. Someone who will see past the wet, angry kitty to the scarred heart underneath that wants to be loved. Just watch out for the claws."

Mackenzie didn't know whether to laugh or get mad at her description of Aaron. "I'm not sure that's exactly how it is…but okay."

Sabine laughed and hugged her again. "Trust me. You're exactly what he needs."

"I don't know about that."

"After what he's been through, you're perfect. Like fresh air."

Mackenzie wasn't completely convinced, but she was willing to trust this woman.

Aaron's door opened. Mackenzie looked back in time to see him scowl at them over the roof of the car. "If you're done having girl bonding time, can we go? There are people trying to kill us."

As if she could forget.

"'Bye, Sabine."

"Take care."

Mackenzie climbed in the front seat and buckled up. "So where to?"

Aaron huffed out a breath. "Let's just get on this. We'll start with Eric's partner."

Mackenzie wanted to ask how his shoulder was, since he had his hand in his lap and wasn't using it to drive. Did it hurt? But she kept her mouth shut, figuring the timing wasn't right to start her campaign to tame the angry kitty.

The corners of her mouth curled up. Aaron looked at her and did a double take. "What's funny?"

"I'll tell you later. But first, answer me this. Why Eric's partner that he mentioned?"

Aaron shrugged what she now knew was his good shoulder. "Eric seemed to think there was something there worth looking into. So until Sabine sends me all the info on the people he works with, it's a place to start, at least. And it's better than sitting here while Eric's in jail."

THIRTEEN

Mackenzie shifted in her seat beside him. They were parked outside a modest adobe house in the suburb of Scottsdale. The sun beat down on the hood of the car; just another day in Arizona. Her eyes were on the house, same as his.

He frowned at the back of her head. "Are you sure you want to do this today? You did get kidnapped this morning."

"I said I did. I wasn't lying. We have to help Eric."

Aaron rolled his eyes. He was exhausted, and his shoulder hurt something fierce. Rest would strengthen them both for the fight ahead. But no, Mackenzie didn't want to take a break. It bothered him, but why not admit to himself they had something in common, at least?

Why couldn't she see that he wanted to help Eric just as much as her? More, since Eric was *his* brother.

They were all tied up in this now. Sooner or later he was going to be arrested for kidnapping Mackenzie, and Eric would go to jail. But still, he was trying to be gracious. This wasn't her fight. She needed to concentrate on Carosa's threat to her life and let Aaron, Doug and Sabine help Eric.

"I just don't know why we can't leave it until tomorrow. It won't hurt anything to wait." She really did look as though she wanted to take a nap, and his shoulder was screaming with fire from having his arms restrained. Hers had to hurt, also.

"It'll hurt if more people's lives are ruined."

She rubbed at the marks on her wrists from the ties the mercenaries had used on her. His were the same, so when Aaron reached over and grabbed her hand, they matched. Her fingers were warm, her skin softer than anything he'd felt before. "Don't rub. You need to let it heal."

He should have bought some cream for her wrists, or a bandage, when he was picking up a prepay phone. Why didn't he do that? He sighed. He could be a real jerk sometimes.

"Are you okay?" Aaron studied her, but she didn't look at him. She just kept her eyes on the house they were watching. "My brother is innocent. Eric's record will speak for him and we'll help any way we can. You don't have to take on his cause, Mackenzie. You have enough to deal with."

He didn't want to leave his brother hanging, but sitting here with her, Aaron had to fight the urge to buy two plane tickets and get her out of there. Run. Never look back. It wouldn't solve either of their problems, but it sounded good anyway.

Mackenzie never answered. She just pulled up the email on Aaron's brand-new unregistered phone and read aloud, "1485 North Harrell is the home of Arnold Schweitzer, U.S. Marshal for the past fifteen years. Forty-seven years old. He's married, wife's name is Marcy and the kids are Helen, who's twelve, and Amy, nine. Now, tell me why we're sitting on the street four doors down from Mr. Schweitzer's house."

"It's called a stakeout."

"Okay..."

"You've never watched a cop show?"

She looked over at him. "I don't have a TV."

"Seriously?"

"Not everyone sits glued to a screen for hours on end. I do it enough at work with the computer. It's the last thing I want when I'm home."

"So you just sit around until bedtime?"

Mackenzie rolled her eyes. "No, I read. I had a five-thousand-piece puzzle that I was working on, but it was taking me a while because most nights I work late at the center."

Aaron pulled the phone over so he could see the file. He scanned down the page. "Eric didn't have anything he could pinpoint without an unsubstantiated illegal search into the life of a man he's supposed to trust. Sabine looked into his financial records, and there's nothing fishy, but at this point Eric's instinct is the best we've got."

"So...what are we doing now?"

Aaron glanced up at the roof of the car and sighed. "We're observing. Rule one of investigation is gathering information. The second is what we're doing right now. Looking for details to add to what we know."

"You mean like how the school bus came by and neither of the girls got off?"

"What?"

Mackenzie motioned to the house. "Why don't we go ask the neighbors why Marcy might be gone when her car is in the driveway, and why the girls didn't come home from school?"

"Fine." Aaron sighed. "You stay put, and I'll go talk to the neighbors."

"But if we split up, then we can cover twice as many houses."

"Which we're not going to do, because you need to rest. There's no point in overdoing it and not having time to regroup and get your strength back."

She looked over at him, her eyes narrowed. "Sounds like that's coming from experience."

Aaron shrugged. "I've been a soldier for a long time."

"So you've been injured?"

"Mostly fractures to fingers, toes, stuff like that. Busted ribs, concussions." He smoothed out a crease in his jeans. "Some injuries that were…worse."

"Like you were shot? Is that what happened to your shoulder?"

He zeroed in on the tone in her voice. "Why are you so fired up to talk about this? It's not fun. I'd think you would want to discuss anything else in the world than guns and war."

Hurt flashed on her face. "I was just making conversation."

Aaron sighed. "Let's go talk to the neighbors."

It didn't bode well how easily he was giving in to her just for the sake of avoiding *that* conversation. He badly needed to shore up his conviction and not let the pain in her eyes get to him. But it was tough. He had to remember this was about Eric, and Mackenzie was just a by-product. *Yeah, right.* Her death would be collateral damage, and he was trained to avoid that. That was why he was here. Doug and Sabine were perfectly capable of helping Eric clear his name.

By the time he got around to her door she'd already climbed out, and they walked together across the street. The neighbor's house was sun-bleached yellow with vinyl siding and a lawn of brown grass between the front door and the street. Blinds in the front window were pulled back, showing a wide-screen TV tuned to kids cartoons.

Aaron rang the bell and pandemonium erupted in the form of kids screaming and crying at the prospect of visitors. A woman answered the door with a stain on her T-shirt, her hair in a ponytail and no makeup. She squinted at the bright light outside. "Help you?"

"Is there anything you can tell us about the Schweitzers next door?"

The woman's eyes darkened. "Who wants to know? You guys cops or what? I'm not answering no questions to cops. I know my rights."

Mackenzie nudged him aside and got between Aaron and the woman. "It's nothing like that. We're friends of Marcy. We were supposed to visit with her today, but we must have missed her and Helen and Amy."

The woman corralled a toddler boy trying to crawl out the door between her feet. She looked back at Aaron and Mackenzie and sighed. "Helen and Amy come by after school most days to help me with the kids, unless they have soccer or whatnot. A week ago she texts me. Going to her sister's, she says. Family emergency or some such. And what am I supposed to do? I've got a business to run. Who's going to help me, huh?"

"We must have been mistaken, then, got our wires

crossed or something. Thank you for your time." Aaron backed up, taking Mackenzie with him by her elbow.

Mackenzie waved at a couple of the kids. "Sorry to bother you."

When they reached the street, Mackenzie pulled her elbow out of his grip. Aaron snagged her hand with his, his mouth opening to say something, but when the warmth of her fingers folded around his, all thoughts left his head. This wasn't good. There weren't supposed to be any feelings between them. Aaron dropped her hand and ignored the glance she shot him. "Okay, so that was a pretty good idea. Now we know the wife and daughters went to her sister's, if we can believe it. We need to check the story and focus our attention on old Arnold."

She nodded and they climbed in the car.

Aaron pulled around the first corner and parked out of sight of Schweitzer's house. "Stay here."

Her eyes went wide. "Where are you going?"

"I'll be back in five minutes."

"What if you're not?"

He looked her in the eye. "I will be."

"Aaron—"

He shut the car door. Who knew how long it would be before the neighbor saw the news and called the police to report their whereabouts? If he needed to check out Schweitzer's house, he had to do it fast.

Mackenzie cranked the air-conditioning to max and slouched down in the seat so no one noticed her. Aaron had disappeared between two houses. A couple of doors up from the car an older teenage boy mowed a lawn, his shirt ringed with sweat. Across the street, two preteen girls lay out on their front lawn on deck chairs watching the show. Life was going on as normal. A car drove by, a low-to-the-ground model with a long hood.

Mackenzie sucked in a breath and squeezed her eyes shut. The sound of the engine diminished as it got farther away. It wasn't rational to be scared of every little thing just because there were a lot people looking for them. She couldn't live her life in fear. Not anymore. Wasn't there something in the Bible about that? Not being anxious or something.

The numbers on the dash clock clicked five minutes, and she watched for Aaron's return. Alone, Mackenzie could admit that attraction had stirred. She wanted to get to know him better and see where it could lead. But while they had been close in proximity, him comforting her when she needed it, he still seemed so far away and removed from her.

Mackenzie had plenty of secrets of her own, but for the right man she was more than willing to open up. Could Aaron say the same? She wasn't sure.

At the six-minute mark, she had grabbed the door handle, ready to go after him, when another car, high-end and not like she would have thought a government employee would drive, pulled around the corner. Mackenzie lifted up an inch and checked out the driver. It was the same guy whose picture had been on the email: Schweitzer.

She slid back down in the seat.

There was no way to warn Aaron that Schweitzer was coming. If he found Aaron in his house, he would surely shoot him, especially when he saw who it was. Or he would arrest Aaron for kidnapping her, and then Mackenzie would be on her own.

She opened the door just as Aaron jogged around the corner.

"What are you doing?" He hissed, "Shut that door."

"Schweitzer came back. I thought he was going to kill you."

Aaron climbed in. "Buckle up. Now."

She waited until he buckled his seat belt and then said, "What took you so long? I was worried. I really thought he was going to find you in there and kill you."

"Seriously?" He pulled away from the curb. "I wouldn't let that happen. I wouldn't leave you on your own."

"I was worried about you."

"Because you'd get left alone."

"I would have been fine." *Hopefully.* Mackenzie crossed her arms. "Am I not allowed to worry about you?"

"Don't know why you would. Most people wouldn't think I was worth it."

Except for Doug and Sabine, who seemed to have a profound devotion to this man. That alone seemed to indicate there was something special about him, despite what he seemed to think. "Schweitzer didn't find you?"

"I was just having a look around. Heard his car pull in, headed out the gate in the backyard. Everything's fine, Mackenzie."

That wasn't true. But it was nice of him to say it. As though if it wasn't then she could trust him to make it that way.

"Please tell me you didn't actually break into that house."

"Rest assured, no laws were broken. I just looked in the back windows."

Had she really been worried he might have killed Schweitzer? Sometimes Aaron acted all no-nonsense soldier and other times he came across like a smooth old West cowboy. The first, she was recognizing, was his work mode. She wondered if the other was the real him. It seemed so...practiced. Was he purposely trying to be charming?

"So what did you do in there?"

He studied the road as he drove, giving plenty of attention to his rearview mirror. Was he looking to see if someone was following them? Mackenzie should probably learn how to do that. It might come in handy... what with there being a man trying to kill her and all.

He gave her a double take. "You okay?"

Mackenzie turned and nodded to the window. "Sure."

"That wasn't breaking and entering, what I did back there. I only break into criminals' houses when I'm asked, and there's nothing concrete to suggest this guy isn't legit. At least, not yet."

She looked at him. "You break into criminals' houses?"

He was smiling, but he didn't look happy. "For my job. The one I do far from here, in hot-as-a-sauna countries where innocent people have no voice and no one to fight for them."

"Wow." It just came out. Mackenzie wasn't sure why she said it, only that it was an honest response from her heart. "Is that why you do it?"

"Pays the bills."

"So you don't want anyone to know you have a heart, or that your job involves some kind of higher purpose? You'd rather brush off the notion that you have an in-grained sense of honor." Mackenzie looked away again.

When Aaron spoke, his voice was flat. "We can't all have some grand calling like you, helping turn around at-risk kids. Not everyone feels a sense of destiny at their jobs. For most people, work is just work. You go, you suffer through it and then you go home and try to escape the fact that you have to do it again tomorrow."

Mackenzie frowned. Was that really what he thought of the world, that life was drudgery? "I happen to think it's a big deal that you are a soldier, putting your life at risk for the cause of freedom. It is honorable. Something to be proud of."

He pulled the car to the side of the road and looked away, out the side window. When he spoke, his voice was low. "You're wrong."

FOURTEEN

"Aaron—"

His head whipped around, his eyes desolate. What
she'd been about to say dissipated and she cleared her
throat. She couldn't ask him what he meant. From the
look on his face, it would be a while before she could
go there. "At least tell me if you learned anything, looking around at the Schweitzers'."

He sighed. "Kitchen sink is full. Counters looked
crowded with cereal boxes and empty jars of peanut
butter, so the neighbor was probably right about the
wife being gone. The only other window I could see in
was the patio, just a view of the hall. But the shih tzu
wanted out pretty badly."

"They have a puppy?"

"A very unhappy one. Nearly yapped my ear off
when it saw me over the fence."

Mackenzie sighed. "So all we have is a bunch of
dirty dishes and a dog?"

"No signs of a struggle that I saw, no broken windows. The wife is most likely fine, at her sister's with
the kids—"

"In the middle of the school semester. Without taking the car."

"Even so, it's the most likely conclusion." He started up the car. "We can follow Schweitzer and see where he goes from here. See if it leads us—"

The fancy car went by them again, this time in the other direction.

"That's him."

Aaron pulled out into traffic, a ways back from Schweitzer's car.

Mackenzie chewed her lip. Somewhere along the way their conversation had taken a turn for the worse. Aaron was no longer deflecting her with lighthearted banter. He had shut down completely into some kind of business-only mode. So why did that make her want to dig deeper and draw him out of his shell?

Aaron kept a solid distance, but his eyes were on Schweitzer's taillights. If this was a mission, he would have someone tracking Schweitzer's phone and giving him the location so he could hang back out of sight. There would be more than one car following the target, and all of this would have been coordinated ahead of time.

As it was, all he had was a sullen Mackenzie and his training, which hadn't amounted to much when everything that could've gone wrong had. She wanted him to open up and tell her about it, but he just didn't want to see the look on her face when she found out he was a complete failure—that because of him, a friend of his, who was a good man and a good soldier, was now blind.

Aaron sighed. He should probably just quit the army as soon as he could. That would be better than living with the shame of what he'd done to the team. He could start his own business, though that would probably take more money than he had. Doug's idea of a partnership sounded pretty good, not that Doug would be the secretary. Sabine wouldn't put up with that either, so they would probably have to hire someone to run the office.

He could maybe see what Mackenzie thought about it. She seemed to have set up a new life pretty well and found something that made her happy. How did she know what that was?

Schweitzer drove into downtown, which was busy with cars on this hot summer evening. People moved everywhere, some of them probably on the lookout to save the "unnamed woman" from the big bad abductor. Schweitzer turned left well before they reached the Downtown Performing Arts Center. Mackenzie's disappointment was plain, but it was for the best. She needed to stay clear of places where people would recognize her.

They followed Schweitzer to a parking garage and wound around the ramp to the top floor where he'd parked. Aaron pulled into a space across the aisle, several cars down from Schweitzer. Aaron turned their vehicle around and backed in so they could see Schweitzer and get out fast if need be.

Aaron wanted to call someone, to let people who could help them know what they were doing. He needed his team, but he and Mackenzie were all alone. How long would it take before his heart realized his team was never going to accept him back?

Schweitzer headed for the doors, the entrance to a chain hotel above the garage. But he didn't push the button. He checked his gold watch and just waited.

Mackenzie glanced at him. "Should we get out and follow him?"

"Let's just hang here and see who he's waiting for."

A car passed them, a red soft-top Mustang he'd seen before. The woman driving the car was the same woman he'd seen at the center. What was her name?

Mackenzie sucked in a breath. "Eva."

She grabbed the door handle. Aaron put his hand on her arm. "Don't. You need to stay here."

Mackenzie stared at the scene in front of her as Eva parked and sashayed to the elevator, hitting the button to lock her car over her shoulder. She strode right to Schweitzer, and then there was no doubt. Mackenzie couldn't pass it off as coincidental when Eva flung herself into the marshal's arms and they kissed...for long enough that Mackenzie had to look away.

But if Schweitzer was dirty, that meant Eva was involved in more than just an illicit relationship with a married man. She was involved with Carosa, too. How was that possible?

Aaron started the car and pulled out of the space, not saying anything while her heart tore open. In all the years since she'd had an actual real friend, she had never expected that the first person she would actually want to be friends with would betray her like this.

As they drove away, a gunshot echoed through the garage.

Mackenzie squealed and looked out the rear window. Schweitzer lay on the ground. Eva was standing over him with a gun in her hand, pointed at his chest.

"She killed him. Eva killed him."

Aaron didn't say anything; he just kept driving, as if

the dissonant fragments of Mackenzie's life hadn't just crumbled all over again.

"Why would she kiss Schweitzer and then kill him?" Mackenzie sucked in a breath, fighting against the tightness in her chest. "Why did she come to the center? I thought she loved the kids, but she's a killer, too. She betrayed me."

"I know." He pulled up to the exit and handed the guard five dollars while Mackenzie wrung her hands and tried to get her breathing under control.

"Why would she do that?"

Aaron pulled forward and slowed the car to a stop at the exit.

The windshield splintered, Aaron grunted and the car moved forward as if his foot had slipped off the brake. He gripped the steering wheel again, and they pulled out into traffic.

Mackenzie saw the red on his face. "You're bleeding." She gasped. "You've been shot!"

He drove, blinking even though blood now tracked down his cheek. It was running freely and he was squinting to see out the shattered windshield.

"You need a cloth or something."

"I need a car I can see out of." He pulled onto a side street but looked out the side window. "And a rifle so I can return the favor."

He winced, and Mackenzie dug around in the glove box but found no napkins. What kind of person didn't keep napkins in their glove box? She grabbed her backpack and found her shirt from yesterday. She balled it up and pressed it against his temple.

Aaron winced but kept driving. He reached up and took over with the cloth.

Mackenzie looked down at her hands.

There was blood on her.

Again.

Black spots peppered her vision. Mackenzie struggled to breathe. Aaron called her name, but she couldn't reply.

Aaron pressed the pedal to the floor and the car tore down the street. He wished he could take his frustration out on whoever had shot at them. Mackenzie was out of it, lost in whatever had made her eyes go distant. But he couldn't help her right now. If they hung around, they could get picked off by another shot from that sniper.

He kept one hand on the balled-up piece of cloth, pressing hard against his head. It wasn't more than a scratch, though it had been made by a sniper round.

The thing had barely grazed him, going as fast as it had, but the heat and the speed had been close enough to his head that it felt like being kissed by fire. Hopefully his free-flowing head wound would quit bleeding soon and wouldn't need stitches, because they didn't have time to stop off at the hospital.

They were running *again*. It wasn't in his makeup to turn tail and do anything other than fight his way out of a situation, and yet that seemed to be what he was doing with Mackenzie at every turn. He should be toe-to-toe with these mercenaries, making Mackenzie safe and clearing Eric's name, but he was driving away instead.

He slammed the heel of his palm against the steering wheel.

This whole situation had done nothing but go from bad to worse, and now Mackenzie's friend was involved. How could that be possible? There had to be a link between the Carosa family, Eric's partner at the Marshals Service office and Eva. Though evidently Schweitzer and Eva had been having an affair...at least up until the point she shot him.

Aaron had already found the on-ramp to the freeway going north. Without really thinking about it, he knew where he was taking her. There was nothing either of them could do for Eric. All Aaron needed was to make sure Mackenzie was safe, and there was nowhere better for that than the cabin.

Technically he wasn't supposed to be there, since it belonged to the team. He hadn't exactly left in good standing, and it grated that he couldn't go visit his teammate in the hospital. But hopefully when they found out about Mackenzie they'd forgive him for intruding on their private space.

Then again, Aaron's face had been all over the news. If his team had seen it, they probably thought he'd gone completely off the rails—from failure to abductor in just a week. How would he ever get his career back after this?

The cabin would give him and Mackenzie the space they needed to regroup instead of being forced to react to what was happening at every turn. They needed to get ahead of the curve so Aaron could turn all this in their favor for once. He'd always hated playing defense.

A low moan came from Mackenzie. Aaron reached over and squeezed her hand to try to alleviate the heavy feeling in his chest. "You okay?"

She drew in a shuddering breath. "Are *you* okay? I mean, your head and everything."

Aaron touched the skin around the wound. It had

stopped bleeding finally. "It's just a graze. Head wounds bleed a lot."

"I'm sorry I freaked out." Her eyes were dark with something he couldn't see. "It was like a nightmare, but while I was still awake. I was right back in the hotel room with Carosa pointing his gun at me."

Aaron focused on the road again. "I'm sorry, Mackenzie."

Her face was turned to the side window, and her voice was low when she said, "It felt as though it happened all over again. My chest still hurts."

"You were shot?"

She nodded and pressed her fingers just below her collarbone on the left side, high enough that the damage had healed—because any lower and she'd be dead.

Aaron squeezed the fingers of the hand he still held in an effort to give comfort, as much for himself as for her.

Mackenzie was just a friend, if that. It certainly wasn't rational to think there was anything more between them. So why did he want to stand in front of her like a shield and protect her from everything in the world that might harm her?

He was no hero.

But considering what had already happened to her, there wasn't much Aaron could do to make it worse. Or better, really. And that made him feel useless all over again—knowing she'd already nearly died and spent half her life in hiding. He was torn between anger at his powerlessness and the overwhelming urge to hug her. There were no do-overs, but if he had the power to wipe it all away for her, he would have.

Eventually the mercenaries would catch up to them

again. Which begged the question…how did they seem
to know where Aaron and Mackenzie were at all times?
First on the way to the restaurant, then the park, the
hotel and now exiting the parking lot, they'd been found
over and over again. It was a wonder they were both
still alive.

Aaron found a rest stop and pulled off the highway
to a far corner that wasn't lit by streetlight. The whole
area was deserted except for a lone semi by the restrooms. "Give me your bag."

"Why? Are we leaving the car? How will we get
anywhere on foot? There's nothing but desert here."

Aaron swiped the backpack from the floor by her
feet and rummaged through it. "We're not walking.
Those mercenaries seem to know where we are every
time we turn around. We need to figure out how they
are tracking us or we'll never get away."

Mackenzie grasped for the backpack. "Where's your
bag? Are you going to give it to me so I can search
through it as if *you're* a criminal?"

Aaron shuffled her things around. "That's not what
I'm doing." His fingers found a rip in the lining at the
bottom. Inside was a solid object. He pulled it out.
"Thought you didn't have a cell phone."

"I don't." Mackenzie's eyes widened. "I've never
seen that before."

"Really?"

He studied her. There was no reason to believe she
would lead the mercenaries to them. It was more likely
that the phone had been planted there. But he had to be
sure. "Are you certain?"

"Some of the kids have phones like that. I've never

used one. I didn't buy that." Was this really happening? "This is unreal."

"Actually, it's very real. This phone is on, which means someone is tracking us. They've been tracking us this whole time."

"Get rid of it then! Throw it out the window, or, I know! Run over it with the tire!"

Those weren't bad ideas, but Aaron had more questions. "Could Eva have put this in your bag?"

"She didn't know about my go bag. It was in my hall closet at home. It's just for emergencies, and since Eric's the one who told me to have a bag like this, he brought it to me."

"Was she at your house any time when you were in a different room, when she could have put it in your bag?"

"To plant a cell phone on me? That would mean she knew…about Carosa. About everything."

Aaron's voice was hard. "She was having an affair with Schweitzer. She probably *did* know everything."

Mackenzie could barely look at Aaron. Shame filled her in a hot rush that was all too familiar. "I just don't know how she could have fooled me. Do you think she's behind all this?"

"I don't know, Mackenzie. But we'll figure it out."

"Why would she do this to me?" She sighed. "Do we have to follow her now? Because I don't know if I can stomach that."

Mackenzie didn't ever want to see Eva again.

"We're not following her. We need time to rest and space to regroup, and we're not going to get that on the lam with a bunch of mercenaries following us." He yanked the door handle and got out for a second, crouching at the front tire. "Your suggestion on how to deal with the phone wasn't bad."

He got back in, gunned the engine and drove over the phone. Then he brought his foot up over the dash and kicked out the shattered front windshield.

FIFTEEN

Hours later Aaron drove down the highway with the wind blowing in his face. There had been a hole in the middle of the glass where the bullet had punched through the windshield.

Mackenzie had crawled into the backseat to sleep. She hadn't wanted him to drive alone, but the exhaustion on her face was clear. That was why he'd suggested she get some rest. There wasn't much more of this she could take.

The unsettled feeling in Aaron's stomach dissipated as, for the first time in a long time, he prayed for Eric, and for Doug, who was by now gathering information to prove Eric's innocence. Because he *was* innocent. Everything about Eric was innocent, it always had been.

Aaron could admit—to himself, at least—that sometimes prayer was the only option to offer a shred of hope. And right now, that was all they had left. Hope. For the first time Aaron was willing to consider the possibility that his foster mom was right, that Doug and Eric were right. Maybe it was worth it to put his faith in God.

Especially when he had nothing else left.

The career Aaron had spent years building, brick by brick, had come crumbling down until he was left with nothing but failure. Since he'd signed up for the military just out of high school, he'd always known who he was and where he was headed. Now the road was shrouded in mist, and there was nothing to light the way.

Just before five o'clock in the morning, the new phone he'd bought at a superstore buzzed. It had been a tough decision, but staying out of contact completely meant not knowing what was happening with Eric. Though having to get a car charger and a Bluetooth had cut into his cash reserves significantly. But he wasn't going to stop driving, not even to take a call.

He tapped the button on his Bluetooth. "Yeah."

"Where are you?" Doug's voice was groggy.

"On the highway."

"Are you going where I think you're going?"

There was a shuffle in the backseat. Mackenzie had awoken, even though he'd been talking quietly. "You know it's the only place, the safest place to regroup."

"Did you figure out how they've been tracking you?"

Aaron blew out a breath. "Yeah, after one of their snipers winged my temple."

"You okay?" Doug's voice cleared of all trace of fatigue.

"Doesn't even need stitches." Not that Aaron had checked—he just assumed by the fact that it'd finally stopped bleeding. At the last rest area he'd found a first-aid kit in the trunk and stuck on a bandage while Mackenzie slept.

He told Doug about Schweitzer and Eva.

Doug growled. "They found Schweitzer's body. You're saying Eva shot him?"

He gripped the steering wheel with one hand and saw the turnoff for the access road. Slowing the car, Aaron removed his foot from the brake, flipped off the headlights and took the turn. To anyone following, their car would have simply disappeared.

"Looked like some kind of tiff. They were clearly having an affair, but he did something to make her mad or else she was done using him."

"I'm going to grab Sabine from her hotel room and we'll head to Schweitzer's house now, and then the Marshals Service office. We'll find out what's going on. Hopefully there's something there that will get Eric in the clear." Doug paused a beat. "You guys stay safe, yeah?"

"Got it." Aaron tossed the Bluetooth in the cup holder, slowed to a crawl and flipped the headlights back on to light the way up the mountain to the cabin.

"Is everything okay?" Mackenzie asked.

He nodded. "Doug and Sabine are on the case." And he hoped all that desperate prayer would help. They definitely needed it.

"But no one is going to believe us that Eva killed Schweitzer. They think we broke the law, too, don't they? That we're in league with Eric, you kidnapped me and no doubt I probably did something illegal, too."

"We don't need them to believe us, Mackenzie. The evidence will speak for itself. There were probably security cameras in the parking garage. And if Eva does manage to get away with it, then Doug and Sabine will find proof she's involved with Carosa. There has to be something linking them more than Schweitzer, if his relationship with Eva is what made him betray the marshals. Maybe she works for Carosa or owes him money or something. Who knows until we find out for sure?"

She brushed back hair from her face. There was an

endearing crease on her cheek from where her head had rested on her sweater. "So where are we?"

Aaron steered around the switchbacks up the mountain. "It's a hunting cabin the team uses. No one knows about it except us, and its ownership is buried so deep no one would ever be able to trace it back to us. It's a little rough, but we'll be safe here."

After their slow ascent up the dirt track to the top of the mountain, Mackenzie followed Aaron into the rough cabin. Apparently their definitions were different, because she might have been a millionaire pop star in her former life, but she was in no way overreacting. This place wasn't fit for a family of mice.

She took a deep breath and swallowed what she was going to say. Aaron had chosen this place for them to be safe, and it wouldn't help them if she put up a fuss now. Unless he'd lured her there to kill her, but she didn't think that was likely. It did pay to be cautious, though.

"Just needs a little sprucing up and it'll be fine."

Mackenzie turned to him, able to feel the way her face had morphed to incredulity.

Aaron burst out laughing. "Okay, so it'll keep the wind and rain out. The rest we can fix with a wet rag and a broom."

"Right." Mackenzie couldn't help but smile at the mental image of Aaron wearing rubber gloves with a bandanna tied around his head.

There was a table and four rickety chairs, an outdated kitchen with grime in the sink, but a stocked cupboard of cleaning supplies that looked as if they'd never been used. The bathroom walls were a weird shade of green, and the bedroom had two twin beds with bare mattresses.

The back door led out to a clearing. Mackenzie watched the trees sway in the breeze, closed her eyes and breathed in fresh air, feeling it rush through the cabin from front to back to air out the structure.

There was a rustling, and she opened her eyes. A deer stepped out of the trees and sniffed at the ground. Here in the middle of nowhere. What state were they in? Wherever it was, they were a world away from Carosa and the responsibilities she'd heaped on her own shoulders. That hardly seemed to matter now, here, where the world rustled instead of buzzing and shouting.

A boot clicked on the wood of the deck. Mackenzie spun around and Aaron stilled, holding a man-size overcoat out in front of him. "Just me. I thought you might be cold."

Mackenzie let him wrap the massive coat around her shoulders. "Thank you." She studied his face. "How's your head?"

Aaron shrugged.

"Does anything bother you?"

His lips twitched. "Like my brother being in federal custody while I can't do a single thing about it, or like a Colombian drug lord on our tail every time we turn around?"

"I can't believe that reporter thinks Eric had anything to do with this." She sighed. "It feels as though, if it wasn't for me, he wouldn't have been targeted."

"This isn't your fault, Mackenzie. Eric knows what he's doing and he's not alone."

He looked so dejected.

"What happened on your mission?" Mackenzie gasped. She'd said it before the thought even registered.

Why had she pushed him that way? Things were nice and now she'd ruined it. "I'm sorry. That was uncalled for. You don't have to tell me something so personal."

As much as she might want him to open up, it couldn't be because she had pushed. It had to be because he wanted to share. She turned to go back inside, and he snagged her elbow.

"Stay. Just for a minute."

Mackenzie nodded.

Aaron looked out at the clearing. The deer had moved on, leaving only whispering branches and the chill of morning. "There's a lot I can't tell you because it's classified. But it was a bad plan, drawn up by someone who didn't seem to care either way that our lives and the lives of civilians who lived around the compound would be at risk. We were in the middle of a firefight, but taking the designated route out would have resulted in too many casualties. Civilians. I just couldn't do it. So I ordered my team to hold tight. It was my decision. It took longer, but we got out. And the cost was still high."

Mackenzie stepped closer but didn't dare touch him when his body was coiled this tight.

Aaron's eyes flickered and darkened. "At the end of the day, the results of the mission are on me. We did what we were sent in there to do, but one of my teammates was blinded in the fight."

He turned to her then. "I have to live with that. It will color my whole career, but I have to face what happened. I did what I thought was right, but then I always knew I wasn't a hero."

* * *

At the sound of a car, Aaron grabbed the loaded rifle he'd stashed on top of the bookcase and strode out the front door. He needed Mackenzie to realize he wasn't the kind of guy a girl like her should fall for.

Mackenzie probably wanted to run now that she knew the whole sordid tale of his failure. It was for the best, even if he did feel like mourning the loss of what might have been.

He'd heard the sound of an engine approaching before he could finish his speech, and sure enough, a black-and-white car was parked out front. It had a light bar on top and the word *sheriff* emblazoned on the side. Aaron held the weapon loosely, angled to the ground so he could bring it up and be firing a round in seconds.

He'd been expecting this visit, but a person could never be too careful.

The tall, wiry man folded himself out of the vehicle. His lean body was exactly the same as it had been when he and Aaron had served together. Aaron's old teammate walked over, his eyes narrowed. "Hey."

Aaron lifted his chin. "Slow morning?"

The sheriff's lips twitched. "You tripped the sensors when you went inside. I drove by, saw the tire tracks in the road and wanted to make sure it was you. Figured you'd come here, what with needing to hide that girl you abducted and all." He lifted his chin. "So who is she?"

Aaron didn't answer. "The media didn't figure it out yet?"

The other man cracked a smile and shook his head. "You never did like sharing. Do I need my gun, too?"

Aaron walked back to the cabin and set the rifle

down so it leaned against the wall beside the door. "Mackenzie, you wanna come out here?"

The door cracked an inch. Her eyes were wide and darted between him and the cop car. "Is it safe?"

Aaron nodded. "There's someone I want to introduce you to." Plus it would clear up the idea the media had that he'd been mistreating her, since Aaron was the one with the head wound.

She came out and stood behind him, so his body shielded her from the local lawman. The fact that she still had faith in him to protect her felt good. "Is he going to arrest us?"

Aaron took her hand and pulled her to where the other man stood. "Mackenzie Winters, this is Sheriff Jackson Tate."

"Nice to meet you, ma'am."

She nodded. "Uh...you, too."

They shook hands, but Mackenzie hadn't completely pushed off her nervousness. Aaron squeezed the hand he still held. "Jackson and I were on the same Delta Force team a few years back. We're old army buddies."

"He's not going to arrest us?"

The sheriff laughed. "I was never here. Except to give Aaron this." He strode back to the car and opened the passenger door to retrieve a taped brown box the size of a small TV.

Aaron studied the address labels. "We get mail now?"

"They sent it to me on the off chance you might stop by here during your, uh...convalescence." Jackson smirked.

"Mackenzie knows about that." Aaron tucked the box under his arm.

"Right. I was sorry to hear about Franklin."

"Not as sorry as I am."

SIXTEEN

"Anyway, I might be able to help y'all. If you need it." The sheriff glanced between them. "Keep an eye out. I can watch the cabin's perimeter when I'm not working, that kind of thing."

It was too risky. "We're good."

Mackenzie glanced at Aaron. "He's offering to help. And we've sure needed it so far. You have a bullet wound, and Eric's in jail. The sheriff is offering to help. I thought you guys worked in teams?"

"This isn't one of our missions, and Jackson has enough to worry about. If he gets tangled up in this it could mean he loses his job. It's a gray area for him to even be here in the first place. If anyone found out he knew we were here and didn't bring us in, he'd get in a whole heap of trouble."

The sheriff leaned forward. "For what it's worth, he's right. I knew he wouldn't let me help, but that doesn't mean I won't have my eyes and ears open while you're here, whether Aaron likes it or not."

"Jackson—" Aaron growled his friend's name.

But Jackson waved his hand. "Deal with it."

Aaron raised his eyebrows. The man was willing to

risk his family? "How are the girls? How old is Lena now? Six? Seven?"

"Six."

Aaron put his free hand in his pocket and rocked back on his heels. "And Ellie, how's your wife these days?"

Jackson practically pouted. "She's pregnant."

"Congratulations, Jackson."

Point made.

Jackson sighed. "Fine I won't help. At all."

"It's just not worth risking them." The risk to himself wasn't worth mentioning. But then he didn't have a wife and a family.

Jackson's lips thinned. "Enjoy your package."

"Thank you. I will." But his hands shook when he took it. He turned and strode inside.

Mackenzie glanced at the front door of the cabin, which, surprisingly, hadn't fallen off its hinges with the force of Aaron's mood. "Is he mad at you?"

The sheriff's face creased in a way that let her know he smiled often. "He doesn't want me putting my family at risk. It's okay, Mackenzie."

"I get the feeling he only cares about his brother, and maybe his friends. He and I hardly know each other."

"The Aaron Hanning I know never leaves anything unfinished. It's a pain when you have to cut and run because that's what you were ordered to do, or when the situation turns and everything goes sour. There are few things Aaron despises more than not meeting the expectations he set for himself."

Mackenzie blew out a breath. The more she got to know Aaron, the more the layers peeled back. She'd only scratched the surface. "Maybe we shouldn't be talking about this. He might not want to share that stuff with me."

"One more thing and I'll get out of your hair."

Mackenzie smiled. "What's that?"

He reached back and Mackenzie wondered for a minute if he was going to pull a gun on her. She must have reacted, because his eyes widened as he pulled out his business card. "Just in case."

She looked down at multiple phone numbers and an email address for Sheriff Jackson Tate. "Thank you."

"Call if you need anything."

Mackenzie watched him drive away and ached to leave this place, to go somewhere—anywhere—simply for the sake of being free of Carosa. But that wouldn't work. He would hunt her until one of them was dead.

It might be little more than a dream, to think about being a free woman one day. Every single time was a struggle, but the more she practiced, the easier it would be to keep giving control of her life to God. But the reality was, she also had to let go of the past.

Until then, all she had was the dream of what could be. Even if she didn't believe it would ever come true.

Aaron looked out the window as his friend drove away. Good. Jackson really needed to get back down the mountain to his family. The longer he spent with Aaron and Mackenzie, the bigger the risk that he would be caught in the cross fire. Aaron had no intention of giving bad news to Jackson's wife and daughter. Not when it would be all his fault.

He already had enough on his conscience.

Aaron slumped onto the couch and ran a hand down his face just as the door shut.

"Does it hurt?" Mackenzie settled beside him. She touched the bandage on his temple, and he gritted his teeth to keep from swatting her hand away. "It looks better. Not that that's saying much."

The couch moved again, but he kept his eyes closed.

"So how come Jackson knew about this place when you said no one would find us here? I thought this was some kind of secret hideout for your team. How can it be if the local sheriff knows about you?"

"I told you, he was part of the team before."

"And he just decided to move here on a whim?"

Aaron shrugged. "It helped to have someone to look out for the place, and his wife wanted to get out of the city. They were in Los Angeles, and she was worried about little Lena."

There was a minute of silence, so he turned. She wanted to ask him something, so he waited.

"At least tell me what state we're in. Utah? Nevada?"

Aaron smiled. "It's not as though I blindfolded you."

"I was asleep. Same thing."

"We're in Colorado."

"Huh."

He motioned for her to continue, since she was apparently going to talk nonstop the whole time they were here. Aaron briefly wondered if there were any noise-canceling headphones in the cabin.

"It's just... I've been to Denver and all. So I've done the Colorado scene, but that was years ago. And I haven't even been out of Phoenix since I moved there. It's part of being in WITSEC. Not that you can't vacation, but I've been to nearly every major city there is, so it doesn't leave many options for traveling and meeting the requirements of witness protection so that I stay where people won't recognize me."

"You don't camp?"

"Uh…no." She shuddered hard enough it shook the couch.

"Fish?"

She shook her head.

"Surf?"

"I tried it once. I couldn't stand up. Like, at all. It was too wobbly, then I hit my head on the board and I thought I was going to throw up. It wasn't a good experience."

Right. Aaron studied her. "So you just work at the center now? Nothing else. No hobbies or anything?"

"Nope."

"What about before?"

"I was all about the music. And then suddenly I wasn't allowed to play anymore because someone might hear me sing and realize who I was. I risked it at the center, late at night. Enough years had passed, and people had pretty much forgotten about me."

She chuckled but without any humor. "Which makes me feel great. Sometimes it's enough to hear someone singing, but I get to the point I can't breathe if I don't play guitar. I need the music. Otherwise it's as if I can't…feel anything."

Aaron nodded, though he didn't really get it. There wasn't anything in his world that made him feel alive like that.

"So what was in your package?"

"Don't know. I didn't open it yet."

She glanced at the back of the cabin. "Do you want me to go in the bedroom?"

Aaron grabbed the box and pulled it across the table. "That's not necessary."

He hesitated with the flaps. The inside was packed with balled-up newspaper. Aaron dug it out and found a plastic container with half a dozen chocolate chip cookies in it. Below that was a game console wrapped in bubble wrap. A remote and a stack of games were with it. Car-racing games mostly, nothing that involved shooting bad guys, since they got enough of that in real life.

"This doesn't seem bad."

Aaron kept his eyes on the box and nodded. They'd told him not to visit Franklin in the hospital until he was asked. So why this, why now?

Mackenzie shifted forward on the couch. "They must not have thought it was so bad that the mission went wrong. Not if they sent you a care package."

Aaron pulled out the games and set them on the table. At the bottom of the box was a white envelope. He ripped down one end and dumped the contents into his palm.

The silver dollar was cold and sat heavy in his hand.

"Does that mean something?"

Aaron bit his lip.

"Aaron?"

"Yes—" He cleared his throat. "It means something."

He got up and went outside with the coin gripped in his fist. Wetness tracked down his face and he swiped it away. The screen door snapped back on its hinges and he turned away, hoping she wouldn't see the emotion on his face.

"There's a note."

He turned. Mackenzie held up a piece of paper. He took it from her and unfolded it.

Franklin told us.

"Your friend who was blinded? What did he tell them?" She backed up a step. "Sorry. You probably don't need me butting in. It's none of my business."

Aaron grabbed her hand and pulled her to him so their shoulders touched. "When it happened, they needed someone to blame for us getting in that situation. It's tough to think straight in the middle of a firefight. Your focus narrows, almost to a single point. Between the four of us we could cover the area surrounding us, but that meant they didn't see the shot that ricocheted and blinded Franklin. They were firing, covering us as we moved, and it was up to me to watch out for the man beside me.

"Franklin was injured and they needed somewhere to put their anger. Honestly, I was fine with it. Now I know they've blown through their ire and they're ready for me to come back."

"And you didn't tell them it wasn't your fault?"

She really thought that? "I'm the team leader, so it was on me. My responsibility. They were right to say what they said." Aaron squeezed her hand. If he was honest, he didn't ever want to let go. "They know I couldn't have changed the outcome. This is their apology for shutting me out, but not for blaming me. And that's okay."

"Cookies?"

He laughed. "Works for me."

"But you still feel responsible."

"I am responsible. Franklin will never be a soldier

again. It was my first time being team leader and this happened."

Something clicked in his mind, and Aaron got why faith had come so easily to Eric. His brother also understood that his actions dictated the consequences he had to live with. But Eric seemed to have been able to give that up to God—to let Him wash away Eric's culpability.

Aaron had to live with the consequences of what had happened on the mission. So why should he seek forgiveness for something that was his fault in the first place? Where was the fairness in that?

"The coin means Franklin is on the mend. It means I can visit him in the hospital and there won't be any resentment."

"That's good."

"It is. Because they've been part of my life for years now. A family, a group of brothers. I'll need their support when I get back." He looked at Mackenzie and smiled. "I know you didn't have much choice in it, but I'm glad you're here."

She smiled back and it warmed him. "I'm glad I'm here, too, and that we can be friends, even if we don't always see eye to eye."

"Me, too." It was a reflex, agreeing. Was he happy with being friends? What if he wanted more? He didn't know if that was even possible, but he liked the idea.

Aaron's unregistered phone rang. He drew it out and hit the button to answer Doug's call.

"Dude, you are not going to believe this."

Mackenzie saw the shift in his eyes as his concentration turned to the phone call. Aaron really thought leadership of his team made him responsible for his actions. Maybe in the army it did. But she couldn't help thinking sometimes awful things happened that couldn't be controlled.

She hadn't known her manager was involved with the Carosas, not until the police had told her. Witnessing the double murder of him and her security guard because her manager had been in over his head wasn't something she'd been able to avoid.

Wrong place, wrong time was right.

There was nothing she could do about that, but she had been able to control how she went forward. Recovering from her wounds, Mackenzie had agreed to testify, and her decision had shifted the power back into her hands.

Aaron was doing the same thing, except that his actions were chewing him up inside.

He sat on the arm of the chair, the phone to his ear. "What is it?" His eyes darkened further. "You're kidding me....No....Yeah, let me know."

He ended the call and looked at her. Maybe she didn't want to know, but she asked anyway. "What is it?"

"Eva is—" He blew out a breath. "I don't know how to soften the blow other than just saying it. Eva is Carosa's daughter—the Carosa who you put away, not his brother."

SEVENTEEN

Mackenzie's body tightened, but she couldn't help it. Her friend was the daughter of the man who had murdered two people and tried to kill her. Eva must have been just a teenager when Mackenzie had testified against him. Now Eva was tied up in all this and Eva's uncle was trying to kill Mackenzie.

The link was undeniable.

"Doug said there's a warrant out for her for the murder of U.S. Marshal Inspector Schweitzer. Eric's on the road to being cleared, but there's still no sign of Carosa. Doug and Sabine can't get involved in a federal manhunt, so they're coming here to help us."

Her mind was awash with the betrayal, and she could barely process what he was saying. "They are?"

Aaron nodded.

"We'll need to clean the place up, then, if there's going to be multiple people staying here."

"Mack—"

She went inside, grabbed some cleaning supplies and dumped them on the counter in the bathroom. Probably a good place to start. She ducked into the bedroom then and changed clothes. Once it was clean she'd be able to take a shower and wash off some of the grime of the past couple of days. When she was finally free of Carosa, she would book a hotel room and take a bath in one of those big spa tubs.

Maybe then she would be clean of the stink of being betrayed.

Mackenzie tied her hair up and got to scrubbing, taking all her frustration out on the grime on the tiles.

When she was almost done, his boot steps stopped at the door. "Wow, I feel sorry for the soap scum."

She glanced back over her shoulder. Aaron leaned against the doorjamb, clearly confused as to what was happening. Why couldn't she just say the words? *I hate my life.*

She was exhausted, physically and mentally, and had the feeling they were far from the end of all this. She didn't want to sleep, but she needed to. She didn't want to relive it all, though. In a vicious trick of the mind, the past would blend with the present and replay the scene back in the hotel room so long ago. Only now she would dream it was Aaron and not her security guard who jerked with the force of a bullet and collapsed into her so that they fell together to the ground.

She turned back to her scrubbing. "Why don't you get started on the kitchen?" Mackenzie shut her eyes at how curt she sounded, but he had to know she didn't want to talk. What? He could have space, but she couldn't?

"Are you mad at me?"

She huffed at the wall. "Why would I be?"

Now she sounded childish. Fabulous. She moved over and started on the next batch of tiles. The exhaustion of years of being hyperattentive to everything around her piled on top of days of running made her feel as though everything was dragging. But she wasn't going to sit around when they had guests coming.

"Eva's the one who betrayed you. Why are you taking it out on the tile?"

"It's not just her." She turned and pointed the sponge at herself. "I'm on the run from a guy who wants to kill me. I have no family, no friends—at least not anymore." And didn't that sound totally depressing? "I had to leave the life I've been building and I have no idea if I'm even going to be alive long enough to find out if I can build something from the nothing I have left."

His eyes softened and he stepped into the bathroom. "So you've resorted to cleaning as if your life depends on it? Sabine isn't going to care."

"I'm being a good host." She put one hand on her hip, only she still had the sponge in it and she was squeezing it, getting the shirt all wet. *Yuck.* She tossed it in the bath.

Aaron smiled. "I'll help, okay?"

She turned back. "Suit yourself."

Why was she taking it out on him? She wanted to kick herself, but that would be less pretty than this attitude. And also awkward. He was helping her, and she was snapping at him.

"Mackenzie—"

"I'm trusting you."

"I know that."

"With everything I have. Which, granted, isn't that much compared to some people, but still—"

"I *know.*"

She looked him in the eyes. "My safety, my future, everything that's good that I've done over the past sixteen years. All the things I've accomplished trying to be the kind of person I want to be. I'm putting all of it in your hands."

He nodded, and his eyes seemed to convey he understood the gravity of what she was saying. "I get all of that."

"That's all I need to know." She fingered the hem of the T-shirt. "It's not that I'm not grateful for what you've done…what you are doing. I am, you know that. I'm just saying…"

Aaron stepped closer to her. "I know what you're saying, and I'm going to do my best not to let you down. I can't make promises, I don't know the future and I won't pretend everything is going to be fine. I'd rather you were prepared for whatever the outcome will be. But I'll do everything I can to keep you safe until Carosa is caught."

"You might not know the future, but I believe God does. He'll keep me safe, even if that means using you to do it."

Before Aaron could check it, his body tensed. "Sure He will."

"You don't believe it?"

He shrugged. "I grew up going to church. But it's not as if it has to be a big deal, or anything. When I need God, I'll ask Him for help. Like after the sniper bullet grazed me, when I realized we were in really deep trouble. I prayed then because there was no other hope. But that was just in the moment."

Faith was an important part of life, and knowing how he saw it gave her more insight than she'd had before. "I'll be sure to ask Him now for the both of us."

Aaron gave her a short nod. Was he going to stay, say something more? But he blinked and whatever was between them dissolved.

She sighed to his back as he walked out of the bathroom. It hit her then. Just as she trusted him with everything, Aaron in turn was also giving everything to see that this was done. He had a life to go back to, and he must have considered the thought that something could happen that might jeopardize his ability to do his job.

What would she do if he was injured, or worse?

Mackenzie squared her shoulders. She could walk away now and spare herself the guilt, but she wouldn't last long before Carosa caught up with her. Maybe it was better that he was keeping this impersonal.

God, keep him safe. It doesn't matter what happens to me, just help Carosa be caught and don't let anything happen to Aaron. And help him to trust in You. He needs You.

He came back in then. Just walked straight up to her and put his arms around her shoulders. Mackenzie stilled, and then squeezed her eyes shut and put her arms around him, too. The simple hug touched her more than she ever would have thought possible.

They stayed like that for a while, before he said, "I'm sorry about Eva."

"Thank you." Mackenzie sniffed. "I'm sorry I'm being a pain."

Aaron chuckled, his chest shaking. "It's kind of cute, actually."

"You are not serious."

He touched her cheek then. He hadn't moved away. In fact, he might be even closer than he'd been a minute ago.

"Aaron—"

He touched his lips to hers, a kiss of comfort and companionship. Never mind that her stomach fluttered and she had to grab his elbows to steady herself.

Then he leaned back, and the corners of his lips

curved up in a smile. "I'll go make up the extra beds and then get started on the kitchen."

Mackenzie watched him walk away. Aaron was a great distraction from the drama that was her life. There might be something between them, something she hadn't experienced before with anyone else. She didn't really know what to call it or what to do with it. But that didn't mean it was the real thing.

He seemed content to have their closeness be about friendship and him supporting her, and she loved that he was that kind of man. But even if he probably had a pretty good idea already, she still couldn't let him know just how much he affected her.

Because there was no way he felt the same way.

Aaron stepped outside a few hours later when Doug and Sabine pulled up in a silver car so out of place in the wilderness it was ridiculous. He eased the door closed without a sound and trotted down the steps. Something had awoken inside him when he'd kissed Mackenzie. It had been a whim, meant to comfort her in the face of Eva's betrayal, but he'd had to pull back before it quickly became a lot more meaningful.

She might be completely out of his league, but she made him want to try to be better. More open.

Now he was struggling with what to do, because Mackenzie had sparked something. And yet, women and his emotions weren't something that usually went together. Friendship maybe, but not love. He'd never understood the point of falling so deeply for someone that he lost his own identity in the process. Not to mention self-control. Turning into a blubbering, simpering mess just because a woman turned her sweetness toward him wouldn't make him a better soldier.

"Nice car."

Doug pulled him in for a hug that was just this side of painful and involved vigorous backslapping. "Fake ID. Rental. You know how it goes."

"Sure, but a hybrid?" Aaron gave Sabine a side hug.

She shot Doug a grin that he returned. Then Sabine smiled up at Aaron. "So where's Mackenzie?"

Doug nodded his shaved head. "Yeah, where is this mystery woman you're supposed to have abducted?"

"I persuaded her to take a nap. She was pretty wrung out."

"You look a little peaked yourself."

Aaron folded his arms. "Thanks, that was really helpful."

Sabine studied his face. "Oh, no. What happened?"

"Nothing." Did he really say that? As if Aaron was some junior-high kid with a secret crush to hide. "I should be asking you what you're doing. Care to share, since I'm not convinced you're just here to help out?"

Doug nodded to the cabin. "Let's head inside."

Aaron helped with their bags, and Doug hauled in two cardboard boxes. How long were they staying? He'd just set the bags down inside when Mackenzie poked her head out of the bedroom.

"You're up."

She swiped hair back from her face, her eyes still tired despite the nap.

"Sleep okay?"

"A little." She came over and stood by him, eyeing Doug with hesitation.

"Mackenzie, this is my former team leader, Doug Richardson. Sabine's fiancé."

They shook hands, and when she stepped back, Aaron put his arm around her shoulders. She glanced up at him, but he ignored it. "Why don't you just tell us the news that I can see on your face, Doug?"

The big man nodded. "Okay. But let's sit first."

"I'll put a pot of coffee on."

Mackenzie's attention zipped to Sabine. "Oh, the coffeepot…" Her nose wrinkled.

"Girl, tell me about it." Sabine laughed, pulling back the flaps of a box. "Brought my own."

Sabine drew out a coffeemaker and plugged it in. Aaron could appreciate this woman's idea of roughing it.

They made small talk while the mugs were all filled, and then Doug sighed.

"Just spill it already."

He shot Aaron a look. "Fine. Your girl here is all over the internet. The kids at the center must have figured out who she was, because they got a photo of her back when she was Lani and paired it with one taken recently. It was a nice gesture, 'Stay safe, we love you,' but the meme went viral, or whatever you call it. Now everyone knows who she really is." Doug sighed. "The media is running the story now."

Mackenzie strode to the window. The world outside was quiet. If she closed her eyes, she could almost forget other people even existed. *Or she could try.* It was a nice dream. Too bad it might get her killed.

Her identity was supposed to be a secret, and now everyone knew the shame she felt over the girl she had been. Wasn't it enough that Aaron and his friends knew she used to be Lani? Now the whole world would know the selfish girl who was Mackenzie's former life. She touched the glass with her fingertips and hung her head. Hadn't she paid enough?

Aaron made his way to her, but she couldn't deal with his comfort. If he was kind, she would lose it. This was all too embarrassing.

"No way."

Mackenzie glanced over at Sabine, ignoring Aaron now beside her. "What is it?"

Sabine was on a laptop, tapping away at the buttons. She was probably touching base with contacts of hers who might be able to shed light for them on Carosa's whereabouts or something. Why did everyone seem to know what they were doing here except for Mackenzie?

"I don't believe this."

Mackenzie sighed. "What now?"

"See for yourself." Sabine turned the laptop on the table.

On the screen was a social media website. In the middle were two pictures side by side.

The left hand one was Lani Anders at the height of her career. The picture on the right was a snapshot of Mackenzie that had been taken from someone's phone. She remembered the day, one of the kids' seventeenth birthday. Mackenzie had brought cupcakes for every-one. She hadn't thought she was in any of the shots.

That must be what Doug had been talking about.

"So what? Isn't that what Doug just said? Why do we all have to look at it?"

Except that underneath the picture it now read, "$1,000,000.00, Dead or Alive."

EIGHTEEN

"Before it was nothing more than a nice message that might have outed your former identity. We weren't going to let anything happen to you, so it wasn't the end of the world. This meme has the same pictures, but someone doctored the words. Now it's a bounty for your capture."

"Or my death."

"Yes, that might pose a problem."

Mackenzie rolled her eyes. "Right, because Eva betraying me and mercenaries trying to abduct me wasn't enough of an issue, we needed things to get even more complicated. Why won't Carosa just leave me alone? Why is he sending all these people after me?"

"I actually have a theory about that."

Aaron and Doug both looked at Sabine, but it was Mackenzie who said, "What do you mean?"

"Well, maybe they're working together and they hired the mercenaries to get you. But what if Carosa didn't know where you were until now? It's also possible that everything that's happened to you since your tires were slashed is on Eva. She could have hired the mercenaries to get you and keep herself removed. She used Schweitzer and killed him. Maybe she's working with Carosa and she's going to deliver you to her uncle, or maybe she's after revenge for herself. Or both."

Sabine pushed back her chair and stood. "Look, no one knows we're here. If anyone did get the idea of chasing us down, there's enough ammo to take care of it."

The two men stood behind Sabine with similar looks of pity on their faces.

Mackenzie pressed a hand to the spot where she'd been shot. "I'm really trying not to be melodramatic here, but it's really hard. Everyone who sees that…"

"It's called a meme."

Mackenzie stared at the picture. The teenage face, the pop-star clothes. She squeezed her eyes shut. "They're all going to know who I was. And then Carosa's going to come and *kill me*."

Sabine frowned. "I used to listen to your music when I was in high school. It was pretty good. Is it really such a big deal if people find out who you were?"

"Yes."

"Why?"

Mackenzie's chest heaved. "Because I hate her. That spoiled, selfish little… She makes me so mad!" She pointed at the picture on screen. "The girl in that picture didn't care about anyone or anything but herself and what she could get. Her parents might not have cared one bit either, but that didn't excuse her behavior."

"You're ashamed." Sabine's words were soft.

"Of course I am!"

"I understand."

"You can't possibly—"

Sabine came over and caught Mackenzie's hand,

squeezing some warmth into it, but Mackenzie couldn't let herself accept the comfort.

"God can wipe it away. He takes our sin and makes it as though it never happened. Do you believe that?"

"I'm a Christian. But it doesn't just disappear. I should know, because it's been years and it's still right there in my head. All the time." Mackenzie looked away. "Maybe your sin is as if it never happened, but mine isn't. It can't just get swiped away. There's no such thing as a clean slate."

"You're wrong." Sabine's voice wasn't full of judgment, but compassion.

Mackenzie blinked away the tears and looked back at her. "No."

Sabine reached for her hand. "You've been holding on to your guilt all this time. There's no need. Not when you can give it up, ask for forgiveness. It's not a trick that sends it away all of a sudden, it's living in grace. In God's love…for you."

The nausea from seeing herself on the computer for the world to see sat in her stomach like bad shrimp. She had to get rid of it, but she didn't know how to let go of the shame.

Sabine took a step closer to her. "Mackenzie, it's just—"

"No." She shook her head so fast everything blurred, and backed up into the hall. She couldn't let Aaron see her like this. It was too embarrassing. He was supposed to think she was good and strong, but she wasn't.

Aaron strode over. "Mackenzie. None of this changes—"

She slammed the door in his face.

Aaron rubbed his nose where the wood of the door had grazed it. He could hear the hitch in her breathing.

She was crying. He shut his eyes and put a hand to the door, wishing he could shove his way through and get her to listen to reason. Was she really so embarrassed that they'd seen her picture?

His heart broke for this talented, beautiful woman, full of promise and life. She had probably gotten used to fine things as a singer. Now she was a woman with a mission to help kids discover what they could do. What could he give her? And yet he couldn't ignore the way his heart seemed to have opened to her.

When it came down to it, she was as damaged as he was.

And yet Sabine seemed to think God could wash it away. As if it had never happened. Aaron was scared to believe that was even possible. What if he got his hopes up, and it didn't go anywhere?

Sabine sat at the kitchen table. "I didn't mean to upset her."

Doug laid his hand on her shoulder and squeezed.

Aaron forced his tired body across the room and lowered himself into a chair opposite her just as Doug did the same. "It wasn't your fault."

Sabine's mouth flicked up at the corners, but her gaze stayed on the computer screen. "It probably could've been better, though. But you know what I've learned from all the fights I've had with Doug? People get upset and angry because they care. It says something about how she feels about you that she's making sure she attacks you first because she's scared that what you're going to think will hurt."

Aaron winced. "I'm such an idiot."

Doug leaned back in his chair. "I could have told you that."

"Just you wait. I'll charm her yet, and you'll be eating your words."

Doug tipped his head back and laughed. How could this man have given up Delta Force? The guy was born for the military and yet he was interviewing for a private security company and building a life with Sabine. Ahead of them was marriage, a family.

Part of Aaron wanted that with Mackenzie.

He turned to Sabine. "Do you really believe that, what you said about living in God's grace?"

She nodded. "I know it's real, because it happened to me. I had to give up my preconceived notions of what faith is like, but now I know. It's freedom."

Doug put his arm around Sabine's shoulders. "Why don't you give us the update?"

Aaron was glad for the change in subject. Had his friend seen his discomfort and given him the out?

Still, Sabine's earnest belief and the change he'd seen in her since she met Doug all testified that God's love really did change a person.

Sabine reached for the laptop. "So the meme the kids did for Mackenzie is now some kind of twisted wanted poster."

Aaron's hands tightened into fists. "Maybe she should be on the first plane somewhere Carosa will never find her."

Doug's mouth twisted in a grin. "She's the one."

"What are you talking about?"

"Just something my dad said to me. I didn't believe he could've seen it until I saw the look on your face just now. This girl is it for you. She's the one."

"And I might have figured it out too late. I can try, but clearly she doesn't want me in her life past this joyful experience and I don't blame her. I haven't been thinking about her at all. Just myself."

Sabine squeezed his hand. "You're going through a lot, as well. You were trying to protect what you have left. And help Eric. You've been in a rough place, wondering what will happen when you get back and—"

Aaron shook his head. "Don't try to make me feel better."

"Mackenzie cares for you, and she thinks you don't feel the same. She's so scared of it, she's pushing you away the same way you pushed her away."

How had Sabine seen what he'd tried to keep to himself? "Mackenzie doesn't love me."

"Once she calms down and gives you a chance to explain, you'll see I'm right. Most of what that was is Mackenzie's own internal stuff. She's going through a lot with this."

"You think I don't know that?"

Sabine smiled. "But you are a guy, so I'm going to say it. You can get mad if you want, but she's dealing with a lot of guilt and shame over who she was when she was Lani Anders. It's been buried for a long time, but seeing that meme finally brought it out. She needs time to deal with her former identity being exposed. Then you can tell her how you feel."

"That's the problem. I've actually got to get her to listen."

Sabine tucked some hair behind her ear. "I get the impression she's lived so far under the radar she hasn't really let herself get close to anyone. A lot like the way you've never committed to anyone because you'd rather keep things light. It has to be hard to be confronted with all these feelings she's never had before…maybe even overwhelming."

Aaron rolled his eyes. "You know, you could actually try to be comforting."

Sabine burst into laughter. Doug swung his arm around his fiancée's shoulder. "That's my girl. She says it like it is."

"Yeah, no kidding." Aaron squeezed his neck. "Do you think I can do this relationship stuff? I've never really tried."

Doug shook his head. "You don't know for sure that you can't. I never believed a relationship would work, or that a woman would ever want to marry a soldier who's always gone. Now I'm in a different place. If she's the one for you, then you walk it together. You keep her in the loop, and she does the same for you. It's communication."

"Great. Communication was never my strength. You know I'm much better with action."

Sabine grinned. "I'm pretty sure she already figured that out."

He hoped so. This relationship stuff was complicated, and Aaron didn't want to mess it up. Mackenzie deserved his best effort if they were going to make something out of this.

But first, he had to get her to talk to him.

Two hours later, Mackenzie was trying to focus on a book Sabine had brought for her. Wrapped up in an oversize sweater she suspected was Aaron's, she was on the couch, cocooned and trying to pretend Carosa wasn't out there. As if the world was, in fact, a safe place to live.

The men had been in and out, patrolling the perimeter. They were acting as if this was a war zone, but maybe they just needed something to do. She sure did. The book was supposed to an epic wartime love story, but her heart wasn't in the right place to get lost in someone else's emotions.

Sabine ran out of the bedroom with her laptop. "Something's going on. It's all over the internet."

"I can't believe there's even a connection up here. We're in the middle of nowhere."

Sabine waved off her comment. "The guys set it up like that. There's a hut across the way that hunters sleep in occasionally, when they find it. The satellite internet goes to there and we're directly connected to it. But to intercept the signal you'd have to literally dig up the cable between that hut and this cabin and cut into it."

She set the laptop on the table. "It's all really technical, and I don't totally understand it. But suffice to say, there would be plenty of warning if someone tried to find us by tracing my IP address and trying to discover where I'm connecting to the internet from. And all it would lead them to is an even smaller, more run-down hut a quarter mile north of here."

"So what's going on?"

"Check it out." The screen blinked on the laptop and a local Phoenix news reporter with wide eyes came on. Shell-shocked. "Our sources at the police department say the vehicle was a black van."

A picture of the center came on screen. Mackenzie gasped and stepped back. That was her center. What was going on? The front windows of the building were shattered. Police and rescue vehicles blocked the street.

Mackenzie's heart jumped to her throat.

"Around nine-thirty last night gunmen opened fire on the Downtown Performing Arts Center, wounding several people, including minors. We're getting word of multiple injuries and that one girl—a teenager—is in critical condition." The news reporter cleared her throat. "We'll keep you updated as further information is related to us."

Mackenzie gasped. "No."

"I'm sorry." Sabine's eyes were wet even though she didn't know any of the kids.

Mackenzie took in a breath that shuddered through the band of emotion that had a lock on her chest. Just children. Her children. In harm's way because of her.

"I'm so sorry, Mackenzie."

"I have to go."

"No—"

"I have to be there. Sabine, I can't just sit here. My kids are in the hospital. They got shot at last night."

"They're getting help, Mackenzie."

"That's not good enough!"

Aaron stepped through the door. Mackenzie was freaked. "What's going on?"

Sabine answered, "Someone shot up the center. There are wounded kids, and some of them in the hospital."

He went straight to Mackenzie. She tried to flee, but he caught her and wrapped her in his arms. When her legs buckled, he swept her up and carried her out to the porch swing. Keeping her in his hold as he sat, Aaron rubbed her back while she cried.

So much weight she carried. There wasn't much more

she could take before she broke in a way he was worried she'd never come back from.

"I'm going to help you through this, Mackenzie. I'm not going anywhere."

Aaron closed his eyes and kept rubbing Mackenzie's back, though her crying had tapered off to little sobs. If he gave everything over to God, that meant giving God control of his relationships, too. Did God want Aaron to risk everything he had that way? Everyone else seemed to believe it was the right thing to do, but did that mean he had to adopt it, also?

Mackenzie would be worth it. He didn't doubt that. But if he were to risk the pain of heartbreak and things with Mackenzie went bad... He blew out a breath. When it was over, there wouldn't be much left of Aaron worth speaking of, and he'd failed enough for this lifetime. Franklin's blindness was proof of that.

He could see how God could use Mackenzie as a blessing in his life to make it richer. Yet something in him still held back to the point he pushed her away. Was he strong enough to overcome that? Because while it took a lot to risk his life every day as a soldier...risking his heart?

That was a whole different story.

NINETEEN

Mackenzie rotated the handle slowly and eased the door open so as not to wake Sabine, who was asleep in the other bed. Her head was still stuffed up from crying, and she was exhausted but couldn't seem to be able to fall asleep. All she did was lie in bed and think about the kids from the class she'd supervised the last day she was there. Those frustrating traits of obstinacy and the air of bad attitude that surrounded so many of them now seemed almost endearing.

They'd suffered so much already in their lives. Neglect, poverty and some even abuse. They hadn't needed this, too.

Mackenzie crept into the living room. It was lit by the yellow light above the oven, and she could make out the couch and coffee table. The rug was soft under her bare toes, and she curled up in the armchair, knees to her chest with the sleeves of her sweater pulled down over her hands.

When was all this going to be over? Would there even be a center to go back to? The front of the building had been destroyed, and several of the kids were wounded. Mackenzie squeezed her eyes shut for the millionth time, but there were no more tears. It was all her fault for trying to help them. For not being satisfied with living a simple, quiet life.

She'd tried to help them realize how talented they were, but all she'd done was put them in harm's way.

She'd walked away from her life once. She could do it again, but it would still cost her to begin anew. Another house in another city surrounded by new people and places; having to put down roots all over again, always prepared to run at any time. Carosa would still be out there, and Eva would still want revenge for her father's death, so she'd have a new WITSEC handler. It was like a sentence, life in prison, but without the locks and bars.

Would she ever be free?

Mackenzie laid her cheek on the back of the chair and stared out the window. The night sky was still, the trees outside unmoving as they enveloped her in a silence that meant she could block out the rest of the world. Pretend there weren't people out there who wanted her dead.

Something shifted, and she turned. Aaron was on the couch, sitting up. He pushed aside a blanket and came to sit on the edge of the coffee table in front of her, rubbing sleep from his eyes. His white T-shirt stretched across his chest, showing the tone of his arms and making her mouth dry. "Mackenzie?"

In the dark she could just make out a small smile on his face. He looked exhausted from being on alert protecting her, another casualty of her selfishness. "You okay?"

Mackenzie looked back at the window. There was no point in getting used to having him there. She needed to know how to live without him.

"Thinking about leaving?"

The longing she felt was there in his voice, too. Mackenzie looked back at him. This wasn't going to last, so why was he acting as if it would bother him to see her leave?

"You look so lost. I wish I knew what to do, how to help."

Mackenzie had to not come on too strong. Just because Aaron was being open with her didn't mean he was willing to accept everything she had to give. What if he pulled away again? She needed to keep her own feelings locked up tight. He couldn't know that she was falling for him, because if he left there was no way she'd be able to come back from it. She had to guard her heart.

His gaze roamed over her face, but he didn't seem satisfied. He sighed. "Couldn't sleep?"

"I've never slept that well. At first it was dreams of watching Daniel die and seeing Carosa's eyes when he shot me."

Aaron bit his lip. "Daniel?"

"He was my head of security. We were friends, and I foolishly hoped for more. Then Carosa shot my manager, and Daniel and I walked in just in time to see it happen. Carosa shot Daniel before he could fire back, and then shot me."

Mackenzie touched her fingers to the spot just under her right shoulder. "Right here. It went through pretty cleanly, but left a nice hole in my lung. I actually stopped breathing before he left the hotel room. The person in the next room heard the shots and someone got the paramedics there quickly enough to bring me back. All because my manager didn't pay his debt to the Colombians."

Aaron's head tipped to one side. "It sounds as though God kept you here for a reason."

Mackenzie stilled. "Why would He do that?"

"All the kids you brought into the center. You've made a difference in each of their lives, something they needed. It's an amazing thing you've done with them, giving them confidence in their talents and making them feel loved and valued. And me…"

"You?"

"You've made a difference in me, Mackenzie."

He might be able to claim that, but the kids wouldn't be able to say it about her. Not now that she had destroyed their lives, too. A tear slid down her cheek.

"Hey." Aaron wiped the moisture away with his thumb. "Don't be sad. It's a good thing. I like the idea that God knew I needed you in my life. I care about you a lot. More than I've ever cared about a woman before."

Mackenzie shook her head. "Don't say that. I'm not who you think I am. Not anymore. The center is gone, and I'll be gone, too, still running from Carosa. What's the point in hiding out here if he's going to keep killing people until he finds me? Or Eva? Maybe she'll be the one I'm looking over my shoulder for for the next sixteen years. It's never going to end, Aaron."

"Of course it will. What do you think we're doing here?"

"Hiding?"

"More like mounting a defensive position on high ground while we wait for the enemy to attack."

"So we just sit here for however long it takes?" Could she even do that? "I won't ask you all to put your lives on hold for me. It's not fair to any of you." If something happened to them, she would never forgive herself.

"There are just too many ways to track someone that it's virtually impossible to hide anymore. Not with all the technology we have, or Carosa's resources. But I'm not giving up, Mackenzie, and I'm not going to let anyone hurt you. I've found something here, with you. And I'm not leaving until I know how it's going to turn out."

Aaron was ready to tell her everything. He'd been satisfied for a long time with shallow relationships that didn't force him out of his comfort zone. But something was missing. He'd been living life to the fullest, pushing the boundaries of what he was capable of physically—playing hard at his job and on vacations rock climbing and skydiving, but that wasn't life.

In fact, those things seemed almost meaningless. They challenged his strength but didn't let him feel anything past the rush of adrenaline. For the first time he actually felt something—compassion for Mackenzie's situation, and then coming to know her heart and her strength it grew to more than that.

It had changed him. He was proud of her achievements. And knowing the heart behind everything she did was about helping troubled kids, well…

Aaron had to admit, that uncomfortable feeling in his chest was love for her. Love she would be hesitant to accept, feeling as if she didn't deserve it when nothing could be further from the truth. She was an amazing woman.

"Mackenzie—"

The front door of the cabin opened and Doug rushed in. "The hut has been breached." Aaron stood while he strode over and set his night-vision goggles on the table. Doug stood straight and tall, battle ready. "Four men at the other cabin. They found the source of the signal and they're headed up the mountain now on foot, spread out in formation ready to take this cabin."

"Armed?"

"They're not carrying water guns." Doug went to the bedroom door and knocked before he cracked it open and stuck his head in to where Sabine was sleeping. "It's time."

Seconds later, Sabine came out with her pistol. Doug took a rifle from on top of the fridge and tossed it to Aaron before he grabbed the other for himself. Aaron checked the weapon, making sure it was loaded and ready to fire.

Mackenzie came over, her eyes darting between his face and weapon. "What's going on?"

"The mercenaries are on their way. They'll have the back exits covered, and they'll be prepared. They're pros, Mackenzie. But four of them don't outmatch Doug, Sabine and I. Remember how you said you were trusting me with everything you had? Well, I need you to do that now, even though it's going to get scary. Whatever happens, just keep your head down, and if I tell you to do something, you don't hesitate. Got it?"

She bit her lip and nodded. He didn't like going back to giving terse orders, but she looked so scared it would surely make her hesitate when she needed a clear head.

If the guys coming up the mountain were the same ones who had been chasing them for days, they were likely supremely angry and looking for revenge. He figured this wasn't so much about their doing the job anymore, but about saving face after being bested by Sabine and outsmarted by Aaron. They didn't know Sabine's skills were off the charts since she'd been trained by the CIA.

Aaron looked around, satisfied they had what they needed to keep Mackenzie from being taken again. This time he wouldn't have to watch her walk away.

He looked at her again. "Trust me."

The words sounded far away. She blinked at the weapons all around her. The magnitude of firepower in the room was overwhelming, and she backed into the kitchen until she hit a chair. She grasped it with trembling fingers and sat down, breathing deeply. It was like some Wild West siege scene in a movie. And everyone except her had a gun.

This was her life now. Not just running and hiding, but fighting. And the fact these people were prepared to kill in order to keep her safe? Her brain wouldn't quit spinning. They could die. Or one of them could be seriously hurt.

Trust me.

Could she do that when she knew what loss felt like? Carosa might take Sabine, too—a good person who was only here because she cared what happened to Mackenzie. And Doug, about to get married and spend the rest of his life with the woman he loved. The price was too high. There was no way she was worth their lives.

Years ago, she craved being the focus of what was going on. Lani would have soaked up the attention, but Mackenzie didn't know what she would do if something happened to one of these precious people, so honorable that they would risk their lives. For her.

Sabine and Doug stood beside the windows, their bodies angled to scan the night outside. Aaron walked through the cabin, turning off lights—except for the light of the laptop on the table. Each of them was completely focused on what was happening. Aaron's movements were precise, as though he'd done this a million times. He'd trained for stuff like this? It was unreal.

On the computer screen, a window blinked. It disappeared, and then flickered and appeared again.

Sabine spoke, "Bogey at two o'clock."

Doug didn't move. "Me, too. I've got one at ten o'clock."

Aaron brushed by Mackenzie, nodding at the computer. "Shut that off." He moved to the fridge, pulled it out and yanked the plug from the socket in the process. He dragged the appliance across the floor and pushed it up against the door, blocking that entrance, and brushed off his hands. "The other two are probably around back. What are they waiting for?"

Mackenzie clicked on the pop-up window. It was an instant message. But from whom?

You in the cabin. Send out the girl and no one has to die.

TWENTY

She should just close the lid. Mackenzie didn't want anyone to die, but what else was she supposed to do? The three of them were trained. This was what they did, so she should just trust that they would keep her safe. And yet, none of them knew what the outcome would be. Mackenzie wanted to pray, but all she could think was what she would do if one of them was hurt. Or killed.

Just the girl. That's all I want.

Her fingers hovered over the keys for a moment. She tossed aside the prick of doubt at what she was about to do and typed, If I come out, you have to leave them alone.

The response came almost immediately: You have my word.

Eva. She must be out there, if the mercenaries were hers. Or it could be Carosa. Mackenzie should have known that neither of them would leave it to chance after so many failed attempts to capture her. But what was the alternative? Live a life where every crazy person came out of the woodwork to collect the million-dollar reward? Never having a moment's peace? Her dreams of home and a family couldn't be part of her future, and she just needed to accept that. But that didn't mean Doug, Sabine and Aaron had to.

Mackenzie looked over at the living room. Doug and Sabine still had their attention on the front windows. Aaron would be a problem. He stood at the entrance to the back hall, his eyes on the rear door. The only other option was…the bathroom window. She prayed it wasn't locked.

Mackenzie typed the message that would seal her fate: I'm coming out the side window.

She didn't wait for the response. It didn't matter anymore that Eva and Carosa would win. Her life wasn't more important than three people who would go on without her because they didn't need to have their lives, their missions, cut short.

When she stood, her knees shook. Mackenzie willed strength into her legs to carry out what she was about to do. She slipped on her shoes and went to Aaron. "I have to use the bathroom." She didn't meet his eyes, and hoped he wouldn't hear the tremble in her voice.

"Right now?"

She prayed he was too honorable to come between a woman and her personal needs.

"Be quick."

Mackenzie pushed out a breath through tight lips and looked up. "I just want to say thank you. For everything."

He frowned. "Mackenzie—"

She backed up and pushed open the bathroom door. "I really have to go."

"Leave the light off. You don't want to draw attention to yourself."

Mackenzie closed the door and squeezed her eyes shut. Waiting a minute, she flushed the toilet, using the sound to cover the scrape of her opening the window. She gritted her teeth and pulled herself up to the frame.

A man dressed in black appeared out of nowhere. He wore those weird goggles like Doug had done, covering his eyes. Green-and-brown paint was slashed across his face in wide swipes, and he had a huge gun in his hands. He let go with one hand and motioned for her to come.

Mackenzie kept her eyes on the outside. If she looked back at the closed bathroom door, knowing Aaron was just beyond it, she would lose her nerve. This was the best way, the only way. She held her breath and crawled out. The night air was frigid enough to cut through her sweatshirt and yoga pants and make her shiver. Breath puffed out in white clouds in front of her as she crossed the open stretch of grass to the soldier.

When she got near, he grabbed her upper arm in a tight grip. She sucked in a breath, but he didn't loosen his grasp, just pulled her along. Farther and farther from the house.

He pressed a button on his vest. "I have her. Get rid of the others."

He kept going, too fast so that she stumbled to keep up. "What do you mean—"

Gunfire erupted behind her. Long spurts from the weapons of the men hired to collect her for Carosa.

"She gave me her word she wouldn't hurt them."

The soldier shook his head, goggles still covering his eyes and focused on the path they were cutting through the brush.

"She promised me." Mackenzie didn't even know who had sent these men for her.

"And you believed it? No one is trustworthy, least of all who you're dealing with." He snorted. "Case in point, we dumped the woman since the drug lord's son pays better. So it's off to Carosa you go."

Mackenzie looked back at the house. Everything was still and quiet. So fast. Were they dead?

"Don't bother looking. No one will be coming for you this time."

She stumbled and went down on one knee to the cold, hard ground. He jerked her arm so hard she cried out. They walked and walked through the brush. Her limbs grew stiff, the feeling permeating all the way through to her heart.

She felt nothing but the cold.

Aaron, Sabine and Doug were all dead because of her. Everything she had done was for nothing, a complete failure of her effort to do the right thing.

Aaron smashed the sole of his boot into the door, just beside the lock. It swung open, hit the bath and bounced back splintered. The window was open.

Mackenzie was gone.

"No!"

Gunfire discharged like a deafening wave of fireworks. He dived to the floor as shards of wood and insulation rained down on his head. He peered out at the living room. Doug and Sabine had done the same thing. Both were prone with their arms covering their heads as bullets peppered the front of the cabin. Doug brushed a splinter from his ear and crawled to his fiancée.

The front door was kicked in and the fridge was

shoved aside. Aaron lifted his weapon and fired, the sound muffled to his ringing ears. His aim was off, but he succeeded in distracting the two men and giving Doug and Sabine time to rally. They got to their feet and surged at the two mercenaries hand to hand, almost in sync. Before he turned away, Sabine already had her man on the floor.

Aaron raced for the back door at the end of the hall, hoping and praying he wasn't too late. Carosa must have gotten to her. Maybe she was just outside and he could reach her in time.

He flew out the door and scanned the area with his weapon ready. Black earth and dark sky, lots of stars and a full moon meant good visibility. Once his eyes adjusted, he would be able to see as clear as if it were day. But she wasn't here. It had been only minutes since she'd entered the bathroom, but Mackenzie was as good as long gone.

Footsteps shuffled through the shrubs behind him, and before Aaron could turn and face his attacker, someone slammed into him. He hit the dirt with at least two hundred fifty pounds on top of him and the breath burst from his lungs. Aaron rolled, using the momentum to push the guy off so he could gain his feet.

The guy looked ex-military but didn't hold his stance like any of the Special Forces branches Aaron was aware of. More like a grunt who thought too highly of himself. Left-handed. He punched before the guy had straightened, catching him off guard. But not for long.

The mercenary swung with the butt of his rifle. Aaron ducked and punched again. The exhilaration of a fair fight rushed through him, lighting his nerve endings. With the hyperawareness that came from intense combat, Aaron deflected and drove forward with the force of his strength and training and pinned the guy on the ground.

"Where is she?"

The mercenary didn't answer. He labored for breath under the force of Aaron's knee and shifted to get a grip, but Aaron was determined.

"Where are you supposed to take her?"

The guy looked up. His face morphed in to a sneer. "I have no idea. Payment upon delivery, you know how it goes."

"Unfortunately, I do."

Aaron released his grip and the guy slumped to the ground, wheezing. Sickness churned his stomach as he got up. This guy was nothing more than a thug for hire without an honorable bone in his body. And Mackenzie had willingly gone with them, most likely to her death.

Who did that?

Doug raced out the back door with Sabine right behind him. Blood trickled from a cut on his cheek.

"You guys okay?"

Sabine was out of breath. "We're good. Where is she?"

Aaron lifted his hands and let them fall back to his sides. "They got to her."

"What?"

"I should have known." He kicked at a rock on the ground with every bit of strength he could muster. "She climbed out the bathroom window and just gave herself up to them. I knew when she said thank-you that something was off. I knew it. I should have asked what was wrong, but there wasn't any time and I wanted her to be quick."

How had she duped him so thoroughly? What made

her get that idea in her head in the first place? He had no idea why someone would make that decision. There must have been something to trigger it, because it wouldn't have come out of nowhere.

Aaron's hands curled into fists and he growled. *The computer.*

"What is it?"

Aaron ignored Doug's question and raced inside, down the hall to the kitchen table. The computer's screen was completely smashed, a hole in the middle where a bullet had torn through it. The answers to all of this might have been right there, and now there was no way to find out, to understand why Mackenzie had walked away.

Why she'd left him.

Aaron ran his hand down his face. For all his trying to be honest with her, wanting to share his feelings so that she knew where he stood, at the end of the day Mackenzie had chosen not to trust him. His heart ached, the feeling so foreign he wanted to rip the thing out of his chest just to be rid of the pain.

He sank to the floor. The one woman in the world he wanted to understand him, and it was as if she didn't even care. Why else would she have left him without saying anything?

Doug crouched beside him. "Dude, talk to me."

"She didn't trust me."

Sabine's forehead crinkled. "I don't think it was about a lack of trust."

"She said goodbye to me and I didn't even realize." Aaron pinched the bridge of his nose. "She thought she didn't have anything else to live for, so she walked to her death like some kind of condemned prisoner. No fighting. Everything was over so she might as well give up. Who does that?"

Sabine crouched on his other side. "Someone who'll sacrifice themselves to save the person they love."

"We were fine. We're all trained for this, and she knew that. It doesn't make any sense."

"To you." Sabine squeezed his shoulder. "Because you knew we had the skills to survive. All Mackenzie knew was that men were coming for her—just her. We were surrounded. She acted, albeit unwisely. She should have shared what she was planning. But she probably didn't because you'd never have allowed it."

Doug scoffed. "Of course he wouldn't."

"Why? You both sacrifice every day, putting your lives on the line to make the world safer. Why shouldn't Mackenzie do the same?" Sabine glanced between the two men as though what she said was the most obvious thing in the world.

A smile curled Doug's lips.

Aaron squeezed his eyes shut. "She thought she was saving us."

"Seems like that to me."

He looked up at his friends. "So how do we save her?"

The more miles they drove, the more certain Mackenzie was of where they were going. In the early hours of the morning they pulled up outside the Downtown Performing Arts Center. The huge building looked ominous, lit by the glow of streetlamps that highlighted the boarded-up front windows. For years she'd loved coming here, knowing she was finally doing something good with her life.

The idea of going inside made her want to scream

and rage against the injustice of simply being in the wrong place at the wrong time—and getting shot in the chest for it. Why couldn't Carosa just leave her be?

She flexed her hands. The tight, thin plastic of the tie her captors had used again cut into the skin of her wrists. The soldier walked around the car and opened her door from the outside, the only way it could be opened. She'd learned that the hard way from attempting to jump from the vehicle after he'd forced her into it.

Being laughed at was not one of her favorite things.

Mackenzie sat in the car until he reached in and hauled her out by the arm. She bit her lip, not giving him the satisfaction of knowing he'd hurt her. The street was deserted. It was as though every living being had run for cover. Marched into the building by the force of the large man's will, she scanned every corner for help. Inside was just as desolate.

The soldier shoved her, and she stumbled into the room. Carosa stood there, arms folded across the silk shirt he was wearing. A gold chain hung around his neck. Khaki pants and brown loafers completed an outfit that looked more like something a used car salesman would wear than the middle-aged son of a senile drug lord.

Where was Eva? She'd assumed her former friend would be here, wanting her piece of Mackenzie, too. Or that Eva had been the one bringing Mackenzie to her uncle.

His eyes fixed on her. They were so much like his brother's dirt-colored ones that for a moment she was back in that hotel so many years ago. But she wasn't going to back down.

Carosa sneered. "Very good. Now we finish this."

TWENTY-ONE

Mackenzie held her body tight against the trembles that stretched down to her toes. *God, help me. This is so much worse than stage fright. Why did I think I could fight it?* Except that this whole thing had come about because of her decision to sacrifice herself for Aaron and his friends.

She hadn't prayed once or asked God to help her do the right thing. So what right did she have to cry out to Him now? Mackenzie hung her head. The weight of guilt bore down like a thousand pounds on her shoulders.

"And my money?"

She looked up, surprised to see the soldier still in the room.

Carosa crossed to them. "I have one more job for you." He handed the soldier two small packages. "Place these at opposite ends of the building. Ground level. And if I was you, I wouldn't accidentally drop one."

"That'll cost you double."

"Done." Carosa motioned to the door with his chin. "The money will be wired to your account. Once you've placed the bombs, you may leave."

"Whatever, man. Just so long as I get paid."

Mackenzie watched him saunter out, and then turned back to Carosa.

"Now the real fun begins," he said.

She backed up, but he grabbed hold of her bound hands and pulled her across the room. She wanted to kick and scream, but the strength had evaporated from her limbs. Her pulse pounded in her fingers. She was pushed to sitting and her brain spun, unable to latch on to a single thread of thought.

Where was help? Who was going to come and save her? Did she even have the right to expect a rescue? She had to face the fact that it was possible no one would find her here. She needed the courage to fight, despite how bad the situation looked. She had to be strong if she was going to get herself out of this alive.

"You won't get away with this."

"Thanks, Sabine. I owe you big-time for this."

Aaron ended the call and threw the phone in the cup holder. He raced through surface streets across the heart of Phoenix, already certain where Mackenzie was even before Sabine confirmed it for him.

"What did she say?"

He shot Doug a glance. "She hacked Eva's email account. There's a bunch of messages between her, Schweitzer and Carosa. Apparently she was playing them off against each other. In one of the emails, Carosa said he's going to end things tonight at the place where it started. She said it reads like a suicide note."

"The place where it started—wouldn't that be the hotel where Carosa's brother killed Mackenzie's manager and security guy?"

Aaron shrugged. "That's what I thought at first, but there's no way he could get her to a hotel in New York if it's all going down tonight."

Doug glanced out the window. "How far away are we?"

"I'm driving as fast as I can."

"I'm just saying, there's no time to lose."

"You think I don't know that?"

"Fine. It's just, I've been there. I know what it feels like to worry about the woman you love until you finally see her. The relief when you do is about the best thing you can ever feel. Until then…not so fun."

"Oh, thanks. That's helpful." Aaron made a right turn so fast that Doug grabbed the dash to brace himself.

"That's me, Mr. Helpful."

Two minutes later they pulled onto the street that backed onto the center. Aaron cut between a law office and a restaurant and parked. They scaled a chainlink fence and sprinted forward. At the back door of the center, Doug gestured that he would lead and go right and that Aaron should go left.

They crept inside, and Aaron searched the halls with his gun drawn. He passed Mackenzie's office, dark now, and kept going to the end of the hall, where he came upon one of the mercenaries. He was crouched, doing something with a package.

Aaron hit the man on the back of the head with the butt of his gun. The soldier slumped to the ground, leaving the package exposed. And beeping. Aaron set his gun down, pulled a pocket tool out and clipped one of the wires.

Silence.

He blew out a breath, grabbed his gun and sent Doug

a text to watch out for bombs on the other side of the building. Faint voices drifted to him from a room—a man's and Mackenzie's. He had to get to her before he lost her forever. Aaron crept toward the door.

Mackenzie tried to sound confident while inside she was shaking. "Do you want to end up in jail like your brother?"

"What if I do? What business is it of yours?"

She stared at Carosa in shock. "But why? Are you going to go after the man who killed your brother in that prison riot?"

"That scum was dead the day he laid a hand on my brother. My only lament is that it was not me who stuck him like a pig." Carosa pulled a chair over and sat with his knees only inches from hers. "Now that you'll be dead, too, I find I've lost interest in the chase. There is little left to live for, you see."

"You're planning on dying with me."

"Clever girl."

"You don't want to be with your niece?"

His eyes flickered with something that actually looked like surprise. "My what?"

"Eva. Your niece. She works for me. She's the reason you found me."

"You lie. I have no relatives save my decrepit father. And this Eva you're talking about is nothing but a stupid girl who shouldn't have stuck her nose in something not her business just because she needed money. But I'll deal with her, too."

"She's your niece."

He shook his head. "Impossible."

"I'm telling you the truth."

"And I should believe you?"

There was movement in the doorway, but when Mackenzie looked no one was there. Just wishful thinking that Aaron had found her when there was no possible way he could have. She would die here, at the whim of this psycho. Alone. Just like always.

Unless she could buy some time.

Mackenzie pushed aside the rush of cold. "I'd rather you didn't kill me. I mean, who's going to clean up the mess?"

Carosa shifted in his chair. "I feel as if I should say a few words to mark this occasion. Since it will be the last either of us ever sees on this earth."

"How about I say something?"

Mackenzie gasped. He was really here. Aaron had found her.

Carosa shot up out of his chair, his gun pointed at Aaron. She squeezed her eyes shut, unable to bear the sight of the man she loved being killed. A gun fired and someone fell, but it wasn't Aaron. In front of her lay the gruesome sight of Carosa's dead body, and beyond Aaron, at the door, stood a woman.

Eva had shot Carosa.

"Drop your gun."

Her former friend pointed a gun at his head. Aaron crouched and placed his weapon on the floor. He spun and his leg flew out, catching Eva behind her knees with a swipe. She yelped and fell backward, and her gun fired.

Mackenzie screamed. The bullet hit the wall behind her head.

Aaron grabbed the side of Eva's neck, and Mackenzie took in deep breaths, not wanting to see Aaron kill someone she'd thought of as a friend, even if Eva had betrayed her. But Aaron held on to her until she was limp but still breathing, and he set her on the floor.

Then he pulled Mackenzie to her feet and his breath came warm on her ear. "Mackenzie." The sound of it was like the chiding of a small child. "Why did you leave like that? Didn't I promise I would keep you safe?"

A sob worked its way from her throat, followed by another until the tears flowed freely. Aaron cut the ties and freed her. He massaged her hands until blood circulated again and then wrapped his arms around her.

"You came."

His chest rumbled with laughter. "You doubted me?"

"I wouldn't let myself believe it. I thought I didn't deserve to be saved."

Aaron drew her away from him and touched his warm palm to her cheek. "You don't ever have to doubt me. I'll always be there for you."

Undeserved, just like God's grace. She didn't have to do anything to earn it. God would always love her no matter what she did or the kind of person she was. She wanted to laugh now, thinking of the years she'd spent trying to prove she was worthy of His love.

Here in front of her was all the proof she needed. Not because of the atonement she'd done, but for who she was. God had taken the bad and used it to make Mackenzie's life into something beautiful.

Aaron's face dipped until his lips touched hers. It was just starting to get interesting when his phone rang.

"This had better be good, dude." His smiled dropped. "You're kidding me." He hung up, already pulling her out of the room. "Doug couldn't disarm the other bomb. We have to get out of here. It's going to go off."

"Not so fast."

Aaron's body froze. Mackenzie looked over his shoulder as he turned. Eva. She was up on her feet with her gun pointed at them again. "Neither of you is going to get out of here alive."

Aaron spun around. She'd been down. Out. How could he have been so careless as to assume Eva was no longer a threat? In his haste to get to Mackenzie, he'd made a rookie mistake. One they were all going to pay for.

He straightened and stared down the barrel of Eva's gun. "The whole building's going to blow in a second. We have to get out of here or we'll all be dead."

"You think I'm just going to let her walk away after what she did to my family? I've been waiting years to get back at her without it looking as if I did it! I didn't hire gang bangers to kill you in a drive-by and then bring in mercenaries to abduct you only to have them double-cross me..." She dissolved into a rant. "All that work to look innocent and they go and ruin it. And I'm *not* leaving just because you say there's a bomb. Nice try." Eva's lip curled. "I'm not about to leave the two of you—"

A boom shook the building like an earthquake, gone in a flash. Eva's confident facade slipped. The building creaked and shuddered. Mackenzie screamed as the room started to list to one side. Eva's eyes darted around the room. Aaron seized the opportunity, rushing her when her focus was elsewhere, and grabbed for her gun a split second before her eyes came back to him.

She fired off rounds, one after the other, while they

grappled for the weapon. Aaron had to keep it away from being aimed at Mackenzie and not get shot himself, but he managed it. Finally he had control of the gun, his elbow pinning Eva to the floor.

Chairs and tables slid across the room to the lowest point. Metal shrieked as it contorted, and drywall cracked and broke apart around them. Aaron glanced at Mackenzie and a sharp right hook slammed into his temple. Sparks filled his vision and he was pushed aside as Eva scrambled to the door and ran.

Aaron shook off the daze. They had to get out of there now.

He worked his way to Mackenzie and grabbed her hand. "Come on!"

Mackenzie ran with every bit of strength she could muster through the center's maze of halls. She glanced back. Eva was running in the other direction. The floor rumbled, and Eva fell through, screaming.

Mackenzie turned back just as Aaron jumped a hole where the floor had fallen away, hauling her with him. Twice they had to backtrack for a way out that was clear of debris. Aaron pulled her along, his speed giving her an extra boost so she took oversize steps.

Air rushed down the hall and whipped at her hair. Aaron's step faltered, and he turned. The look on his face went from intense concentration to wide-eyed. The floor began to shake, and yet another boom of thunder rent the air.

Another bomb?

"Secondary explosion."

Mackenzie didn't realize she'd spoken aloud until he answered her.

The floor splintered beneath her feet, and then she was falling. Aaron's grip tightened until it almost crushed the bones in her hand. They dropped through the floor into the basement.

Mackenzie slammed into the concrete and her ankle buckled beneath her weight. She cried out, but the sound was muffled with the roar of the explosion. Aaron hauled her up, and they kept moving forward. His hand was outstretched as he felt their way through. It was the boiler room.

The building shuddered and fell around them, encasing them in a concrete tomb. Aaron shoved her through a door, into another room sided by thick cinder block walls. Mackenzie stumbled and fell.

With her free hand outstretched, she scrambled around and watched as Aaron fell under the weight of the water heater. His head hit the concrete, and the heater slammed onto his lower body. Ash rained down on her, the hot air from the explosion all around them, sucking the moisture from the room.

Mackenzie collapsed.

TWENTY-TWO

God, help us. Mackenzie scanned the dark of the space they were in. The building creaked and groaned, and she heard the distant sound of sirens and people shouting. Help was here. They just had to last long enough to be dug out. But how long would that take? She scrambled to stand under the highest point, which was barely above her head.

"Help! We're trapped in the basement!" She screamed until her voice broke and then crumpled to her knees, coughing. "You have to help us."

Aaron moaned and shifted under the weight of the water heater. Mackenzie winced. When she'd first purchased it, it had taken two men to muscle the thing off the cart and into place. A moment that had marked the building of her new life; now it was all destroyed.

Mackenzie crawled to him and brushed a smudge of dirt from his forehead. It smeared. "Aaron." She whimpered. "You have to wake up."

He didn't move.

"Aaron, I need you to wake up."

A groan came from deep in his throat.

"I'm right here, Aaron. Someone will get us out, I

can hear them. Only you have to stay with me. Don't leave. I can't do this without you. That…that's not life."

He grunted and shifted as though he was trying to fight the pain. Maybe he shouldn't do that. "Lie still. They'll get us out, okay?"

Life without him would be…desolate and empty. Like it was down there in the boiler room, nothing but smoke and rubble and the remnants of something that used to be great. She refused to drown in despair. That wasn't going to help them get out of there. Instead Mackenzie picked her way to the nearest wall and felt around.

"Call for help."

She rushed back to his side. "Aaron."

He grunted and held up his phone.

There was a deep crack in the screen and no power. Her stomach turned over. What good was technology now?

All around them were beams of wood and bits of what used to be the walls of her building, and the concrete walls of the basement. "It's going to take them forever to dig us out of here."

"Don't have forever."

She moved back to him and crouched low so her face was close to his. Her heart broke at the stark pain in his eyes. "Tell me."

"Can't breathe."

The heater wasn't on his upper body, so his back was clear. Had he fallen wrong? Circling around his head, she went to his other side.

There was a pool of blood beside his torso.

She looked, but couldn't find where it was coming from. At least it wasn't a lot of blood. But if he couldn't breathe, that didn't mean anything good. Right?

"Aaron—"

"Back to me."

She did as he asked, coming back around so he could see her face. Her eyes were full of tears, but she didn't hide them. One spilled out and tracked down her face. She swiped away the grit.

"Talk."

"You want me to distract you?"

The nod of his head was the slightest of movements she'd have missed if she wasn't looking right at him.

She took a deep breath and exhaled. "I don't know what to say." How precious it was, just to be able to breathe. Air was something easily taken for granted, but the ability to simply inhale oxygen was a gift.

God, You made our bodies, You made Aaron's. Heal him. Don't let him die.

"Macken—"

"Okay, okay." She smiled for him. "I don't really know what to talk about."

"You'll think...of something."

She laughed. "Hey! That's charming. Well, I'm about to talk your ear off, so you'd better get ready, buster. Let's see..." She bit her lip. She had never told anyone else what she was about to tell him. "Well...sometimes, I still play music."

"Know that."

"I also write songs. I've been writing them all down in this notebook...that was in my office. I guess it's destroyed now, but I have a lot of them. Songs, that is. I don't know... I mean, I used to only sing songs other people had written for me. That's just how it works when you're a 'star.' I hate that word. Anyway, writing down my thoughts helps me process what's going on. Especially back when I didn't have anyone to talk to."

She clenched and unclenched her fingers. "It just seemed so natural to put them to music. What I was feeling, what I wanted to say to God. Things I was learning."

"Sing." His voice was a whisper.

Mackenzie didn't think about it.

"The air is still, silence all around.
But You are there.
My heart cries, 'Lord come and save me.'
You are there.
The final curtain falls, flowers fade and clouds come in.
You are the light that breaks the night, bringing morning.
The Son that gives His life, bringing freedom.
Jesus, You are there."

She kept singing, wondering why she had spent so many years trying so hard to please a God who simply loved her without demands. Sabine was right that she'd been too stubborn to listen.

Well, no more.

Mackenzie had nothing to atone for. God had forgiven her—she just hadn't found the courage to accept it enough to forgive herself. But she would, because she could be free of that burning, gnawing need to make up for the girl she'd been.

Thank You, Lord.

She looked down at Aaron and the sound died on her lips.

"Aaron?" Mackenzie touched his shoulder and shook him gently. "Aaron, are you awake?"

Eyes closed, his lips parted to expel a breath.
"Aaron, don't do this. You have to wake up."

Aaron couldn't move. His whole body was numb.
Why was that? And why was he floating? From what
sounded like the end of a tunnel someone was singing.
The voice was full and rich and very familiar.

She sang of light and morning.

Of life.

If he could wake up, he would tell her that he loved
her. See the smile on her face when he did, knowing it
would surprise her.

For as long as he could remember, he'd been living a shadow of a life. Going through the motions but
keeping his heart guarded so closely that he didn't feel
anything. Not even his brother ever truly got through.

What he needed was… Mackenzie. That was who
was singing. Her sweet voice warmed him where there
had been only cold and pain. Love rushed through his
cells and awakened every part of him to the fact that
he was completely hers.

If he could only wake up, then everything would
be all right.

God, I want to be with her. Was it was even possible?
*You brought me this woman to love. So I know You can
get us out of here.*

So that he could love her, because that was what he
was born to do. Mackenzie was made for him and him
for her. He'd never believed in that stuff before, but he
wanted to accept it. There was nothing else he could
do except trust God.

In his personal life, or his professional life, it was
the same—he simply needed to trust God for all things.

Aaron felt as though he was being lifted. Pain tore through his body, and he groaned.

"Aaron?"

He blinked. The rotors of a helicopter beat above his head. Wheels scraped concrete, and he blinked again. Mackenzie's face was right there. He tried to smile but everything hurt too much.

She touched his face, her skin so soft. He closed his eyes.

"Stay with me."

He needed to tell her. Aaron tried to summon all the strength he had, but it was hard. "Love you."

"Stay with me, Aaron."

His lips formed the words. "Love you."

And then there was nothing.

Mackenzie's foot tapped a staccato beat on the tile floor. National news played at a low volume on a small TV tucked in the corner of the ceiling in the hospital waiting room. People passed by the door, going about their business. Nurses, doctors. Across the room an elderly couple sat in silence, holding hands. The hum of noise was like a swarm of bees, relentless and threatening to drive her insane.

Mackenzie squeezed her fingers together, wrung her hands until the joints in her fingers ached. After firefighters had made a way through the rubble of the center, they had found her and a barely breathing Aaron just in time. Movement had erupted, people suddenly rushing and shouting instructions, and she was escorted to an ambulance so they could check her out. But what was the point if he wasn't okay?

Aaron had been freed from under the water heater,

and the decision had been made to airlift him to the closest hospital because there was no time to lose.

Barely hanging on.

Those words would stay with her for the rest of her life.

Mackenzie went with him, which meant she got to see that one glorious moment when he'd opened his eyes. The words he had mouthed set her heart to flight, but then his heart had stopped beating and the paramedics had to shock him back to life. It was the most gut-wrenching thing she'd ever witnessed in her life.

Movement at the door caught her attention, but it wasn't the doctor. Sabine led Doug into the room. His hands were bandaged from digging at the rubble in an attempt to burrow down to the last place he'd seen them.

Mackenzie stood. Her legs were stiff from sitting for so long, and they gave out. Sabine yelped and Doug lunged for her. Mackenzie managed to grab his forearms, avoiding his injuries, but he still winced. "Sorry."

Doug helped her sit. "Don't apologize. You've been through enough tonight."

"Yes." Sabine settled on his other side, looking around him at Mackenzie. "How are you doing?"

"Bruises on my knees and some scratches, but nothing more than feeling as if I got pummeled. Not like—"

Doug lifted his elbow, and she grasped it like a lifeline. He gave her a small smile. "Have the doctors told you anything?"

"I'm not a relative, and I've asked for an update so many times they've started ignoring me. As far as I know, he's still in surgery."

Eric tore through the door. "Mackenzie, thank God you're okay."

He swept Mackenzie up in a hug. She held on even tighter, reveling in the feel of strong arms around her. A sob worked its way up in her throat.

"I thought you were in jail."

"My office got a package. Proof that my partner was the mole responsible for every file that was leaked. He was colluding with Eva, so he was the link between her and the Carosas, too. I still had a lot to explain to them before they would believe me, but when Doug called and told them what happened to Aaron, they let me come."

"So you're not free?"

"I'll be fine. It's mostly just paperwork from this point." His eyes strayed over her shoulder to where Doug was, and something passed across his features that she couldn't discern.

"But—"

Eric gave her one last squeeze and then released her. "I've already seen the doctor. I figured it couldn't hurt to have a federal badge in their faces to make them cough up some information, so I went straight there. They're sending someone in right away."

Mackenzie sucked in a breath and nodded. "Thank you, Eric."

He squeezed her hand.

True to his words, a white haired man in blue scrubs strode in. "I'm Dr. Palmer."

He shook Eric's hand. "I understand it was a water heater that fell on him?"

Mackenzie nodded. The doctor turned back to Eric. "The weight crushed his left patella, and he has multiple fibula and tibia fractures. He'll need further surgeries to repair the damage since we had to stabilize him first. The injury to his torso was more extensive—"

Eric gasped. "More?"

Mackenzie's breath evaporated.

"I'm afraid the shard of wood was long. It entered his right side just below his ribs and cut through his diaphragm, puncturing his lung. We repaired that damage, but all in all you're talking about months of downtime in order to heal. Aaron has a long road ahead of him, but I'm confident he will recover."

"But not fully." Doug's words were somber.

The doctor gave them a small conciliatory smile. "We won't know for some time. Right now, Aaron is stable. The nurse will let you know when he's ready for visits, as long as you keep it short."

Mackenzie stepped away from the huddle. She'd been so happy just knowing he was alive. What if he didn't recover all of his mobility? She squeezed her eyes shut. He might never be able to be a solider again.

God, give him comfort. Give us the words to say. Help him through this.

She stumbled back and sank hard into a chair.

An hour later she walked into a dimly lit hospital room. Monitors beeped a steady rhythm to mark each heartbeat, each breath. Eric turned away, but she'd seen the sheen of tears in his eyes. He crossed to Mackenzie and squeezed her forearm as they passed each other in the doorway.

Aaron's face was too pale, his fingers too cold. She held his hand between both of hers, trying to give him some of her heat, and leaned down and put her lips to his forehead. The last words he spoke to her played in her head.

"I love you, too."

TWENTY-THREE

Aaron eyed the small cream-colored plastic pitcher. Condensation beaded on the outside, making his mouth dry just looking at it. He swallowed, tasting fuzz and an odd chemical. His chest was wrapped with layer upon layer of bandages. It was as if he had a flak jacket on. The pain was dull but present enough that he wasn't going to try to move anytime soon.

If only the water was closer.

He stretched out his hand for the pitcher but couldn't get near enough to grab it on the high table beside his hospital bed. He grunted, testing the limit of his reach without moving the rest of his body.

Useless. Just like he was now. Just like he'd caused Franklin to be.

If he twisted, bent or leaned the wrong way, he knew his chest would be on fire. He wasn't even going to think about his legs, except for flexing his toes every so often just to make sure there was some sense of functionality.

They were still there, and he could feel them, which meant things could have gone a lot worse. He'd seen army brothers who were amputees and had more than a ton of respect for how they dealt with it. Mostly, Aaron was just thankful to be alive. He wasn't going to think about what could have happened if the water heater had landed anywhere other than on one of his legs.

The damage to his torso from the wood was enough that even an inch difference and he wouldn't be lying here. How could he be anything other than over-whelmed with thanks to God for still having, at least, his life? After so many years of taking it for granted, it seemed strange to be grateful just to be able to breathe in and out. Life itself was a gift. Why hadn't he noticed that before?

But he *was* thirsty.

He reached again for the pitcher. The door to his matchbox-size room opened and he nearly groaned. He wasn't too happy about having to undergo another round of poking and prodding by perky nurses who were seriously annoying, or doctors who looked down their noses and nodded a lot. He'd rather they all left him alone with his prognosis. He would let them know if he needed anything.

No one else could help him process the idea that he couldn't be a solider anymore. Why did they think a counselor would help him? He just needed time. And space.

Whoever had come in was close to the side of the bed.

"Want some help?"

Mackenzie's voice brought with it a rush of vitality that made him feel as though he could leap from the bed. Visions of pulling her into his arms, dipping and kissing her brought a smile to his face. But he kept his eyes focused on the prize, still reaching to the opposite side for the water. She didn't need to know how desperately he didn't want her to leave. But she would. Eventually she'd have to decide where she was going to go now that the threat was over.

"Aaron? Do you need a drink?"

Why was she still here? Did she really think she was helping him when it was torture having to smell her vanilla perfume and pretend he didn't see how upset she was? It was as though she was taking the end of his career worse than he was.

He sighed. If only it was an inch closer or if he could roll the table nearer… He gripped the edge and pulled. Mackenzie reached across him to help, but not fast enough.

The table jerked and the pitcher toppled and fell over, dousing the whole surface with ice water. It ran onto the bed, bathing his hip in water. He groaned at the pain.

Mackenzie rushed around the bed. She pulled the table away and ducked into the bathroom, came out with a towel and began mopping up the mess—including his side.

He bit back what he really wanted to say. If she wanted to baby him, fine. But he didn't have to like it.

"I'll get you some more water, okay?"

He didn't answer.

Mackenzie stilled beside him. In the corner of his vision, her white knuckles gripped the towel in her hands. He looked up. Her eyes were soft, but she was trying to hold it back. As though she didn't want him to know she pitied him.

"Will you let me help you?"

Honestly, Aaron wasn't sure he even knew how to do that. Yeah, he was alive. But he hated feeling so helpless, wondering why this had to happen. God could have brought him out of that basement with no injuries, yet here he was: incapacitated, his career almost over. His future for once not clear, but shrouded so that he couldn't see what lay ahead.

Where would he be in a year? What would become of him? He hoped Mackenzie would still be here, but he didn't want her to see him so weak. Couldn't she come back when he was strong again?

Mackenzie sighed. "Here, take this." She pulled a bottle of water from her purse and twisted the lid off before handing it to him.

Aaron gritted his teeth. He could have opened it himself. Maybe. Okay, probably not, but he didn't need her making it so obvious. Next thing she'd be trying to cut his meat for him…when they let him have some.

He watched her walk out the door and sighed. Why couldn't he be a better man? One who knew how to say what he was thinking and feeling. He stared at the closed door and listened to the click of seconds on the wall clock.

The handle turned, and Aaron fought the urge to roll his eyes. Wouldn't anyone let him have five minutes of peace?

Eric stuck his head in and a smile immediately broke over his face. "Brother, you look like death warmed over."

"Thanks." He sounded like a frog. Aaron cleared his throat before he took another sip of Mackenzie's room-temperature water. It would do until she got back with the pitcher. Eric sat in the chair beside the bed, the one Mackenzie had slept in, insisting she needed to be with him even when the nurses had told her she should go home. He was sure it wasn't comfortable at all, but she hadn't complained. "They pulled Carosa's body out of the rubble this morning. Single shot to the forehead. You don't mess around, do you?"

"It wasn't me."

"Then, who—"

"Eva. Did they find her body, too?"

Eric set one foot on his opposite knee. "Under a pile of concrete. It wasn't pretty, but she's gone now. She can't hurt Mackenzie anymore."

"What about your job?"

"I'm headed to a meeting with my boss next. The charges were dropped since Doug managed to find enough proof Schweitzer was the mole, but that reporter still outed me as a WITSEC inspector. I need to find out if I'm being fired, or transferred to another part of the marshals."

Aaron nodded.

Mackenzie swept back in. "Eric, it's so good to see you."

Eric rose and enveloped her in a hug. "You, too, Mackenzie. You look lovely."

She tucked hair behind her ear with slender fingers. "If you say so."

Aaron sniffed. "Did you bring my water?"

She turned to him then, the warmth in her eyes deepening. "Yes, with ice." She took the bottle and handed him a cup with a straw. He tossed the straw onto the table and took big gulps, downing the entire cup before lifting it up for her.

"I guess you were thirsty."

Eric coughed, sounding a lot like he was laughing.

"Well, I just thought I'd check in, but since you're in such good hands I'm going to leave you two to it."

"I actually need to talk to you a minute." Mackenzie motioned to the door. "Can we step outside?"

Aaron pressed his lips together. What was all this about? Why did she need to speak privately with his brother?

Eric reached out to shake Aaron's hand. "Take care."

Aaron held on a second longer and gave it an extra squeeze. "Sure. You, too."

Mackenzie closed the door behind them and pulled the piece of paper from her back pocket. "I signed it."

Eric grinned. "Does it feel good knowing the threat is over, that you don't need to be in WITSEC anymore?"

She blew out a breath, trying to push off the stress of being around Aaron when he was this closed off. And of not knowing what the future was going to bring for them, only what her heart was telling her. But she could hardly throw herself at him in his condition.

"Are you okay?"

Mackenzie huffed out a laugh. "I honestly have no idea. Things are all so up in the air right now I'm not sure what to do, or if I should even just go. Aaron doesn't seem to want me here."

Eric squeezed her shoulder. "God hasn't brought you this far to let go of you now. And as much as Aaron might act like he doesn't want you around, he would be even more insufferable if you left."

Mackenzie laughed. "Thank you. I needed to hear that." She smiled. "It's going to be strange not having you around in case I need something. But I feel lighter now that Carosa is gone. I'm just not used to it yet."

"You have the rest of your life to get used to that feeling, Mackenzie. And I'll always be just a phone call away, okay? No matter what happens with you and Aaron."

She nodded, and Eric pulled her in for a tight hug. "Take care."

"You, too."

Mackenzie had been back in the room half an hour, but still neither of them had said anything.

Aaron held her gaze, knowing there was a lot to say. But the energy he had was fading, making him wonder why she insisted on hanging here with him. "Don't feel like you have to stay." He settled back against the pillows. "I think I'm going to take a nap."

Mackenzie pulled a magazine from her purse and settled back in the chair. "I'm fine right here."

Aaron closed his eyes, but he could still see her. This woman was with him, in his mind, his heart. He could see her eyes, full of fear, and feel her hand touching his cheek. Why couldn't he just tell her what he wanted?

Stay with me.

But she was staying with him in his hospital room, without even asking him if that was what he needed. Not in a pushy way, more like quietly letting him know that she cared. What had he ever done to deserve this? Aaron exhaled, falling asleep with Mackenzie's name on his lips.

TWENTY-FOUR

The sound was so slight. Mackenzie looked up, certain she had heard him breathe her name. Like a sigh or a prayer. He seemed so distant, always holding back, as though he was forcing himself not to explode, which was what he really wanted to do. It was obvious he was frustrated by the situation. Anyone would be.

Recovering from surgery, talking with doctors about more procedures, unable to get up or do much of anything without help. He seemed as if he was trying to convince them all that everything was fine. Why couldn't he talk to her instead of holding it in all the time?

God, help us know what to say to each other. Give me the words that will touch his heart.

Mackenzie went to his side and perched on the edge of the bed. She watched the rise and fall of his chest, tucked her hand in his and spoke, keeping her voice low. "I want you to know something. I've felt it for a while and I'm thinking... Well, it just seems like the right time to tell you. I know you're uncertain about what's going to happen, unsure what the future holds for you, but I want you to know that you can do anything. I really believe that you'll find the path, because if anyone can, then it's you."

She stroked her thumb over the back of his hand. "You're always so strong and together, as if you know who you are. Sure, I'd love it if you told me what you're feeling. Or how you're doing sometimes, just so I know where you're at. But that's okay. It's part of who you are. And, well... I love you."

Warmth enveloped her, and she could finally accept the fact that she didn't want to live her life without Aaron being part of it. But how would it ever work? What would they do?

She bit her lip and blinked back tears. "I don't know what's going to happen. I don't really know where to go now or what I'm supposed to do. I guess we're in the same boat that way. And maybe that doesn't have to be a scary thing, because we can navigate it together. We could find a way to make this work, to stay together."

She blew out a breath that shuddered in her chest. A lump had worked its way up to lodge in her throat.

"I wish we could do that. I've gotten used to you being around all the time. If you left, or you told me to go—" Her voice broke. "I don't know what I'd do."

The bed shifted, and a motor whirred as the head of the bed rose. Mackenzie looked up. Aaron's eyes were down, focused on his finger pressing the button. What was he doing? When he was finally upright, he looked up at her.

She blinked and tears ran down her face. Mackenzie opened her mouth, but he covered it with his fingers, cutting off the sound.

"I love you, too."

She stared at him. "I thought you were asleep."

He sighed. "I should have told you. I'm not so good at all this emotions stuff. You're going to have to stick with me as I navigate it. Maybe we could row that boat together, too?"

His lips curled up at the corners. He was teasing her.

She sat up straight, folding her arms and trying to act as though she was mad. "Are you making fun of me? Because I was pouring out my heart, and I don't think it was very funny at all."

He touched her cheek, the roughness of his palm abrading her skin. Mackenzie closed her eyes as his fingers slid into her hair. The facade of being mad evaporated, and warmth hummed through her.

"I said I loved you."

She didn't open her eyes, but she did purse her lips. "I heard you."

"And all that stuff you said? I'm in. So long as you add a small wedding at this private beach I heard about. But I'm only dancing one song. And we're going on a honeymoon. As for the rest of it, we'll have to see how things play out. I have some ideas, but one thing I do know is that wherever you are, that's where I'm gonna be."

His words echoed in her mind and she held her breath.

Aaron laughed. "You might wanna breathe, babe." "Yes."

He tipped his head back, smiling full on now. Mackenzie smiled back, and he tugged her toward him.

"I don't want to hurt you more."

For the first time, his eyes were open all the way to his soul and Mackenzie saw the answers to everything she wanted to know, right there on his face. He continued to pull her close, so Mackenzie put her hands to the bed on either side of him, keeping her weight from pressing on his injury.

Aaron motioned to her with his chin. "Come here, Mackenzie. I wanna kiss you."

When she leaned in to kiss him, she was smiling. Aaron's hand went to the back of her head, holding her close as their lips moved in a melody that soared. She shifted and touched his cheek with one hand, feeling the warmth of his skin. So alive.

She pulled back and touched her forehead to his, seeing the smile playing on his lips.

You brought him back to me. Thank You, Lord.

Mackenzie found there, in that moment, that she didn't need a cause. She didn't need anyone to save. She could live her life content, because she would be with him. There would be no protection team, or marshals there to help her navigate her life now, but she certainly wouldn't be alone.

She would never be alone again.

EPILOGUE

Mackenzie waited at the edge of the crowd of people milling on a downtown Dallas street. Thankfully it wasn't yet nine o'clock in the morning, so instead of being deathly hot, the heat was only mildly oppressive.

Aaron walked toward her, a smile playing on his lips. He wore the khaki pants and light blue button-down shirt with ease, as though looking that good was the most natural thing in the world. It still astounded her, every time she looked at him, that a guy like him could fall for a girl so far from the put-together star she'd been.

The limp in his stride from his injury was still there. He'd thrown away the cane weeks before everyone thought he should have and declared that he refused to be an invalid any longer. Mackenzie had warred between being concerned he'd reinjure himself and being intensely proud of him for the fight he showed in working toward recovery. Together they'd found new direction, a shared dream for the future.

She brushed her hand down the skirt of her blue dress, a shade darker than his shirt. He must have seen her bite her lip, because when he drew close to her, his arms slid around her waist. His kiss was light but lingered. "You don't have anything to worry about. You look beautiful."

He kissed her again.

Mackenzie chuckled. "We have to go. We're late already and everyone's waiting for us."

He gave a mock sigh. "I suppose. Ready?"

Aaron squeezed her hand, and they picked their way through the crowd to the front doors. They had bought this former theater for a song and spent months—and a considerable chunk of change—to establish this place. This was the legacy of what their lives would be about, no longer atonement.

Mackenzie stopped at the front of the crowd, where people had created a pocket of space just outside the front doors of the Lani Anders Center for the Arts and Sports Complex.

The mayor's assistant saw Mackenzie and motioned for her to come to the front. She walked to the perky young woman, smiling as if she wasn't nervous at all, and faced the crowd. It had been a long time since she was the center of attention. She squinted in the sun's glare, and Aaron gave her a thumbs-up.

Mackenzie stood beside the mayor, shaking hands. She held the pose while photographers snapped a million pictures of her smile frozen in place. When he finally let go of her hand, he gave her a hilariously large pair of scissors. She turned to the wide red ribbon pinned across the front doors of her new dream.

She hesitated and glanced at Aaron, but he smiled to encourage her to go ahead. She held out her hand to him, and her fiancé didn't hesitate before coming to her side. His hand rubbed between her shoulder blades and cameras erupted in flashes.

Together they snipped the ribbon, officially open-ing the new center. It was a twin of the one her staff in Phoenix now ran. After the old center had blown up, a number of local benefactors had emerged, willing to rebuild the place despite everything that had happened there. Mackenzie had been overjoyed that they believed in her vision of bringing the arts to inner-city kids, and immediately commenced talks to open a new center. But Arizona wasn't where she was supposed to be.

The kids at the center in Phoenix were all at dif-ferent stages of their recovery. They would be fine, but they didn't need Mackenzie when there were good people still there.

When Aaron had suggested Dallas, she'd been cau-tious about moving. Then the moment she stepped off the plane, she knew it was the place for her...for them.

The noise of the crowd soared with cheers. Aaron leaned down and touched her lips with his.

With the business of the ceremony done, people poured inside to tour the new facility and the sports complex that was attached to it. Sabine had been jeal-ous that the view from Mackenzie's window would be a bunch of guys showing off their talents. Mackenzie had laughed with her friend. Now she would see Aaron at the sports complex every day from where she worked in the performing-arts portion of this new center and know he was always close to her.

The top floor of the building was being renovated into a condo. Right now Mackenzie was living with Aaron's pastor friend—another old army buddy of his—and the guy's wife. Aaron was sleeping on a mat on the floor of what would be their home after they were mar-ried. Despite her concern, he'd insisted on doing the bulk of the renovations himself, and she had to admit he was doing a fantastic job.

She fingered the simple diamond on her left hand. In a month she would be walking down the aisle to him. She couldn't wait.

A TV anchorwoman toddled over to Mackenzie on her four-inch spike heels. A big guy carrying a camera on his shoulder followed close behind. The woman cracked a perfect smile and stuck her microphone in Mackenzie's face. "Lani, darling! Tell the viewers what it was like being on the run in witness protection."

Mackenzie smiled. "It's been a long time, Adelyn, but I wouldn't trade the journey for anything else. Sometimes life throws you a curveball and you have to move with it, or let it pass you by." She glanced at Aaron, talking to the mayor. "I'm glad I didn't let opportunity slip through my fingers."

"Delightful! And who is this?"

Mackenzie turned as Aaron slid an arm around her waist. "This is my fiancé. Aaron is a former soldier and the brains behind the sports-complex side of the center. All of the staff are former servicemen and women who have made tremendous sacrifices for this country. It is our great honor to have them come alongside to help serve the young people of this community, young people so often dismissed or overlooked."

Mackenzie didn't think it was possible to smile any wider, but she did. "I can tell you, I am one extremely blessed woman."

"Sounds like it. How wonderful!" A sly smile lifted the anchorwoman's mouth. "And when is the wedding?"

Mackenzie could have laughed out loud. Reporters were always trying to get details of the small ceremony they were planning. Aaron squeezed her hand and answered for her. "Less than four weeks and I get to make this incredible woman my wife. Can you imagine? Talk about being extremely blessed."

The anchorwoman wrinkled her nose, probably upset that she wasn't going to get anything juicy out of them. "Thank you for talking with us today, and best wishes for your venture."

The anchorwoman moved away and Mackenzie turned to Aaron.

He kissed her. The noise of the crowd dimmed as he swept her up in the moment and the sweetness of his strength. After a minute, he leaned back. "I came over here to tell you something. I forget what it is, though."

She laughed.

"Right, now I remember." He glanced back over his shoulder. "There's someone here to see you."

Mackenzie looked past him, to a face she hadn't seen in years. The sight of her mother, thinner and so much older than she remembered, brought tears to her eyes. It had taken weeks after Aaron's accident and the drama with Carosa being over before she found the courage to look up her mom and dad.

Mackenzie's father had passed away a number of years before from liver cancer. Her mom had been living alone in a condo in Miami. At first their communication had been awkward, neither really knowing what to say to each other. But when Mackenzie began to open up about what the years had been like and what she had come to realize about God's grace, her mom had broken down, crying over the phone. It turned out that her mom had discovered a relationship with God after Mackenzie's dad died and she'd been praying for her daughter every day since.

The relief, the joy that they could have a relationship where they had both moved on from the past, was indescribable. It wouldn't be an easy road, but both of them wanted to begin anew. Like so many things in their lives had.

Aaron squeezed her shoulder and whispered in her ear, "Go say hi to her."

Mackenzie shot him a smile and crossed the distance to where her mom stood off to the side of the building's entrance. She stopped short a ways away, suddenly unsure of herself despite all she'd accomplished. Mackenzie looked at the sidewalk, praying no one noticed her discomfort. This was the woman who let her walk away, valuing her own lifestyle more than her daughter. She took a deep breath and looked up, finding a smile she didn't have to force.

But when she looked at Clara Anders now, Mackenzie saw nothing of the woman from years ago. Instead there was only delight in the eyes full of tears.

Mackenzie stepped closer. "Hi, Mom."

"Mackenzie." Clara expelled a lungful of air. "That sounds so strange, calling you that. Are you really going to keep that name?"

Mackenzie nodded. "It's who I am now."

Her mom nodded. "I wasn't sure before, but looking at you now, I understand."

She wrapped her arms around her mom. It took a second, but the smaller woman reached up and did the same. Tears ran down her face.

"This is a wonderful thing you and Aaron are doing

here. You should be very proud of yourself." When they broke apart, Clara smiled. "I met your young man."

Mackenzie had a rush of nerves wondering what her mom thought of him.

"He's wonderful. I'm very happy you found the man God made just for you." Clara's eyes dimmed. "Your father was that man for me."

Mackenzie stiffened, not really wanting to dredge up what was gone.

Her mom continued, "Somewhere along the way, we lost our direction. But from the beginning there wasn't a doubt we were it for each other. There's never been anyone else for me, then or since." Clara shook her head. "Don't mind me. I'm happy for you, my darling."

"Thanks, Mom. That means a lot to me."

"And can I hope that I'll be part of your life going on?" A wistful smile crossed her face. "I quite like the thought of being a grandmother."

Mackenzie laughed. "I'd like that, too. But we'll have to see what time brings."

She might have missed a lot of years and have a lot of history with her mom that both of them would rather forget, but that didn't mean the future couldn't be bright. She loved the idea of her mom being a part of their lives and the lives of the kids she and Aaron might have together. They could leave the bad stuff in the past and forge a new family dynamic together. Build for their children what she and Aaron never had.

Thinking of him…she turned and scanned the faces around them. He was talking with Pastor John.

As though he felt her gaze on him, he looked up and caught her staring. His face brightened into a smile, and she wondered that this man who had been so contrary and who held everything so close to himself, never giving away his feelings, now practically glowed with joy.

He crossed the room, stepping around people milling and talking, partaking of refreshments. He ignored a waiter's offer of a flute of sparkling grape juice and made a beeline for her.

He slipped his arms around her waist. "Caught you."

"You certainly did. And I'm glad. Very glad." The rush of emotion brought tears to her eyes.

"Hey, no crying. This is a happy day, remember. What's going on?"

She sniffed. "No crying. I'll try to remember that."

He gave her a gentle shake. "What's up?"

"I'm just really glad you found me and I found you, and God brought us together. Or however that all works. I'm just glad it did."

He cleared his throat. "Me, too. You have no idea how alone I felt before you came along. And you wouldn't let me do what I'd always done. Thank God you weren't content to let me hold back. You'd have walked away and I would have been…well, it definitely wouldn't have been pretty. At all."

One corner of his mouth tipped up. "I'd probably be sitting in my boat, all alone with two days' worth of stubble and a fishing pole that I'd run out of bait for, wondering where on earth I'd gone wrong."

Mackenzie laughed. "I love you."

"And I love you."

* * * * *

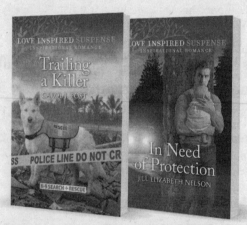

LOVE INSPIRED

Stories to uplift and inspire

Fall in love with Love Inspired—
inspirational and uplifting stories of faith
and hope. Find strength and comfort in
the bonds of friendship and community.
Revel in the warmth of possibility and the
promise of new beginnings.

Sign up for the Love Inspired newsletter
at **LoveInspired.com** to be the first
to find out about upcoming titles,
special promotions and exclusive content.

"I elbowed him. Think I broke his nose. He ran after that—didn't even take his stuff with him." She gestured over to the counter.

As proud as he was that she'd successfully defended herself, the pride didn't ease his panic at the sight of the shower curtain and clothesline. She could take care of herself, but that didn't make it any easier to accept that she'd been targeted. He didn't know if this had anything to do with the case—but the shower curtain and line the assailant left behind suggested it did. They might have just caught a break, but at what expense? He wouldn't risk Cecile's life even to catch a serial killer.

She rubbed her arms and he spotted goose bumps on them. "I'd better go clean up before someone sees me like this."

She walked across the hall into the bathroom and shut the door. He checked the rest of the windows and then double-checked the locks. The house was as secure as he could make it for now—but that wasn't nearly as secure as he'd like.

The presence of the shower curtain and clothesline seemed to suggest she'd been deliberately targeted. Josh prayed the blood evidence would provide them with a DNA match, but that would be days, maybe weeks, away. They couldn't wait that long. He'd already lost Haley to a killer.

He couldn't lose Cecile, too.

Don't miss
Texas Buried Secrets *by Virginia Vaughan,*
available August 2022 wherever
Love Inspired Suspense books and ebooks are sold.

LoveInspired.com

IF YOU ENJOYED THIS BOOK, DON'T MISS NEW EXTENDED-LENGTH NOVELS FROM LOVE INSPIRED!

In addition to the Love Inspired books you know and love, we're excited to introduce even more uplifting stories in a longer format, with more inspiring fresh starts and page-turning thrills!

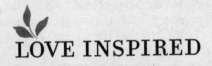

Stories to uplift and inspire.

Fall in love with Love Inspired—inspirational and uplifting stories of faith and hope. Find strength and comfort in the bonds of friendship and community. Revel in the warmth of possibility, and the promise of new beginnings.

LOOK FOR THESE LOVE INSPIRED TITLES ONLINE AND IN THE BOOK DEPARTMENT OF YOUR FAVORITE RETAILER!

Within ten minutes of her call, Cecile's home and property
were surrounded by sheriff's deputies and forensics
personnel.

Josh was one of the first to arrive. He found her on the
couch. He'd never seen her look so fragile before. It worried
him—even though her demeanor changed the moment she
saw him. She slipped on her mask of confidence as she stood
to face him.

"What happened?" He resisted the urge to pull her into
an embrace. Not only would that be unprofessional, but he
didn't want to blur the lines between them any more than
they already were.

"A man broke into my house." She explained hearing the
glass breaking and then finding the broken glass and dirty
shoe print. "He grabbed me from behind and knocked my
gun out of my hands, but I managed to fight him off."

Josh glanced at the trail of blood. She'd connected with
the assailant.